FRANKLIN HORTON

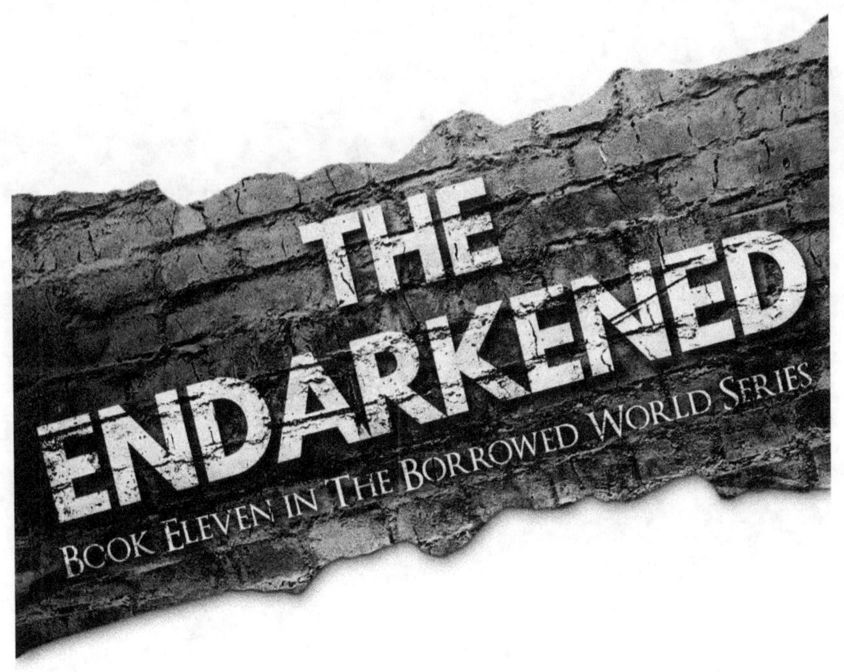

ABOUT THE AUTHOR

Franklin Horton lives and writes in the mountains of Southwestern Virginia. He received an English degree from Virginia Common-wealth University and has written over thirty novels. He lives a hermit's life on a remote mountaintop along the Clinch Mountain chain, splitting his day between writing and tinkering in his shop like one of his characters.

You can follow him on his website at franklinhorton.com.

While you're there please sign up for his mailing list for updates, event schedule, book recommendations, and discounts. He's also active on social media so follow him on Facebook or Instagram to keep up with the latest releases.

ALSO BY FRANKLIN HORTON

THE ENDARKENED

1

Jim Powell was working the ax, splitting the lengths of red oak that Pete stood on the chopping block. When the wood split, Charlie picked up the pieces and tossed them into a rusty wheelbarrow. A couple of years ago Jim never would have needed this much firewood. Now firewood was essential for heating, cooking, and the occasional bonfires that formed the centerpiece of their social gatherings.

Although for many people this task was drudgery, Jim had always enjoyed it, even before the collapse. He wasn't complaining about the tools they'd recently acquired that made the job easier. When he was opening the Reset Roadhouse in town, he'd arranged a trade with a hardware store owner to acquire his inventory of battery-operated drills and saws. Included in the deal were several battery-powered chainsaws and he was impressed with their capability. They might not cut the monster logs that his Stihl chainsaw had once cut, but they were more than capable of cutting wood to stove length.

While Jim, Pete, and Charlie split firewood like a finely-tuned machine, Lloyd sat on the porch steps playing the banjo. In his eyes, he was making a valuable contribution to their effort by playing music that lifted their spirits while they were working. While Jim indeed felt that Lloyd's playing provided a contribution, it was not the kind Lloyd imagined. With each stroke of Jim's ax, he imagined that he was smashing a banjo, which explained the satisfied smirk on his face.

Pops came out of the house and rested his elbows on the porch rail. "You can quit any time, Jim. You're probably not going to need all that firewood. President Lightspeed is saying we should have power soon. I heard it on the radio."

Jim brought the ax down on a new chunk of wood before answering his father. "I'll believe it when I see it. Besides, when did you become such a fan of Lightspeed? Once we found out he'd declared himself president, you spent the first couple of weeks ranting that it was an unlawful coup and he should be arrested."

"I have reevaluated my position," Pops declared. "When a man actually begins to deliver on the promises he makes, you can't dismiss him as easily. I'm impressed. We may not have power yet, but he's delivered aid into the region just like he said he would."

Jim sank the ax into the chopping block and mopped his face with the tail of his shirt. His dad had been involved in local politics for much of his life and Jim understood it was difficult for him to accept anyone who deviated from traditional politics. As much as Jim would have enjoyed badgering his father about his acceptance of Lightspeed, he kept his mouth shut because he hated discussing politics in general.

Jim was just about to signal the boys to take a break when an odd noise hit his ears and caused him a momentary pang of anxiety. It was the rotors of an approaching helicopter.

It wasn't completely uncommon to hear a helicopter passing overhead. Even though Jim's region mostly existed at a nineteenth-century level, there were parts of the country where the sight of helicopters and moving vehicles was commonplace. The military and those working for the government used helicopters as their primary mode of transportation since the condition of the public roads had declined so significantly.

Jim was always relieved when the helicopters remained high in the air and kept going. When they stopped in his community it never meant anything good. He couldn't forget about the helicopter that had arrived months back carrying men intent on killing him. He'd never hear another one without going on alert and experiencing a moment of panic.

Everyone heard it now and they shaded their eyes, searching the sky above them for the helicopter. Usually, the choppers flew by at maximum speed, on their way to some other destination. This one was flying slower, as if it were searching for something, perhaps a place to land. They only caught a brief glimpse of it before it was lost in the trees, veering off toward Clinch Mountain.

"Well, that's my cue," Jim said. "It's time to throw on my gear and see what's going on."

"Ignore it," Pops said with a dismissive wave. "Stay home and mind your own business."

Jim wandered over to where his gear was stacked on the porch steps and took a long pull off a water bottle. "That strategy never worked for me. Ignoring things that happened outside this valley nearly got us killed. Remember?"

"Eh, I remember, but take someone with you. You need adult supervision, so you don't shoot someone. Besides, Lightspeed said on the radio that we needed to be on the lookout for power installation crews—"

"I know what Lightspeed said," Jim interrupted. "We can't assume those are Lightspeed's people. We need to get eyes on them and make sure. Never assume anything. That's another lesson we've learned, right?"

No one answered, but they all knew it was true.

"Remember that you said you needed to get *eyes* on them, not crosshairs," said Lloyd. "We ask questions with our mouths and not our rifles."

Jim scowled at his oldest friend. "How about you stick with the banjo, Deliverance Boy. Leave the thinking to the grown-ups."

Lloyd mumbled a curse and turned away like he was offended. Pete and Charlie laughed like hyenas.

"You need us to get our gear and go with you?" Pete asked.

"No, you guys keep working on this firewood. I'll radio Hugh and have him join me. I think he's up at his place this morning." Jim shot Lloyd a look. "Maybe Lloyd will help you with the firewood if he can pry his butt off those steps."

Again, Lloyd looked offended. "I'm helping with my musical accompaniment. Everyone knows that music helps men forget their burdens and makes work less taxing."

"I agree," Jim said. "*Music* does *all* those things. Banjo does *none* of that."

"Besides, I have trouble gripping the ax because of my missing fingers," Lloyd complained, holding up the hand with the missing digits. "I'd hate for it to fly out of my hands and kill someone."

"Then let one of the boys split and you can stack," Jim suggested.

"If those are Lightspeed's people, please don't kill them or drive them off," Pops said. "Lightspeed said on the radio that he didn't have time to argue with locals who weren't receptive to his efforts. He said he'd pass over folks who gave his people a hard time and they'd be the last to get power. We *need* power, so put on your friendliest smile and be nice."

Jim offered his dad a smile that was somewhere between a grimace and a manic grin. "This better?"

Pops cringed and held up a hand. "Please, that's enough. How about you just try to be nice and forget about the smile. You smile like Lloyd plays the banjo."

Lloyd and Jim looked at each other, then at Pops. With one verbal swipe Pops had offended them both.

Jim grabbed his rifle and strode toward the barn. "Someone let Ellen know where I'm going," he called back. "I'll radio as soon as I can."

When he reached the barn, Jim tapped a metal feed bucket against the wall of the barn, luring his horse in from the pasture. He had no grain to offer it, so when the horse trotted up to him, he rewarded it with a knotty apple from a bushel basket. The best of the local apples were used for apple butter, preserves, or applesauce. Some were sliced, then dehydrated in the sun, and those were a favorite snack for nearly everyone. The small, knotty, or worm-eaten apples were collected in buckets and used as treats for the horses.

Although Jim had never been a horseman before the collapse, he'd quickly learned their value after his long walk home from Richmond. Now, after a little over a year without running vehicles, he'd become much more proficient at both saddling and riding them. He was no longer terrified of the experience and his saddles no longer loosened a few minutes into the ride.

Once his horse was ready, Jim mounted up and rode from the barn. He waved in the direction of his people, ignored their warnings to behave, then nudged his horse into a gallop. As he rode, he radioed Hugh to see if he was available to chase down the helicopter.

"Already on it," Hugh replied. *"They were going low and slow, like they were looking for something. The pitch of their engines isn't changing any longer, so I assume they've either landed or they're getting ready to."*

"Tell me where you're at and I'll catch up with you."

Once Hugh relayed that information, Jim adjusted his course to intersect his friend high on the shoulder of the mountain. Hugh thought the chopper had been hovering over a particular section of the ridge that capped this stretch of the Clinch Mountain range. Jim was very familiar with the area. Much of the ridge consisted of little more than a narrow, knife-edged trail, but there were a couple of places where the ridgetop sprawled out into broad meadows.

Those meadows must have been cleared over a century ago when some brave pioneer decided to live on the mountaintop instead of in the valleys. Those meadows had primarily been used for grazing and growing hay up until the collapse. The one exception was a period in the 1970s when they'd been used for large-scale marijuana cultivation since the meadows were isolated enough to escape detection.

It took Jim a bit longer to reach the tree line since he was starting from the valley floor and Hugh's place already sat high on the shoulder of the mountain. Hugh had stopped to wait for Jim where a logging road led into the dense forest and eventually to the clearing where they suspected the helicopter might have landed.

Hugh sat his horse like he'd been pulled straight from the Old

West. He wore camouflage pants, a grubby desert tan t-shirt, and his ever-present boonie hat. He wore a plate carrier so battle worn it had begun to look as if it were part of him, an exoskeleton grown to conveniently carry extra tactical gear. He had a scabbard on each side of his horse. One carried his M4 and the other carried a Remington 700 in case he needed a longer shot. Hugh liked to be prepared.

He tipped his head toward Jim's mount. "You need to rest that horse?"

"Nah. He'll be fine if I walk him for a while and let him cool off."

Hugh checked his watch. "The helicopter engines quit seven minutes ago."

"Quit or trailed off to where you couldn't hear them anymore?"

"Quit. I heard them wind down somewhere up on the ridge."

"It has to be the big meadow. That's the only place they could land one."

"Agreed," Hugh said.

Everyone in their group had hunted the ridge for deer and bear. Game was plentiful, but tougher to hunt in the unforgiving terrain of the wooded mountain range. The largest of the meadows was one of the few places where a hunter could post-up and get long sightlines.

It was late summer and the day was warm, but fall was in the air. Nights were getting cooler, leaves were changing color and dropping from the trees, and the summer garden was dying off. They followed the overgrown bulldozer road which wound up the mountain through a series of switchbacks. Their horses shuffled through dried leaves. Rabbits and squirrels fled at their approach. Grouse exploded from cover like feathered grenades.

After nearly an hour of riding, they reached the top of the ridge and the logging road flattened out. From there, the big meadow was perhaps a quarter mile to the west. They dismounted, tying their horses off where they could pluck at the sparse grass emerging from a dusting of topsoil.

The men communicated with hand signals, moving slow and watching their steps for anything that would make noise underfoot. The tall poplars, oaks, and maples that lined the road up the mountain were fewer here. Tall trees couldn't withstand the winds this high on the mountain. Stunted cedars and twisted mountain laurel replaced them, standing ancient and gnarled like arthritic fingers. Here and there they encountered pockets of sand spilling out from beneath boulders, a reminder that this mountain had once been the coast of an inland sea that spanned much of the eastern part of the country.

When they reached the meadow, the helicopter sat near its center, its blades still and its cargo disgorged onto the ground like the entrails of a gutted animal. They watched through binoculars as a team organized the unloaded gear and set up a camp. A heavily armed security guard nervously paced the perimeter of the operation, no doubt anticipating that the arrival of the noisy aircraft would inevitably bring company. The rest of the team members wore body armor and carried handguns, but Jim didn't see any more rifles.

"What now?" Hugh asked.

"We try to introduce ourselves without dying in the process."

"Or killing anyone else. According to the radio, we don't get power if we kill Lightspeed's people."

"Sounds reasonable." Jim stood and let his rifle hang across his chest. "You hang back until I call you, okay? You know what to do if this goes south."

Hugh nodded grimly. "Indeed I do. Cover your ass."

Jim raised his hands above his head, a posture he truly detested. He hated feeling helpless and the word "surrender" wasn't in his vocabulary, but he didn't want to appear threatening. He'd be totally at the mercy of a team of people he knew nothing about. He let out a long breath and walked into the clearing.

2

Jim made it less than a dozen steps from cover before the guard picked up his movement and spun on him, snapping his rifle up and leveling it. Jim stopped in his tracks, noting that the guard's finger was already resting on the trigger. He hated being on this end of a gun barrel.

"Easy there," said Jim. "I'm not here to cause trouble. I live in the valley to the north. I heard you land and decided to check it out. Are you Lightspeed's people?"

Jim's appearance had put the entire team on high alert and all work had stopped. The crew was frozen in their tracks, waiting to see how this situation unfurled.

"What's it to you?" the guard snapped.

Jim smiled wryly. "If you have to ask, it's obvious you haven't spent much time out here in the wild. For most of the last year, a helicopter showing up in the community meant nothing but trouble. I needed to confirm you were here to begin the power restoration and not here for nefarious purposes."

Jim remained there with his hands in the air, waiting for someone to tell him if they were Lightspeed's people or not. When they didn't, he felt the need to press the matter.

"We've been listening to Lightspeed on the radio. Obviously, if you're here to work on the power, we'll do everything we can to assist and make you comfortable. On the other hand, if you're here to cause trouble, we won't be so welcoming."

Finally, a woman stepped forward and held a hand up to calm the guard. "Why don't you lower your rifle, Meyers."

"I'm not comfortable doing that, Danielle."

"Look down, Meyers."

The guard didn't do as she asked, not taking his eyes off Jim. Jim understood the guard was being cautious, but he also knew what Danielle was trying to tell the guard. Hugh had Meyers in his sights.

"Listen to her, Meyers. Look down at your chest, just above your plate carrier. What does that glowing red dot tell you?"

Meyers looked down and saw the red dot of a laser beam resting just above the upper edge of his body armor.

"How about we all lower our weapons and play nice for a moment?" Jim asked. "There's no need to make this unpleasant. The soil on this mountain isn't even deep enough to dig a decent grave."

"Lower your weapon, Meyers," Danielle repeated. "We have a lot more communities to visit, and we can't treat everyone like they're the enemy. We're supposed to be here to help."

"You stick to the installations," Meyers said. "Keeping you guys safe is my job."

"My job isn't just installations, Meyers. I'm also the community liaison *and* the team leader. I'm in charge here."

"If it's any consolation, Meyers, I understand your dilemma," Jim told him. "A lot of good people have died in the last year and it's thrown off the natural balance of things. The ratio of assholes to decent folks is all out of whack and it might be a while before we thin the assholes out."

"Which are you?" Meyers had raised his cheek off the rifle, looking at Jim overtop the optic, but he hadn't lowered the weapon yet.

Jim cringed. "Geez, you had to ask, didn't you? If you ask me, I'm a decent guy. If the people in town had to vote on it, I'm afraid they'd give you a different answer. I don't make friends easily and I don't play well with others. Guess that makes me equal parts good guy and asshole."

Oddly enough, Meyers apparently could relate to Jim's blunt assessment of himself and he finally averted his rifle.

Jim slowly lowered his arms and the tension eased from the moment like water squeezed from a sponge. "Can I bring my buddy out now? I promise we won't get in the way or hold you up. I just wanted to ask some questions."

Meyers and Danielle exchanged glances, then she gave a nod of assent.

Catching the gesture, Jim called to Hugh, "Come on out!"

Seconds later, Hugh stepped into the clearing, his rifle at a low ready. When he reached Jim, the two of them moved closer to the group of visitors.

"I'm Jim Powell. Like I said, I live in the valley below here. We've been looking forward to your arrival, but you have to understand that folks are a little on edge out here in the wilder parts of the country. I don't know how much of the collapse you've seen firsthand, but we've been through a lot of crap out here. Most of the outside visitors we've had brought nothing but trouble."

Danielle stepped forward and extended her hand. Despite the rough setting of their fieldwork, Jim couldn't help but notice that her hands were clean and her fingernails painted. Her hair was fashionably cut and her clothes were in decent shape. The same appeared to be true for the rest of the clean-cut crew. It was a far cry from the state of most people living the collapse day to day. In Jim's community, like most others, grooming standards had slipped. Most people were wearing clothes that didn't fit right due to weight loss and they were all in need of repair.

"I'm Danielle Johns and I'm the team leader for this install crew."

Jim shook her hand, introducing himself and Hugh.

"If you've been listening to Lightspeed's public addresses, you might know that we've been at this for a couple of weeks now. We've got a barebones grid set up across most of Virginia now. Barring any problems, we should be here three days at the most, then we return to base to resupply. Right now the plan is that we keep doing that until the entire nation has electricity, which could take a year or more. You guys lucked up by being on the East Coast, so we got to you pretty quickly."

Jim thought those return trips to base every couple of days probably explained the condition of this crew. Regular showers, regular meals, clean clothes—all the luxuries that most people in the nation were missing. He didn't begrudge them that. If people had access to better resources, they'd be idiots to not take advantage of it. Everyone he knew would jump on the opportunity for better food, clean clothes, and a nice haircut if they could get it.

While Jim and Danielle spoke, the rest of the install team returned to what they'd been doing before Jim popped out of the woods. Meyers remained there at Danielle's side, not ready to fully trust Jim and Hugh yet. He took his job seriously.

"Listen, I know you have a lot of work to do," Jim said, "and I don't want to hold you up."

Danielle grinned. "The longer we stand around, the longer it takes to install your power."

"I assumed that, but I would like to hear some news of the world. Is there any chance you guys might want to join us for dinner at my place in the valley tonight? It's only a short hike. I could even send a wagon to come get you so you wouldn't have to walk."

"We can't leave the install site," Meyers interjected. "We can't risk the gear being stolen. Not to mention the helicopter."

Danielle nodded in agreement. "He's right. Our orders are not to leave the install site."

"What if we brought dinner to you?" Jim offered. "That might be easier anyway."

Danielle and Meyers looked at each other, as if trying to gauge the level of risk presented by this offer.

Meyers shrugged at Danielle. "As you just reminded me, you're the boss."

Danielle frowned at Meyers before replying. "That sounds

wonderful. The second step of the installation requires a local partner anyway, so this might be a good opportunity to see if you're the right person for that role."

Hugh grinned.

"What?" Danielle asked, catching the expression.

"Nothing. Jim is an icon of the community. A figurehead of high society. Loved by all, from old ladies to stray puppies."

Danielle looked suspicious. "I feel like you're teasing me."

"I am," Hugh admitted. "Jim is an asshole, but in his defense, he's a fair and dependable asshole. He might just be the right guy for whatever you need."

Danielle laughed. "I guess we'll find out tonight, won't we?"

As they made arrangements for dinner, Jim felt a sense of relief. It had been a while since there had been strangers in the valley who weren't trying to kill him. Maybe this was a turning point—that singular event around which the future revolved. The power these people were bringing could mean a new beginning for everyone. A chance to rebuild and revive their way of life. A point from which they could begin to heal. Despite the temptation to see this as the end of this horrible, disastrous period in American history, Jim couldn't let himself go there yet.

A few minutes later, Jim and Hugh said their goodbyes and left the install crew to their work. Walking back to their horses, Jim was lost in thought.

"What's brewing in that brain of yours?" Hugh asked.

"I was just thinking about what happens next, Hugh. Restoring power won't be a magic bullet. Once word of this gets out, everyone is going to think that going back to their old lives will be as simple as flipping a switch, but I'm betting that won't be the case."

"There's not nearly as many people as there used to be, for one thing," Hugh pointed out. "Nature thinned the herd."

"The people who are left are different. It'll be a different country. People may think they're ready for it, but I'm not so sure that getting power back will be the end of hard times. I hope so, but my gut tells me no."

3

Cookie had wanted to hold his meeting in the boardroom where the county board of supervisors had once held their regular meetings, thinking that would make the meeting feel more official. He'd already told people that was where they were going to meet, which may have been a little premature since he hadn't cleaned the room out yet. In fact, he had not even been in there since the collapse. Now that he finally stood inside the boardroom, he was questioning the wisdom of his choice and wishing he'd never told anyone they'd meet there. The place was a wreck.

Cookie had never been much of an organizer or a leader before the collapse, but the disaster had brought something out in him. He'd worked in sales at the local building supply store and had no interest in politics or community service, but he understood efficiency. Everything that was happening in town was the opposite of efficient. Everyone was running around like chickens with their heads cut off and much of their effort was wasted because they were so disorganized.

He knew the people of the town needed to do something, but he wasn't sure exactly what. He found a few people who thought like he did, and they approached another local man, Jim Powell, who had a good grasp on survival skills. No one in the town would have listened to Jim if he'd tried to organize them. Most of them didn't trust him because he was rude, abrasive, and way too blunt for most people.

Even so, Cookie understood that Jim had skills they needed. Under Jim's tutelage, Cookie had spent the spring and summer organizing the town to work together. They had people assigned to caring for livestock that grazed the athletic fields. When one of the animals was slaughtered, they worked together to make sure they got maximum use out of the meat, distributing it to everyone who wanted some. It was much less wasteful than the previous system, in which people were randomly killing animals, hacking off a few crude cuts of meat, and leaving the rest to rot.

Cookie also organized people into improving the water system so people had clean drinking water. They installed a few primitive solar systems so people could recharge batteries and access power if they needed it. Some gardened, some gathered wood, and some repaired occupied homes. Together, there was less wasted effort and more efficiency. Now Cookie was ready to take it a step further.

He'd brought his family along with him to help clean the boardroom since he couldn't find anyone else interested in volunteering their labor for the cause. Everyone else said they had their regular jobs to do and no spare time for another project. Cookie's wife Caroline had started throwing him looks as soon as they stepped inside the office building, wondering what he'd gotten them into. His teenage son and daughter were much more vocal in their criticism. They'd complained and mumbled nonstop since they arrived.

"What is that *smell*?" his daughter Amelia asked. She gagged dramatically, a palm pressed to her chest. "I think I'm going to die."

Indeed, the air inside the room was stale, having been trapped in there for over a year without the benefit of heating or air conditioning. The air was damp and lay on their bodies like an oily film. Even beyond that musty smell, there was an undertone of other unidentifiable odors. Though Cookie didn't want to let his mind go there, he couldn't stop it.

"This place smells like butt!" Anthony was pretty much a fifteen-year-old version of his father. Same stocky build, same red hair.

"Anthony!" Caroline snarled. "I don't like you talking that way."

"It's true," he protested. "I feel like I just walked into a dead deer's butt after it's been roasting on the highway for a couple of days."

Amelia's gagging only got worse at that image. Still, the accuracy of Anthony's description hit home for all of them. Even Cookie was feeling a bit queasy.

"Do we have to do this?" Caroline asked. "Are you sure it's worth it?"

Cookie cocked his head and spoke as if he had a larger audience than just his family. He sounded like a TV dad lecturing his family about something they had to do for their own good. "Listen, if we don't do this, who will? Our community is a lot smaller now since so many people left or...passed. Everyone has to step up."

Caroline shot Cookie a look that temporarily made him lose track of what he was saying. The death toll from the disaster was a sensitive subject since both kids had lost friends and were still struggling with the trauma of that. Some had simply disappeared with their entire families and no one knew where they had gone. Others had died in one of the multitude of ways in which one could expire these days—violence, illness, starvation, even freezing to death.

With an apologetic shrug to his wife, Cookie continued. There were only so many ways to sugarcoat things without lying outright. "My point is that we all have to buckle down and shoulder some of the responsibility for bringing back our community. Look at it like the early pioneer days. There's a lot of work and only a few people to do it. We're pioneers rebuilding society."

"Did it smell like roadkill butt in pioneer days?" Anthony muttered.

Cookie shot his son a disapproving look. "I find your attitude disappointing, Anthony."

"That's my attitude too," said Amelia. "I don't care if it's disappointing or not. I feel like I'm going to hurl."

Cookie looked at his wife again and saw that she was siding with the kids on this matter. "Okay, how about I go down the hall and check out the boardroom? Once I see what it looks like, I'll come back and give you a report. How's that sound? Then we can decide what we're going to do."

"We'll wait outside," Caroline said, immediately sweeping the children toward the exit.

Left alone in the vast, empty office building, Cookie let out a sigh before heading down the hall. All around him there were signs of what had taken place in the building over the past year. Stained ceiling tiles revealed places where the flat roof had leaked. Some of the damp tiles had eventually broken and lay crumbled on the floor, leaving gaps in the flat plane of the ceiling grid. Office chairs were scattered throughout the hall, as if left behind after some impromptu and disorganized meeting. Scattered papers littered the carpeted floor. On a wide expanse of white wall, someone had used markers to draw pictures, most of them crude and pornographic. When they grew bored with their work, they'd stabbed their drawing instruments into the wall and left them stuck there like knives.

Cookie reached the boardroom and stared at the heavy door with its walnut stain. Beneath the sign that said "boardroom," someone had carved the words "bored room" into the wood. Cookie shoved the door open.

The boardroom was dimly lit by sunlight filtering through a row of high windows that lined one wall. A thick film of grime coated the outside of the windows, giving the light an amber cast. Opening the door had disturbed the layer of dust that coated everything, and motes floated in the air, illuminated by the sharp, angular light. It was like entering some ancient tomb.

Cookie walked to the center of the room, the scuffing of his shoes on the low pile carpet the only sound in the silent space. The room was in shambles. The chairs were overturned, and the table was covered in dust, broken ceiling tiles, and other debris. Cookie pulled out a handkerchief and covered his nose and mouth, but it did little to block the stench.

He understood that part of the odor came from mildew, both

from the building being closed up with poor ventilation and from the roof leaking. However, that wasn't all of it. A sleeping bag lay stretched out on the conference table and the crusty stiffness of it made Cookie wonder if someone had died in it. But if so, why on Earth did they leave the bag behind? They should at least have had the decency to toss it outside.

More of the smell was explained when Cookie caught sight of a metal chair with the bottom knocked out of it. Someone had put it in the corner and used it as a toilet. Judging from the heaped pile of waste beneath it, whoever had been staying there had stayed for a while.

Cookie shook his head at the state of the room and muttered, "Filthy animals."

There was no way he could bring his family in here and ask them to clean up this filth. The entire building needed to be gutted down to the studs. It would need drywall, paint, ceiling tiles, and new carpet. It was simply too much work and it went way beyond a simply cleaning.

Cookie suddenly felt exhausted and wanted to sit down. He couldn't see a single place to sit that wasn't filthy. He stood there feeling totally defeated. He wanted to keep the momentum of the summer projects going. With the summer's work over, he wanted to find new projects to keep his volunteers busy. Additionally, he wanted to bring in even more people, so they'd get more accomplished. Having the meeting there in that room would have been symbolic, a sign of people governing themselves and doing a better job of it than the politicians who'd failed them.

He blew out a hard breath and tried to pump himself up, to regain his earlier momentum. "This is not going to stop us," he said aloud to the empty room. "This is a bump, not a roadblock."

He knew he sounded ridiculous. He was spouting empty expressions into an equally empty room in an attempt to inspire himself. He had to keep going. This destroyed boardroom was one room in one building in one town. Their town was only one small part of a collapsed nation. If he couldn't muster the courage to keep going in the face of hardship, what hope was there for the nation as a whole?

Cookie left the room, headed down the hall, and exited through the unlocked front door. His family sat on the sidewalk and they all looked up at him with dread in their eyes, fully expecting to be ordered back inside.

"We're going home," Cookie announced. "We'll find another place to have the meeting and maybe I can get some volunteers to start cleaning this building. Once I got in the boardroom, it was even worse than the hallway."

His stoic and downcast family started grinning and clapping exuberantly. A chorus of cheers went up and they jumped to their feet to wrap him in a collective hug. It was a short one. Almost immediately they backed off, noses crinkling in disgust.

Amelia covered her mouth, her chest heaving as she fought not to throw up. She staggered a safe distance away from her father and sucked in a deep breath of fresh air.

"You need a bath," said Caroline. "I'm not even sure you can go in the house smelling like this."

"You smell like roadkill butt." Anthony cackled. "Dead, rotting skunk butt."

4

Jim had learned a long time ago that food could get you through a lot of doors. In their dark world, where currency was useless, food was perhaps the single best way to win someone over. That was exactly what Jim had in mind when he offered to feed the power installation crew. That evening, he led a small group from the valley up the mountain to the meadow where Lightspeed's team was working.

They had two packhorses loaded down with coolers. Some of the coolers held warm foods, while others held foods they'd "refrigerated" in the cold water of their springhouse. The group consisted of Jim, Hugh, Ellen, and Gary. Randi, Lloyd, Pete, and Charlie were all working at the roadhouse that evening while Ariel stayed home with her grandparents.

When the riders finally reached the meadow, Jim found the power installation crew packing up their tools for the day. While they'd all been fresh, clean, and energetic that morning they now looked like different people entirely. Jim almost felt sorry for them in their dirty, sweat-stained clothes, moving slow and stiff from the exertion of the day. Their faces were smudged with grime and grease, their expressions weary. It was as if they were unused to this level of physical exertion, but if they kept doing these installations, that would probably change. It appeared to be heavy, exhausting work.

"Hey there," Jim called out, throwing a hand up in the air as they approached.

Meyers, the security guard, had heard them coming before they got close. He'd been waiting for them with his rifle ready, then lowered it upon recognizing Jim and Hugh.

"I promised you a meal." Jim gestured at the packhorses. "I hope you guys are hungry."

Though the crew had been wary of Jim this morning, exhaustion and hunger forced them to push aside their suspicion, just as Jim had expected it would. They wouldn't question a man bearing food.

Danielle smiled wearily. "You're just in time. We're knocking off for the day and no one enjoys MREs. No one."

Hugh grimaced. "Me neither."

Jim's group dismounted, then set about unloading the coolers and packs of gear they'd brought along with them. Even while they worked, no one let their rifle stray too far from their reach. Although things had been mostly peaceful as of late, they all operated under the awareness that an attack could come from anywhere at any moment. They'd learned to stay ready.

"What's the situation like around here?" Meyers asked, approaching the group.

Hugh led the horses a short distance away and tied them off, while Ellen and Jim worked to clear a fire circle so they could reheat the food. Gary stood by with his rifle hanging around his chest, acting as an additional sentry.

"Right now things are pretty calm," Jim said. "It hasn't always been that way. We've fought thieves, rogue cops, criminals, neighbors, strangers, foreign soldiers, and UN peacekeepers. I've killed people who might have been from our own military and others I don't know what the hell they were. There was also some guy who called himself a regional sheriff, a politician or two, and some guys who might have been government contractors."

Meyers stood there listening to Jim rattle off his list with a disturbed look on his face, like he was waiting for a punch line that never came. When Jim stopped, he asked, "Seriously?"

Jim's brow furrowed as he considered what he'd just said. "It *does* sound like a lot when you list them all like that. It's been a tough year, but I haven't kept a body count. I prefer not to know."

Jim, Gary, and Hugh gathered rocks for a circle, while Ellen gathered kindling. Jim lugged a pair of grapefruit-sized rocks to the circle, dropped them, then nudged them into position with the toe of his boot.

"I wasn't aware things were that bad for the average person," said Meyers. "I've mostly worked as a contractor since the collapse and it's kind of been business as usual."

"Seriously?" Jim said. "You had no idea we've all been fighting for our lives out here?"

Meyers shrugged. "I've seen some shit, but it sounds like you've seen more action than I have. I've mostly worked protective details with VIPs. I might have killed two or three guys, but that's it."

"I'm not proud of it, but there's been days I've killed that many before lunch," Jim said.

"We've seen more action than we wanted to see." Gary added two more rocks to the circle. "Jim and I used to work together, and we figured out a long time ago that we thought alike. We were both preppers, but things got way worse than we expected. In fact, my family had to move out of our community because we couldn't defend our home. We were under constant attack."

"I've heard stories like that," Meyers said.

Danielle joined them, wiping her hands on her pants. "I have too."

Ellen struck a lighter to a compacted ball of dried grass. It flared to a larger flame, a wisp of smoke rising as the fire spread to the twigs Ellen piled atop it. In less than a minute, she had a decent fire going. It wasn't enough to draw attention from down below but was hot enough for reheating food.

"I think it's been way more violent than anyone expected," said Hugh. "There's always someone wanting to take your stuff."

Jim placed a metal grate over the fire, resting it on the rocks. "Or someone ready to kill you just for the hell of it."

"There's an army of install teams out there doing the same thing we're doing," Danielle said, wiping her face with a bandana. "The only consistent thing they're reporting back is that there *is* no consistency across the country. Admittedly, we're in the early stages and we haven't gotten past Virginia yet, but there's a huge variation in how communities are doing. It's like America has split up into thousands of little regions and subcultures."

"Really?" Ellen opened a cooler and removed some foil-wrapped items to place on the grill.

"It's everywhere on the spectrum," Danielle said. "We dropped into some rural communities in eastern Virginia where we never saw a single living soul the entire time we were there."

"What happened to the locals?" Gary asked. "Did they die off from disease or starvation?"

Danielle shook her head. "Some were driven out by violence, judging by the shot-up houses, the bodies, and the shell casings. Some looked as if they'd gotten sick from bad water and didn't have the meds to treat it. And yes, there were even those who looked like they wasted away due to a lack of food. It's been heartbreaking."

Jim pulled a clear water bladder from a pack and hung it from a tree, then tested the spout to make sure it would dispense properly. "We've seen plenty of violence, but I don't know of any local communities that have turned into ghost towns."

"You guys are lucky," Meyers said. "You've got isolation and remoteness working for you. These mountains are the kind of place where strangers might be less likely to show up and try to take over."

Jim laughed. "Flatlanders might be all about inclusivity during good times, but the minute the grid goes down they're back to thinking all of us hillbillies are inbred, gun-toting, paranoid wackos."

"They'd only be wrong about the inbred part," Hugh pointed out.

Everyone laughed.

"But we've still had strangers show up," Jim said. "Some wanted to rob us. Others wanted to run us off and take our land. The fact that we're here and they're not should tell you how that went."

"Can we talk about something more pleasant?" Ellen got to her feet. "How many people do you have, Danielle?"

"Eight total."

"We brought fresh water to drink if you need some. I wish we could have brought iced tea or something, but our supply of coffee, tea, and drink mixes is nearly gone," Ellen said. "We prepared for the worst, but we didn't expect the worst to last so long."

"Hopefully the worst is behind us," Danielle said.

Ellen pointed down at the grill. "We have shish kebabs made with beef, chicken, onions, peppers, and chicken of the woods mushrooms we harvest off the mountain here. There's also homemade flatbread, which is what I call my tortillas when they turn out too thick."

"They're fine," Jim said.

Hugh's face lit up. "They're amazing."

"Thanks, guys." Ellen flashed them a smile. "There's also a fruit salad made with fruits and nuts that come from our valley. One of the coolers is full of corn on the cob from our garden. There are jalapeno poppers stuffed with homemade cheese and some baked potatoes, along with plenty of homemade butter."

"God, I'm drooling," Meyers said.

"You came at a good time," said Jim. "Right after gardening season there's always more to choose from. A few months from now it'll all be preserved foods, except for the meats."

"You guys can dig in when you're ready," Ellen said.

Danielle waved the rest of her people over and Ellen handed out paper plates, another thing they were nearly out of. Now they used real plates at home and took turns washing them, which was a job no one enjoyed.

Jim added a few more pieces of wood to the fire since the smoke helped keep biting insects at bay. Once everyone had filled their plates and taken a seat in the grass, Jim and his people dug in.

"Are all of you from this community?" Danielle asked, sweeping a finger to indicate the people in Jim's group.

"I lived in this valley behind us even before the collapse," Jim said. "My wife and I have two kids. I was out of town when the shit hit the fan, which is a story in itself. While I was gone, my parents moved in with my wife and kids to help them out."

Jim went on to recount the story of how he and Gary got home from Richmond, then the events which led Gary, Randi, and Charlie to end up living in the valley. By the time he was done, the members of the install team appeared to be in shock. The things being described to them were clearly outside of their range of experiences.

"What about you guys?" Ellen asked. "Tell us about Walter Lightspeed. He's fascinating."

Members of Danielle's team took turns spinning the story of Lightspeed and how he came to assume the presidency of the United States. They talked about the Punch List he'd used to eliminate those in government who were working against the best interests of the American people. The most surprising element of their story was just how many people were determined to kill Lightspeed even now that he was turning the lights back on.

"That's hard to believe," Hugh said. "You'd think someone could put a stop to that, whether it's the military or one of our allies."

"No one knows where to point the finger," said Meyers. "There are foreign governments trying to take him out. Members of our own government. Other billionaires who decided if Lightspeed could take over the country, then maybe they'd kill him and take it for themselves. It's like *everyone* wants him dead."

"Except for the average American sitting home in the dark," Jim added. "That guy doesn't care. He just wants light, heat, and clean water again."

"Hopefully we can provide some relief for that guy," said Danielle. "It'll take us two more days to get the repeater in position, then it's only a matter of installing the converters in individual homes. When we leave, we'll be dropping the converters off with a local representative and training them on how to install them. It's a simple process that only takes a couple of minutes."

"Is that what you were telling Jim about earlier?" Hugh asked.

Danielle nodded. "Yes, I was hoping he might be interested in serving as our local partner and distributing the converters."

Ellen let out the same laugh Hugh had earlier that day.

Danielle looked at her warily. "Okay, I'm starting to get a little worried. This is the second time someone has burst into laughter when I suggested Jim might be a good local partner."

Ellen held a hand up. "No, he'll be fine. He'll be responsible for it. It's just that my husband is a bit of a controversial figure in the community. Anything that involves him, regardless of what it is, creates drama."

"Should I ask someone else?" Danielle asked Jim's group.

Despite their laughter, no one suggested that she do so.

"He'll be fair," Hugh said. "Even if he has to kill a few guys to keep it that way."

Danielle chuckled until she saw that no one else was laughing. "I'd rather you not have to kill people to distribute our electrical components."

"Same here," said Jim. "I'd rather not have to kill anyone in the process."

"The power isn't the only thing you'll be getting soon," Danielle said. "There's a road clearing crew working their way in this direction. They don't move as fast as we do, but they're making progress. Once they get here, you'll begin receiving regular aid deliveries by truck. At least that's the plan."

"How far along are they?" Gary asked. "The adults in my family are faring okay, but I still have some grandchildren in diapers and we ran out of those a long time ago. I hope those aid shipments include diapers."

"I've helped load a few of the trucks," Meyers said. "The shipments include infant formula and over-the-counter medications for children, but I don't recall if there are diapers or not."

When she was done eating, Danielle set her plate down in front of her and took a long sip from her water bottle. She extracted a packet of cigarettes from her pocket, flipped one from the pack, and placed it between her lips, lighting it with a butane lighter.

From across the fire, Hugh was watching, mesmerized. He'd smoked nothing but hand-rolled cigarettes for months.

Catching his stare, Danielle asked, "Would you like one?" She removed the pack from her pocket and held it out in his direction.

Hugh took the pack and removed one, then handed it back over. He slowly dragged one of the store-bought cigarettes below his nose as if enjoying the bouquet of a fine wine. He released a sigh of contentment, then lit the cigarette and inhaled deeply. Everyone around the campfire was watching him with amusement.

"I can't believe that after months of smoking pure unadulterated tobacco you can even enjoy one of those things," Jim said, a disturbed look on his face.

"Hand-rolled cigarettes satisfy the craving." Hugh held the lit cigarette out in front of him as if it were a thing of beauty. "But you quickly realize it's the toxic chemicals that make them taste so good."

Everyone but Hugh laughed at that comment. They talked for two more hours until members of the install team began to yawn, their eyes glazing over as the fire lulled them into a hypnotic state.

"We need to go," Ellen said.

Jim had pressed the team with questions the entire time, wanting to take full advantage of this rare opportunity to learn more about the outside world. He reluctantly gave in, understanding that Ellen was right. He didn't want to overstay his welcome.

"If you'll mark your house on our GPS, we'll deliver those converters to you when we head out day after tomorrow," said Danielle.

"Can I get you to drop them off in town?" Jim asked. "That'll save me the trouble of hauling them."

"Will they be safe?" Danielle asked. "There's a black market for these things."

"We have a place in town," Jim said. "A kind of restaurant/bar/trading post. We started it as a way to monitor what was going on in our community, but it's grown into something else."

"You can store the converters there?" Meyers asked.

"The place is guarded twenty-four hours a day," Hugh said. "No one will be able to steal them."

"Sounds interesting," Danielle said. "I look forward to seeing this business of yours."

5

Jim arrived at the Reset Roadhouse midmorning the next day. He'd ridden into town alone since all his people had other things going on. Hugh was up on the mountain, having decided to assist Danielle's installation crew with the electrical repeater. He was fascinated with the technology and wanted to understand how it worked. He'd asked a million questions at dinner the previous night and Danielle told him the easiest way to understand the device was to watch it being installed.

Although the roadhouse wouldn't open for another hour, there was already activity taking place when Jim stepped inside. Ed was in the far corner of the room, monitoring his brewing and distilling operations. Jim had brought him to the roadhouse from a nearby town after a fire had destroyed his brewery. Ed lived at the roadhouse full-time and was content with the arrangement. He enjoyed making beer and liquor more than running the establishment that served it.

Another new resident of the roadhouse was Ian, the vendor they'd met at the local farmers market who sold homemade stabby things. He had a house in town and had been living there since the collapse. He'd done all right, selling and trading homemade weapons to keep himself fed. It was late summer now, though, and the idea of spending another cold winter alone in his house didn't appeal to him. The arrangement worked well for everyone. Because they stored weapons, food, and other merchandise at the roadhouse, they had to guard the place at night. The more people they had living there, the safer it would be.

In the colder weather, there was also the matter of keeping the fires stoked. The large building required multiple woodstoves to stay warm. If the temperature was allowed to drop too much, it could take days to warm the building back up. That many woodstoves required a lot of feeding and Ian would also help with that. He'd taken one of the spare offices and converted it into a bedroom, bringing a few things from home, including the tools of his trade. Jim allowed him to set up a booth in the roadhouse. There, Ian could work at his trade and sell his wares year-round.

Ian waved when Jim entered the building. He was seated at a pedal-operated grinding wheel, converting cheap Chinese screw-drivers into icepick-style weapons. "Morning, Jim."

"Morning! How were things around here last night?"

Ian smirked. "Lively."

Jim cocked an eyebrow. "What did I miss?"

"We had a big crowd. I am not sure exactly why, but it was a spontaneous vibe. Like the warm day made people realize that there wouldn't be very many more of them before winter hit, so they wanted to take full advantage of it."

"Sounds like a party."

Ian checked his watch. "It was, and it only ended about four hours ago."

"You're kidding. That might be the record."

"The party would probably still be going on if the music hadn't ended."

"What happened to the music?" Jim asked.

"It passed out."

Jim laughed. "You mean Lloyd quit playing while there were still people here? That's not like him."

"I don't think Lloyd had any choice in the matter. The liquor made the decision. One minute he was playing, the next he was tipping over like a felled tree." Ian nodded toward the far end of the roadhouse.

Built against an end wall a short distance from the loading dock, a crude stage elevated the performers a few feet above the crowd. Lloyd had chosen the spot because he said it provided the best acoustics. Apparently, it also offered good sleeping because Jim could make out a lump on the stage.

"I'm guessing that's Lloyd. Is he in a sleeping bag or a body bag?" Jim asked. In an apocalyptic roadhouse, either was a possibility.

"Sleeping bag. We covered him where he fell."

"Any trouble?"

"Out of Lloyd or anyone else?"

"Anyone."

Ian shook his head. "Things were cool. Becky sold all the food that had been prepared for dinner. She had Pete and Charlie hustling in the kitchen making popcorn and homemade potato chips, which she sold as fast as they could make. She also had eight pounds of deer jerky and sold every bit of it."

"That the jerky Shade Wolford gave her?" Jim asked.

"Yes, but I heard her telling folks last night that her boyfriend made it, so I assume Shade is more than just a regular at the bar now."

Jim shrugged. "You had to wonder why he was here in town so often. He lives a good distance out and he's been at the bar almost every night since this summer."

"I don't think Shade has been going home, if you know what I mean. He's been staying here in town, with Becky, but they don't want to make a thing of it."

"He's a good man. I like having him around." Jim winced. "I don't know about that jerky of his though."

"It must be good. People were eating it like it was going out of style."

"You ever talk to him about his jerky?" Jim asked.

Ian shook his head. "We've talked about a lot of things, but the topic of jerky has ever come up."

"We had that conversation once. Shade and I were talking about preserving meat and he made an offhand comment that any animal with enough meat made decent jerky if you prepared it right."

Ian stopped his work and gave Jim a disturbed look. "*Any animal?*"

"Raccoon, possum, groundhog—"

Ian cut him off. "Please tell me the man doesn't make jerky out of dogs."

"No dogs because I asked him the very same thing. He told me he didn't consider dogs to be animals. They were a step above the rest of them. He did mention that he'd once made jerky out of a mule that had broken its leg and a blue heron just to see if it could be done."

"I'm not eating anymore of Dr. Frankenstein's beef jerky," Ian said. "Thanks a lot, Jim."

"What about the store?" Jim asked, changing the subject.

"Randi was hustling all night. I don't know what all she sold, but she was constantly haggling with someone."

"I'll check the ledger. Sounds like a good night. Guess I better check on Lloyd and make sure he's breathing."

The roadhouse had once been a factory and most of the building consisted of a single open space. When converting it into the roadhouse, Jim had added woodstoves and they'd used old cable spools as tables. As Jim wove his way through the tables, he spotted Gary's family entering through the side door.

Operating the roadhouse required the effort of their entire clan. They rotated duties, and this week Gary and his family were responsible for preparing the single meal that would be sold as lunch. It was usually something simple, such as a sandwich or a stew. People who brought their own bowl or mug received a discount.

Jim climbed up the side steps onto the three-foot-high stage and glanced down at his oldest friend. Ian wasn't kidding when he said Lloyd passed out. It looked like he'd simply fallen over backwards and lost consciousness while playing the banjo, just as Ian had described.

Aware that customers would be showing up soon for lunch, Jim didn't want to leave Lloyd here in the public eye. He gripped one corner of the sleeping bag and tugged it off him. He was amused to see that someone had taken chalk and drawn an outline around Lloyd's banjo-toting body as if he were a corpse at a crime scene.

The movement of the sleeping bag being dragged off him made Lloyd stir. Jim expected a pained groan or perhaps even a bout of dry heaving, but what happened was even more disturbing. Lloyd sat upright so quickly it was as if he were spring-operated. He made a loud strum across the banjo strings and immediately launched into a clawhammer banjo version of "Good Old Mountain Dew," a song about making bootleg whiskey.

After his quiet, peaceful morning, the loud banjo assaulted Jim's senses on every level. It was an affront to everything serene. He winced and covered his ears, then nudged Lloyd with the toe of his boot. "Hey! Hey! It's too early for that. Give it a rest."

Lloyd quit singing and his fingers gradually slowed their strumming as if he were some animatronic musician whose plug had been pulled. He looked around the room with confusion. "Where is everybody? What happened to the audience?"

"They're gone, Lloyd. It's the next day and almost time for the lunch crowd to begin rolling in. I don't need you lying here like some hobo at the bus station."

"The next day?" Lloyd was clearly confused. Somehow, he thought that he'd simply quit playing and was picking up where he left off.

"You need more sleep," Jim said. "Take that infernal instrument of torture with you and go lie down in a back room somewhere."

"Uh, you're right. I'm not hitting on all cylinders yet."

Lloyd slid off the end of the stage and wobbled his way through the empty tables, still confused as to what had happened to his audience. Jim watched him go, shaking his head in disbelief. Just as he hopped off the stage to touch base with Gary, he spotted someone he recognized entering the side door.

"You're a little early for lunch, Cookie."

From the corner of his eye, Jim saw Ian, Ed, and Gary all watching this interaction. The three of them had enough experience with Jim to know that anything was possible when he met with the community. The situation could go from friendly to nuclear in the blink of an eye. They were relieved to see the man at the door was someone Jim got along with. Most likely no blood would be spilled.

Cookie extended a hand. "Morning, Jim. How's it going?"

Jim grinned. "Not too bad. Just sweeping out the drunks left over from last night."

Cookie smiled back. "Copy that. I might have been swept out of here once or twice, myself."

"The general public gets swept out at closing time. Friends can lie here till morning."

Cookie held up a thick stack of handmade posters. "I've been running around town this morning putting up signs. I wanted to see if I might be able to post a couple here." Cookie gave Jim one to examine.

It was simple and to the point:

*L*ooking *for volunteers to help clean out the courthouse, the community center, and the local government offices. No pay other than a sense of accomplishment and good company. We'll be working there for a couple of hours every morning. Bring your own gloves and masks. If you have shovels, rakes, brooms, or wheelbarrows, those would be helpful too.*

"M*y* k*ids* m*ade* t*he* s*igns*," Cookie explained. "I tried to get my family to help me get started on those buildings, but they were too disgusting. People have been living there and maybe even *dying* there. To call those places filthy is an understatement. It's too much work for one person and I need some volunteers."

Jim handed the poster back. "You're welcome to put them up here. Not sure you're going to get any help out of my staff. My people and I have our hands full between running this place and keeping our homes going."

Cookie waved a hand. "I get it. I just wanted to know if I could stick a poster up in here. You get a lot of traffic and I figured more people would see it."

Jim pointed to a part of the roadhouse where four bulletin boards had been attached to the wall. "Knock yourself out."

Those bulletin boards had become a hive of activity around the community. They were covered with hundreds of notes posted by people passing through the roadhouse. Some people came there not to eat, drink, or buy things, but simply to read the messages on the bulletin board. Jim was fine with that. It was a community service he could perform with minimal effort and yet one more way of easing the longstanding tension between him and the town.

Beside the bulletin board there was a table there with blank paper, ink pens, and thumbtacks for anyone wanting to leave a message. Some people posted notes asking if anyone had information on a missing person. Others were attempts to locate specific goods they needed, such as eyeglasses, wheelchairs, medications, or diabetic supplies. Families with young children listed clothes and shoes they had available for trade. There were people selling services and others searching for people to perform a certain service. Some needed chimneys cleaned or firewood supplied. There was a man delivering coal from a local mine with a horse and buggy. There were people selling all manner of livestock or looking for animals to grow their herd. Others were selling food, homemade items, or goods they'd come across one way or another. To the community, this bulletin board was like Craigslist, the local news, *Dateline*, and Tinder had all come together in one singular place.

"Everyone who comes in the roadhouse spends some time at that board, Cookie. It's the closest thing this town has to a newspaper or Internet these days. Sometimes I get sucked into the damn thing and can barely pull myself away. All these missing and desperate people... there's an entire tragedy written here."

Cookie offered a somber shake of his head. "I can hardly allow myself to think of that. It's too much."

"I know exactly what you mean." Jim stared at a blurry photograph with the word "missing" scrawled across the top.

"I better be going. I've got more signs to put up and if I get sucked into this board, I won't get anything done."

As Cookie was walking off, Jim asked, "What's the point in cleaning those offices out? I can't imagine anyone will be working out of the courthouse or government offices anytime soon. Even when we get some power back on, those institutions are going to be paralyzed for a long time."

Cookie stopped and thought for a moment. "You remember when I approached you at the farmer's market?"

"I remember," Jim said sheepishly.

"You'd pretty much cussed the whole town out and told us we should be working together instead of sitting around feeling sorry for ourselves." Cookie chuckled at the memory. "I took you seriously. You knew what you were talking about and the rest of us were running around like chickens with our heads cut off."

"You and your friends have done a good job with that, Cookie. This town is in a lot better shape going into winter than they were going into summer. You should be proud of what you've done."

"It's been interesting," Cookie said. "I never wanted to be a politician, but that's kind of what I feel like. I spend a lot of time coercing people into doing things that need done. It feels like a big waste of my time, but I can't do everything by myself. Although people are working together, it's taken a major effort to make it happen."

"I get that. My plan was always that my family would work together to take on any disaster by ourselves. We'd hole up, hide out, and wait for it to be over. Didn't take me long to realize we needed help. The only way we all survived was by working together. It was a hard lesson to learn. I realize now that a lot of my logic was flawed."

"At least you'd thought some of this out. I was blindsided," Cookie said. "As far as cleaning out those offices, I don't care about the stupid things government used to do there, like vehicle registrations, county taxes, and registering deeds. There are other things we could do in that space that might actually be useful. Things that would help the community."

"Like what?"

"Maybe we could get a clinic going. I'm sure there are doctors and nurses who would be willing to practice in exchange for barter goods. Obviously, we couldn't do complicated lab work, advanced diagnostics, or even prescribe many medicines, but surely they could provide some basic services. Same with dentistry. Perhaps even counseling for some of the people suffering from PTSD from this whole mess."

Jim frowned. "Show me someone who doesn't have PTSD. I'm probably on the fringe of being a sociopath and this whole situation has still messed me up. I don't think anyone who has lived through it will ever be the same again."

"You mentioned something once about creating an emergency shelter for the elderly," Cookie said. "A place for people who might freeze this winter because they can't take care of a fire, put in wood, or just don't have the resources to keep going. Seeing the way you heated this place with a bunch of stoves made me think we might be able to do the same with parts of the government offices."

"I'd be glad to help you figure that out if you need me to. I've got a lot of experience with stoves and I know where a few are to be found."

"I may take you up on that, *if* I can get those buildings cleaned out."

"You'll get it figured out," Jim said. "You're doing this for the right reason. You're trying to help people, not take advantage of them. That makes a difference."

Cookie smiled at Jim's comment. "I appreciate you saying that. Most of the time this is a thankless job. I've never wanted to be in the public eye, but it feels like the right thing to do. Like, if each person did a little something to try and restore normality, there would be a momentum that took over and carried us forward."

"I wish each person *would* do that, but most people are just concerned about themselves. I've been guilty of it at times," Jim admitted.

"We all are," Cookie said.

"Hey, if you'd like the chance to plead your case in person, why don't you come by here tomorrow night? We're having our first open mic night. People from the community can come up on stage to sing or play a song. It should be a blast. I'll give you a few minutes on stage to ask for volunteers if you're interested."

Cookie shifted uncomfortably. "I've never been much of one for public speaking, but it comes with the territory. I'll do it, even if I know it's going to suck."

Hearing Cookie say those words reminded Jim of his own personal struggles early in the collapse. After a difficult walk home from Richmond, he wanted nothing more than to be left alone with his family, yet there were constant demands placed upon him. His friends and neighbors were struggling. They needed a leader, and as much as he wanted to disappear into the background, that was not an option. He was the only person with the knowledge and skills for the job.

"Maybe the best leaders aren't those who want the position," Jim said. "They're probably created by the situation. They're the ones who only take the job because there's no one else to do it and they refuse to allow it to go undone any longer."

Cookie nodded. "That pretty much hits the nail on the head. I'll come back tomorrow."

6

"I got it," said Herring.

Everyone in the crew perked up at those words. The searching was always the most stressful part of their job. Even though they could track them on GPS, catching up to them on horseback took a while. Weeks ago they'd managed to get a satellite tracker onboard one of Lightspeed's helicopters so they could track one of the crews installing the electrical repeater stations in Virginia. With each installation, electrical power was gradually being restored to more people.

"About damn time." Foley got to his feet and took the binoculars from Herring. He smiled when he verified what Herring had seen. The bright orange balloon that held Lightspeed's wireless power repeater was indeed being inflated on a nearby ridgeline.

It was hard to miss the repeaters once they were sent aloft. They were like gigantic orange weather balloons tethered in place by steel cables and attached to anchors driven deep into the earth. They were usually mounted on high peaks, like cellular towers, so Lightspeed could get maximum coverage from a single repeater.

Foley returned the binoculars to Herring. "Saddle up, boys. Let's hit the road."

Once the GPS tracker told them that they were close to the helicopter, Foley's team of rogues would post up on a mountaintop and take turns scanning the nearby peaks with binoculars, like fire spotters searching for a blaze. Once they spotted the balloon being inflated, they'd mount up and ride without pause until they neared the installation site. Then it was just a matter of keeping the install team under surveillance until the job was completed.

"I wish we could just steal them from the installation team," Mickelson said.

Mickelson was new to the team and Foley wasn't sure he was going to make it. He was proving too soft for this line of work, constantly complaining about the long hours in the saddle, the bugs, and sleeping on the ground. Foley had already decided that if Mickelson continued whining, he was going to cut him loose. Mickelson's first run could well end up being his last.

"We can't steal them from the installers," Foley said with a tone of a man tired of having to explain himself over and over. "If we do that, Lightspeed is just going to put more security on the installation teams, or he'll change the process for distributing the wireless converters. The way we're doing things right now works, you just have to be patient."

"I never was good at waiting," Mickelson griped.

"Then maybe you should shut your trap and go home." Herring tossed his saddle blanket over his horse. "I'm sure I'm not the only one tired of listening to your bellyaching."

Mickelson stuck out his chest and tensed his muscles. He pointed a finger at Herring. "If a son-of-a-bitch is going to run his mouth, he best have the ass to back it up. If not, he's liable to get his nose mashed in."

"Pull up your diaper and bring it," Herring said.

"You two knock it off and get your gear together," Foley snapped. "I'm tired of listening to it. First man to throw a punch is going to answer to me."

Foley and his men had followed this same installation team most of the way across Virginia. After each install, the helicopter returned to Lightspeed's base to resupply. A few days later it would be back in the field, ready to install another repeater a couple of miles west of the last one. With each new install, Foley and his team were hot on their heels.

When they were finally mounted and underway, Herring asked, "How far off you reckon that team is?"

"GPS says twenty miles," Foley replied. "That's as the crow flies, but things are different in this steep terrain. All this up and down adds miles. Makes everything farther than you think."

Mickelson groaned in frustration.

"You say something, boy?" Foley snapped.

Mickelson scrambled to come up with something to say that wasn't another complaint. "Uh, yes, I was wondering how you got in this line of work to begin with."

"Random chance," Foley replied. "A few months back, Lightspeed had just started rolling out electricity and the installation crews never left enough wireless converters behind for all the people living in the community. You could always request more, but that could take days or weeks and some people didn't want to wait. I heard some rich guy that lived in the same town as me bitching that he'd missed out on the first delivery. He was telling everyone he'd be willing to pay if someone could get him a wireless converter before the next shipment came. That sounded like something right up my alley."

"You steal one for him?" Mickelson asked.

"I asked him how much he would pay first. Of course, money was no good, but he had other ways to pay. I ended up getting a nice handgun out of the deal, which was good because I didn't have any guns, being a convicted felon and all."

Mickelson pulled his ball cap down over his eyes. The bright sunlight in his face was starting to give him a headache "And it took off from there?"

"Not immediately, but soon after. After we did our deal, the rich guy told me he had a buddy who would pay the same if I could get him one. So my new friend and I ended up forming a partnership."

Mickelson snorted. "A partnership? What the hell do you need him for? You're the one taking all the risk."

"Maybe, but how many rich assholes you think I know, Mickelson? It's not like I can put up signs advertising my business. Someone who'd had their converter stolen would track my ass down and kill me. I needed someone who was part of the *club* and knew other rich people."

"I guess that makes sense," said Mickelson.

"It was the right call. The business scaled up faster than I could've ever done it alone. My partner is a businessman and he knows how to do this stuff. I'm just a thug with more balls than sense." Foley burst into laughter at this characterization of himself and the rest of his team joined in. "You laughing back there, Tibbets?"

Behind the other riders, the fourth and final member of the team had a slight grin on his face. It was the closest any of the others had seen him come to laughing.

Foley jabbed a finger in Tibbets' direction. "That's what I like about you. You're quiet. Mickelson here could learn a thing or two from you. These young punks think they need to say everything that passes through their head, like the rest of us give a shit."

"And we don't!" Herring piped in, shooting Mickelson a hard look.

Mickelson, the youngest of the riders, clammed up and pouted. He wasn't used to being ganged up on like this and didn't like it one bit.

"Let's pick up the pace, boys. It's going to take us all day to reach that install crew." Foley nudged his heels into the ribs of his horse, urging it into a trot.

The group rode for most of the day. They ate in the saddle, only stopping to water the horses, refill their canteens, and relieve themselves. Back in the flatter part of Virginia, the area that Foley called home, he could have covered this distance in half the time. In this godforsaken region they frequently came upon hills too steep to be climbed. Because of that, they followed roads when they could and trails when they had to.

Twice, the trails they were following led them into rhododendron thickets that were too dense for their horses. They had to backtrack and lost precious time. Once they ran into a fat, late-summer bear that terrified their horses. Even though they were able to drive the bear away with shouting, it was nearly thirty more minutes before they could coerce their scared horses into continuing down the trail.

That evening, as the sun gradually sank over the distant horizon, Foley called the men to a stop. They were on a grassy forest service road that wound up the side of the steep mountain. "Boys, we have to be getting close. I figure we're within a mile or two, but we're losing light and I'm afraid we'll spook them if they see our headlamps moving around in the dark. It's probably best we settle in here for the night and get an early start tomorrow."

It wasn't like any of the men were going to protest Foley's decision. Mickelson in particular had been ready to stop several hours ago. He was so exhausted he didn't even care if they ate dinner at this point. All he wanted to do was lie down and fall asleep.

Herring mopped sweat from his face with a crusty bandanna. "You're probably right. This road is the only flat ground we've seen in some time. We might as well call it a night and camp here."

Foley looked at Mickelson. "You good with that, boy?"

All the men laughed but Mickelson was confused. He didn't get the joke, even though he knew he was the butt of it.

"You look like a stiff breeze would blow your ass right off that horse," Foley taunted. "You're going to have to toughen up if you want to work with us. This ain't the life for a housecat."

Mickelson bristled. "I ain't no damn housecat. You all get in a pinch and you'll find out real quick. I might be small, but I'm mean and I ain't afraid to kick a man's ass."

This made the men laugh even harder. Mickelson climbed off his horse, cursing under his breath, and unbuckled his saddle. He was going to show them one day. They were going to get in a tight spot and he was going to save their asses. Either that or they were going to keep messing with him until he killed them all in their sleep one night. That thought was the first thing to make him smile all day.

7

Lunch was usually the quietest time of day at the Reset Roadhouse. With a few exceptions, most people weren't drinking at that time of day. They were more interested in a meal. Folks would start rolling in about midday, most of them bringing their own bowls and cups. At this time of day, the roadhouse was like a combination food court and soup kitchen, if the food court only served one selection and half the patrons were armed.

The place had several regulars, people who met up there each day to have a meal together. Some of these folks had done the same thing in the days before the collapse, meeting at one of the local fast-food joints. Some of them, long retired or disabled, had been fond of sitting along the low stone wall in the center of town known for generations as the Deadpecker Bench.

Jim personally knew many of the patrons and was meeting more each day, while others were people he'd never encountered during his time in the town. Some folks, eating alone, were conversational and talked about their past. Others were grim and demoralized, not saying any more than was required to barter for their meal.

Since Jim didn't take cash at the roadhouse, people had to barter for the things they bought there, whether it was food, drink, or an item from their growing store. Randi was responsible for assessing the value of customer's barter items in the evening, but either Jim, Ian, or Gary would perform this function during the lunch shift. The most common currency continued to be ammunition, with different calibers assessed at different values. The oddball rounds, those that Jim had no use for, went directly into the display case to be resold to patrons.

Jim tried not to spend too much time looking at the display case as it contained a lot of grim reminders. There were weapons, ammo, and other gear taken off the dead. There were packs, clothing, and sleeping bags obtained the same way. Despite the morbid nature of this trade, Jim saw no sense in leaving such items behind after a fight when there were so many people in need of basic gear.

The lunch shift was quiet until the unmistakable thrum of an approaching helicopter overpowered the murmur of conversation. Most of the patrons were uncertain as to what was going on and all looked wary. Like Jim, most of them were aware that throughout the collapse, the arrival of helicopters rarely meant anything good. Only Jim had any inkling of what this visit might be about.

Noting the anxiety of his patrons made Jim wonder if it had been a mistake to have Lightspeed's people deliver the wireless power converters to the roadhouse. Had he directed the helicopter to deliver them to his home in the valley, there likely would have been no witnesses at all. No one would have known anything about those converters until Jim brought them to town and started handing them out.

While he'd been trying to avoid the hassle of having to haul them into town, now he would have an audience to whatever transpired when the helicopter arrived. Not only would the customers at the roadhouse witness him receiving the converters from Lightspeed's people, there would certainly be others in town drawn by the sound of the helicopter. There could potentially be a hundred witnesses, and that many eyes meant Jim would lose control of the narrative. The secret would be out and word would spread like wildfire: power had returned to their community and was available to them.

"Easy, folks!" Jim said, speaking loudly so everyone in the road-house could hear him. "I'm expecting this helicopter and there won't be any trouble. These are good folks here to help us. This is something we've all been waiting on. I'll tell you more about it in a minute, but I need to get outside now and direct them to a landing zone."

Jim jogged toward the raised loading dock door, left open to capture some of the warmth from the sunny day. He hopped off the dock, then walked out into the enormous gravel lot that had once been employee parking. Without regular vehicle traffic, weeds now poked through the gravel. There was plantain, dandelion, chicory, and jimson weed. Jim waved his arms as the helicopter approached. When it slowed to a hover, he knew he'd been spotted. He directed them to land in the parking lot, then sprinted clear.

The chopper landed, and Jim shielded his eyes against the dust and debris stirred by the rotor wash. Leaves, twigs, and dust pelted him. When the pitch of the engines changed and the rotors began to spin down, Jim removed his hand from his eyes. Through the wind-shield he could see Danielle, the team leader of the installation crew, giving him a friendly wave. Jim smiled and waved back. The doors opened and the installation crew piled out into the parking lot. Danielle headed over to speak to Jim.

"Any trouble finding us?" he asked.

Danielle shook her head. "The waypoint you plugged into our GPS led us right here. Your town looks like it's holding up pretty well."

Jim shrugged as if he wasn't so sure about that. "You really think so?"

"Definitely. I've flown over hundreds of small towns as we've worked our way across Virginia. Some of them look like war zones. Streets lined with shot up cars, entire neighborhoods burned to the ground, businesses looted, and trash strewn up and down the streets. Despite everything, this place looks like it held up well."

"That surprises me, but I'm glad to hear it. Things didn't always feel very peaceful here. We've had our share of trouble."

Danielle flashed a sad smile. "Hardship doesn't always bring out the best in people. We'd like to think it does, but history has proven otherwise."

"Hopefully, we can do something about that lack of power now," Jim said, eagerly watching the installation crew unload boxes from the helicopter. When they'd unloaded six boxes, they climbed back inside the aircraft and buckled into their harnesses. Jim frowned. "That's it? That's our entire allotment of converters?"

Danielle nodded. "There are three hundred in those boxes. They're smaller than you think. Lightspeed designed them to be light and compact. Before America collapsed, he developed this technology as a way to provide electricity to remote regions around the world. He wanted places that never had electricity before to have a dependable source of power. He thought these converters should be small enough that they could be carried into remote locations in a backpack. He imagined military units using them in the field or backpackers using them in the mountains."

Jim shook his head, trying to wrap his mind around what she was saying. Even if those six boxes did not contain enough converters for the entire community, it was incredible to think of the potential they contained. There were thousands of little things that people had lost the ability to do when they couldn't access electricity. Now they would be able to resume some of those activities.

They could charge phones and power laptops, microwave a meal, leave a lamp on and read in their bed at night, and they could watch old VHS tapes of birthdays, weddings, and school plays. Some people had been able to do those things throughout the collapse because they had some level of solar power, but it had been a small segment of the population. This would restore a small degree of normality to a larger group of people.

But only to three hundred homes. That was going to be an issue and Jim had no idea yet how it would be resolved.

Danielle pulled him out of that spiral of thought. "Let me show you how to install one, because you'll need to teach the people of your community." She removed a backpack she'd been wearing, then fished around inside it until she found the device she was looking for. "This is a converter. It's very simple."

She handed the device over to Jim and he examined it. It was around the size of a small Frisbee or dinner plate, probably two inches thick, and encased in black plastic. There were some LED lights on the front and instructions molded into the plastic on the back. Jim hefted it in his hand and decided that it must weigh close to a pound.

"I used to work in construction," Jim said. "Just looking at this, I already have a basic idea of how you'd install it. This should be fairly simple."

Danielle took the device back. "I mentioned that Lightspeed planned that his wireless power could be used in remote locations. That requires a different type of converter—a portable one. This one was designed for powering homes after a natural disaster. Specifically homes that once had grid power and are now in the dark because of infrastructure damage."

"So I can't use this one to run an electric blanket on a camping trip?"

Danielle offered a wry smile. "Nope. This one will only power homes, small businesses, or any other electrical installation that once received metered power from the grid."

"I assumed that after I saw the back of it. It's similar to the meter that the power company installs at your service entrance."

"Yes, installation is intuitive if you know anything about construction, but there are some important steps that have to be taken for safety. First, you need to open the electrical meter base where you want to restore power. For most installations, that means cutting the safety tag that the power company installs on the meter base, removing the lid, then pulling the electrical meter and setting it aside."

"When someone powers their grid-connected home with a generator, they have to be careful not to back-feed power into the grid or they can injure a lineman," Jim said. "Is that a risk with this device? Do you have to disconnect from the grid?"

Danielle shook her head. "Not a risk with this. The technology is designed to only deliver power on the house side, not the grid side."

Jim nodded with appreciation. "Nice."

"Once the meter is removed, you align the prongs on the back of this disc and push it back into place where the meter used to be. Then you close the door to the meter base and secure it so no children or dumbasses stick their hand in there and get shocked."

"That sounds easy enough."

"It is. I'm sure you noticed the instructions are molded into the plastic. It'll be self-explanatory for some people. Others might need assistance."

Jim asked, "How do you turn it on or know if it's working?"

"It's all automatic." Danielle pointed to the row of LEDs on the front of the converter. "There's a chart on the back that tells you what these lights mean. One shows that the device has a good connection to the wireless repeater up on the mountain. That light will continue to flash while the device does a quick diagnostic test to make sure that the electrical system in the home is not grounded or faulty. This can be useful if the home has sustained some kind of damage or if the electrical system has been tampered with."

"That's handy."

"Yes, Lightspeed took into consideration that there may be homes partially destroyed by falling trees or high wind. You don't want to power a home up if restoring electricity is going to cause a fire. If the electrical system tests good, the LED turns green to show that power is now passing through the converter. The wires going from the meter base to the breaker box are now carrying electricity."

"What if the device determines that the home's electrical system is damaged or unsafe?" Jim asked. "What if it fails that diagnostic stage?"

"Then you get a flashing red LED that stays on until it determines that the wiring is safe. That could be something as simple as turning off the breaker to the damaged section of wiring. This can be tricky if the homeowner doesn't understand some of the basics of residential wiring. But if the red LED is flashing, no electricity is being provided to the home."

Danielle handed the converter back over to Jim and he flipped it over in his hands, examining it from all angles. "It's hard to believe what this device can do for the country. I've seen some technological advances in my life—from the Internet to cell phones—but this is next level. It doesn't even seem possible that it can do the things Lightspeed promises. If technology was ever akin to voodoo, this is proof. It's more like magic than science."

"When Nicola Tesla invented wireless power technology, power companies were concerned enough to feel threatened. They didn't want this tech out there in the world, but now it is, and life will never be the same again."

Jim smiled. "I hope you're right. I hope this is the beginning of the end, but I've got a little pessimist in me that regards any promise of normality with a healthy suspicion. I want it to work, but I'll believe it when I see it."

Danielle laughed. "I completely understand your suspicion but spend a few weeks with one of these attached to your house and I'm certain you'll come away a believer."

Jim frowned as he regarded the stack of boxes. "I'm not sure I'll even get one. I don't know how far three hundred will go in this community. I suspect we'll be finding out soon. Once people learn what's in those boxes, they'll be coming out of the woodwork."

"I'm sure you're right but remember you can get more converters. There's paperwork in those boxes with a radio frequency where you can submit a request. It can take a few weeks to get them, depending on when someone is flying over the area."

"Got it," Jim said. He knew full well that anyone who ended up on that waiting list wasn't going to be happy. No one would want to be left in the dark when their neighbor had power.

"I need to hit the road, Jim, get back to base and resupply. Once we do, we'll be installing another repeater a couple of miles down the road in Wise County. Good luck with distributing the converters."

"I need to move those boxes out of the way before you take off."

Jim stepped over to the stack of boxes and hefted one. It was heavy but not unmanageable.

When he turned around to carry the box to the loading dock, he was shocked to see the open doorway packed with people. All the patrons of the roadhouse had abandoned their meals to see what was going on in the back parking lot. Jim had been so focused on Danielle's instructions that he hadn't noticed he had an audience, and it was likely they'd all heard Danielle's explanation of how the power would work.

That meant they knew what was in those boxes. Everyone standing in that doorway likely understood that Jim possessed devices that could make their lives easier in a matter of minutes. Suddenly Jim didn't feel so comfortable leaving that box on the loading dock while he returned for the others. He could imagine those people diving onto the box like a flock of chickens onto a handful of feed, shredding it in their desperation to snatch a converter.

He'd accepted responsibility for distributing the devices and he wanted to do it in an orderly and fair manner. He wasn't about to let this moment descend into chaos. Jim set the box down on the ground and unclipped his radio from his belt.

"Jim for Ian and Gary. I can't see you guys, but I need you on the loading dock to guard something before we lose control of the situation."

While Jim waited for his friends to reach him, Danielle offered him an apologetic smile. "There's a lot of responsibility that comes with being the keeper of light, along with a little risk. Sometimes I feel like I don't clarify that aspect enough, but it's difficult to convey the gravity of the situation."

"You remember how my friends reacted when you told them I was gonna be in charge of handing these out?"

"They laughed and shook their heads," Danielle replied.

"The reason they were laughing is that I might just be the perfect guy for this job. I can manage the risk."

Ian and Gary parted the crowd at the loading dock, rifles in hand.

They hopped down to the ground and Jim pointed to the stack of boxes by the helicopter.

"I'm going to stack these boxes by the dock. I need some crowd control. Make everyone back up. They can return to their tables or go home, but if anyone tries to open a box, shoot them." Jim didn't actually plan on killing anyone just for opening a box, but he did want to make sure that people understood the boundaries.

Danielle cocked an eyebrow at Jim's command. "Perhaps you *are* the right guy for the job. I wish you luck."

"Safe travels, Danielle."

She returned to the helicopter and disappeared into the main cabin. Jim swung his rifle around to his back and shuttled the rest of the boxes to the loading dock. All the roadhouse patrons stayed clear, as they had been ordered to do. Most had heard Jim's warning and no one wanted to test him. Some returned to their tables, not ready to leave until they had an opportunity to ask questions about the cargo Jim had just received.

Jim remained outside with the boxes until the helicopter was in the air and departing. He was in no hurry to go inside and face the crowd. He knew everyone had questions and he hadn't figured out the answers yet.

8

As soon as Jim went inside, roadhouse patrons peppered him with questions. Just because they couldn't get close to the boxes didn't mean they couldn't shout their inquiries at him from around the room. He was never very good at being badgered and he responded even worse when he felt cornered. Even the most stoic people became agitated when others surrounded them like a pack of dogs, and Jim was far from being a stoic person.

Fortunately, Gary had been around Jim long enough to understand what was about to happen. Jim's default reaction was often to overreact and that could get messy. Knowing this, Gary intervened and cleared the roadhouse.

"Hey, folks," he called out, "you should come back later. I assure you your questions will be answered then."

Some of the patrons argued with Gary, insisting their questions be answered immediately. They wanted to know when the power converters were going to be distributed, and wanted to make sure they got one. While Gary understood their reaction, he quickly figured out that being easygoing and friendly was not going to work in this situation.

Though Gary rarely lost his cool, he shouted at the uncooperative customers. "Do you want this to get ugly? Because that's what's about to happen! Remember who you're pissing off here. If you continue to chase Jim Powell around the building like some angry mob, I can tell you how this is going to end. There's going to be gunfire and then getting electricity is going to be the least of your problems."

Gary's outburst cut through the growing chaos. The patrons then understood there was nothing to be gained from badgering Jim when he wasn't going to talk. Gary was right. Jim did have a hair trigger sometimes and electricity wouldn't help dead men. Amidst a murmur of sighing, cursing, and complaining, the crowd shuffled off toward the door, dirty cups and soup bowls in their hands.

An old man wearing a flannel shirt, jeans, and suspenders turned around. He was wearing grubby white sneakers and a ragged green ballcap advertising a seed company. He jabbed a finger in Gary's direction. "I always thought you were the *nice* one. Guess you're a son-of-a-bitch just like that other one."

"I *am* the nice one," Gary replied. "I might've just saved your ass."

The old man scowled. "I might be old but I'm tough. I catch you outside you're in for an ass whooping." He threw a practice punch, then winced and gripped his shoulder.

"Better stretch first," Gary warned.

The old man gave Gary the finger before turning away and stomping out.

Jim went to the roadhouse door and called out. "Come back tomorrow night. I'll make an announcement in the parking lot around dark. Spread the word and we'll start handing these things out. I want rid of them just as much as you want them."

People muttered and complained to each other as they trailed off down the street. Jim shook his head as he watched them go. People were forgetting that social boundaries were different these days. In the old world you could harass and badger someone in an attempt to force them to do what you wanted. That was a much riskier proposition in a world without law. Push someone too far and people died. It had happened to Jim more times than he cared to recall.

It was never safe to assume that other people played by the same rules you did. There were people who fought with words, which might be an adequate weapon in some situations. They fell short when used against the man who preferred a gun.

Jim retrieved a dolly and wheeled the boxes of converters back to the secure storeroom. Only when he'd locked them away did he finally breathe a sigh of relief. "I'll be glad when we get rid of those damn things. This is going to be stressful."

Ian and Gary silently stared at Jim as he leaned against the rusty metal door that secured the storeroom.

"What?" Jim asked. "Why the hell are you guys just staring at me? I didn't shoot anyone."

Gary pointed toward the storeroom door. "You're going to lock *all* those converters in there?"

"Of course. If we don't keep them secure, someone is going to try to steal them."

"*All* of them?" Ian asked. "You're not going to take one out?"

It was only then that Jim understood what his friends were talking about, and he felt like an idiot. He'd spent the last few days thinking about the big picture implications of being able to restore electricity. The smaller, more personal aspects of that opportunity had completely gone over his head. Like the fact that he could now power the Reset Roadhouse.

Jim palmed himself in the forehead. "It completely slipped my mind."

Ian and Gary bobbed their heads in agreement, pleased that their slow friend had finally gotten up to speed. Jim looked down at the storeroom key in his hand, then unlocked the door. He retrieved a flashlight from a nearby shelf and turned it on to search the room. It occurred to him that if one of the devices in those boxes would actually work on his building, this might be the last time he had to use a flashlight to look around this room.

Jim laid the flashlight on a shelf so that it illuminated the stack of boxes, then used his knife to cut through the tape that sealed the uppermost box. Inside, a neat row with fifty converters sat nested in a

Styrofoam cradle. Jim plucked one of the devices out and held it in his hands. Yes, it sounded like a miracle when Danielle was explaining it, but it suddenly carried significantly more weight.

He carried the converter out of the storeroom and relocked the door behind him. The old sewing factory had been in operation for nearly a century. The mechanical systems of the building represented nearly every decade of construction materials. There was PVC plumbing alongside cast-iron, PEX water lines connected to old galvanized plumbing, and the wiring was the same way, with a mixture of modern breaker boxes and old fuse boxes.

With Gary and Ian helping, Jim shut off all of the main breakers. Once they had everything off, they went outside and walked around to the back of the building. Jim had noticed when he was rigging up solar lights inside the building that the place didn't have three-phase power. Although he wasn't sure if it was the age of the building or the size of machinery that had been used, they'd never had anything more than a standard single-phase electrical service.

When they reached the electrical meter, Jim removed a multitool from his belt and used the wire cutters to cut the power company's safety tag from the meter base. He pulled off the cover and set it to the side. The meter itself had copper prongs on the back that plugged into the meter base. Removing the meter was simply a matter of pulling it loose and tossing it to the side.

Jim took a deep breath. While he wasn't exactly nervous, he was anxious to a degree. The moment felt like a turning point. It was a profound point in time that they would all look back on in the future and remember for the rest of their lives. Jim aligned the converter with the plugs in the meter base and firmly seated the wireless converter.

It felt like a long time before that first LED began flashing, but when it did Jim felt an exhilaration he had not felt in some time. The three men watched without speaking while the converter established a connection with the wireless repeater floating high above Clinch Mountain. Then the converter quickly assessed the state of the wiring in the old building. Turning off all the breakers most likely reduced the amount of time required for that diagnostic step.

When the light turned green, Jim almost couldn't believe what he was seeing. Was it really possible they could go inside this building and flip on a bank of lights? That seemed almost unimaginable. After more than a year in the dark, they'd all sadly become accustomed to the state of things. Even though they'd never admit it, they might even have begun to accept that they'd *never* have electricity again.

"I guess we go inside now," Jim said.

Gary pointed at the meter base. "We need to put the cover back on and padlock it so no one steals that converter. I don't want to sound dramatic, but that device is priceless. I bet there are people out there who would pay a million dollars for one of those."

"There's a couple of padlocks in the storeroom." Jim placed the metal cover back onto the meter base. It fit securely over the converter and held it in place. "Once we check the lights, we can come back out here and lock it. If I go inside to get a lock, I'm not going to be able to come back out here until I've checked the lights. There's no way I can pass by that breaker box and not see if this damn thing actually works."

The three men walked back around the building together. For Jim, the short distance became something larger. The magnitude of the moment swelled to consume him in a way he barely understood. The sound of gravel and twigs beneath his feet sounded louder, the clear light of the late summer morning brighter, the sky clearer. It reminded him of other walks he'd taken over the years in those moments when he knew everything was about to change. Walking out of the hospital with his newborn child, moving out of a home where he'd spent a significant portion of his life, walking into the funeral home to say goodbye to someone he loved.

They climbed up the steps by the loading dock and went to the bank of electrical panels. In the old sewing factory the panels were mounted to an interior wall in a neat block. The primary electrical panel only contained a few breakers which served to direct power to several smaller sub-panels. One of the main breakers was labeled "lighting" and Jim started with that one. If everything was working correctly, flipping that breaker should energize the smaller panel that controlled all the individual lighting circuits.

"Should we start with the overheads in the main room?" he asked.

"Go for it," said Ian.

Jim found a breaker marked "production floor lights" and flipped it. A loud humming sound erupted from the ceiling as the long rows of fluorescent tube lighting were energized. Most of the bulbs started with a dim glowing. Sporadically, individual bulbs burst into full illumination. In less than thirty seconds, most of the lights had come to life and lit the dreary room with a harsh, unnatural light. This was significantly brighter than the few scattered bulbs they'd been powering with solar.

"I'd forgotten how unpleasant fluorescent lighting could be," Gary said.

Jim shot a frown in Gary's direction. "Don't jinx us."

Gary offered an apologetic look. "That doesn't mean I don't want power. Geez."

Jim didn't need to activate any of the subpanels that had once controlled machinery, but he did turn on the receptacles in the building. Once they had all of those circuits active, the men wandered through the building making sure everything was okay and there were no burning smells, no sparking.

Ed had been focused on his brewing until the lights came on. Now he wandered around staring at the ceiling with the incredulity of a man watching a UFO land in his front yard. Gary's family was much more animated in their excitement. They danced, cheered, and clapped.

"This reminds me of those *Life* magazine photos taken when World War II ended," Gary said, watching his family's elation. "Community by community, I suspect that's what it's going to be like. People jumping up and down and celebrating as if a war is over."

Noting Jim's grim expression, Ian said, "You look a little disappointed. You having second thoughts about climbing out of the apoc-alypse? You thinking we should stay in the dark forever?"

Jim shook his head. "I admit there was a point where I wanted this collapse. I thought the country needed a reset so people would learn to appreciate what they had. Once I saw how much suffering came from the collapse, I felt a lot of guilt about having wished for it."

"We've talked about that," said Gary, nodding. "I had a lot of those same feelings."

"I've learned my lesson. I would never wish an apocalypse on our country again, but I have a hard time accepting that this is the end of it. Having the lights back on only serves to remind me of just how far our lives have come from where they used to be. Hell, look at us. We're in an old building we don't even own selling liquor, guns, and food to people who mostly pay us with ammunition."

Ian cringed. "And I live in a bar selling homemade stabby weapons. Thanks for throwing the wet blanket of reality onto our moment of celebration, Jim. I really appreciate that. For a moment I'd almost started to feel good."

"Sorry, it's just that this one slice of normality drives home how far we've strayed from where we used to be. If people think having the lights back on is going to give us the life we used to have, they're in for a shock. That old world is gone forever."

Now that they had verified Lightspeed's technology worked, Jim turned the main breaker off. It was an extremely difficult decision. It filled him with a strange anxiety, as if turning the power off might be the end of it and they'd never be able to re-create this miracle again. However, Jim felt like it had to be done. Having the only building in town with working lights would be awkward.

Jim had no doubt that the entire town would show up wanting to know why he had power and no one else did. If a large enough mob came and tried to steal the converters, what would he do? Would it turn into a full-fledged battle where people were killed or injured because they were so desperate for the technology? There was no justice in that.

They would turn the power off and do business just as they'd done it since opening. They would rely on their solar lights, flashlights, lanterns, and woodstoves. Tomorrow night, when the public arrived to hear about the converters, Jim would use the roadhouse's working lights to demonstrate the miracle of Lightspeed's technology. Beyond that, he had no clue what he was going to do next.

9

"You doing okay?" Hugh asked.

Jim was standing behind the bar, watching Becky serve patrons. His mind was elsewhere. "I guess."

"You look a little distracted."

"I am. You know, I was a little wound up when we opened the roadhouse because I didn't know how it was going to work out. We've gotten into a routine now, and this place is like a second home. Most nights are pretty chill."

Hugh grinned. "Despite the occasional stabbing or shooting."

"Yeah, but you can get stabbed or shot anywhere these days," Jim said defensively. "I tell people that all the time."

"True," Hugh agreed. "That still doesn't explain why you're sitting there staring off into space."

Jim looked out over the growing crowd. It was a normal night by any measure. Lloyd was onstage getting ready to perform. The smell of roast pork, wood smoke, and tobacco hung in the air. Jim had bought hundreds of homemade tortillas from a local woman and tonight they'd be selling carnitas with homemade salsa and jalapenos. Beer was flowing and they were offering a special on shots of homemade liquor.

"Having those converters around is making me nervous, Hugh. I feel like I'm in one of those old Westerns where I'm trying to get a wagonload of gold through hostile territory and hoping like hell no one figures out what I'm hauling."

Hugh laughed.

Jim furrowed his brow. "What's so funny?"

"I was just picturing you as Clint Eastwood's character in *High Plains Drifter*. The funny thing is it didn't change the outcome much. Just as many people died." Hugh was still grinning at the thought.

"Very funny."

Hugh slapped Jim on the shoulder. "Chill out, man. You just have to get through tonight. Tomorrow, you'll hopefully be getting rid of most of them. The burden will be lifted."

"I hope so," said Jim. "As much as getting power back will be a blessing, having these converters in my possession is more like a curse. I already sent word to my family that I'd be here all night. I'm afraid to let those boxes out of my sight."

"I'm staying, and I think Gary is too. We should have enough guns to keep anyone from trying something stupid."

"I appreciate that," Jim said. "Then there's Lloyd."

On the stage, Lloyd held a mason jar of liquor high aloft, then let out a long *yeeehawww*. He took a swig from the jar, carefully threaded the lid back on, then launched into "Reuben's Train."

"Then there's Lloyd," Hugh chuckled. "Not much for running a gun but he does provide some comic relief."

"Yeah, there's that. You get anything to eat?"

Hugh nodded. "Those carnitas are out of this world. They're hard to resist with that pork smell wafting through town all day. You'll probably sell out."

"I hope so."

Suddenly, Hugh straightened up, going on alert. He stared toward the main entrance to the roadhouse, intently focused on a group of ten or so people who'd just come through the door. Their demeanor indicated that they weren't there for the food, drink, or entertainment. They were there on a mission.

Hugh made a subtle adjustment to his rifle sling, moving the weapon to the front of his body. He raised his radio and keyed the mic. "Hugh for Team One, Hugh for Team One. I've got a flock of geese at the west entrance. Gentlemen, let's keep an eye on them."

Hugh ran security for the roadhouse and Team One was his security personnel. They used the term "geese" to describe any ill-tempered patron who appeared to be there to complain, raise hell, or squawk. Geese generally were more irritating than violent, though not always. Sometimes they had to be swatted out of the air and stomped.

When the geese finally spotted Jim at the bar, they made a beeline in his direction. There was a click when Hugh moved the selector on his rifle to the Fire position.

Jim reached down to make sure his shirt was clear of his holstered handgun. "I don't see any visible weapons."

"Copy that," Hugh said. "Let's still assume they're packing. Recognize any of them?"

Jim studied the group. After a moment, he groaned and nodded. "Yes, that tall, scrawny one in the back is Blake Justice. You weren't around, but he was here for lunch today."

Hugh nodded in recognition. "Ah, when the helicopter dropped off the converters."

"Exactly, and since they appear to have something on their minds, I assume that's what they're here to discuss." Jim leaned back against the counter, folded his arms over his chest, and waited. He stared at the group as they approached, trying to determine if the man he recognized, Blake Justice, was the leader of this group or not.

That didn't appear to be the case. A short, thick man took the lead as the group closed in on the bar. He looked in his early 40s and probably kept his head shaved in better times to conceal the fact he was losing his hair. He was still trying to rock that look, but his grooming was slipping. Without a supply of fresh razors, his effort was patchy, making the top of his head look like a teenage boy's chin. He jabbed a thick finger onto the rough bar top as if that move commanded attention.

While that move may have worked at the Kmart customer service counter, Jim wasn't nearly as responsive. He hated people who did everything as if they were performing for an audience, which this man clearly was. Jim rolled his eyes. This wasn't going to go well. He could already tell.

"Are you Jim Powell?" the man asked. His voice was high-pitched, tense from anger.

"You might be the only person in town who doesn't know the answer to that question," Jim said.

Hugh grinned. "He must not have seen your wanted posters all over town."

"Wanted posters?" the man repeated.

"I jest." Hugh shrugged. "Jim claims to be the *most* wanted man in town, but it would be more accurate to say that he's the *least* wanted."

Jim frowned at his old friend. "It's a good thing I'm not sensitive."

"I'm glad you two think you're so funny," the man said with a fake smile. "You're a couple of comedians. Maybe you should be on that stage telling jokes instead of tormenting people with that infernal banjo playing. But to answer your earlier question, I'm familiar with your name, but I didn't have a face to put with it."

Jim could already tell this was not going to be a civil conversation, so there was no point in trying to keep it that way. "Well, I'm afraid I don't recognize you. Do you have another name besides 'asshole'?"

Hugh looked at the floor and shook his head. "Oh boy. This went downhill quickly."

Asshole cocked his head to the side and frowned at Jim. "Actually I do. I am *Doctor* Byron Nelson. I just moved here to work at your local hospital a few weeks before the country fell apart, and I must say that there's probably be no worse place in the world to be stuck."

"You're wrong about that," Jim said. "There are plenty of worse places. I walked through a couple of them."

"Please tell me you are a proctologist," Hugh quipped. "That would be too ironic."

The doctor curled his lip at Hugh. "No, smartass, my specialty was rheumatology. Do you know what that is or do I need to translate it into hillbilly?"

Hugh's expression grew hard. He was much more tolerant of unpleasant people than Jim was, but he did have his limits, and this guy was testing them.

"It's an understandable mistake," Jim said, patting Hugh on the back. "It's easy to confuse someone being Doctor Asshole with being an asshole doctor."

There was uproarious laughter from down the bar where Becky was eavesdropping on their conversation. Jim sometimes forgot that she had supernatural hearing, which helped compensate for her vision loss. Hugh also laughed at the joke. Among the group that had come in with Dr. Nelson, no one was laughing.

Blake Justice shoved his way to the front of the group and slapped a palm on the bar. "Cut the shit, Powell! I know you have those converters that Lightspeed's people dropped off. I saw the whole thing. I heard the woman say we could turn the power on at our houses just by installing one of those devices."

The sound of Blake's hand smacking the bar top caught the attention of nearby patrons. They didn't allow the drama to interfere with their drinking, but they did turn in their seats to have a better view of the action. If this was going to get ugly, they didn't want to miss anything.

Dr. Nelson again jabbed a stubby finger on the bar. "We just want what we're entitled to. You have no right to keep those converters from us. We each want one and we want them *now*!"

Jim moved closer to the bar so he wouldn't have to speak as loudly. Blake must have been afraid that Jim was coming for him because he backed up and put some distance between himself and the bar. Dr. Nelson, on the other hand, didn't budge. Jim didn't think the doctor was standing his ground because he was prepared for a fight, but because he was arrogant. He was used to people doing what he told them to do.

"I agree that I don't have the right to decide who gets electricity and who doesn't," Jim said in a low voice. "I do have a responsibility to make sure those converters are handed out in a fair manner. That responsibility was given to me when I agreed to distribute those converters. I'm already wishing I hadn't agreed to it, because I expect it's going to bring me nothing but trouble."

Dr. Nelson shrugged. "First-come, first-served is a fair manner of distributing those devices and you can start right now."

"If we went by that, they'd be gone in a couple of hours," Jim said. "I'm not sure handing them all out to people who just happen to be drinking at the roadhouse tonight is the most responsible approach."

A man in the group, someone Jim didn't recognize, turned red and pointed his finger across the bar. "There you go again, assuming you get to choose."

Jim paused to collect himself. He was never good at these kinds of interactions. There was an old joke about people who shot first and asked questions later, and Jim was the very personification of that expression. There were some people with whom he had endless amounts of patience. Then there were people like this.

"I'm not going to be the one who decides who gets power and who doesn't," Jim said through gritted teeth. "Blake was here at lunchtime today and he heard what I said to everyone. We're going to have a public meeting here tomorrow night and the people of the community can decide their priorities. The public will decide—not me."

No one in the group across the bar appeared happy with Jim's statement.

"The problem with that is that I'm here right now and I'm first in line," Dr. Nelson said. "Who knows where I'll be in line tomorrow? I could entirely lose my shot at getting power just because you're on some kind of power trip, and that's not fair."

Hugh snickered. "*Power* trip? That's kinda funny. Who's the comedian now?"

Jim was too wound up to be amused. "You guys are here for personal reasons. I get that. I understand that we all have to look out for ourselves and our families first, but there might be important community spaces that need power. There was a guy in here just this morning talking about opening a clinic in town. That's something that would benefit everyone and should probably have access to power. Some people may want the library to have power so that they can start schooling their children again. Distributing the converters may not be so simple as just handing them out until they're all gone. But again—and this is my *final* word on the matter—the people who show up here tomorrow night will be the ones who vote and decide."

Dr. Nelson stared hard at Jim, his entire face and head growing red with anger. He wasn't the kind of man used to being refused. Perhaps he was accustomed to his status as a doctor giving him a level of authority, but that wasn't working with Jim. Right now, he was just another asshole.

Blake swept an arm around, gesturing at all the customers in the roadhouse. "There's a lot of people in this building right now. What if I was to get onstage and tell everyone that you have those converters hidden here and refuse to share them? What do you think would happen then? You might have a riot on your hands." He grinned at Jim, revealing yellow teeth.

Jim looked around the room before returning his eyes to the man who'd just threatened to turn their quiet evening at the roadhouse into chaos. "If you did that, people would end up getting hurt. You would be one of them."

Blake glared at Jim. "Are you threatening me?"

At this ridiculous comment, Jim, Becky, and Hugh all burst into laughter.

"He didn't do his homework, did he?" Becky said, wiping tears from her eyes. "What an idiot!"

Jim smiled. "Yes, Blake, I am threatening you."

The group of men pulled into a furious huddle and whispered among themselves. Finally, they turned back around to the bar.

"You haven't heard the last of this," Dr. Nelson spat. "I can assure you of that."

"Yeah," Blake growled, as if he were the muscle for the group, which couldn't have been any further from the truth.

Jim shooed them away with a whisking gesture of his fingers. "Go home before someone gets hurt."

The men backed away from the bar, then headed for the door.

Jim watched them go. "Somehow, I don't think that's the end of it."

"I don't think they liked our sense of humor," said Hugh.

"You're right," Becky called from halfway down the bar. "But I sure got a kick out of it."

"That's what matters," Hugh said. "We're here for your entertainment."

Becky gave him a thumbs-up. "As it should be."

"That could easily have gone sideways," said Jim. "You never know what people are capable of, even when they've never pulled a trigger before. Scared people can be the most dangerous."

"I'll add a few extra men to the night shift," Hugh said. "Hopefully we won't need them, but it's better to play it safe."

Jim suspected they would need them.

10

Foley and his crew of converter thieves had enough experience tracking Lightspeed's installation crews by this point that they had a fairly good understanding of what happened once the repeater was up in the air. The very last step was to deliver the converters to the nearest town so they could be distributed to the public. Foley didn't understand how Lightspeed's people chose who got to hand the converters out, but somehow they picked a local and delivered the converters to them. That brief window between when those poor souls received the converters and when they began handing them out was when Foley made his move.

With a GPS tracking device installed in the aircraft, Foley was able to see exactly where the converters were dropped off. Then it was only a matter of scouting out the location and determining where the converters were being stored. Typically, the team would come back that night and steal them when there was less of a chance of their crime drawing attention. However, if the converters happened to be stored in an occupied residence, sometimes there was bloodshed. Foley and his people didn't get bent out of shape about it. It was a cost of doing business.

When Foley had begun stealing converters in Northern Virginia it'd been no big deal for him to return them to a central point where his partner could sell them to his rich friends. Later, as Foley worked his way farther across the state, delivering those stolen converters to his partner had become more complicated and time-consuming. He lost days going back and forth when his time could have been better spent stealing more converters. Eventually, his business partner had come up with a better solution.

Foley's partner was a man by the name of J.T. Elder. He ran a chain of pawnshops in the Northern Virginia area and had become wealthy from it, though his was not the type of wealth that high society acknowledged. No matter how much money a man like J.T. Elder earned, rich people tended to look down on him because of how he'd made his money. Pawnshops were considered low-class, making Elder no better than those who got rich through dealing drugs, prostitution, or being in the Mafia.

The way his neighbors looked down their noses at him gave J.T. a perpetual chip on his shoulder. For that reason alone, he stuck it to them when it came to pricing his stolen converters. He made sure they paid well, regardless of what currency they had available. Pills, guns, gold, liquor, or food—J.T. didn't care. He and Foley were making a fortune and neither of them had any reservations about making hay while the sun shined.

"Are you sure we can afford that?" Foley had asked when J.T. proposed that they begin using a helicopter to return the converters to their base of operations in Northern Virginia.

"Oh yeah," J.T. assured him. "The pilot contracts with the government so he gets his fuel for free. Delivering for us is just a side job for him. I gave him a converter to secure his services and he gets one more converter for each trip he makes. We're paying him with stolen goods so it's basically free to us."

"You're the businessman, J.T. If you say this is what we need to do, I'll take your word for it." Foley hesitated a moment before adding, "By the way, speaking of taking your word for it, I hope you're keeping a record of all the sales. I trust you as much as I trust anyone, but I want to get my fair share. I'm not accusing you of anything, but surely you can understand my position. I'm not here when you're making the sales."

"It's all on the up and up, as far as criminal enterprise can be, Foley. You keep track of how many converters you're bringing in and I'll account for each one of them. I have a ledger where I write down what I get for each one of them. You're welcome to review it at any time."

Foley accepted that. "I don't need to see it now, but I might take you up on that in the future."

"Then if we're good, I need you back in the field. I'm going to give you a satellite phone so you can send me a set of GPS coordinates once you've stolen more converters. When I have those coordinates, I can send the helicopter right to you. You guys load the cargo onto the helicopter, and the pilot will deliver them to me. Remember, I've got no reason to cheat you on this. We need each other. Without you, I've got no business. We each bring our own expertise to this operation."

Even though Foley had been uncertain about using the helicopter, the idea had quickly proven its worth. The time saved by not having to travel to Northern Virginia on horseback allowed Foley and his team to spend more time stealing converters. In most instances, it was just a matter of creeping into a house at night, perhaps killing a few people, then riding away under the cover of darkness with a load of converters. This most recent job, however, had Foley more concerned than usual.

They'd left Mickelson on the outskirts of town guarding their horses. Foley, Herring, and Tibbets were now hidden in the woods across from the low brick building trying to figure out exactly what they were looking at.

"The Reset Roadhouse," Foley read off the side of the building. "What the hell is that?"

"Judging by the caterwauling coming out of the place, I'd say it's some kind of bar or restaurant," Herring said. "I've seen a few of them pop up in the last year. They're kind of like the trading posts in the old West. They sell a little bit of everything and take a little bit of everything in payment."

Foley took his hat off and scratched his head "You can tell all that by just looking at the place?"

"Call it an educated guess," Herring replied.

Foley snorted. "I call it bullshit."

The normally silent Tibbets chuckled.

Herring shifted, his hunkering position hard on his stiff knees. "Whatever it is, it's going to be a harder target than a normal house. That old brick building doesn't have many windows and those doors look pretty stout."

"I suspect a crowbar will get us through one of those doors," Foley said. "They look old and wore out. Kind of like you, Herring."

"Hardee har har," Herring replied sarcastically.

Foley looked over at Tibbets. "What about you, quiet man? You think we can bust in there?"

Tibbets only grunted in response. Unless you were addressing a subject he was deeply invested in, that was about the best you could hope for.

"Tibbets thinks we can do it," Foley said.

Herring shot Foley a look. "The man didn't utter a damn word. How can you take that grunt to mean he agrees with you and not me?"

Foley shrugged. "I've worked with him longer. I know what he's thinking." He tapped his head for emphasis.

Herring looked doubtful. "Well, since you two have decided we can do this, what's the plan? I guess I'm just along for the ride."

Foley reached over and patted Herring on the back like a mother soothing a child. "Now quit your pouting, honey. Let's go check the place out. If they're serving liquor, I could use a drink."

"Hell, I ain't got no money." Herring patted his pockets. "What do you think they charge for a drink?"

"Nobody has money these days. I'm sure they barter. Everyone does."

"What about you, Tibbets?" Herrings asked. "You up for a drink of liquor?"

Again, Tibbets grunted, but this time the corners of his filthy mouth turned up in a smile.

Herring pointed at him. "Now, I'm pretty sure that's a yes. Let's go."

Herring shot to his feet only to have Foley grip him by the arm and pull him back down.

"We can't go hopping out of the woods like Bigfoot," Foley chastised. "Let's go back a little ways, then climb down to the road and approach the building like civilized men."

Herring didn't see the point of that but acquiesced and followed Foley a short distance back down the road. They cut down the slope, crossed a ditch, and came out on the road. There was still some daylight, but the sun was near setting. Another hour and it would be dark.

"Damn burrs," Foley mumbled, picking burdock burrs from his pants and tossing them away.

In the distance, there were several small groups of men standing around the exterior of the roadhouse, talking animatedly and laughing. The sound of a banjo could be heard, along with something that was either singing or the death throes of a mortally wounded man. Walking toward the roadhouse, they passed a larger group of men coming toward them and engaged in a heated discussion.

Once they were past, Herring said, "Those fellows look a little pissed off. Think they got booted out for some reason?"

"Who knows?" Foley said. "And why do you care?"

"Just curious."

"More like nosy," Foley said. "You need to mind your own business when we get inside and not draw attention to yourself."

When they reached the entrance, Foley halfway expected a doorman, bouncer, or some type of gatekeeper, but there was no one. They strolled in through the door like it was a normal restaurant back in the pre-collapse days. They could have been a group of coworkers swinging by Applebee's to snag a few appetizers and drinks at happy hour.

The interior, with its exposed brick walls and industrial décor, wasn't that different from what one might find in a chic, modern-day brewery. Even the strands of low-voltage lighting—in this case old car headlights—lent the kind of ambiance that one might have found in a swanky bar. The air was thick with a combination of several different kinds of smoke, and that was something one was less likely to find in a bar or restaurant in pre-collapse days.

The cloud of smoke hanging in the room made the place feel like some melding of a medieval pub with an Old West saloon. Some of the smoke came from the woodstoves that provided supplemental heat on the cool evening, and some came from meat roasting over open coals in the kitchen area. Then there was the marijuana and tobacco being smoked at tables throughout the establishment.

At the far end of the room was a crude stage made of salvaged lumber. There was a sound system that appeared to be battery-operated and a few stage lights that might have been powered by the solar panels they'd spotted on the roof earlier. The sound system was entirely unnecessary as the drunken musician pummeling the banjo onstage required no amplification to be heard. Foley noted that the song he was playing didn't have any words. Instead the spirited musician released spontaneous outbursts as if he was driving a team of horses, with lots of "hey," "yaw," "yeehaw," and "whoa."

While they stood there taking it all in, a short, older woman approached with her hand on her hips. "You can seat your own damn selves. This ain't Chilis and we don't have a hostess." To emphasize her point, she pointed toward a crude sign on the wall that said "Seat Your Own Damn Self."

"Yes, ma'am," Foley said. Her tone was so commanding that there was never a thought of arguing with her. All the men immediately obeyed.

"What do you reckon she did before the collapse?" Herring asked as Foley led them toward an empty table.

Foley shook his head. "Drill Sergeant, cop, or a nurse, I'd bet. She's got some authority in that voice. I felt like I was in trouble and I haven't even done anything yet."

The normally silent Tibbets said, "Librarian." He let out a short chuckle, obviously having a thing for librarians that no one wanted to ask about.

"I ain't asking her," Herring said. "You all want to know that bad, you can ask her yourself."

"I ain't asking," Foley said. "She looks like the kind that might whoop my ass."

Tibbets grinned, revealing teeth so nasty they appeared to be covered in yellow moss. "Whooping."

The table they chose was a wooden cable reel that utility companies had once used for stringing power lines. Most of the tables were the same, with a few exceptions. The chairs were the folding type like at a funeral, with a few odd, mismatched items thrown into the mix. There were some pieces of living room furniture arranged for conversation off to the sides of the dining area, making it look like Goodwill had decided to open a trendy speakeasy.

"Quite the place," Foley commented, taking a seat. "I've seen a few bars and eateries during the collapse but nothing like this. It's got a bit of flair to it."

Herring pointed toward the bar. "They got a velvet Elvis wall-hanging. That's how you know it's a classy joint."

The woman who'd told them to find a table appeared shortly after they took their seats. "My name is Randi and I'll be your server. Note that I said *server*, not *servant*. It's a busy night and I'll do my best, but I recommend that you be nice and keep the attitude in check. You be nice, I'll be nice. Act like assholes and we'll take it outside. Are we clear?"

"Yes, ma'am," said Foley.

Herring followed suit and even Tibbets mumbled that he understood.

Randi smiled. "Alrighty then. With that out of the way, what are you boys drinking tonight and how do you intend to pay?"

Foley scratched his head. "Uh, what do you have and what do you take for it?"

"We have bourbon, tequila, vodka, whisky, and scotch. The meal is smoked pork served with tortillas. Payment is in barter, with ammunition being the preferred currency. If you don't have spare ammo, we can negotiate other trades. We also sell ammo, guns, knives, and other gear in the store at the end of the bar if you're in need of anything."

"Damn, you're a one stop shop." Herring grinned. "What's it cost a feller to get a shot of bourbon and an order of the pork?"

"Liquor is all the same price," Randi said. "There's a chart posted behind the bar that shows the price in different calibers of ammunition. A meal runs the same as four shots of liquor."

"Why is all the liquor the same price?" Foley asked.

"Because it's the same liquor," Randi replied. "Just served in different bottles."

Foley cocked an eyebrow at her, watching for any sign that she was teasing him. When he saw it wasn't a joke, he checked out the sign posted behind the bar again. "Then how about we get three orders of pork and three shots of liquor. Can we get water with that?"

"Water is free. The rest of it you can pay for right now. We don't run tabs here at the Reset Roadhouse. It's strictly pay-as-you-go."

Foley reached into the backpack at his feet and withdrew a spare Glock magazine. He thumbed off the appropriate number of rounds, then slid them across the table to their server.

Randi dropped the rounds into her apron pocket. "I'll be back in a moment with your food and drinks."

Before Randi walked away, Foley said, "I've never seen a place like this and I'm kind of curious about it. Can I ask you some questions?"

Randi gestured at the bustling room around them. "You see how many people are in this place? Now look how many servers there are. Not nearly enough. So, no, I don't have the time to stand here and jaw with you. If you need to know something, go to the bar and ask one of those folks. They're used to stupid questions."

As she was stalking away, Herring let out a low whistle. "Damn, that one has got some attitude."

"Firecracker," Tibbets mumbled, grinning like a wolf.

Herring looked at Tibbets and laughed. "That woman must've gotten to you. I've never seen you this talkative before."

Tibbets only nodded, apparently having exhausted his allocation of words for the moment. Meanwhile, Foley was staring at the bar. "Boys," he said to his companions, "I'm going to head to the bar and see what I can find out about this place."

"You thinking about opening a franchise?" asked Herring.

"No, dumbass, I'm trying to get some intel. We need to figure out where they've stored those converters and if they keep security on the place at night."

"Oh, that makes sense."

Foley rolled his eyes, scooted his chair back from the table, and stood. "I'll be back in a minute. If my food gets here, don't you dare touch it."

11

Jim was sitting behind the bar, still talking to Hugh about Blake Justice and Dr. Nelson showing up to demand converters. He didn't immediately notice the man who walked up to the bar and addressed Becky.

"Excuse me, miss, you mind if I ask you a few questions?"

Becky sighed dramatically, like she heard the same questions every night. "Okay, loser, here are the answers. My name is Becky. Yes, I'm from this town. No, I don't know where I've been all your life. No, I don't want to marry you. Yes, I have a boyfriend. Yes, he's big and mean and will drive you into the ground like a fence post if you offend me in any way. Now, do you still have questions?"

"Uh, yes," Foley replied. "Do you happen to be one of the owners of this fine establishment?"

Becky shook her head. "No, you're looking for Jim. He was down at that end of the bar earlier. I can hear him talking, so he must still be there."

It was only then that Foley understood that Becky couldn't see. He raised his voice and spoke slower. "Thank you. I'll find him. You have a good night."

Becky scowled at him. "I'm blind, not deaf, you freaking idiot."

It was Becky's words that got Jim's attention. He turned in her direction to see who she was berating and spotted the man headed toward him. He hoped it wasn't someone else there to ask about a converter. He understood that people's desperation drove them to seek out anything that might improve their family's odds of survival. He would do the same thing and it was only that awareness that helped him keep his attitude in check. It was hard working with the public when you generally hated the public.

"Excuse me, sir," Foley asked. "I was wondering if I might have a moment of your time."

Jim braced himself for a question about the converters. "Sure."

He tried to determine if he knew this man, but he couldn't place him. The number of men wearing long hair and beards had exploded since the collapse and it made everyone look different than they had before. The guy didn't look familiar, but he could have been a local that Jim didn't know or even a stranger passing through from some outlying community.

Foley extended a hand in Jim's direction. "My name is Foley. I'm here with my cousins and we're passing through on our way to Wise County. We have family over that way and wanted to check in on them."

Jim shook the man's hand. "Jim Powell. This is my friend Hugh."

When Foley broke off the handshake, he shook Hugh's hand. "Good to meet you all."

"What can I do for you, Foley?" Jim asked.

Foley gestured at the building around him. "That blind girl over there told me you owned this place."

Becky's finely tuned ears picked up the comment. "That blind girl has a name, jerk. I told you it was Becky. Will you remember it better if I come down there and slap you?"

Foley cringed. "Uh, that won't be necessary. My apologies, Becky."

Jim smiled. "Becky has supersonic hearing. I only keep her around because she keeps me humble."

"You keep me around because most people can't work with a jerk like you!" Becky called back.

"Also true," said Jim.

"Becky is an excellent shot," Hugh told Foley. "Consider yourself lucky she hasn't demonstrated that skill to you."

The thought of Becky waving a gun around visibly disturbed Foley, but he didn't comment on it. He didn't want to further offend Becky and find out firsthand how good a shot she was. "As I was saying, Becky told me that you own this place and I think it's cool. I've seen a few bars and restaurants operating since the collapse, but nothing like this place. It honestly embraces this experience we're all going through right now."

"Thanks," Jim said. "If there's an overall theme to the roadhouse, it would be 'availability.' We decorated with what we could scrape together, and we furnished with what we could come up with for free. We serve one meal a day of whatever the cooks feel like fixing and we sell one liquor under five different names. We've also been selling some beer lately, but we're out at the moment."

"Now that's a shame. It's been a while since I had a good beer," said Foley. "The reason I was asking about your place here is that I've been thinking of starting some kind of business and I might enjoy running something like this. You have much trouble? People can get a little rowdy these days with everyone packing guns."

"In the beginning, I ran into some local resistance. People were saying this was the last thing the town needed, that I should be putting my efforts toward something more productive than sin, vice, and debauchery."

Foley's eyes went wide. "You offer all that?"

Jim laughed. "No, it's nothing like that. I felt the town needed a place where people could come together and forget the hard times for a minute. A place where they could do something normal. On a personal level, it was also an opportunity to put my family and friends to work, and that's been good for all of us."

Jim left out the part about the roadhouse being a way to keep a finger on the pulse of what was happening in his community. Gathering regional intel had been a big motivator for getting the roadhouse up and running. Nearly everything bad that had happened to

Jim and his family could have been addressed earlier if he'd had better intel about what was going on in his community. He wouldn't fail there again.

"What about thieves?" Foley asked.

"People have tried to steal from us, but they were...dealt with."

Jim didn't like going into detail about their security procedures. Between him and Hugh, they had a lot of tricks up their sleeves. If someone tested the rules, the response was decisive and permanent. It was like the sign on the wall listing the roadhouse rules said, "Survivors will be banned."

Seeing that he wasn't going to get any more than that, Foley smiled and pushed back from the bar. "I won't take up anymore of your time. I just wanted to let you know that I appreciated your place. Thanks for taking the time to talk to me about it." He nodded at Jim and Hugh, then returned to his table.

"What did you make of that?" Hugh asked.

Jim watched Foley sit back down at his table and confer with his friends. "People these days aren't usually that polite unless they're wanting something. It was like he was fishing for information."

"Agreed. The question is what was he fishing *for*?"

"Let's keep an eye on that table," Jim said. "Alert all the staff to get a good look at them. I want them to recognize their faces if they show up again later."

"On it," Hugh said, hopping off his stool and wading out into the crowd.

"You think Human Resources will write me up for being a jerk to that customer?" Becky called from the other end of the bar.

"I doubt it," Jim replied. "Nobody died. The standards for a complaint are a lot higher than they used to be."

"So I only get in trouble if I kill someone?"

"Not even then. You only get in trouble if they didn't deserve it. Otherwise we're good."

Becky giggled. "I love working here. It's going to be tough going back to a normal job one day."

Her innocent comment sent Jim down a spiral of thought. There were so many people waiting for electricity, thinking it was going to give them their old lives back. Jim knew that wasn't going to be the case. Surely, they had to know it too. He often said that the genie couldn't be put back in the bottle. It was going to take decades to erase this experience from the nation's DNA.

12

"If I'd known those converters were going to be so much damn trouble, I wouldn't have agreed to take them," Jim growled. "I have a feeling Danielle knew what kind of burden she was laying on me, she just didn't want to say anything about it."

"Not even one of them?" Randi asked.

"Well, maybe *one*." Jim took a sip of his drink, a concoction that in the mountains was often known as "Bourbon and Branch" but was just as often made with moonshine and spring water.

"If it helps at all, I'm not going to ask for one," Gary said. "As long as we have access to power here at the roadhouse, that'll serve our needs until more converters come along."

"It sure would be nice to have power somewhere in the valley," Jim said. "I hope one of our people gets one."

"I'm not as selfless as you, Gary," Randi said. "There are a lot of things I'd like power for. For one, it would be nice to have a hairdryer. If I wash my hair in the winter, it's wet all day. I'd even like some of that stupid stuff that we always took for granted before—a toaster, a popcorn popper, a microwave oven."

Jim shook his head in frustration. "I told Lloyd a million times that he needed to install a small solar system at your house for things like that. He just never got off his ass to do it."

Randi rolled her eyes. "Well, for one, that would have required him putting down the banjo long enough to pick up some tools. And two, it would have meant sobering up long enough to do it."

"I'm right here." Lloyd was about ten feet away, sitting on a worn sofa, and plucking on his favorite five-string instrument of torture. "Y'all are talking about me like I'm not here. I can hear everything you say."

"Then you should be ashamed of yourself," Jim said. "You should have installed that solar system for Randi so she could dry her damn hair."

Lloyd played louder. "Sorry, I can't hear you over the banjo."

Jim drained the last of his drink and set it down on the bar. He got up and walked away so he could hear his radio over Lloyd's banjo banging and keyed the mic. "How's it looking, Hugh?"

At Hugh's suggestion, Jim had kept extra people on at the road-house that night. Normally, Ed and Ian, the two people living there full-time, served as backup for whoever was on night watch. In the beginning it was Hugh, but they had since hired other men who worked under Hugh's supervision. A meal and a beer each day was all they required in payment.

Jim had also stayed on at the roadhouse, along with Randi, Hugh, Lloyd, and Gary. Shade Wolford, Becky's newfound boyfriend, had insisted on staying on as well. Jim was glad to have Shade on his side. The guy was tall, strong, and more than willing to lay a beating down on somebody. He shared a lot of the same values that Jim did, although Shade was a bit more easy-going. Where Jim tended to get wound up over people bugging the crap out of him, Shade maintained the same relaxed demeanor up until the point he was pushed too far. Then it was time to deliver a beating and nothing could hold him back.

"I've got one guy watching the road and another on the woods," Hugh replied. "I'm patrolling the grounds with night vision."

Jim's people had several sets of military-grade night vision, most of which had been recovered as the spoils of battle. They'd fought better-equipped people and come out on top, which allowed them to keep everything they could carry away from the battlefield. While it might have been ghoulish, the practice was critical to survival. It gave them more weapons, more ammunition, and more tactical gear to spread among their people. Anything they didn't want got sold at the roadhouse.

"Have you spotted anything suspicious?" Jim asked.

Hugh shook his head. "Not a thing."

"Hopefully, it'll stay that way. Remember, I've got more people if you guys need a break."

"We're good for now, but you guys stand ready in case things go kinetic."

Jim opened his mouth to say something else when Hugh cut him off.

"I spoke too soon, Jim. Hold tight."

Jim picked up a wet rag that Becky had used to clean the bar top at the end of the night. He slung it at Lloyd, trying to silence him.

"Hey!" Lloyd cried out when the damp, smelly rag struck him in the face.

Jim swiped the tip of his fingers across his throat in a "cut it out" gesture. "I need to be able to hear. We might have company out there."

Lloyd started playing again, mumbling something about how the arts could not be silenced. This time, Jim snatched an empty liquor bottle from the bar top and drew it back over his head. Just as Jim had predicted, the arts were immediately silenced.

Hugh's voice came back across the radio. *"Jim, I've got a group of about two dozen approaching on the street from town. They are not making any effort to hide themselves. I'm headed up to the roof."*

"You see any weapons?" Jim asked.

"I saw a few long guns, but I couldn't tell if every man was armed or not."

"I'll meet you on the roof." Jim placed his radio on the bar while he slipped his body armor over his head. "Folks, we have guests."

Everyone scrambled into gear, armoring up and grabbing weapons. Jim and Gary headed for the roof. Everyone else was assigned to watch the doors inside the roadhouse in case someone attempted to break in.

The welded steel ladder that led from the roadhouse to the roof was a new addition. Originally, the only way to access the roof was to go outside and use the wall-mounted ladder. Those pulling night watch had quickly figured out that going outside to access the roof left them vulnerable to attack. To remedy this, Jim and Hugh cut a hole in the flat roof and used treated lumber to form a curb. They bent flashing over the curb and sealed it to the roof with tar. The lid to the roof hatch was fashioned from a car hood and it managed to keep *most* of the weather out.

Jim and Gary used that ladder now to get to the roof. Like the rest of the men working security, Jim carried an M4 rifle he'd taken off a dead man. It was a select-fire version of the same rifle he'd trained with for the last twenty years. For most interactions, semi-auto fire was fine, but it was nice to have that full-auto option available if he needed it. Jim referred to the full-auto option as "the setting of no return" because it was typically a last resort measure. It also blew through ammo like napkins at a barbecue joint.

Gary was carrying a sniper rifle in .338 Lapua. It had a night vision scope designed for hunting, which was helpful, but that large caliber was overkill for short ranges they were working with. The rifle was Gary's pride and joy, so he refused to carry anything else. While Jim had no idea how many people the rifle's three hundred grain rounds would pass through before stopping, he assumed that "overpenetration" would be an understatement.

"Any updates?" Jim whispered when he got on the roof.

Hugh waved him over to a parapet wall. Jim and Gary headed in that direction, then dropped to a crouch. Jim had been on a lot of roofs in his life. Most of the newer commercial roofs he'd been on used membranes of rubber or a synthetic fabric. The old sewing factory had a flat roof built up from layers of tar and roofing felt. Around the edges, the brick sidewalls rose a short distance above the roof level, offering some degree of ballistic protection. The walls were capped with old clay drain tiles mortared together. Back in the 1920s, this would have been standard construction for a light commercial building in this part of the country.

Hugh pointed into the darkness. "They're still coming this way, but they're not here yet."

Jim's ballistic helmet was another battlefield pick up. He had single-tube night vision so only one eye could see in the dark, but it was still more of an advantage than any of the men coming down the street had. It was unlikely any of them knew they were under surveillance and had multiple rifles pointed at them at this very moment.

At this distance, had Jim's people chosen to open fire, it was likely half of the visitors would have died in the first seconds of the skirmish. Another quarter of them would have been shot when they tried to flee. A few might have escaped if they found good cover, but the odds were against them in the dark. Jim hoped to avoid bloodshed. It wasn't like he was a figurehead of the community or anything, but killing his neighbors certainly wasn't good public relations when he was a business owner.

"Recognize any of them?" Jim asked.

Hugh shook his head. "Not one hundred percent, but if I'm going off silhouettes and intuition, that tall bastard in the front row is Blake Justice. I think Dr. Nelson is beside him because I'm catching the reflection of moonlight off his shaved head."

Jim held a monocular to his eye and studied the group. "You're right, Hugh. The cocky string-bean is definitely our friend Blake. Reflector Head is Dr. Nelson."

"What's our play?" Gary asked.

After well over a year of living in the collapse, Gary had adapted to the state of things. He'd always been a shooter and a prepper, but the level of violence they'd encountered had been difficult for him to accept. Although Gary had always done what he had to do to protect his family and friends, he'd never been comfortable with the number of people he'd had to kill. He didn't hesitate when he had to pull the trigger, but he looked forward to a day when they could put that behind them.

"The question is whether they know we run a night watch or not," Jim said. "I guarantee every low life and criminal in the area is aware of it because that's the kind of information they share among themselves. However, I'm not sure if word reached these townsfolk. I guess we'll find out in a minute."

"How close do you intend to let them get?" Hugh double checked his chamber and verified that the optic on his weapon was on the night vision setting.

"The parking lot," Jim said. "Then I'll greet them, and we'll have a little heart-to-heart talk."

Hugh grinned. "Like a real talk or the kind with bullets?"

"I guess we'll see." More than once Jim's "discussions" had turned into gunfights.

When the mob turned off the street and started across the parking lot toward the roadhouse, they were perhaps eighty feet from Jim's position. He raised his radio and spoke softly. "We have about two dozen visitors entering the parking lot. I'm getting ready to address them and hopefully they'll turn around and go home. If they don't, I'm sure you'll be able to tell."

Hugh patted Jim on the back, the energy of the blow dissipated by his rear plate. "Give 'em hell, Jim. We have your back."

Jim reached down to his belt and unclipped the heavy spotlight he'd brought from the bar. It was an insanely bright rechargeable LED spotlight made for law enforcement or firefighting operations. In the dark, it was almost as good as a weapon at stopping people in their tracks. Jim stood and folded his nightvision out of the way, then powered on the spotlight.

The painful light paralyzed the mob in its beam. People immediately tried to shield their eyes against the head-splitting brightness. One of the men attempted to shield his eyes with his left hand, while drawing a handgun with his right.

"Easy there," Jim said. "I've got a dozen guns on you people, and we'll kill the first man to point a gun in this direction. Just so no one gets hurt, how about you set those guns down on the ground right now? We're not going to keep them. You can take them with you when you leave, but I would prefer not to have any fatal misunderstandings. Killing customers tends to have a negative effect on my Google reviews."

When no one moved to obey his order, Jim repeated the key points of his message. "Set the guns down before somebody gets hurt. Rifles and handguns both. Then I'll turn the light off and we can speak like old friends."

Though none of the visitors looked very happy about the request, they were smart enough to understand that they'd been caught at a disadvantage. One by one, everyone leaned over and carefully placed their weapons on the ground. True to his word, Jim switched off the spotlight. He knew the men on the ground would all be seeing spots in front of their eyes now, with their natural night vision destroyed by the bright light. That temporary blindness would hopefully make them compliant for a little while longer.

Jim handed the spotlight off to Hugh and got a hand back on the rifle hanging across his chest. He dropped his nightvision so he could again see the men standing below him. "Gentlemen, what was the plan here tonight?"

No one said anything.

"Aw, come on, you guys are big enough to come marching down to my place, but not big enough to admit it?"

"You know why we're here," Dr. Nelson said. "And don't make out like it's to steal from you. We have just as much right to those converters as you do."

Jim's gut knotted from frustration. "Dude, we've been down this road today already. You *do* have a right to those converters, but so does everyone else in the community. Like I already told you, I was personally given the responsibility of making sure they were given out fairly. I accepted that responsibility, although I've been second-guessing that choice all day."

"Then give them to us," Blake said. "We'll see that they get handed out."

"Not happening. I told people to spread the word that we'd have a community meeting here tomorrow evening to decide how to distribute them. Just to give you a heads-up of how that might go, I'm leaning toward a lottery system. That sounds like the only fair way to do it."

"First come, first served would be fairer," Dr. Nelson argued.

Jim raised his voice. "I'm done arguing with you! You've got thirty seconds to pick up your shit and get out of here. Anyone still here after thirty seconds won't like how this ends. Electricity will become the least of your problems."

When no one moved, Jim shouted, "One...two...three!"

By the time he reached fifteen, almost everyone had picked up their weapons and was tearing down the road as fast as they could run. Their vision still impaired by Jim's spotlight, the men ran into each other, going down when their legs tangled. One ran into a deep ditch, crying out as the ground disappeared beneath him. Another ran full tilt into a speed limit sign. His friends grabbed the stunned man, got him standing, and hustled him off.

The only man who hadn't left yet was Dr. Nelson. He wasn't done. "If I somehow end up *not* getting a converter, you and I are going to have a problem, Jim Powell." With that, the doctor turned and jogged away.

"We already have a problem!" Jim yelled back. "I don't like you."

13

On the hill opposite the roadhouse, crouched in the woods, Foley, Herring, and Tibbets watched the scene unfold between the owner of the roadhouse and the group wanting to steal the converters. Foley's team had been waiting for hours for the employees to leave so they could steal the converters, but they knew people remained inside. While they'd gorged on smoked pork, they'd counted the men they saw working at the roadhouse and knew some remained behind at the end of the night.

"There's our answer, boys," Herring said, watching the action through binoculars. "They're babysitting those converters all night."

"That's not the answer I was hoping for," Foley replied. "And you heard the man. They're going to be distributed tomorrow. The clock is ticking. Once they get handed out, it's too much work to track them down one by one."

"Maybe we should just move on," Herring said. "There are softer targets out there that present less risk to us. I'm just here to make money. I'm not interested in getting ventilated over a load of converters."

Foley considered this. "When Elder and I partnered up to start stealing these things, he said that times of war were when fortunes were made. That's when money flows and people don't always see where it ends up. This is exactly like that. Most people are starving and desperate but we're building a future for ourselves. Those converters are too valuable to pass up."

"You're the boss," Herring said. "If you say steal, I'll steal, but please don't get my ass killed. I swear I'll come back to haunt you."

"What do you think, Tibbets?" Foley asked.

Tibbets grunted, which Foley took as a statement of support.

Herring shook his head and rolled his eyes. "Damn, Tibbets, can you start doing one grunt for yes, two for no. I never understand what you're saying."

Tibbets shrugged and gave Herring a look that was indecipherable in the dark.

"What's our play then?" Herring asked. "We can't hit them head on. It'll be like attacking a fort. We won't have a snowball's chance in hell."

Foley opened his pack and tucked his binoculars back inside. "We come back tomorrow. Hit them during business hours."

"Are you crazy?" Herring asked. "That'll be even worse. That place will be full of armed men."

"Stealth mode isn't going to work here, Herring. We have to be brazen. Think of this as a bank robbery rather than a burglary."

"A bank robbery?" Herring asked, his tone questioning Foley's sanity.

"Think about it. What makes a good bank robbery?"

"Duh. Getting away with the money."

"Well, obviously that," Foley replied. "But what makes the most effective bank robbery? How do you do it right?"

When Herring didn't answer, Foley continued.

"Terror. You go in and you fire a couple of shots to make sure you have everyone's attention. Then you take a hostage so they know you're serious."

"What if the hostage is somebody they don't like?" Herring asked. "Then they won't care if you kill them or not."

"Geez, Herring. This is like arguing with a kid. Haven't you ever watched a heist film? If firing shots and taking a hostage doesn't produce the effect we want, we kill that hostage and take another. They'll eventually get the point."

"How do we get away?"

"We make Mickelson hang out in the woods with the horses. Once he sees us bringing converters outside, he comes down with the horses. We load up and take off."

"Won't they chase us?"

Foley shook his head. "We take the hostage with us so they don't, then we release them outside of town."

"Sounds risky," Herring said.

"Life is risky, Herring. If you don't have the stones for it, you can start home in the morning. You can't be part of the team and cherry pick which jobs you want to be a part of. You're either in or out. There's plenty of men out there who'd be willing to take your place."

"I'll think on it. I'll let you know by the time we reach camp."

"Good enough," Foley said. "Tibbets, you in?"

Grunt.

"Damn neanderthal," Herring snapped, irritated with how difficult this job had become.

Foley chuckled under his breath. "You best be careful about how much you poke that bear. I didn't bring Tibbets along for the conversation. Keep running that mouth and you'll learn that son of a bitch is tough as woodpecker lips."

Herring huffed out a breath. "Sorry, Tibbets. I'm just pissed this job has turned into such a hassle."

Tibbets didn't even grunt, remaining even quieter than his customary level of quietness.

"You made him mad," Foley said. "He's pouting now. It's probably best you give him a little space for a day or two."

14

The roadhouse didn't open for lunch the next day. Jim not only posted a sign on the door, but out on Main Street so that people would see it well before walking to the roadhouse. It still didn't stop people from showing up and banging their empty bowls on the door to see if they could get a little something to go.

"We're closed!" Jim shouted. "Read the damn sign!"

Some would go away in response to his barking. Others persisted in their attempts to gain entry until someone went to the door and politely told them to come back later. Not everyone was after a meal. There were the drunks who were pleased they had the opportunity to imbibe real liquor again and they weren't happy about being put off.

During the collapse, those with a weakness for alcohol had been forced to fall back on other sources of intoxication. Fortunately for them, drunks were a resourceful lot and had an entire catalog of substances they resorted to when they were in a detox facility, jail, or otherwise cut off from their drink of choice. They drank after-shave, rubbing alcohol, and liniments. They drank diluted Lysol, which gave them fresh pine-scented breath along with their intoxication. They sucked down mouthwash, red wine vinegar, and vanilla extract. Some resorted to eating nutmeg. Others inhaled the fumes from aerosol cleaners, spray paint, gas, glue, paint thinner, and even magic markers.

The drunks were not as easily sent away as those after food. Those in search of a little nip would lay on the histrionics in an attempt to get a sympathy shot. One faked a heart attack and lay there unmoving for nearly thirty minutes while other wishful customers stepped over him.

"I'm in withdrawal," another claimed. "I feel a seizure coming on."

Jim watched from the doorway, unmoved.

Finally, the man got to his feet, scowled, and shook his fist at Jim. "This ain't over!"

"Bring it!" Jim fired back. "Mess with me and I'll put a knot on your head the Boy Scouts can't untie."

Then there were those who'd gotten word of the public meeting Jim was holding at the roadhouse that night. Just like Dr. Nelson's group, they apparently had the impression that they could get there early and somehow improve their chances of getting a converter.

"Listen, I got a jar of silver dollars here that my granddaddy put back in the 1920s," one man said. "It's about the only money worth anything these days and I'll give you the whole jar for one of those power doohickeys."

"No deal," Jim said, exasperated. "Come back this evening. We'll have a meeting then and discuss how they're being distributed."

Although Jim didn't hear the response, it involved a significant amount of profanity.

After the lunch crowd got turned away, those wanting to bargain for early admission continued their campaign. Most of Jim's people working inside the roadhouse had jobs to keep them busy, such as preparing the evening meal, working with the distilling or brewing equipment, or cleaning. That left Jim, Hugh, Lloyd, and Randi to deal with the unwanted guests. Though the people in Jim's group found his growing irritation to be amusing, they knew it could easily reach the boiling point and no one wanted to see how that went down.

Boom! Boom!

Another knock.

"Your turn, Lloyd," Hugh said.

The knock came again before Lloyd managed to get up.

Lloyd groaned and set his banjo aside. "Hold up! I'm coming."

Once he staggered to his feet, he stood just to the side of the door. He didn't open it, nor did he want to stand in front of it in case someone fired through the door. Sentries on the roof were supposed to be watching for armed visitors, but they wouldn't be able to tell if someone carried a concealed weapon.

"Open the door, please!" a woman called. She tried to sound friendly, but that was tough when she had to yell to be heard through the door.

"No. Go away." Lloyd made no attempt to match her friendliness. He was pissed at having to stand up and deal with her.

"Please?" the woman asked. Now she was trying to sound seductive, but again it was tough when she had to speak so loudly. "Are you a single man?"

Lloyd looked around at the rest of the group and cocked an eyebrow, intrigued at what she might be about to propose. "Why, yes I am!"

Before the woman could respond, a pizza pan went sailing across the room like a giant frisbee, striking the wall beside Lloyd. He screamed like a little girl, then noticed Randi glaring at him.

He quickly backpedaled, speaking loudly so the woman outside could hear him. "No! I was wrong! I'm not single. I'm happily...something. Very happily something. Now go away before you get me killed!"

"Is there anyone else in there I could talk to? A single man, maybe? I don't want to brag, but I can—"

Randi was across the room in a flash. She yanked the door open and charged outside. Jim, Hugh, and Lloyd were hot on her heels, ready to drag her back inside. They found a woman in tight jeans and a snug t-shirt flat on her back on the sidewalk, Randi standing above her.

She jabbed a finger in the woman's face. "Listen, girl, there's ten bad bitches in this town and the other nine address me as ma'am. You ever come back here and you'll find out why."

The girl crab-walked backward a few steps, then stood and took off running. Randi noticed Lloyd watching her go, so she reached out, gripped a handful of chest hair through his shirt, and twisted.

Lloyd cried out and went to his knees. "I was just admiring her speed."

"That all you noticed?" Randi asked.

When Lloyd didn't immediately answer, she twisted his chest hair again.

"I noticed she had a coin in her back pocket," Lloyd said.

Randi nodded. "I bet you did. Those jeans were practically painted on."

Despite his pain, Lloyd winked at her. "Pretty sure it was on 'heads' too."

Randi let go of Lloyd's chest hair and shoved him over on his ass before she stormed back inside the roadhouse. "Jerk!"

Hugh and Jim stepped over to regard Lloyd sprawled on his back on the gravel parking lot.

"Think she's mad?" Lloyd asked.

Jim said, "I think you're lucky to be alive."

"That pizza pan almost beheaded you," Hugh said. "She was like an enraged ninja."

"I sometimes have an unsettling effect on women," Lloyd said. "I attribute it to my smoldering gaze. I used to practice it in the mirror."

Hugh and Jim shook their heads at Lloyd, gazing at him pityingly, then they headed back into the roadhouse.

"You better get back in here before the next one comes along," Jim warned.

Lloyd staggered to his feet, stretched his back, and dusted off the seat of his pants. He followed the others inside and locked the door behind him then made a beeline for the couch and began plucking the banjo again. Several times he turned around and grinned in Randi's direction, but she wasn't in a forgiving mood. She slammed, banged, and slung stuff as she prepared for the night shift, which they all expected to be a busy one.

Twenty minutes later there was more banging at the door. Lloyd, Jim, and Hugh let out a collective sigh, arguing over who was going to deal with it.

"It sure as hell isn't my turn," Lloyd said. "I took the last one and nearly died for my troubles."

Randi unleashed a torrent of swearing and slapped a towel onto the bar. She came around the end and stalked toward the door. "Don't worry, I'll get it. Leave it to a woman to fix, just like you always do."

"I was getting ready to get it," Lloyd said, winking at Jim and Hugh.

"Damn right you're about to get it," Randi spat, narrowing her eyes at Lloyd. When she reached the door, she paused and lit a cigarette. "Who is it?"

"I need to talk to somebody." Again, it was a woman's voice.

Randi sighed. "Listen, I just ran off the last woman who came sniffing around here, trying to trade her body for electricity. Am I going to have to come outside and run you off too?" Randi took a drag off her smoke, folded her arms over her chest, and waited for the woman to respond.

"I really need to talk to someone," the woman repeated.

Jim leaned to the side so he could unclip his radio from his belt. He radioed Ian, who was working the roof. "Jim for Ian."

"Go for Ian."

"There's a woman at the door wanting to speak to someone. Is she alone?"

"Negative, Jim. I've got eyes on her and she's with a young girl. Maybe eight, nine, or something like that. I can't tell."

Jim sighed. "Copy that. Thanks." He looked at Randi.

Randi shrugged. "It's up to you. You're the boss."

"They could need food," Jim said. "I'll own up to being an asshole, but I'm not a cruel asshole."

Lloyd stopped playing and gave Jim an accusing, side-eye glance.

"Well, except to banjo players."

Randi hung the cigarette off her lip and unbolted the heavy steel door. When she tugged it open, she found a scrawny woman with dark circles under her eyes standing beside a young girl. The girl was wearing a Barbie backpack and carried a doll in her hands. Her clothes were dirty, her long hair matted, and she should have been wearing something a little warmer than shorts and a t-shirt.

Randi leaned against the doorjamb, blocking the way, and gave the woman an expectant glance. "What?"

The woman came closer and whispered even though there was no one around to overhear what she was about to say. "I hear you all got a thing that will make the power work again."

Randi rolled her eyes. "Damn, lady, can you not read the sign right here on the door? You walked by another one down the street. Both of them say to show up here tonight and there will be a meeting about the power. All your questions will be answered then."

Hugh nodded, impressed. "She's being nicer than I expected."

"She's not done yet," Jim said. "Don't get ahead of yourself."

"I got something to trade," the woman said.

"No trades!" Jim called from his seat on the couch.

"No trades," Randi repeated. "You heard the man."

The woman jabbed a thumb toward the little girl. "I got the kid here." She said it in a lilting voice, cocking an eyebrow suggestively.

"You'd trade your child for electricity?" Randi asked, incredulous.

"Aw, hell no," the woman said. "She ain't mine. She's my niece. Her parents are dead, and I got no interest in raising a damn kid. If I'd wanted one, I'd have had one already."

Randi looked at the little girl, who was staring at her feet, the doll clutched in her arms. "Honey, you step inside a minute. Go sit by that man with the banjo. He ain't much to look at but he's nice and he knows some silly songs."

The little girl did as Randi asked and the woman grinned. "We got a deal?"

Randi dropped her cigarette butt and ground it beneath the toe of her worn-out tennis shoe. She stared at the ground a moment, then let out a breath. The woman thought she had a deal and wasn't expecting the hard right that Randi threw. There was an audible pop when Randi's first punch connected with the woman's eye. The woman cried out and staggered backward, though not nearly far enough to escape Randi's wrath.

Randi lashed out with her left hand and grabbed the woman's shirt, preventing her from going anywhere, and she began raining hard punches onto her face and head. The woman tripped as she backpedaled, and Randi transitioned from punches to hammer fists. The woman was screaming and yelling, trying to block the torrent of blows, but Randi flogged her like a woman possessed.

Back inside the roadhouse, Lloyd was playing and singing, trying to cover up the sounds of the fight happening just outside. While his hope was to spare the child having to hear her aunt being beaten, he couldn't drown out the cries. There was nothing in the girl's demeanor to suggest that the sounds of the fight bothered her. In fact, she was clutching at her backpack and grinning in the direction of the door. If anything, she looked pleased at the ass-whooping her aunt was taking.

"Reckon we should stop her?" Hugh asked.

Jim thought for a moment. He looked at the little girl and tried to imagine what she'd gone through living with such a callous and uncaring woman. What had the aunt told the little girl this morning? Where did this little girl think she was going?

"Nah, let Randi get it out of her system," Jim finally said. "She needs this."

"I'm going to take a peek." Hugh got up from the couch and walked toward the door. When he got there, he looked outside, cringed, and stepped out.

"I better take a look too," Jim said. "You keep an eye on this young lady here, Lloyd."

Jim reached the door and immediately saw what had made Hugh wince. The woman was out cold on the crumbling sidewalk, her face a bloody pulp. Her eyes were swollen shut and her lips looked like two sausages that had split their casings. Randi was no longer pounding the woman. She was pacing around, cradling her right hand in her left.

"Broken?" Jim asked.

"Think so," Randi said. "I was fine until I hit teeth. Think I broke a knuckle."

"She's alive," Hugh said, finding a pulse on the woman.

Randi frowned. "Who cares? Somebody get me a damn cigarette."

"Yes, ma'am!" Hugh said, lighting one of his smokes and handing it over to Randi.

Randi took a pull, got a second wind, and kicked the unconscious woman in the ribs.

"Not sure there's much of a point in that," Jim said. "She's already unconscious."

Randi shot him a dirty look. "The point is that it makes me feel better and she'll remember me for a long time."

"If she lives," said Jim, regarding the battered woman at his feet. "What's your plan? You can't leave her here. It'll be bad for business."

"Can I kill her?"

Jim shrugged. "I'd be the last person to tell someone they *couldn't* kill someone if they had their mind set on it. I'm that kind of friend."

"You're the kind that brings a shovel and helps dig the hole?" Randi asked.

"Depends on the ground," said Jim. "If it's rocky, I'd help you throw her in the river."

"Are we sure we need to kill her?" Hugh said. "I ain't arguing that she doesn't deserve it, but she can't fight back. Maybe you just dump her out of town with a note that you'll finish the job if you ever see her again."

"Obviously I ain't giving her that kid back," Randi spat.

"Yeah, what about that kid?" Jim asked. "This whole thing was a little spontaneous."

Randi glared at him. "You think I should have sent her home with this piece of trash?"

"No," Jim said. "But what are you going to do with her?"

"She can stay with me and my family until we find her a home,"

Randi said. "I've already got kids and babies around the place. She'll have friends and be well taken care of."

"That's between you and the kid," Jim said.

"Then it's settled," Randi said.

"Except for what we're doing with her." Hugh pointed to the woman at their feet.

Randi waved her off. "I ain't got time to fool with her. I got work to do inside and it's going to take twice as long with a broken hand. Throw her across a horse, haul her back into the woods, and leave with that note you mentioned. I've already wasted as much time on her as I'm going to."

"I'll get my horse," Hugh said, heading around the back of the roadhouse.

"Might need to soak your hand in that cold creek back there," Jim said. "Which reminds me, I'm going to find an ice machine and install it in the roadhouse. That's one of the big things we're missing around here."

"Besides offering a liquor *other* than moonshine," Randi pointed out.

"There you go being picky."

Hugh was back in a minute with his horse and the three of them heaved the woman across the back of it.

"You're better go with me," Hugh told Randi. "People see me hauling this woman into the woods like this, they'll think I'm some kind of serial killer or something."

"Okay," Randi sighed. "Get a move on."

The two of them ambled off down the road. Jim couldn't help but think how a person's fortunes could be reversed so quickly. One minute you get the genius idea that you're going to trade your niece for free electricity. The next you're being dumped in the woods looking like you went bare knuckles with Mike Tyson.

When he got back inside, the little girl asked, "Do I have to go with Aunt Karen?"

Jim shook his head. "Nah, you're going to stay with us for a little while. The lady who went out to speak with your aunt is going to take you home with her. She has little girls too."

"Did she hurt my Aunt Karen?"

Jim hesitated, unsure of what to say. Surely the little girl had heard the fight taking place just outside the door. "Uh, maybe."

The little girl grinned. "I hope she did. Aunt Karen is a bitch."

15

When the Reset Roadhouse finally opened its doors on the day of the public meeting, it had never been more crowded. Most people weren't using watches or clocks anymore and had long ago lost track of the actual time. They estimated the time by using the position of the sun or the noises coming from their bellies. As a result, there was a line outside the roadhouse when the doors opened and by 6 PM it was standing room only. Those unable to tolerate the elbow-to-elbow crowd inside the building stood outside near the loading dock area where could still hear the amplified voice of anyone speaking on the stage.

Everyone in Jim's clan was in attendance, from his parents to the families of Gary and Randi. Jim stood behind the counter sipping on a beer that had been cooling out back in the creek. He hoped this was the last batch of beer they'd be forced to cool in that manner. Hopefully after tonight, they'd be back to good old refrigeration.

After he'd drained the last of the beer, he placed the bottle in a rack behind the bar to be washed and reused. He sucked in a deep breath and let it out slowly. "Guess I can't put this off any longer. It's showtime."

Hugh patted him on the back. "You'll be fine. You have a real way with people. Mobs in this town love you."

"Liar."

"Give 'em hell, Jim," Becky said.

At her side, Shade Wolford offered Jim a reassuring nod. "If things get spicy, we got your back."

Jim went around the bar and stepped into the crowd. When people caught sight of him determinedly making his way to the stage, the overpowering murmur of the crowd subsided, leaving an awkward silence behind. Jim heard the scuff of his boots on the gritty concrete floor and the occasional clunk of a beer bottle being placed on a table. He felt like he was at a high-school assembly, on his way to the lectern to make a dreaded speech.

When Jim took the stage, no effort was required to silence the crowd. They were already dead silent and entirely focused on him. The intensity of their collective gaze felt like the burn of the sun on a late July day. It made him want to turn away, but there was nowhere to turn. Nowhere to go.

He flipped the switch on the microphone, then tapped it to see if it worked. He was tempted to make some stupid joke, but he didn't know any that would come close to dispelling the level of awkwardness he was experiencing. Any attempt at humor would likely fall flat anyway. This audience knew him as a killer, not a comedian. It was best to just dive into it.

"Can everyone hear me? This is probably as loud as I can get without feedback."

The murmured response from the crowd indicated that they heard him well enough to understand his question.

"I don't know what you've heard, but I want to tell you my side of the story in case you heard it from one of those ass...*idiots*...I had to run off yesterday."

There were a couple of chuckles among the audience, which Jim found encouraging. He forgot sometimes that there were people in the community who appreciated his attitude. Who understood him.

"Most of you have been listening to the same radio transmissions from Walter Lightspeed that I have. He promised us power, but we had no idea when it might reach us. Well, it reached us the other day and it's like nothing any of us have ever seen before. Just as Lightspeed promised, there aren't any power lines to fool with. There's a converter that you have to install at your home to get power. You'll remove your electrical meter, replace it with this device, and it will wirelessly receive power from that big orange balloon that most of you have probably seen floating over Clinch Mountain."

There was some scattered laughter in the audience now, but Jim knew it wasn't from amusement. Some in the crowd were skeptical of the technology Jim was describing and he fully understood it. The whole concept sounded too bizarre to be real. It challenged every understanding anyone had of how power was transmitted in the US. Jim was prepared for that skepticism.

Jim waved toward Gary stationed along the wall. "Gary?"

Gary disconnected the system that had been providing solar power to the roadhouse since they opened. There was a gasp from the crowd when the interior of the roadhouse went pitch black.

Jim yelled, "Hugh!"

Near the loading dock door, Hugh flipped a breaker on the main panel box and the fluorescent lighting fixtures along the ceiling of the roadhouse buzzed to life. Jim smiled as he looked out over the astonished expressions of those gathered in the room. Such was their amazement that this might have been the first time a lightbulb was ever illuminated. The first time anyone ever witnessed the miracle of electricity demonstrated. They'd been in the dark long enough that the restoration of technology was almost like a miracle.

"See? It works," Jim said. "We installed one yesterday, shortly after Lightspeed's crew dropped them off here. They were delivered here because I agreed to receive them and make sure they were distributed in an equitable manner. I almost wish I hadn't because it's brought me nothing but trouble. There have been rude people, robbery attempts, and people offering trades that I'd be embarrassed to recount."

There was a smattering of laughter until people saw that Jim was serious.

"The only reason I agreed to accept the responsibility was because of the experience I've had with local government around here since the collapse. I don't know how many representatives are left, but I wouldn't trust any of them. They've tried to kill some of us, they've tried to tax us for using a public parking lot as a farmer's market, and they've done nothing to help us. I didn't want to be at the mercy of some public official who kept the converters for his friends or tried to sell them to us when they're supposed to be given away for free."

"Isn't that what you're going to do?" a man shouted from the back. "I heard you didn't want to give them out to people."

"When did you hear about this meeting?" Jim asked.

"Today."

"How would you personally have felt if you showed up here tonight and found out all the converters were already given out or promised to other people?"

"I'd have been pissed off," the man said.

"If I hadn't held onto those converters, there wouldn't be any left by now. They would have been taken yesterday and most of you in this room wouldn't have had a fair shot at getting one. So if some asshole says I was being a jerk about it, that's why. To me, the fairest way to go about this is to use a lottery system with as many people participating as possible. If anyone has a better idea, I'm open to hearing it."

Jim looked around the room. He saw no suggestions but caught Doctor Nelson boring holes in him with his stare. Jim managed to restrain himself from giving him the finger.

"Before this meeting descends into total chaos, I need to mention that Cookie wants to speak to you all tonight. Many of you know him because he jumped in this summer to take the lead on some community projects. He has some ideas worth listening to, so I hope you'll give him your attention when he gets up here. Cookie, you out there?"

From somewhere in the crowd, Cookie raised a hand and waved, but no one paid any attention to him. They were here for one reason and one reason only.

"You going to shoot us if we don't listen to Cookie?" Dr. Nelson called, unable to keep his mouth shut.

If Dr. Nelson wasn't going to restrain himself, Jim decided not to either. He shot Dr. Nelson a middle finger, which drew laughter from the crowd. Jim glared at the doctor, getting some enjoyment from his embarrassment.

"One of Cookie's ideas was to power up some local buildings that could be of benefit to everyone, like the library and the government offices. Even if we can't power the entire building, getting the library going might allow our kids to start learning again. As far as the government buildings go, it's the same deal. I'm not sure if we can power an entire building with a single converter, but Cookie suggested we might be able to get a clinic going if we could clean the place up."

"Why not just power up the hospital?" a lady asked. "There's medical equipment there that could be useful."

"I'm not sure how much you folks know about power, and I don't want this to get technical, but the hospital requires three-phase power and these converters are single phase only. We could try to only power part of the hospital, but it could take a long time to sort out all that wiring. It might be better to power a simpler building now and work on the hospital as time permits."

A man Jim recognized as a local minister stood up. "Our church is near the hospital. My congregation would be okay with me offering it up for use as a clinic. We're only about a hundred yards from the hospital, so it would be easy to access the hospital for supplies, assuming there are any left."

"Good thought," Jim said. "The bad news is that we were only given three hundred converters as a starter set. I took out one for this building and I'm going to pull out one for a clinic. I'm going to take out another for the library. Can anyone think of another building that would benefit the public if we could light it up?"

"Why do you get to keep one for your damn bar?" Blake Justice hollered. "You think this place is more important than any other business? What makes you so special?"

Jim let out a sigh that was clearly audible across the sound system. The sound produced scattered laughter. "I'm taking one of the converters as a tax for dealing with shitheads like you and Dr. Nelson. For anyone who wonders what I'm talking about, those two stormed in here yesterday demanding I give them first shot at the converters. When that didn't work out for them, they showed up here with an armed mob last night to try and steal them. That didn't go as they planned either, but since Blake feels a need to call me out, I'm returning the favor. If you don't appreciate those two trying to steal from the rest of you, you can catch them after the meeting and let them know what you think about it."

A lot of heads turned and glared at Blake Justice and Dr. Nelson. They were not happy looks. As Jim was admiring his handiwork, he spotted another man holding his hand up. Jim pointed at him.

"I used to work at the water plant," the man said. "I know we can't run our equipment off one of those converters because we need three-phase power, but it would sure be nice if we could find a house in town with a private well that we could power up. Hauling water is a major issue for people in town. If we had one house in a central location where we could fill jugs, that would help until we could do something with the public water supply."

"Another good idea," Jim said. "I'll tell you what we're going to do. I'm going to send some people around with scraps of paper. I want every family interested in a converter to submit their name on a piece of paper. One entry per household. If I catch you cheating, you're out of here. We'll draw names for the converters, minus those we already discussed putting aside for public projects."

"What if we don't get a converter in this go around?" a woman asked.

"Good question. The people who dropped them off provided me with a name and a radio frequency for requesting more. I just have to contact them with how many we need and they said we'll have them in a week or two. They only had room for a limited amount on this first trip because of the equipment and people required to do the installation."

Seeing some downcast faces, Jim added, "I know none of you want to wait, but if we all survived this long, hopefully we can survive a little longer. Now I'll start those people around with the scraps of paper."

Jim waved toward the bar and Randi, Gary's family, Ian, and Becky handed out scraps of paper.

"As much as I hate to, I'm going to ask my friend Lloyd to come back up here and play a banjo tune for you while we collect names," said Jim.

There was a scream in the crowd. At first, Jim assumed it was related to the warning about more banjo music, but then he spotted people craning their necks around, looking back into the crowd. Then Jim saw it. The crowd parted and backed away from the screaming woman.

It was Randi, and there was man holding a handgun to her head. It took Jim a moment to recognize him, then the pieces fell in place. It was the man who'd called himself Foley. The man who'd been asking Jim about the roadhouse last night.

At the bar, Herring sprang across the counter and wrapped an arm around Becky's neck. While she couldn't see who'd grabbed her, she recognized the cold steel of a gun barrel pressed against her temple. On the other side of the bar, Shade Wolford, Becky's boyfriend, rose to his full height and shot daggers from his eyes.

"Sit down, big boy," Herring warned.

When Shade didn't immediately follow his orders, Herring jammed the barrel harder into Becky's head and she cried out. Shade gritted his teeth and reluctantly sat back down on his stool.

Still at the microphone, Jim addressed Foley over the noise of the crowd. "What the hell are you doing?"

Foley grinned and made his way toward the stage, his arm tight around Randi's neck, his gun pressed against her temple. "We need to talk."

16

When Foley reached the stage with Randi, the two of them awkwardly climbed the steps together like some four-legged beast. He never removed the gun from her head. He growled at Jim, "Back away from the microphone."

Jim did as he was told, keeping his hands raised and clear of his weapons. He didn't want any misunderstandings, especially the kind that would get Randi or Becky killed. "What do you want?"

Foley moved toward the microphone stand and leaned over to speak into it. "You folks stay where you're at and stay calm. This will be over in a minute." He looked over at Jim. "I need you to hand those converters over to my friend out there. Once we have them, we'll be out of your hair."

"We're not giving you those converters," Jim said. "They belong to us."

"Does someone have to die to prove I'm serious?" Foley asked, wrenching a handful of Randi's hair and making her cry out.

Lloyd unslung his banjo and pointed a trembling finger at Foley. "That's enough. You let my girlfriend go right now."

Foley laughed at the banjo player threatening him. "What are you going to do? Drive me to suicide with your playing?"

Lloyd took another step forward, but Foley lashed out with a foot, sweeping Lloyd's knee and sending him crashing to the stage. When Lloyd hit, he lost his grip on his banjo, and it slid across the stage. Foley took aim and fired, shooting a hole through the banjo hide and taking out two strings in the process.

"Somebody should have done that a long time ago," Foley snapped.

"I can't argue with that," Jim said. "But stop this right now and we'll let you go on your way."

"We're not leaving without those converters." Foley returned the barrel of his gun to Randi's head and searched the crowd. "Tibbets?"

Tibbets had not shown his hand yet, sitting calmly at a table with a shot of liquor in his hand. He hadn't displayed a weapon or menaced anyone up to this point, so no one knew to whom Foley was referring.

That all changed when Tibbets drew a handgun from a shoulder holster and fired at a neighboring table. The round smacked into the head of a man in his early thirties and he collapsed facedown onto the table. His dining companions were paralyzed with shock, their faces splattered with blood.

Foley grinned at Jim. "That one's on you for not taking me seriously. Do you get the point, or do we need to make it two?"

Jim wasn't as shocked by the display of violence as much as he was angered by it. His eyes burned with a hatred that wouldn't be sated until Foley and all his men were dead. Any thoughts of letting them go on their way were gone.

"What do we need to do to end this with no one else getting hurt?" Jim asked.

Foley tipped his head toward Tibbets, now standing in the crowd with his gun in his outstretched hand. "You're going to take my man there to wherever you have those converters stored, then you're going to help him haul them outside. Once we're loaded, we'll take the hostages with us to make sure you don't follow us. If you play by the rules, the hostages will be let off at the town limits and they can walk back here without a scratch. You feel me?"

"I got it," Jim said, starting toward the edge of the stage.

"Not so fast," Foley said. "You unsling that rifle off your neck and leave it on the stage. Don't even touch the weapon, just the sling. Same with your handgun."

Jim did as he was told, not wanting to risk another innocent death. "Can I get those converters now?"

Foley nodded and Jim hopped off the stage, pushing his way through the crowd. People grumbled, expressing their anger at this turn of events. If Jim was reading the crowd correctly, they were more interested in saving the converters than in saving the hostages, but Jim wasn't going to let Becky or Randi die for the promise of electricity.

Once Jim was through the crowd, he reached Tibbets, standing there with a handgun now pointed at him. Tibbets was a wiry man with crazy, intense eyes. His mouth hung open slightly, revealing cracked lips and nasty teeth. He held his weapon with a caution that told Jim he'd probably been in this same situation before.

Jim gave Tibbets a wide berth and headed toward the door that connected the factory floor to the office wing. "They're back here in a locked supply room."

Tibbets didn't say a word, but continued tracking Jim with his handgun, his finger on the trigger. Jim pulled the creaky metal door open and a dark hallway loomed ahead of them, lined with offices, a conference room, and storage rooms. At the far end, close to where the hallway turned right, was the storage room where they locked anything valuable. Jim paused in the doorway, waiting on instructions from Tibbets.

"You want me to go first?" Jim asked.

Tibbets gestured for Jim to keep going, so he pulled a flashlight from his vest and clicked the button on the tail to turn it on. Behind him, he heard Tibbets flipping a useless wall switch.

"This part of the building isn't hooked up yet," Jim explained. In truth, it was simply a matter of flipping a breaker, but he wasn't telling Tibbets that. He hoped the darkness might give him some advantage that would allow him to turn this situation around.

Once Tibbets gave up on the light switch, Jim headed down the long hallway until he reached the wooden door marked with an engraved plastic sign that read "Storage." The old sewing factory had used this room for office supplies. Jim hadn't found a key to the lock installed in the door, so he'd added a hasp and a heavy padlock to secure it.

He turned around to face Tibbets. "I have to get the key out of my pocket."

Tibbets pointed the gun at Jim's head and nodded for him to proceed.

While he fished for the key, Jim said, "Don't talk much do you?"

Tibbets ignored the comment.

Jim extracted the key from his pocket and held it up for Tibbets to see. Tibbets used his handgun to gesture at the lock, which Jim took as a sign to keep going. He unlocked the padlock and removed it from the hasp. Jim kept the lock, aware that a padlock held correctly was just as effective as brass knuckles at beefing up a punch. He turned the doorknob and shoved.

With an ushering gesture, Jim waved toward the room. Tibbets shook his head and used the barrel of the gun to wave Jim inside first. Jim stepped in and Tibbets followed him to the doorway, stopping just outside.

Jim pointed at the cardboard boxes stacked on the floor. "Those are the converters. They're still in the boxes."

Tibbets used his gun to direct Jim to the far side of the room. Jim obeyed, moving away from the boxes while Tibbets pulled a flap open to confirm these were indeed the converters. Once he was satisfied, Tibbets backed out of the room. Jim stood there staring at the man, waiting to see what the plan was.

Tibbets grinned. "Carry."

"At least I know you can talk now," Jim said. "Do you mind if I use a hand truck?" He pointed to a two-wheeled green dolly sitting against the wall.

Tibbets shrugged that he didn't care, so Jim got the hand truck. He couldn't get all the boxes in one trip, but the hand truck did allow him to carry two instead of one. The boxes weren't unmanageable, but they were awkward to carry. Jim stacked two of them, then tipped the loaded hand truck back toward him.

Seeing Jim was ready to move the boxes, Tibbets backed out into the hallway, his gun still on Jim. In an effort to keep a safe distance away from Jim, Tibbets backed down the other hallway so Jim wouldn't have to pass close to him. As Jim was rolling the boxes from the room, he noticed a shadow shift in the darkness behind Tibbets. Before he figured out what it was, there was an explosion of movement so quick that Jim couldn't follow what was happening.

In the glow of Jim's flashlight, Ian emerged from the darkness like a ghost, jamming a finger behind Tibbets' trigger as he latched onto the handgun. Tibbets immediately tried to fire, but Ian's finger prevented the trigger from going back far enough. At the same time he grabbed Tibbets' gun, the man locally renowned as a creator of stabby things used one of his handcrafted weapons to puncture Tibbets' throat.

A torrent of arterial blood sprayed from the end of the weapon, startling Jim. In the harsh glow of his flashlight, it was like a crimson geyser. He'd never seen anything like it. Tibbets quit struggling in seconds and his eyes went glassy as the life drained from him. Ian lowered him to the ground, then retrieved Tibbets' handgun, shoving it in his belt. He yanked his weapon from the dead man's neck with a sucking sound, then cleaned it on Tibbet's shirt.

"What the hell was that?" Jim asked.

Ian grinned. "Stainless steel tubing. I grind an angled tip on it so it goes in easy. It's modeled on the trocar."

"The what?" Jim asked.

"An embalming instrument used for removing bodily fluids."

Jim cringed. "Sorry I asked. Listen, we don't have much time. That guy is going to expect me out there any second. Any thoughts?"

"Hugh ducked in here as soon as things went to shit," Ian said. "He's in the crow's nest with Gary's sniper rifle." The crow's nest was a hidden observation deck where they could monitor the crowd in the roadhouse without drawing a lot of attention.

"Does he have a shot?"

Ian extended his radio toward Jim. "Ask him. We're on a different frequency now, so none of the other staff will hear us."

Jim took the radio and keyed the mic. "I need to get back out there, Hugh. Do you have the shot or not?"

Hugh replied immediately. *"Not a head shot. Foley is tucked in tight behind Randi and I can't see enough of him. He's got his gun arm stuck out like a chicken wing, though. I think I can hit his forearm near the elbow."*

"What about Becky?" Jim asked.

"I can transition to her captor after I hit the guy on stage, but Shade Wolford is only five feet away from the guy. Something tells me that once I pull the trigger, Shade will take advantage of the chaos and deal with that situation."

Jim wasn't happy with the choices available to him but didn't see another option.

Outside, a voice rose over the speaker system. "Tibbets, you good?"

Jim spoke into his radio. "Take the shot, Hugh."

Jim and Ian rushed toward the door that connected the hallway to the factory floor. They were only halfway there when the powerful .338 Lapua fired in the confines of the roadhouse with a deafening blast.

17

Foley was standing onstage, anxiously awaiting word from Tibbets, when a blow hit him like a sledgehammer. A powerful rifle round struck his upraised forearm just ahead of his elbow, vaporizing everything in the proximity of that joint. Bone fragments and blood sprayed both Foley and Randi. There was a clatter as Foley's handgun hit the floor, a footlong stump of hand and severed forearm going with it.

The energy of the round sent Foley reeling backward. Randi was left standing there alone, temporarily blinded by the blood in her eyes. She staggered forward, wiping her face with the tail of her shirt. For once in his life, perhaps motivated by his love for Randi, Lloyd displayed good tactical judgement. Though he had no idea who'd fired the shot, Lloyd dove for Foley's handgun the minute he heard it hit the stage floor.

As Lloyd scrambled to get his hands on it, he shot an eye toward Foley, wondering if he too was going for his dropped gun, however, Foley had other concerns. He was desperately trying to staunch the flow of blood pumping from his ragged arm wound. He had his one good hand on his belt, trying to unbuckle it so he could attempt to tourniquet himself. Lloyd had no intention of letting him get that far, nor would he allow Foley the peace of quietly bleeding to death. Not only had the man threatened Randi, he'd shot a hole in Lloyd's banjo.

Lloyd pounced on the bloody handgun, then rolled to his side. Over the top of the sights, he saw Foley whip his belt loose. Lloyd fired once, striking Foley in the left side. Foley flinched but didn't give up on his tourniquet. Lloyd got to his knees, his hands now smeared with blood from the gun. He took a two-handed grip and fired again. Then again. Then again.

Finally, Foley quit moving. The arm holding the belt dropped and the buckle clattered against the floor. The blood pouring from the stump of his wound slowed to a trickle as his heart ceased beating.

Lloyd stood and stuck Foley's gun in the waistband of his pants. He managed to get a hand on Randi before she walked off the edge of the stage. She screamed at his touch, uncertain who had her by the arm.

"It's me, Randi. He's dead." Lloyd pulled off his jacket, then his shirt, and used it to blot Randi's face.

"Water," she said. "Pour water on me. Get his blood off me!" She was frantic.

There was a table at the back of the stage. Lloyd had a banjo case there, along with a pitcher of water and a jar of liquor. He hurried over and got the pitcher, then slowly poured it over Randi's upturned face. As he poured, he saw that the bar was engulfed in sheer chaos.

18

Shade seethed with fury, never taking his eyes off Herring as the man held Becky at gunpoint. After a lifetime of loss, after thinking he'd never fall in love with anyone ever again, Becky had come out of nowhere and stolen his heart. He'd once beaten a man nearly to death over abusing a dog and he knew already this was going to be way worse. Unless Herring emptied that entire pistol into him, Shade had not a single doubt he was going to kill him with his bare hands.

When the powerful sniper rifle fired in the roadhouse, the tremendous boom startled nearly everyone. Around the room, people screamed and took cover, flattening themselves against the floor or ducking beneath tables. Becky jerked with surprise. Even Herring was caught off-guard, inadvertently taking the gun off Becky's temple when he tried to catch a glimpse of what was going on.

Only Shade did not break his concentration, so intently was he focused on Becky and Herring. The second Herring looked toward the stage, the second his handgun wavered and pointed away from Becky's forehead, Shade snatched a heavy beer mug off the bar. There were only five feet separating Shade from Herring and he threw the mug with the accuracy of a farm boy who'd grown up heaving gravels at asshole roosters or throwing apples and snowballs at his siblings.

The mug hit Herring on the side of the head, stunning him temporarily. He staggered and tried to blink away the blood, tried to figure out who'd hit him, but there were too many people crowded against the bar. Then Herring caught a glimpse of the tall, rawboned man hopping the bar with the proficiency of a farmer hopping a fence. It was the same man who'd been staring at him so intently since he took his prisoner.

Herring tried to swing his gun around to put a bullet in Shade, but it was too late. The man was on him.

The second his feet touched down behind the bar, Shade grabbed Herring's gun and diverted it upward just as Herring pulled the trigger. The gun fired, the concussion of the exploding powder temporarily deafening everyone in proximity to the weapon. Shade's tight grip kept the slide from cycling and chambering another round. When Herring pulled the trigger, nothing happened.

It was the first gunfire in this part of the room, and the sound sent the bar patrons scattering in all directions, screaming and shouting. Becky was screaming too, and Shade shouldered her to the side, pushing her clear of the scuffle and putting his body between her and Herring.

"I got him, darling!" Shade yelled.

Shade wrenched the pistol hard to the side, and Herring cried out when his trapped trigger finger snapped like a pretzel. Shade could have pistol-whipped Herring at that point. He could have drawn his gun and shot him dead on the spot. He could have whipped out his sheath knife and stabbed, sliced, or diced Herring. Instead, he grabbed another hefty beer mug by the handle and wielded it like a pair of brass knuckles, punching Herring in the face with it.

The mug shattered and Herring screamed as the glass ground into his face. It punctured an eye and ground against the bones of his nose and skull. Shade drew the bloody remnants of the mug back and checked its condition. The mug had shattered but there was still enough to punch with. Still enough to turn Herring's face into ground beef.

Throwing his head back, Shade let out a roar that drowned out nearly everything else in the roadhouse. He seized Herring by the collar and set upon him with the shattered mug. Shade only got in a half-dozen solid punches before the rest of the mug shattered, nicking his knuckles and slicing his palm.

Shade was oblivious to the pain of his cut hand, which was nothing when compared to Herring's injuries. Herring had no fight left in him. He tried to speak, but the garble of broken teeth and a detached upper lip made it difficult. The bones of his nose were crushed and exposed. Both eyes were gone, oozing a gory and viscous fluid that streaked with blood as it ran down his face.

Perhaps Herring's words were an attempt to yield or surrender. Perhaps they were the prayers of a dying man. They might even have been an entreaty for Shade to kill him and end his misery. The wet, garbled words were impossible to understand, more choked out than spoken.

When the mug shattered, Shade tossed the pieces to the ground, then shook his hand hard to dislodge the chunks of glass embedded in his flesh. He wrapped an arm around Herring's waist and unleashed another powerful bellow as he heaved Herring onto the bar like a two-hundred-pound sack of feed. Herring flailed around, but he was too incoherent to mount a defense and too blind to escape. Shade rolled him onto his belly, leaving Herring's head hanging off the inside of the bar. He'd have been staring at the floor had he been able to see.

Shade latched onto Herring's neck like a man wrestling a steer, then flexed his hard muscles. His teeth gritted and his mouth contorted in rage. Immediately, there was a muffled pop and Herring went limp, his neck broken. A woman near the bar doubled over and vomited. Others nearby cringed and hid their faces.

Shade jumped up onto the bar and drew his handgun. The man who'd been holding Randi on the stage was down, and Jim was at the stage now.

"All clear?" Shade called across the bar.

"There's one more out there somewhere. They have a man watching their horses," Jim called back. "Ian and Hugh are on the roof looking for him now."

Becky called for her boyfriend. "Shade?"

"Right here, baby." He sidestepped on the bar top until he was closer to her.

Becky latched onto his leg and hugged it tight. Shade glared at the crowd, then reached down and hauled Herring's body up with a single hand. The dead man's head lolled to the side with its internal armature disjointed.

When Shade spoke, his voice was raw, abraded by hate and violence. "Let this be a lesson to you people! Tell everyone you know what you saw here today. Anyone *ever* lays a hand on my Becky again, this is what they have to look forward to. That's a promise."

With that, Shade tossed Herring's body out onto the concrete floor of the roadhouse. People cringed when blood splashed onto their legs. A man gagged at the sight of Herring's destroyed face.

Shade's adrenaline was still up, his breathing hard, and his nostrils flared with each exhalation. When he saw he'd made his point, he hopped off the bar, his heavy boots thumping when they hit the floor. He leaned over and wrapped his arms around the much shorter Becky. As soon as he had her in his embrace, she erupted in sobs.

19

Jim took the stage and snatched up the microphone. Behind him, a one-armed Foley lay dead and draining into a pool of his own making. Lloyd and a blood-smeared Randi were locked in an embrace, though it was unclear who was supporting whom. Surprisingly, the crowd was mostly still there. The arrival of power was such a landmark event that nothing short of their own demise would have dispersed this crowd.

Jim jabbed a finger at the audience. "This is the kind of bullshit we've had to put up with, so I don't want to hear a single word about us keeping one converter for the roadhouse. We just killed three people to save your power. Don't forget that."

A hand shot into the air. It belonged to someone who would have been a typical soccer mom before the collapse. Now, with her oily hair, dry skin, and dirty pink sweats she looked like a feral troll. When she noticed Jim looking at her, she asked, "Are you still handing out those things tonight?"

While Jim could have taken a moment to call out her callous nature, what was the point? This wasn't the spoiled, delicate society it had once been. If a person had to step over a body to get something they needed, then so be it.

"Damn right I am. You think I want to keep them here another night and have to deal with even more thieves and criminals? Hell no! You're going to have to wait a few minutes, because these people have one more man out there and none of us are safe until we get him. Please bear with us."

Jim started to leave the stage but had another thought and backed up. He leaned into the microphone again. "If there's any more sonofabitches out there who think they're going to steal from us, I'd advise you to leave now, or you'll end up like these folks."

People in the crowd looked around with suspicion, trying to gauge whether there were more thieves in attendance.

Just then, Jim's radio squawked. *"Hugh for Jim."*

"Go for Jim."

Hugh's response was brief. *"Got him."*

Jim hopped off the stage and raised his radio to his ear as he shoved his way through the mob. "What do you see?

"A lone rider coming through the woods across the street. He's leading three saddled horses and two packhorses. It has to be their accomplice. You want me to drop him? I have a clear shot."

"That's a negative, Hugh. We need to speak to him first. You guys stay on the roof. I'm going to get Shade and intercept him out front."

"Copy that," Hugh replied.

Jim raised an arm over his head and shouted down the crowd. "Hey, there's liable to be some shooting out front. Do me a favor and stay inside for the next few minutes. If you die, you don't get a converter."

After the trauma they'd witnessed, the crowd was a little slow on the uptake, struggling to decide if Jim was joking or serious. Like many of the things he said, it could be taken either way. Jim headed to the bar, finding Shade still comforting Becky. His bloody arms were wrapped tightly around her and his blood-spattered face was resting on her head.

"There's still one of them out there, Shade, and he's headed this way. I need backup."

"Hell, have those boys on the roof shoot him. Why risk going out there?"

Jim shook his head. "I want to ask him some questions, *then* we kill him."

A voice chimed in from behind Jim. "Uh, we have a jail. Are you sure you need to kill that man?"

Jim turned around, wondering who was spouting such nonsense. He found Dr. Nelson standing there with a defiant look on his face, Blake Justice at his side.

"The converter issue aside, the violence has to taper off at some point," the doctor said. "We must return to being a civilized society. Maybe tonight is as good a time as any to start reclaiming our humanity. Certainly, enough blood has been shed." He cast a look toward Herring's crumpled corpse laying only a few feet away.

Jim sighed and gestured for Dr. Nelson to follow him. He didn't want to turn this into a public debate. He didn't choose his course of action based on public consensus. He never had and he never would. He also didn't have a lot of patience with people who suggested coddling criminals because there was no legal system or law enforcement in place. Jim was aware that civility would need to return sometime but he wasn't interested in pioneering that approach. All in all, the bullet seemed more effective.

Once they were away from the crowd, Jim said, "Do you know what's involved in arresting someone right now?"

Dr. Nelson smirked. "Simply locking them in jail, I would assume."

"Guess again. It means you *personally* finding an unlocked cell or the keys to a locked one at the jail. As far as I know, no one has found the keys to the jail cells yet and they've been looking. They assume a former inmate tossed them away out of spite. If you do manage to find an open cell, someone has to physically manhandle your prisoner into the building and force them against their will into an unlocked cell. You up for that?"

Dr. Nelson didn't respond, turning this information over in his head.

Jim continued. "Once you manage to get your prisoner padlocked into a cell, then you *personally* have to take responsibility for feeding them, delivering them water, and carrying out their waste in a bucket every day since the plumbing doesn't work. How long are you willing to do that, and for how many prisoners? How do you decide when to release someone? What are you going to do this winter when it gets too cold to stay in the jail? Are you going to take them home with you?"

Dr. Nelson held up a hand to stop Jim's barrage of questions. "I get what you're saying. There's no system for incarceration in place yet. Obviously, I don't have the answers to all the questions you've thrown out there. So maybe you just let them go with a warning?"

Jim belched out a laugh. "Society figured out a long time ago that doesn't work. When there's no punishment for crime, other people see that and decide they're going to start stealing too. A society can't function that way. Things are bad now, but it's not anarchy. Let people get away with stealing and that's where we're headed."

Shade kissed Becky on the head, snatched up his rifle, and came around the bar to join Jim. They headed toward the main door of the roadhouse. When Dr. Nelson and Blake Justice didn't move, Jim beckoned them to follow.

"Oh no, you guys need to see this. Let's *all* listen to what the last member of this gang has to say, then you can tell me if he should be released with a warning."

When they reached the doorway, Dr. Nelson and Blake were reluctant to step outside. Jim urged them forward and Shade closed the door behind them. Whatever happened out there, they didn't need the eyes of the entire roadhouse upon them.

Jim couldn't see anything. The bright electric lights of the roadhouse had fried his ability to see in the dark. He raised his radio. "Jim for Hugh. We're outside but I can't see shit. Where's our Lone Ranger?"

"We have eyes on you," Hugh replied over the radio. *"Our boy is still in the field, about forty yards from reaching the paved street. I'd say we'll*

*hear his horses on the pavement in another minute or two. Fighting all
those horses by himself seems to be getting the better of him."*

"Good," Jim said. "Little does he know that his night is about to
get a lot worse."

"Why am I here?" Dr. Nelson demanded.

Jim replied in a low growl, "Shut up." He spoke into his radio
again. "I heard Foley radio this guy and tell him they had things
under control, and he should meet them at this door. He should
assume that's still the case and ride right up to us."

"I'm sure you guys can handle this without us," Blake said, nerves
changing the pitch of his voice.

"I was going to handle it, but if you and Dr. Nelson are so dead set
on arresting people, I can step back and let you handle it." Jim
grinned into the night as he spoke those words. He already knew
what Dr. Nelson would think of that idea.

Dr. Nelson cleared his throat. "Uh, why don't you take the lead on
this one. If he's willing to turn himself in and go peaceably, we can
discuss options at that time."

Shade chuckled at the doctor's response, his laughter a low, stac-
cato rumble like the growl of a menacing jungle cat stalking the darkness. It was not a friendly laugh.

Jim smirked. "You start working on those options, Dr. Nelson, and
I'll let you present them. Hopefully, the guy won't put a bullet in you
during your presentation."

Shortly, they heard the clatter of several horses walking along
asphalt.

"One rider approaching," Hugh's voice said from the radio.

Jim retrieved a tiny flashlight from his pocket. Using the thumb
switch on the back, he flashed it a couple of times, signaling the rider
as he imagined the man's compatriots might do if they were trying to
get his attention. The rider called out in acknowledgment, then
steered his string of horses toward the door.

Jim, Shade, Dr. Nelson, and Blake remained in the shadows until
the rider was close, then Jim hit him with the beam of the flashlight.

He drew his handgun and leveled it on Mickelson. Shade moved forward and latched onto the bridle of the lead horse.

"Easy there," Jim said. "We have guns on you from all sides. I'm going to need you to get down off that horse." When the young man didn't move, Jim took a few a few steps toward him. "Don't be stupid, kid."

To emphasize Jim's point, Hugh and Ian stood up on the roof. The rider saw the profile of the two shooters silhouetted against the night sky. Hugh double-tapped the switch on his Steiner laser illuminator and a green dot appeared on the rider's chest. When the rider looked back down, Shade also had a gun pointed at him.

Mickelson huffed, then climbed down off his horse. "Dammit! What happened?"

"First things first," Jim said. "What's your name?"

"Mickelson." The rider turned his head and spat.

"Well, Mickelson," said Jim, "your boys tried to rob us and things didn't go their way."

"What happened to them?" Mickelson asked.

"They're deader than dogshit," Shade grunted. "You're the last man standing."

The gravity of his predicament hit Mickelson like a hammer, and he started trembling. His voice quavered as he spoke. "Listen, let me take my horse and go. You'll never see me again. This is my first trip with this bunch. I swear."

"You're *thieves*," Jim said, his tone summarizing his feelings on the matter, the belief that being labeled as such made you unworthy of salvation or second chances. Even in the old world, he would not have been averse to the idea of cutting a hand off repeat offenders.

"And one of you scared my girlfriend," Shade said, his tone implying that this was the gravest offense of all. "That's his blood I'm wearing."

"I didn't run this outfit," Mickelson said. "I was their flunky. I gathered wood and watched camp. I fetched water and cooked. Hell, I'd have gone home weeks ago if I could have found the way. I didn't know what I was getting myself into when I signed on with this bunch. I was just looking for a way to get by."

"Yet here you are," Jim said. "You rode off that hillside ready to ride away with our converters. You were ready to steal the hope from all these people gathered here tonight. Stealing is one thing but there's no making amends for taking the hope from people."

Mickelson hung his head, unable to muster a response to the accusation.

"Where you from?" Jim asked.

"Woodstock, Virginia."

"Were you all just passing through town like that Foley guy told me?"

Mickelson shook his head. "We're working our way west."

"And you just spontaneously decided to steal our converters. How'd you even know we'd received them?"

"We...those guys...only stole converters," Mickelson said. "It was like a business for them. They have a tracker on one of the helicopters and follow it around to new installations. Somehow Foley knows that converters get dropped off on the last day of each install, so they watch the GPS to see where the helicopter leaves them. Then we show up and steal them before they get handed out."

"Where do you sell them?" Jim asked. "How do you sell them?"

"Foley had a partner back in Northern Virginia," Mickelson explained. "They used a helicopter to pick up and deliver the converters back and forth. Foley had a satellite phone and he'd text the pilot once we had a load. He'd resupply us, then take the converters back with him. Foley's partner would sell them and split the money with Foley. He paid us in whatever currency we wanted. Food for our families, ammo, silver, whatever."

"What payment did you accept?" Jim demanded.

"What do you mean?" Mickelson asked.

Jim bristled and repeated his question. "I mean, what did he pay *you*? What was the payment *you* took?"

Mickelson shrugged. "Just an old gun and some ammunition. A little silver to put back. Why?"

Jim let out a disappointed sigh. He reached forward and put a hand on Mickelson's shoulder, yanking him away from the horse. "Cover me, Shade." Jim holstered his handgun and searched Mickelson, removing a handgun and two spare mags. "This all?"

"My rifle and the rest of my gear is on the horse. All our gear is on the horses. After we took the converters, we were going to get well clear of your town and arrange for the helicopter pickup." Mickelson swallowed hard. When he spoke again, the pitch of his voice had gone up. "Look, you can have all our gear and all our horses. You didn't lose any converters. Just let me go."

"Too late for that," Jim said.

"What's happening here?" Dr. Nelson asked. "I feel like I'm missing something."

Shade intercepted the question. "A man who worked to feed his family might get a pass. Any husband or father can understand that level of desperation. That ain't what this fellow did."

"He profited," Jim said. "It was business for him. He knew what he was doing and still did it."

"Man like that doesn't get a pass," said Shade.

"Unless one of you wants to take him to jail," Jim asked the doctor and Blake. "If that's the case, I'll hand him over right now."

Dr. Nelson was taken aback. "You mean like right now?"

Jim nodded and shoved Mickelson toward the doctor. "Right now. By yourself. You were the one presenting jail as an option. I don't do incarceration."

"Uh, I'm not ready for that," Dr. Nelson replied, backing away from Mickelson. "I'm not prepared. We're not prepared."

"Then you'd do well to quit thinking out loud," Shade said. "Don't be throwing out ideas unless you're prepared to act on them."

"You might be right in this case," Dr. Nelson said. "Not about everything, mind you, but maybe in this one case."

Jim gave Dr. Nelson a light punch on the arm. "Maybe there's hope for you yet, Doc."

"What will you do with him now?" Dr. Nelson asked.

Mickelson blinked. "Yeah, what happens now?"

"I got this," Shade said. "I still got a fire in my belly over these people scaring my Becky."

"What the hell does that mean?" Mickelson asked.

Shade grabbed a fistful of Mickelson's shirt and yanked him away from the group. Mickelson was protesting, demanding answers, but all he got was silence from the big man dragging him off into the darkness.

"Where are they going?" Blake asked.

"Shade doesn't need an audience," Jim replied.

Both Blake and Dr. Nelson jumped when a single shot was fired off in the darkness. They were the only ones not expecting it.

After a moment, Dr. Nelson said, "I don't get it. What was the purpose of going off into the dark to do that? Everyone in the road-house heard the shot. They'll know what happened. We all know what happened."

Shade ambled out of the darkness, a heavy revolver in his hand. He holstered the weapon, clicked on the headlamp he wore over a cap, and removed a tin of tobacco from his shirt pocket. In the glow of his headlamp, Shade efficiently rolled a cigarette from tobacco he'd grown, dried, and cured on his farm. Everyone remained silent as they watched the rhythm of his fingers performing a task they'd likely performed tens of thousands of times.

When Shade finally spoke, his voice was low and as natural as the frogs croaking in the night. He was a man comfortable in the darkness. Comfortable in solitude. Comfortable in himself. "When a man kills like that, he doesn't go off to hide his actions from other men. He goes off to hide his shame. No matter how much someone deserves to die—no matter how certain you are that you can't release them back out into the world—there ain't no pride in it. It leaves you feeling dirty in a way you can't wash off."

20

Jim had expected to face a roomful of accusing stares when he went back inside the roadhouse, but that was not the case. Business had resumed somewhat. Lloyd was onstage either picking a song or tuning his banjo, it was hard to tell which. Staff were behind the bar serving drinks as fast as they could pour them. The rest of the crowd was simply milling about, engaged in conversation. One of the staff had thoughtfully placed wet floor signs around Herring's body, still piled up near the bar.

Shade headed for the bar. "Reckon I need to clean up my mess. Becky slips in all that blood, I'll hear about it."

"She might give you a pass since you saved her bacon," Jim said.

"A man can always hope," said Shade.

Jim searched the crowd and spotted Cookie talking to a group of men. He went over and placed a hand on his shoulder. "You ready to speak to these folks?"

Cookie looked a little green around the gills. Jim couldn't tell if it was from nerves or from all the chaos that had ensued before they were even able to get down to business.

"I guess so."

"Then follow me," Jim said.

The two of them wove their way through the crowd to the stage. Once they were up there, Jim silenced Lloyd by gripping the neck of his banjo and muting the strings.

Lloyd was appalled. "This old girl survived being shot tonight. She's trying her best to entertain this crowd with a bullet hole in her hide and a new set of strings. How dare you?"

"I dare," Jim replied. He stepped to the microphone. "Let's get on with it before some other shit happens. We left off collecting names for the converter drawing. We're going to pick back up with that. While you guys are writing down your names and putting them in the hat, Cookie is going to talk to you about a project he's working on."

Jim stepped aside and gestured for Cookie to approach the microphone. He then hopped down to help with collecting names.

"Can you hear me?" Cookie asked, removing the microphone from the stand and holding it in front of his face.

There was a murmured response that indicated the audience could hear him well enough.

"I came here and spoke to Jim yesterday about a project I've been working on. Feels like years ago now because so much has happened in the last day or two. It's been a long night and I know we're all ready to get on with it, so I'll keep this short. I've been wanting to clean out the courthouse and some of the government buildings. They're trashed. People have been squatting there and left a mess behind. There's fire damage, mold, trash, and human waste to deal with."

"Why?" someone in the crowd yelled. "What's the point?"

"We have to start somewhere," Cookie said. "I believe all of us would like to return to a more civilized society. Obviously, as the events of tonight confirm, we're a long way from there. I'm not running for an office. I'm not wanting to clean those offices out so the government can try to tax you again. I feel like those are public spaces that the public has paid for. We own those damn buildings and we should be able to put them to use for our benefit."

"Like what?" another person asked.

"For one thing, we could use a clinic. There are plenty of doctors, nurses, and physician assistants in this town. If we could gather enough of them, we could staff a clinic every day. They could take shifts and people who needed their services could pay with barter. It's not a perfect plan, but it could be a start. Jim even suggested cleaning out the library so people could use the building to start teaching their kids again."

Seeing that the audience was more interested in power than in hearing his vision for the future, Cookie cut it short. "Anyway, I appreciate you listening to me. If anyone wants to participate, we'll be meeting at the government offices by the farmer's market every morning until we get the job done. If you want to participate, show up. If you have them, bring masks, gloves, shovels, rakes, and wheelbarrows. Buckets might help too. Thank you for your time."

Cookie replaced the microphone in the stand and climbed down from the stage. Jim started clapping and was joined by an unenthused smattering of applause. Jim hoped people would show up to help Cookie. He appreciated that the man was trying to be positive and useful when the rest of the community was bogged down by its own inertia.

Lloyd didn't let the microphone sit idle for very long. "Did I hear applause?" He gave his damaged banjo a loud strum. "It's time for some Grandpa Jones. How about some of that good old Mountain Dew!"

Lloyd started stomping his foot and pounding the banjo like a man possessed. He bawled out the words of the Old Time classic and many in the audience clapped their hands to the tempo. The song was a favorite of Shade's, and he tossed back his head to express his appreciation with a loud hillbilly yell.

Jim let Lloyd play, waiting until he'd finished the song to retake the stage. It took a moment for the cheers and applause of the enthusiastic crowd to subside. They apparently liked that tune too.

Standing at the head of the stage, waiting for his opportunity to speak, Jim couldn't help but think about how surreal this moment was. He was about to hand out devices that could restore power to people who had been living in the dark for over a year. He was sharing the stage at an apocalyptic roadhouse with his lifelong best friend and a one-armed dead man still cooling in a pool of his own congealed blood. If things got any weirder than that, Jim wanted no part of it.

When the crowd finally settled down, Jim leaned into the microphone. "Historic night here, folks. Hell of a strange one too, but we're going to roll with it. If you're ready, I'm going to start drawing names for converters."

A cheer went up from the crowd. Randi approached the stage with a clear gallon-sized pickle jar filled halfway to the top with folded scraps of paper. Jim reached in and stirred the names, doing it slowly so the audience could see what he was doing. He didn't want any accusations that he'd cheated.

After stirring and shuffling the names for a good thirty seconds, Jim drew a name out and read it aloud. "Elmer Buchanan."

A man shot to his feet and cheered. A group that must have been his family joined in the celebration.

"Elmer, if you'll head toward the back of the roadhouse, I got people there ready to hand out the converters. They'll be glad to explain the installation process to you."

Elmer skipped toward the back, as elated as anyone Jim had seen since before the collapse. Jim drew the second name and handed out the second converter, then continued the process for four more hours.

21

It was the wee hours of the morning when the staff finally ran the last of the patrons out of the roadhouse. Although everyone was beat from the adrenaline, the pace of things, and the long night, no one was ready to leave. The doors were locked and many from Jim's clan were still present at the roadhouse, even if they hadn't been scheduled to work. Everyone had wanted to be there to see the converters handed out. It was an historic moment.

Someone had plugged a speaker in and they were playing music from an iPod. A refrigerator was running and they'd packed it with beverages, hoping they could actually sell and enjoy cold beer tomorrow. It was strange not only to have electricity, but to be enjoying it in some place other than their homes.

After the thieves had been dealt with, Hugh had gone through their gear. He had it spread out on the bar, explaining what he'd found to Jim. Jim and Shade split the horses as their fee for dealing with the thieves.

"This is interesting," Hugh said. "This device is the satellite tracker Mickelson mentioned. You turn it on and there's an icon that follows the helicopter our installation team used. I also found the satellite phone they use to arrange pickup. They charge it with a folding solar charger."

"I used a solar charger like that on my walk home from Richmond," Jim said. "Anything else interesting?"

Hugh shook his head. "The usual stuff. Guns, ammo, food, some camping gear."

"Spread the word," Jim said. "Our group gets first dibs. Anything that doesn't get claimed can be sold here at the roadhouse."

Hugh held the satellite phone up. "Obviously we need to keep this, but I had an idea I want to share with you."

Jim put the satellite tracker back on the bar and took a sip of his drink. It was the darker moonshine they were calling bourbon, even though the only thing that distinguished it from the others was the color. "Go for it."

"I want to call for a pickup," Hugh said.

"A pickup of what?"

"Converters."

Jim cocked an eyebrow. "I'm not following you."

"I've gone through this phone and I see how they did it now. There's a number they message with their location. I've read the old messages and I know exactly what they say."

"I see that you figured out *how* to do it, but I'm still not seeing *why* you'd want to do it."

Hugh pointed to a stack of empty boxes piled near the bar. "I'm going to take those empty boxes up on the mountain and call for pickup. Once the chopper gets here, I'm going to force the pilot to take me to the location where he delivers the stolen converters."

"And then?"

"I'm going to bring back as many stolen converters as I can lay my grubby little hands on."

Jim drained his drink, looking doubtful. "How do you know they have a stockpile of converters? They may sell the things as fast as they get them."

"I'm willing to that take that chance."

"You'll also be taking the chance of getting stranded somewhere far away."

"If Foley's partner still has converters, the people they originally belonged to have probably already requested and received replacements. Besides, we have no idea where they came from. They could be of some benefit to our community. There were a lot of sad people who left empty-handed tonight. If I could get more converters, we can help some of them."

"How do you know the pilot won't fly away once you get where you're going?"

"This isn't my first rodeo, Jim. I'll drag his ass out of the chopper and cuff him to the landing gear. He'll stay there until I bring back more converters or figure out there aren't any to be had. Then I make him fly me home."

"I don't know," Jim said. "Sounds risky."

"It's risky as hell, but I'm not asking anyone to go with me. I'm running this as a solo op and I'm comfortable with the odds."

"I'm not comfortable with the idea of losing you. You're an asset to our group."

Hugh smiled. "Then let me go off and do what I do best."

"When do you want to do this?"

"I'm going to ditch this place right now and head back to the valley. I can get my gear together, catch a few hours' sleep, and call for pickup in the morning."

"What can we do to help?" Jim asked.

"Give me Pete and Charlie for a few hours in the morning. I'll need to haul those boxes up in the mountains and find a good spot for a landing zone. Once we do, I'll offload my gear and the empty boxes, then send the coordinates to the chopper. Pete and Charlie can head back home with the horses."

Jim mulled this over. "They won't be exposed to any danger?"

"Negative. They'll be long gone by the time the chopper arrives."

"Go for it, Hugh. If your mission goes south and you get stuck somewhere, we'll keep an eye on your place until you find your way home. It's a long walk. You can take my word for it."

Hugh nodded and finished the last of his drink. "I'm going to take what I need from this gear and you guys can deal with the rest tomorrow. Can you have Pete and Charlie at my house a little after sunup?"

"They'll be there," Jim said. "We'll haul these boxes home with us tonight. You grab your gear and get out of here. You'll need to rest up."

Hugh checked his watch and his eyes went wide. "Shit, I'll be lucky to get two hours."

"You can nap while you're waiting on the chopper."

22

Jim was up at dawn the next morning, feeling as if he'd just laid down minutes earlier. He still wore yesterday's clothes and his mouth felt like an old sock tasted. He crept quietly from the bedroom and wandered into the kitchen. He went to the sink and filled a glass with cold, gravity-fed spring water. They'd been out of coffee for a while now so spring water had to serve as a morning stimulant, and it was a poor substitute. Occasionally, someone wandered into the roadhouse with coffee they wanted to trade off, but it didn't last very long.

Usually it was immediately brewed there at the roadhouse and shared among whoever was working that day. Where coffee was concerned, all the rules of politeness and sharing went out the window. To a person, they had the patience and generosity of junkies when it came to caffeine.

Once Jim had drained his disappointing glass of water, he wandered outside with his radio. The morning was cool with a heavy dew. With Lloyd now shacking up with Randi, Pete and Charlie had been staying in Lloyd's house, which had previously been Buddy's house. Jim felt a little better about the two young men staying there by themselves now that life in the valley had calmed down some. The boys were getting older and for some time they'd had to shoulder more responsibility than kids their age were used to managing. They weren't children anymore and Jim had to respect that, even if he still worried about them.

He raised the radio. "Jim for Pete or Charlie. Jim for Pete or Charlie."

"Go for Pete. Morning, Dad!"

"Morning, Pete. I just wanted to make sure you guys were up since Hugh was expecting you."

"We're already awake and riding up the mountain," Pete replied. *"We set an alarm on one of the old cellphones we use for playing games. It felt weird to get up to an alarm. I was almost afraid I'd have to go to school for a minute."*

Jim laughed. "That day may come."

"I might be too old to go to school once it reopens."

Pete was joking, but Jim felt a pang of sadness at those words. While the collapse certainly wasn't his fault, he hated to think about this generation of kids who'd missed out on vital years of their education. They'd never be able to make up for these lost years, and he wondered how it would impact them.

At the same time, maybe their educational deficits would be the least of their problems. It might be more challenging to overcome the memories of the violence they'd seen and the losses they'd experienced. They'd never be the same as the kids who'd come before them. They'd always have that harder edge. They'd be less likely to rely on law enforcement to solve their problems, react to perceived threats with boldness and finality, and they'd be less likely to concern themselves with consequences because they'd come of age when there were none. A wild animal might be tamed, but could the same be done with a creature born into a world of rules and order, who was then allowed to go feral? Jim didn't think so.

"Charlie is with you?" Jim asked.

"Yep. We're each leading a packhorse carrying those empty boxes."

"Good. You guys be careful. As I understand it, Hugh is going to send you guys back with the horses after he reaches the landing zone."

"That's what he told us," Pete said. *"We're going to bring his horse and all the packhorses home so we can store the tack in the barn and turn the horses out in the field."*

"You guys stay safe. Even though things are calm right now, don't let your guard down for a minute. Keep your guns loaded and handy. Come straight back here and radio us as soon as you're within range. Someone will be watching for you."

"Copy that, Dad. We'll be fine. We'll be careful."

"Good. I'll see you when you get home. Love you guys."

"Love you too, Dad."

"You never quit worrying about them, do you?"

Jim spun toward the voice and found his father standing in the door. He came out onto the porch with a steaming mug in his hand.

"What are you drinking?" Jim asked, wondering if his dad might have some secret stash of coffee he didn't know about.

Pops scowled. "Some kind of herbal mint tea crap that Ariel and Ellen came up with. I know they're just trying to help us survive coffee withdrawal, but this tastes like something you'd scrape off the bottom of your mower deck."

"Yet you're drinking it."

"Of course I am. I'm supposed to be enjoying my golden years—fishing and drinking coffee out of a thermos. Then the world got too dangerous for fishing and the coffee ran out. Pretty darn bad timing for a retirement if you ask me. I'd rather go back to work than sit here drinking grass tea. Sadly, that's not an option."

Jim shrugged. "Can't help you there, Pops. I can barely solve my own problems."

Pops plunked himself down on the porch swing, the chains popping as they went taut with his weight. "I didn't expect you could." He took a sip of his tea, grimaced, then choked it down. "As if getting old doesn't suck enough. Your mother and I should be going to church, hanging out with other old people, and visiting our friends before they turn into worm food."

"I know the lack of socializing is tough. It's been tough for everyone."

Pops huffed dismissively. "What do you know about it? You hate people. I get a charge out of them. I like talking with people who saw the things I saw and shared the same experiences. People who grew up driving cars out of the 1940s and filled them up with gas for a dollar. People who drank bottled Nehis and Orange Crushes out of coolers filled with chilled water. People who listened to the Everly Brothers and went to all-day Western matinees at the movies to see Roy Rogers and Lash Larue."

"I can't do anything about the state of the world, Pops. If I could, I'd have done it a long time ago. As bad as things are, though, you need to focus on the fact that we've had it better than most. We've had food, running water, and a little solar power. We've had friends and family. We've survived when most people didn't."

Pops grumbled an unintelligible response. Jim understood that no amount of rationalizing was going to elevate the mood his father was in, so he went inside and left him out there sulking at the world. Jim snatched a biscuit off the counter, tore it in half, and filled it with homemade apple jelly. He ate it over a plate to avoid leaving a trail of jelly through the house, something he may have been accused of doing on occasion.

Jim gathered the gear he'd need for a day away from the house. Most of his family was still asleep after the late night at the road-house, so he tried to be as quiet as he could. When he was finally ready to go, Jim left a note on the counter telling Ellen he was headed into town. He stepped out the front door wearing his pack, his chest rig, and carrying his rifle. Even with things being more civilized than they'd once been, a man couldn't let down his guard and go out unarmed.

"I'm headed to work, Pops."

"Can I go with you?"

At the edge of the porch, Jim stopped in his tracks and turned around slowly. "You serious?"

Pops stood up, the swing rocking behind him, and dumped his mug over the porch rail. "Grasses to grasses, dust to dust. Yeah, I'm serious."

"You better wake Nana up and tell her. I'll head to the barn and saddle two horses. You realize you have to ride a horse, right?"

"I'll be fine," Pops told him. "I might need help getting on and off, but it's the least you can do. I'm sure I helped you on a horse or two in your life."

"You did."

"Then saddle me a horse. I'll be back in a minute."

Jim lured a couple of horses from the pasture with a bucket of knotty apples. By the time he had them ready, Pops was back on the porch. As Jim led the horses from the barn, he couldn't help but smile at his dad. He wore a straw gardening hat, a sweater that looked as if it was made from a Pendleton blanket and wore a holstered pistol dead center over his abdomen.

Tying his horse off to the tree they used as a hitching post, Jim led the other horse alongside the porch. He'd removed a section of railing there to make it easier for Ariel to mount a horse. It worked the same for Nana, Pops, or anyone else who struggled to pull themselves up into the saddle. Pops had stiffened some over the decades, but he managed to climb onto the horse and take up the reins. When Jim was satisfied that Pops was stable, he mounted his horse.

"What's that shooting iron you're carrying there, Pops?" Jim asked as they rode down the driveway toward the main road through the valley.

"Ruger .22."

"Got ammo?"

Pops huffed. "Yes, smartass, I have ammo, and I don't want to hear any cracks about the caliber. You ever been shot with a .22?"

"Nope."

"Want to be?"

"Uh...no." Jim wasn't entirely sure if the question was rhetorical or if his dad was threatening to shoot him.

"Besides, I don't want to kill anyone," Pops said. "But I have no qualms about sending a man home with a couple of painful holes in him."

"Geez, Pops, it's probably more merciful to just kill someone outright than send them home to die a slow painful death from infection."

Pops furrowed his brow. "Never thought of it that way. Might have to reconsider my weaponry next time."

Jim dismounted to unlock the gate, then held it open for Pops to ride through. Jim led his horse out, relocked the gate, and mounted up. Pops was already plodding down the road ahead of him. Jim nudged his horse into a trot until he was alongside him.

"You were a pretty good shot with that thing back in the day," Jim admitted.

"Probably still am, but I haven't shot it in years."

Jim didn't bring up the fact that shooting was a perishable skill if you didn't practice it regularly. Jim had learned to shoot handguns with the very Ruger that his dad was carrying now. He'd spent years plinking with .22 rifles before his dad ever allowed him to handle the pistol. His dad and grandfather had started by letting him shoot at cans, then before long they moved on to pennies and Lifesavers. If you grew up squirrel hunting with a rifle, shooting targets the size of cans taught you nothing.

"So what got into you, Pops? You usually don't want to come to town."

"It depresses me to see the state of things. If I stay at your place, I can pretend town is like I remember it, even though I know it's not. If town was really the way it used to be, I'd be at my house and not yours."

"Maybe we can get you back there one day soon," Jim said. "We should have more of those power converters soon. If we can install one on your house, we should be able to get it habitable. We'll probably have to make some repairs since it's been sitting empty a while, but it shouldn't be too bad."

"You think our house is mostly still in good shape?"

Jim nodded. "Pete and Charlie have been going out there regularly since we opened the roadhouse. They keep an eye on the place. If we get power at your house and you decide to move back, the boys could stay with you for a few weeks and help get things back in order."

Pops grew enthusiastic at that possibility. "That would be great, Jim. You can't imagine what it would mean to your mother. This whole thing has been rough on her. She's aged a lot."

"And not you?"

Pops straightened his back. "I remain as fine a specimen as I've ever been."

23

The roadhouse was still locked up when Jim and Pops got there. Ian was asleep in his room, having pulled an all-nighter watching from the roof. Ed was going at it like a mad scientist—distilling whiskey, brewing beer, and preparing to bottle some of each. Gary and some of his family arrived shortly afterward, not looking very excited to be back at work.

"It feels like we just left here," Gary announced as he dragged into the roadhouse.

"We did," Gary's wife said.

"For what it's worth, you can use electric appliances now," Jim said, flipping the breaker that turned on the bank of overhead lights. "Maybe we can even manage to get a dishwasher hooked up soon."

Despite their lack of enthusiasm, Gary's family cheered at that idea. No one liked washing dishes.

In anticipation of this moment, ever since Lightspeed had promised them power, Jim had been gathering appliances they could use in the roadhouse. He wasn't sure if Lightspeed would ever accomplish was he said he was going to do, but in case he did, Jim wanted to be ready for the return of modern conveniences. They'd found a couple of residential refrigerators and freezers, hauling them to the roadhouse in Shade's wagon. They'd done the same with stoves, toasters, blenders, food processors, and a few other things that would indeed be handy if the power did come back on.

Since they'd opened the establishment, they'd been cooking on the massive woodstoves scattered around the main room. It had proven to be a constant challenge. Baking was difficult and the results inconsistent. Sometimes thick stews scorched on the hot stoves, leaving them with a bitter taste that no one could stomach. The big woodstoves would still be required to heat the massive building since the building's original heat source was propane, but everyone who worked in the kitchen was excited about the possibility of reliable electric ovens with timers and thermostats.

Gary opened one of the refrigerators that had been plugged in and cooling all night. He removed a bottle of beer and held it against his face. "Wow! I never thought a refrigerator would seem like magic."

"Hitting it early, aren't you?" Jim asked.

Gary frowned. "I don't drink, but I can appreciate the miracle of a cold bottle that didn't have to be left in the creek overnight."

Jim laughed. "What's on the menu?"

Charlotte, one of Gary's daughters, was stirring a large pot that had been simmering on a woodstove all night. "Chicken soup."

"Now that we have power, you might be able to expand the menu to two items," Pops said. "Can you imagine?" He laughed at his own joke, then took a seat at the bar.

The clatter of hooves and the rattle of tack against wood announced the arrival of Shade's wagon. Shade helped Becky down, then walked inside with her. "Morning, folks."

"Pops is going to help you today," Jim told Becky. "He was bored sitting around the house."

Becky gave him a thumbs-up. "Good. I'll sit on my ass and take it easy. He can do the work while I criticize him."

Pops laughed.

"She'll do it, Pops," Shade warned. "Watch and see."

Becky headed for the bar, prepared to open it for the day, and Pops rose to help her.

"I'm going to make a run out in the Belfast direction," Shade told Jim. "There's a couple of families out that way that I know from the livestock market. Some of them produce crops that I haven't seen down this way. Thought I might ride up there and see if they had anything they might want to trade."

"Like what?" Jim asked.

"Sunflowers, different kinds of corn, peanuts, and even pumpkins."

"I love pumpkin pie," Pops said.

"Who doesn't?" Becky gushed.

"Corn has obvious uses," Shade said, pointing toward one of Ed's liquor stills. "He's burning through his supplies at a pretty fast clip. There are also people who've asked about liquor for trying to run vehicles, but he can't make enough of it for that right now. He sure as hell wouldn't get as much for it as fuel as he's getting for intoxication."

"That's probably true. What about the sunflowers?"

"There's plenty of folks here in town started raising chickens," Shade said. "Thought I might buy it as a feed supplement and see if there was a market. You could also serve them as a snack."

"That would be nice," Jim said. "Sounds like a worthwhile trip. Let me send some trade goods with you. If you see anything we could use at the roadhouse, pick it up. Any other stops while you're out?"

"There are a few people with exotic livestock. Might be able to pick up some ostrich, beefalo, emu, or llama."

Becky crumpled her face. "You can eat a llama? Gross!"

"It's actually a South American delicacy," Shade said. "Low fat, like venison."

"I'd eat it," Pops said. "Anything to get some variety back in our diet."

"I expect I'll be gone all day, Jim," said Shade. "I'll try to make it back here before you close so I can haul Becky home."

"Be safe, Shade. Wish you had someone to ride shotgun with you. Where's your brother Nooner been?"

Shade dismissed him with a wave. "He's been keeping with a lady over toward Dickenson County. Her son makes liquor. As you can imagine, Nooner instantly fell in love with her as soon as he heard that. She's also a drunk and I bet they ain't got seven teeth between them."

"Love is blind." Jim shrugged.

Shade shook his head. "Love is drunk."

24

Hugh was uncertain how long he'd been napping when he heard the helicopter. As soon as Pete and Charlie had left with the horses, Hugh stacked the empty cardboard boxes in a clearing high on the shoulder of the mountain and used Foley's satellite phone to text the pilot for a pickup. He'd held his breath while awaiting a response, unsure if the message would be received or if the man on the other end might somehow know that Hugh was an imposter. Maybe there was some kind of signal or code that he wasn't aware of, something he was supposed to send to convey that all had gone well.

When the response came, it was a simple message from the pilot stating that he should be there in around four hours. Hugh took the opportunity to catch up on his sleep. Between the late night at the roadhouse, having to pack gear for this operation, and riding up there at the crack of dawn, he was exhausted.

He was instantly awake now, rolling to his knees and blinking the sleep from his eyes. His gear was concealed in the brush, along with his rifle, his camouflage jacket, and his ever-present boonie hat. He'd opted for wearing a coat and hat that had belonged to one of the men killed at the roadhouse, hoping it might conceal his identity long enough to get within range of the pilot.

With it already being midday, Hugh didn't have to do much to guide the pilot in. When the pilot slowed over the coordinates he'd been given, Hugh caught his attention by waving his arms, then stood clear while the pilot landed. The pilot killed the engines, unfastened his harness, and moved from the cockpit to the cabin. Seconds later, the cabin door slid open, and the pilot used his foot to nudge a cardboard box to the edge of the door opening.

Hugh suspected the box contained resupply for the thieves, food and any gear they'd requested. The pilot had not detected that Hugh wasn't one of the men he normally worked with. It was on. The operation was a go.

Hugh picked up one of the empty boxes that had once held converters and carried it toward the helicopter. He kept his head lowered so the pilot couldn't see his face. The rotors were still winding down, stirring dust and leaves, filling the air with a steadily decreasing whine.

When Hugh reached the helicopter, the pilot stepped aside so Hugh could leave the converters in the doorway. Hugh set the box down, then immediately grabbed the pilot's legs and swept them out from under him. The pilot crashed hard on his back, his head bouncing off the deck. Hugh used his free hand to latch onto the pilot's shirt, then shoved his handgun under the stunned man's chin.

The pilot's eyes went wide when he saw his attacker. "You're not one of the men I work with. Who the hell are you?"

Hugh grinned but there was nothing friendly about it. It was the menacing expression of a man aware that he was completely in control of a situation. "I'm the man who can kill you here in these woods or let you go safely home at the end of the day. It's your call."

"Please don't hurt me," the pilot said. "I have people depending on me. A family."

"Then do exactly what I tell you and you won't get hurt."

Hugh rolled the man onto his stomach and used zip-ties to secure him. Once he was bound, Hugh yanked him the rest of the way out of the helicopter and let him drop him to the ground. The pilot grunted as the wind was knocked out of him.

"You need to understand that I mean business," Hugh said. "If I have to use pain to assure compliance, I'm more than capable of doing so."

Hugh searched the pilot, removing a satellite phone, a large folding knife, and a Sig 226 handgun the pilot carried in a shoulder holster. Hugh cleared the weapon, then took one more look at the pilot and decided to take his shoulder holster too, for good measure. Once he was sure the pilot was clean, Hugh dragged him to a sitting position. He used another heavy zip-tie to secure the pilot to the landing gear, then retrieved his gear from the bushes. He stashed the pilot's weapons in his pack, then stowed all his gear into the cabin of the helicopter. A search of the aircraft turned up a compact pump shotgun with a pistol grip and no buttstock, which Hugh unloaded and seized. The rest of his search turned up nothing unexpected.

Hugh hopped out of the helicopter, yanked off the jacket he'd found in the thieves' gear, and tossed the hat into the bushes. Once his boonie hat was back on his head, he felt like himself again. He lit a cigarette, hunkered down in front of the pilot, and studied his face. The pilot's long hair was in his face and his clothes were rumpled. There was dried grass stuck to his face and he appeared to be nervous. He had good reason to be.

"What are you going to do to me?" he asked.

"You know what cargo you're flying?"

The pilot looked away, sighed, then nodded. "Yeah."

"The men you're here to pick up are all dead. You're fixing to join them if you don't do exactly what I say."

The pilot's eyes were back on Hugh then, imploring. "I don't want to die. I'll do whatever you say, just let me go home to my family."

"Then listen to me very closely because I'm a man who does not tolerate bullshit," Hugh said. "I might look like some backwoods hillbilly, but I'm smarter than you, better trained than you, and a damn sight meaner than you. Are we clear?"

The pilot nodded.

"Tell me what you do with those converters once you pick them up in the field."

The pilot hesitated a second, his eyes flickering sideways as he searched for a lie. Catching the gesture, Hugh lashed out and slapped the pilot so hard his ears rang.

Hugh pointed a finger at him. "That's for even thinking about lying to me. Do it again and you'll lose teeth. Now answer the damn question."

"I fly them to Northern Virginia. There's a guy I know, lives on a golf course. I land there and we offload the converters into his garage."

"What does he do with them?"

"He sells them to the highest bidder. Other rich dudes he knows."

"How many converters have you picked up and delivered to him?"

The pilot shrugged. "Hell, I don't know, man. We've been doing this for a month or two. A lot. Thousands. Maybe tens of thousands."

Hugh couldn't help himself. He slapped the pilot again, the blow ringing off the bound man's face.

"Hey! I'm being honest with you!" the pilot sputtered. "What the hell was that for?"

"That's for consorting with thieves and stealing from the suffering. Now here's what we're going to do," said Hugh. "So help me God, if you deviate from the plan, I'll kill you and I'll make it really, really special. You read me?"

The pilot nodded.

"Now I'm going to cut you loose and we're going to get inside the helicopter. You're going to fly me to that golf course and we're going to steal back some converters."

The pilot's eyes went wide. "I can't do that, man. This dude will kill me. He's shady as hell. I don't know if he's mafia or what, but he's something."

Hugh winked. "I'm something too."

25

The Reset Roadhouse was absolutely slammed for lunch that day and Jim didn't think it was only for the refrigerated beer. The presence of electricity in the town had reinvigorated people and restored hope to their lives. Many locals still didn't have power yet because they'd run out of converters. Most were still living in deplorable conditions without enough food, were weak, and had unmet medical needs. They'd lost friends and loved ones, suffered untold traumas from which they'd never fully recover. Still, there was a spark present that hadn't been there weeks ago. It had to be the power.

It was evident in the way the crowd enjoyed their lunch. Often it was like a soup kitchen with depressed people silently eating an equally depressing meal. Today there was laughter and conversation, enthusiasm and excitement. As he walked around the room, Jim overheard people planning and discussing projects they wanted to do.

The restaurant got even more crowded when Cookie showed up with a large group of dirty and starving people.

"Where'd you wrangle up all these folks?" Jim asked, pulling a couple of tables together to accommodate the group.

"They showed up to help clean buildings today." Cookie couldn't hold back a grin. "There's a lot of work to be done but it's a start."

Jim patted him on the back. "Congratulations! Motivating people under these circumstances is no easy task."

"While we were working, there were several folks with medical backgrounds who came by and said they'd be glad to provide services for barter. I collected their names and addresses and said I'd get up with them when we had a space set up. There were enough of them that it shouldn't impose too much of a burden on any single person. There were doctors, nurses, pharmacists, physician assistants, and a couple of EMTs."

"That's encouraging. Are you going to set them up at the government offices or at the church the minister offered you?"

"I'm thinking the church," Cookie said. "It's way cleaner than the government offices. We're going to meet there tomorrow and build a list of the things we need to get it operational. I'm still going to have some people working on the government offices. If nothing else, we can move some of the vendors from the farmer's market inside for the winter."

"Good idea." Jim pulled Cookie to the side. In a low voice, he asked, "Any rumbling about last night? About the way the converters were distributed?"

Cookie shook his head. "Surprisingly, no. Those I spoke to who didn't get a converter last night felt confident they'd get one soon. Several people mentioned that they got their converters up and running as soon as they got home last night. I suspect people will be good about sharing power with their neighbors until everyone has access to it."

"Hopefully that will be soon."

Cookie rejoined his group and Charlotte took their orders. It was a rather simple process considering the limited menu. Soup and water, soup and beer, or soup and liquor. That was about all there was to it.

Jim was milling around, speaking with lunch customers when Pops flagged him down from the bar. Jim headed over to see what his father wanted.

Pops was talking with a bubbly young woman in her late twenties.

He gestured toward her with a flourish. "This young lady is Catherine Anderson. She'd like to speak with you."

The woman shoved a hand in Jim's direction. "Most people call me Cat."

"Most people call him ornery," Pops said, gesturing toward Jim. He laughed at his own joke.

Becky and Cat joined in politely. Jim wasn't nearly as amused.

"I'm Jim." He shook her hand.

"I've never met this young lady before," Pops said. "But I've known her people going back generations. You won't find many people in this town I don't know."

"I'm aware," Jim said. "What can I do for you, Cat?"

"I'm getting together a group of people interested in starting various businesses. It's like a business incubator kind of thing. We'll help each other brainstorm ideas. Talk about how we might be able to earn an income in this new economy."

"Okay, what can I do for you?"

"We wanted to meet here tonight. I just wanted to make sure that was okay. I have no idea how many people will show up, but this place is a good option because we can order drinks and stuff."

"I'm cool with you guys meeting here," Jim replied. "Especially if you're buying stuff. Would you like us to set up some tables off to the side so you can hear each other better? This place gets a little noisy at night."

Cat reached out and touched Jim on the arm. She made an animated sigh, as if the circumstances around tonight's meeting were the greatest burden weighing upon her at that moment. "That would be *amazing*. Could you do that?"

"I just offered," Jim said.

Pops leaned toward Cat. "See? I told you he was ornery."

"You can come to our meeting too, Mr. Powell. You've obviously built a successful business under very challenging circumstances. I'm sure you have insights we'd all benefit from."

Jim was noncommittal. "Maybe, but I stay pretty busy here at night. Depends on what kind of crowd we have."

"You can play it by ear," Cat said. "You'd be welcome too, Pops. I'm sure you know way more about this town and its people than I'll ever know."

Pops gave Jim a smug look. "Why, I'd love to. I have quite the broad range of expertise."

"You've never run a business in your life," Jim said.

"No, but I know a lot of people and many of them have run businesses," Pops said.

"Then come to our meeting, Pops. We're hoping to meet around dark."

"I shall. I'm always glad to share information with those who appreciate it." Pops shot Jim a look, clearly accusing him of not being so receptive to the insights he regularly offered.

Cat clapped her hands enthusiastically. "I need to get out of here and make sure everyone knows this is where we're meeting. I'll see you folks later!" She hurried toward the door.

Becky began mixing a drink on the bar. Someone had recently traded them an entire case of powdered lemonade mix so a lemonade moonshine cocktail was one of their "specials" right now. "She's a little bundle of energy. People like that get on my nerves."

"She's adorable. And it's about time someone recognized the breadth of my knowledge," Pops said.

"Don't dominate their meeting," said Jim. "Someone else might want to talk too."

Pops narrowed his eyes at Jim. "I can't help it that my talents go right over your head, son."

Becky cackled. She loved it when people gave Jim a hard time.

26

"This the point where I'd usually contact J.T.," the pilot said, checking his primary navigation display.

"He's the guy?" Hugh asked.

"The one who sells the converters. Partner to the men you killed. J.T. Elder is his name."

Most of the flight had passed in silence. Hugh didn't engage in casual conversation with his prisoners. The distraction could cause him to let his guard down. Sometimes it could make it tougher when he had to pull their plug.

"How do you contact Elder?"

"I text him on the sat phone you took from me. I tell him I'm inbound, then I land on the golf course, practically in his backyard. If he's around, he comes out to meet me. If he's not home, he tells me where to leave them."

Hugh pulled the confiscated sat phone out of his pocket. "What's your passcode?"

The pilot replied immediately, remembering the powerful blow Hugh had delivered to the side of his face the last time he hesitated. Hugh plugged in the passcode and the phone unlocked. He scrolled the previous calls and found there weren't very many. The only text messages in the entire phone were to the contact labeled "JT."

"How far out are we?" Hugh asked.

"Twenty minutes or so."

Following the example of the previous texts, Hugh fired a text message telling Elder that the helicopter would be there in approximately twenty minutes. He received a reply in less than a minute.

"I'm around. I'll meet you with a golf cart when you land."

Hugh read the message off to the pilot.

"He has an electric golf cart he uses for hauling the converters from the helicopter to his garage. If he's not home, I have to carry the boxes to his place by hand and that sucks. He's going to be pissed when he finds these boxes are empty."

"That'll be a short-term problem," Hugh said. "He won't live long enough for it to become an issue."

The pilot grew nervous at that comment, shaking his head and mumbling to himself.

"What is it?" Hugh demanded.

"Look, if you're going to do this, you better do it right. If Elder comes out on top, he's going to kill me just for bringing you here. That's the kind of guy he is. He lives to make an example of people. I've seen it before."

"Don't worry about that. You just get me there," Hugh said. "If you do what you're told, you might make it home to your family tonight. Speaking of which, how's your fuel holding out?"

"We'll need to refuel before I can take you back across Virginia, assuming that's what I'm doing. Getting fuel won't be a problem. I have a contract with the government and they have fuel depots where I can refuel for free."

"Good. We'll take care of that as soon as we've visited your friend."

The pilot was still on edge, but Hugh was fine with that. He wanted the man to be scared and cooperative. As far as his state of mind went, Hugh was fine. He was relaxed and knew what he was going to do. Should his primary plan fail, he had multiple backup plans ready. If Hugh had a happy place, this was it—an irregular operation with a tangible benefit for him and his friends.

"There's the golf course," the pilot said a short time later. "With the leaves gone, you can see J.T.'s house there in the trees, just east of that little pond."

"Land where you normally land. As soon as you touch down, kill the engine. I'm going to secure you in the back so you don't get any stupid ideas while I'm gone. Don't fight me and you'll be fine."

"I'll cooperate."

Hugh reached in his pocket and extracted a billfold. "I'm not sure why any dumbass feels the need to carry his billfold around during the collapse, but your bad decision is part of my insurance policy." Hugh opened the wallet and extracted the pilot's driver's license. "Your street address is right here. You try to sabotage my plan or try to escape, I'll find you and kill your whole family. If for any reason I come back with those converters and you're not here, this address is my next stop."

Hugh might kill the pilot, but he had no intentions of harming the man's family, although he wasn't going to tell him that. He wanted to let the pilot's mind race to the worst possibilities. That could only work to Hugh's benefit.

The helicopter slowed to a hover and began to descend. It settled gently onto the overgrown golf course and the pilot killed the engine as asked.

"In the back," Hugh ordered, gesturing with his handgun.

He quickly secured the pilot's hands behind his back with two sturdy zip ties, then shoved him into a jump seat against the wall. He threaded a long zip tie through an anchor point on the wall, then snugged it around the pilot's neck.

"That's a little tight!"

"Good," Hugh said. "Remember, it could be tighter."

The pilot shut up and Hugh added a few more zip ties, securing all the pilot's extremities. There was no way he was getting loose without help. Any movement would only put more pressure on his neck and threaten to choke him. Hugh expected the pilot would do nothing but sit still and pray for his quick return.

With the pilot secured, Hugh moved to a window and watched for the golf cart. Several minutes passed before it sped into view, following a well-worn path in the high grass. There was only one man in the vehicle. He was overweight and wore a polo shirt with aviator sunglasses. With his black pants and white shoes, he looked like he'd stepped off the set of *The Sopranos*.

Hugh waited for Elder to stop the golf cart before he made his move. While Elder was distracted by the effort required to squeeze himself from the cart, Hugh slid open the cabin door and raised his rifle. Elder was hitching his pants up when he turned around and saw Hugh. He was so startled he stumbled backward, nearly losing his footing.

"Get those hands up!" Hugh ordered.

The man was too stunned to obey the command.

"Up! Now! Turn away from me!"

This time Elder did as he was ordered. Hugh rested the barrel of his rifle against the base of the man's skull while he performed a hasty search. He removed a Desert Eagle .44 from a holster and a .380 automatic from an ankle holster, tossing them to the ground beside him.

"Are you J.T. Elder?"

"Who's asking?"

Hugh delivered a short jab to the back of the Elder's head. The rubberized armor of the glove protected Hugh's hand, but the blow was hard enough to shove the prisoner's head into the roll cage of the golf cart.

"Ouch!"

"Answer the question or the next will be worse."

"Yes, dammit, I'm J.T. Elder. Who the hell are you?"

"I'm not here to answer questions. I'm here to talk about converters."

"What the hell is a converter?"

This time Hugh spared his fist. In a blur of movement, he flipped his rifle around and clubbed Elder in the back of his head with his rifle butt. Elder staggered, collapsing against the side of the golf cart. Taking advantage of Elder's condition, Hugh zip-tied him, then stood him back up against the cart.

"Wrong answer, asshole. I know who you are. I killed your gang of converter thieves and now I've come to kill you too."

Elder's eyes went wide. Hugh had his attention.

"Listen, buddy, I don't know what they told you, but I'm not part of any stealing or looting. I'm an honest businessman."

"Save the bullshit," Hugh said. "I don't have time for it. Show me where you store the converters."

JT started to protest but shrank away when Hugh raised the butt of his rifle again. "Okay, okay. I'll show you."

Hugh flipped the rifle around and pointed it at Elder's face. "You get one shot at this and you better not screw it up. You try to trick me or set me up, you die. You lie to me, you die. You try to escape, you die. Those are the rules. We clear?"

Elder swallowed, then nodded. Hugh stuffed his prisoner into the golf cart, securing his feet together, then zip-tying his neck to a part of the roll cage.

Elder wasn't happy about that. "This path is bumpy as hell. I'll choke to death."

"Tough." Hugh slid into the driver's seat and turned the key. He punched the accelerator pedal and the cart spun the tires, throwing chunks of sod before it caught traction. "Where are we going? That house up there?" He pointed to the house nearest the landing zone.

"The garage behind the—" Elder's words choked off when a bump tightened the zip-tie around his throat. He squawked, "Slow the hell down!"

Hugh was running short on sympathy. Everyone in America had been forced to confront their personal morality during the collapse. They'd ventured into ethical gray areas and done things to survive that they weren't proud of. This man, however, had stolen hope from people. That was a hard thing to forgive.

Even thinking about it enraged Hugh. He set his jaw and intentionally swerved the golf cart back and forth several times, tossing Elder around. It was only the zip-tie around his neck that kept Elder from bouncing out of the cart. His red face, watering eyes, and abraded neck attested to that.

As they neared the house, Hugh asked, "Is there anyone else home?"

"No," Elder choked out, gasping. "My son is visiting a friend in the neighborhood. My wife rode her bike over to her mom's house."

"You better not be lying. What do you think will happen if they surprise me out here?"

"I'm not lying! Now can you loosen this thing around my neck? I'm choking to death."

"No," Hugh spat, rolling to a stop in front of the four-car brick garage. He turned the key off and sat there for a moment, listening for any sign that Elder had been lying to him about there being people at the house. "Do you have converters here now?"

Elder didn't answer. He hadn't yet learned the lesson the pilot learned, which was that Hugh didn't tolerate hesitation in these situations. He was about to learn.

Hugh lashed out with his right fist, delivering a hammer blow to Elder's paunch. Elder coughed and sputtered, his body trying to double over, but choking each time he pulled against the zip-tie around his neck.

Hugh didn't wait for Elder to collect himself. He climbed out of the golf cart and advanced on the garage with his rifle at the ready. He tried the knob on the side door and found it locked. Without hesitation, he raised a heavy boot and stomped the door right beside the knob. The jamb splintered and the door flew open hard, rebounding off an interior wall. Hugh glanced at Elder to make sure he was still subdued. Satisfied the big man wasn't going anywhere, Hugh activated his weapon light and crept inside.

The first thing Hugh noticed inside the massive space was the humming of refrigeration equipment. The second was there were several LEDs glowing in the darkness. Aware now that the garage had power, Hugh held his rifle with his right hand and groped for a light switch with his left. When he flipped it, the garage lights burst to life and Hugh couldn't hold back a grin. One entire parking space was filled with the familiar cardboard boxes.

Jackpot.

Hugh hurried over and tore into one of the boxes, finding it packed full of factory-fresh converters. A quick estimation told him there could be as many as forty-eight boxes. If they were all full and held one hundred converters each, that should be forty-eight hundred more converters for his community. There was no way that many cardboard boxes would fit, even in the spacious Bell Long-Ranger, but if he could quickly repack the converters and ditch the protective Styrofoam trays, he just might be able to make it work. Hugh didn't intend to leave any of them behind.

He carried his primary handgun, a Glock, in a drop-leg rig on his battle belt. There was a nylon holster fastened to his plate carrier, and it held a backup handgun he'd received as a gift from Barb Maguire when she'd visited him in the valley. It was a Ruger .22 with integral suppression and perfectly tuned to function with subsonic ammunition. Barb said that her father, the Mad Mick, had made it in his shop. It was the perfect assassin's weapon. Hugh confirmed there was a round in the pipe and went back outside.

"You got your converters," Elder growled. "What are you going to do with me?"

Hugh's reply came in the form of a .22 caliber mag dump into Elder's heart. The prisoner arched against his bonds, pissed himself, then slumped dead in his seat. Hugh efficiently inserted a fresh mag into the Ruger and holstered the weapon. He drew a wicked blade from a sheath on his plate carrier, cut Elder loose from the golf cart, then dragged his body into the garage.

Searching the wall, Hugh found the button that raised the garage door, and activated it. Elder had been kind enough to leave just enough room inside the garage to back the golf cart inside. Hugh felt that had to be intentional, for easier loading and unloading of the cart. Once the cart was backed inside, he closed the garage door, and dug into the boxes.

Hugh understood the purpose of the bulky Styrofoam trays the converters were nestled in. These converters had likely made their way to America from some overseas factory and Lightspeed had needed a way to make sure they weren't damaged in transit. Hugh quickly figured out that the foam trays took up most of the box, with the actual converters only taking up a third of the space. By ditching the trays and repacking the converters directly into the boxes, Hugh managed to reduce the forty-eight cardboard boxes down to sixteen.

Once he was done, he managed to load eight of the heavy boxes onto the golf cart. Any more than that and he was afraid one might roll off. There was no way he wanted to waste time out there in the open having to chase down stray converters. He stuck his head out the side door, carefully listening and looking for any unwanted guests. When he didn't see any, he opened the garage door, drove the golf cart out, and headed back down the trail to the helicopter.

"I see you managed to work something out with Elder?" the pilot asked, still bound to the rigging.

Hugh wasted no time on small talk. "I managed to kill him. That made negotiations simpler."

The pilot turned his head away, unable to conceal the fear that this might be the fate that lay ahead for him as well.

Hugh quickly placed the eight boxes inside the open door of the helicopter. He shoved them as far as he could reach but didn't climb inside to secure them. He'd worry about repacking once he had all the boxes safely onboard the aircraft.

Once all the boxes were offloaded, Hugh climbed back into the golf cart and zipped up the path toward Elder's garage. He whipped around in front of the open garage door, then more carefully backed up to the stack of remaining boxes. He'd never be able to forgive himself if he backed into the stack and damaged them.

Hugh made one more quick scan in front of the garage, even searching the house windows to make sure he wasn't being watched. By himself, there was no way he could secure the area, so the operation was a balance between risk and speed. He had to be as safe as he could, while working as fast as he could. He was as relaxed as he could be in this type of situation, not being prone to panic or nerves. Still, he wouldn't breathe easy until he was back up in the air and headed toward home.

He let his rifle hang from the sling while he transferred the last eight boxes onto the golf cart. Feeling like the Grinch stealing the last ornament from Whoville, Hugh even found the garage's electrical meter and snatched the converter that powered Elder's garage. He decided to leave the one installed on the house. Elder's family shouldn't have to suffer any further just because they lived with a dirtbag.

Before he pulled out of the garage, Hugh looked around with longing. The place was crammed with all manner of items that Elder had probably taken in on trade for converters. There were freezers full of food, stacks of gun cases, and ammo cans that could contain nearly anything. The survivalist in Hugh wished he had time to sort through the gear and see if there were things his people could use. The practical operator in him, the voice that had always got him home alive from missions, told him it was time to go. Hugh heeded the voice and drove back to the helicopter.

He offloaded all the boxes, then climbed inside once he had room to shut the door, then used his knife to cut the pilot loose and held a gun on him while the man climbed into the cockpit. The pilot was pouring sweat as he sat down and buckled into his seat. He rubbed at the impression a zip-tie had left embedded in his neck, wincing when he touched the abraded flesh.

"A little cool for sweating," Hugh commented, arranging the last of the boxes. "It's about mid-fifties outside." Hugh took his seat and fastened his seat belt.

"It was all I could do to *not* pass out. I felt like I was going to throw up, but I was afraid I'd choke to death if I did. That zip-tie made it hard to swallow."

Hugh shrugged. "Remember that next time a thief offers you work. In the words of Batman, crime doesn't pay."

"I'm pretty sure I won't be forgetting that, if I live long enough."

"You do what I tell you and the worst is over. Refuel the chopper and take me home. I'll direct you to the landing zone once we're over the town."

"Copy that. Fuel stop in about twenty minutes."

The pilot did his thing and the engine began to whine. Soon the rotors were spinning and the helicopter lifted into the air. Hugh let out a long breath when they left the golf course behind them. He hadn't stressed over this op, but it was always nice to be walking away at the end with no leaks, no broken bones, and having accomplished the objective he set out for.

It was a good day.

27

Cat Anderson showed up about thirty minutes early for her meeting at the Reset Roadhouse that evening. She seemed like the kind of person who always showed up early so she could personally oversee every detail, not wanting to leave anything to chance. Before the collapse, the person facilitating the meeting might show up with a copy paper box full of materials. These days, with people having to walk everywhere they went, Cat arrived with hers crammed in a backpack.

Before she even took her pack off, Cat stood on the gritty concrete floor assessing the tables Jim had pulled to the side for her. He wasn't sure exactly what she was looking for, but she stood there for a surprisingly long time before determining that Jim's arrangement would do. Once that was decided, she removed her pack and began organizing the items she'd brought.

"You look prepared," Jim said.

"It's a little embarrassing," Cat said, rolling her eyes. "A few years ago, you'd never have caught me handing out *used* ink pens and note pads at a meeting. Everything had to be just right. Now we have to make do with whatever we can pull together. It's absolutely primitive."

"What are those cardboard strips for?" Jim asked, pointing to the one stack of items on the table he couldn't immediately see a purpose for.

"Placards. Everyone writes their names on one and places it on the table in front of them. That way we know who everyone is."

"That's...*thorough.*"

"Look, I know it's a small town and I know everyone I invited, but that doesn't mean they all know each other. Plus I told them to invite anyone they thought might be interested, so there could be a few new faces."

"You don't have to explain yourself to me, Cat. I hope you have a good turnout. In fact, I brought on an extra server tonight just to make sure you guys are well taken care of."

Cat patted Jim on the shoulder. "Oh, that's so sweet. Thank you. You're totally welcome to join us, since you're a successful businessman here in the community."

That took Jim aback on several levels. For one, he didn't particularly think of himself as a businessman. He'd opened the Reset Roadhouse for entirely selfish reasons. It was a strategic move, not a financial one. The roadhouse was originally intended to be a hub for collecting intelligence, not earning money. While Jim had always liked being an outsider, that decision came with consequences, such as not always knowing what was going on around him. Turning a blind eye to his surroundings had almost got him killed several times. He was a slow learner, but he'd finally got the lesson.

"I might drop by and see how things are going," Jim said. "I stay pretty busy around here, but if I have a moment, I'll stop in."

Cat moved closer. There was nothing flirtatious or intimate about the gesture, but she was one of those people who conducted every conversation as if it were a conspiracy, standing close and speaking in a low voice. Jim had *big* personal space and didn't like people entering it. It was restricted airspace and required a special permit as far as he was concerned. If someone was within arm's reach, they were too close. He took a step back.

Cat cast him a weird look, surprised by his reaction. "I was going to ask about appetizers. I know you mostly sell soup, beer, and liquor, but are there any other options? Anything we could put out on the table for people to share? Something snacky?"

"You're in luck. There's a Mexican lady in town who's been making tortillas for us. I don't know where she gets her ingredients, but she cranks them out by the hundreds, and we've got fresh garden salsa. Since we can use ovens now, we've been baking tortilla wedges into something like a cracker that you can dip salsa with. It's pretty good. I tried some earlier."

"What will that cost us?" Cat asked. "I know you're not running a charity."

"I don't know how much time you've spent here at the roadhouse, but this is a bartering establishment. Ammo is the currency of choice, although we take other things as well."

Cat smiled. "I don't shoot a lot of people, but I do come from a family that overmedicates. We take pills the way drunks eat mints."

Jim laughed. "There's always a medication market. It's another popular currency. What do you have?"

Cat reached into her backpack and pulled out a gallon bag full of pill bottles. She rattled it like a maraca. Jim panicked briefly and latched onto it with both hands, stopping her motion. He looked back over his shoulder and saw a lot of heads turned their way.

"Not a good idea," he whispered.

Cat's eyes went wide, though there was an amused look in them. "There used to be an old joke about rattling a pill bottle being the Appalachian mating call. Is that real?"

Jim shrugged. "To an extent. Carrying around a bag of pills this size is a good way to die. You need to be careful. Don't let anyone else see that."

"Sorry, I forgot." She held the bag in front of her face and studied the labels of the individual bottles. Finding what she was looking for, she reached inside and selected one. "Ninety Xanax."

Jim looked appalled. "Who the hell takes ninety Xanax? What is that—a year's supply?"

"Try a month. That was my grandmother's. She claimed to be

afflicted with 'bad nerves.' I've probably got five or six more bottles just like that and I haven't even broken into my mom's stash yet." Cat handed the bottle over to Jim.

He studied the label. "That will pay for a hell of a lot of chips and dip."

"If you'll take meds as payment, I'll cover the whole meeting tonight. Drinks, appetizers, food, whatever anyone wants. You can either return what we didn't spend at the end of the night or keep it and give me credit against future meetings."

"That's a deal." Jim pocketed the bottle. "I'll make sure the staff know to keep you guys happy. You need anything at all, you let me know."

Jim wandered off and left a gleeful Cat to setting up her meeting table. Having worked at a large state agency prior to the collapse, Jim had known a lot of people over the years whose lives were all about meetings, preparing for meetings, and performing administrative tasks. He wondered what all those people had done to keep sane during the collapse.

Of course, there was also the possibility that those people had *not* remained sane, or even survived. If the restoration of electricity was indeed a small step toward the country becoming civilized again, Jim couldn't wait to see what kinds of people emerged. There had to be more Cats out there—people who'd been waiting for the dust to settle before they came back out and resumed their place in society.

Pops had put in a full day at the bar, losing steam as day moved into evening. Ellen wisely sent Pete and Charlie into town just before dark to see if Pops was ready to come home or if he was going stay at the roadhouse until closing. Pops looked glad to see the two boys he called his "old grandson" and "new grandson." He gladly accepted their offer.

Jim helped Pops mount his horse at the loading dock. "Thanks for the help, Pops. I'm sure Becky appreciated it."

"I'm sure she did. I'm not sure how you guys keep this place running without me."

Jim smiled. "I'm not sure either, Pops."

Pops nudged his horse into motion. Pete and Charlie fell in along either side of him and the three plodded off toward the valley. As they rode away, Jim heard Pops launch into a story.

"I ever tell you boys about the time I decided to raise Chinchillas? It was 1953 and I saw this ad in the back of a comic book about how I could become rich in the fur trade."

Jim was still smiling at those three when he went back inside to see if Becky or Randi needed any help. When things got busy, he sometimes filled in at the store selling guns, Ian's stabby things, ammo, and whatever other gear they had in the row of display cases. He was surprised to see that Cat's tables were quickly filling up.

"I'm going to go get them another table," he told Becky.

Against a far wall, they had a stack of folding tables they could set up when they needed them. Jim set one up alongside Cat's other tables, then wrangled up enough chairs to fill it.

"Quite the turnout, isn't it?" Cat said, obviously pleased with herself.

Jim nodded. "It's encouraging."

While Jim had noticed the tables filling up, he was now close enough to get a good look at the people seated there. He recognized a few faces from around town and from booths at the farmer's market. While he was standing there, Ed, the brewmaster and distiller for the roadhouse walked over and took a seat.

Jim shot him a funny look. "Ed?"

Ed held up a hand. "I'm not quitting the roadhouse, Jim. There are some folks here who want to explore the idea of brewing alcohol for running vehicles and I told them I'd share some of what I knew."

"Good enough. Your server should be here in a second. I'll check back with you in a bit."

"Jim!" Becky yelled from the bar.

Unable to see Jim, she resorted to paging him at the top of her lungs. While it sometimes startled those enjoying a drink just a few feet from her, it was an effective means of locating anyone in the building.

Jim hurried over to the bar before she yelled again. "What is it?"

"I just got a call on the radio from my man," she said. "He's turning onto the street right now."

"That warms my heart, Becky. I'm glad you decided to share this tender moment with me."

She sneered. "Get baked, asshole. I'm only telling you because he wanted you to meet him at the loading dock."

Jim laughed. "Yes, ma'am. Headed there now."

28

The night was cool enough that the dock door was closed. Jim opened it, hearing the sound of Shade's horses and wagon approaching. Shade's wagon wasn't one of those lightweight buggies that a doctor from bygone days would have used for making house calls. He'd told Jim on several occasions that his style of wagon was the tractor-trailer of its day and he'd added several modern upgrades to this one, such as rubber tires and softer seats. Shade also pointed out that his massive horses had pulled loose many stuck trucks over the years, mired in mud or snow. Jim had no doubt. He found the massive horses to be terrifying.

When the wagon finally reached the loading dock, Shade expertly made his horses back the wagon up to the dock just as a semi-truck might.

"Oh, now you're just showing off!" Jim teased.

Shade laughed. "I don't want this team to get out of practice."

Jim squinted to make out the contents of the wagon in the low light, then he felt like an idiot. He almost palmed himself in the forehead when he remembered he had other options now. He walked over to a bank of light switches, flipped a few up, and floodlights along the dock area burst to life.

Shade covered his eyes against the bright, unnatural light and unleashed a torrent of profanity powerful enough to curdle milk. A circle of men stood outside smoking hand-rolled cigarettes of tobacco or marijuana. They squinted, shielded their eyes, and recoiled like vampires thrown into daylight.

"Quit being dramatic," Jim said. "You'll all live."

Shade set the parking brake on his wagon and climbed down. He was still rubbing his eyes. "Damn, Jim. After an hour of driving in the dark, it feels like you stabbed me in the brain."

"You old folks always get an attitude about technology." Jim waved a hand dismissively. "These are the days of electric lights and the horseless carriage."

"Bullshit! You have a horse to thank for this delivery." Shade untied the tarp, then pulled it back for Jim to see the sacks piled there.

Jim climbed into the back of the wagon to get a closer look. "What's all this?"

"There are sunflower seeds, sacks of corn, honey, molasses, beans, and a few other goodies. There are peanuts in there too. You can roast those and sell them. What's a roadhouse without peanut shells on the floor?"

"All this came from people you know on that end of the county?" Jim was surprised because goods at the farmer's market had been drying up over the last month, like the folks who'd been selling there on a regular basis had exhausted the supply of things they were willing to sell.

"Every bit of it. There's a lot of farmers up in that part of the county that haven't had any contact with people down this way. They stay to themselves and mostly trade with each other. They're not doing farmer's markets or anything like that because they don't want to draw attention to themselves."

"Smart play, but they were willing to sell to you?"

"Yeah. Like I said, I know a lot of them from the livestock markets and extension agency events. I visited a couple of folks I knew, had a few sips of liquor, and spent some time catching up. Amazing what you can do when you're not an asshole." He cut Jim a sideways glance and winked at him.

Jim laughed. "So I've heard. Maybe I'll try it sometime. Learn anything interesting?"

"Oh yeah," Shade said. "There's a couple of National Guard armories up that way. One in Richlands and another in Bluefield. That Lightspeed character has been delivering aid to those armories. People have been lining up to get canned goods, powdered milk, flour, baking powder, and a lot of other stuff. I hadn't heard a word about it. I managed to trade for some of those supplies. We might need to see if we can get in on that."

"I'll send a few folks up that way on horseback to check it out. Anything we could get like that would help."

Shade stuck a hand rolled cigarette in his mouth and lit it with a wooden match. "They had some questions for me too, especially once I mentioned we'd just got power. Those folks want power, and they were pissed they didn't know about the converters and didn't get a shot at drawing for them like people here in town."

Jim frowned. "Hell, Shade, I can't be responsible for riding through the whole community like the town crier, letting everyone know what's going on. If those people want to know what's going on in town, they need to make a point of showing up here every once in a while. I learned the same thing when I stayed in the valley and never came to town. Hermits miss out on a lot. That's just how it is."

Shade held up a placating hand. "I get it, Jim. The same is true with me. I didn't realize how much I was missing until I started staying in town more. Those people I talked to today aren't mad at you in particular, they just want to make sure that people in outlying communities aren't passed over."

"They could well be passed over. It's up to them to make their voices heard. That's reality. If they want converters from us, they need to get down here and say so."

"That's pretty much what I told them," Shade said. "I'm not even sure what the range is on those electronic gizmos. I didn't know if they'd work on that end of the county or not."

"It's not about range. They have to be in line of sight with that big orange balloon floating over the mountain."

"Oh, they can see that. They call it The Great Pumpkin. I also told some of them about the roadhouse, so you might see a few new faces in the next week or so. I told them to ask for you if they had questions about the power. I knew you'd appreciate me giving your name out."

"Greeeaat," Jim drawled. "I'm well known as a friendly customer service representative. This reminds me of when we first got the internet in the region. Within days, everyone wanted it. Installers couldn't keep up with demand."

"Sounds like a good business to be in."

"While it might be, I'm not in the power business," said Jim. "I don't make a dime off it. All I get is the damn headaches."

Jim went inside and got a cart, which the two men used to haul the supplies to the storeroom in the back of the roadhouse. Once they were done, they headed for the bar, and Jim got them two beers.

"I'm here for a cold beer and a warm hug!" Shade boomed, wrapping his arms around Becky.

Jim left Shade to catch up with Becky and took his beer back to the table where Cat and her business incubator people were meeting. He needed to sit down and rest his back for a few minutes so he took a seat with the group, hoping he wouldn't regret it. The conversation slowed as he joined them, and Cat paused to welcome him. Looking around the table, Jim was amused to see that everyone had a placard with their name on it, just as Cat had planned. Beneath their names, they'd each listed the business or idea they were interested in developing.

"I was going to ask what I've missed, but it looks like I've missed a whole lot."

"You have!" Cat was loud, animated, and bubbly. She was obviously thrilled to be back in her element, facilitating a meeting and socializing with people. "Everyone has been talking about their ideas and why they're in a good position to launch that particular business. These aren't the days of the internet where anyone can start a multinational corporation from their garage."

"No more eBay empires," one of the people seated at the table remarked.

Cat nodded. "Exactly. We're using business models from a century ago and thinking local. *Local* sales and *local* supply chain. The next thing we're working on is developing a list of action steps— the things each person has to do to get their business up and running."

Some of the businesses were throwbacks to the past, such as sewing, shoe repair, and chimney cleaning. With others, Jim couldn't tell from their placards what kind of business they were describing.

Jim pointed at a guy in his late twenties whose business idea simply read "carts." "What does yours mean? What kind of carts are you talking about?"

"My uncle had a business rehabbing and repairing old golf carts. Since it could be a long time before we have gasoline again, I thought it might be useful for some people to have electric golf carts for getting around town. I've been running one using solar for a while now, and with more people getting electricity, this could be a viable solution for a lot more people. Especially the elderly and those with mobility issues."

"Too bad your golf carts can't haul a heavy payload," Jim quipped. "Having to use horses to move supplies back and forth in wagons is a little slow."

"That's where my business comes in," another man spoke up. "I had a franchise that sold frozen foods door-to-door. Our fleet was powered by natural gas. Even though we have natural gas available locally, I can't use it for fuel because we need power to compress it into tanks. Now that we have power, we should be able to do that. I want to get my truck fleet up and running so I can offer vehicle services regionally."

"What kind of vehicle services?" Jim asked.

"We have a lot of vehicles in our fleet. Pickups, vans, a service truck, and nearly thirty freezer trucks. I could offer heavy hauling, delivery, or moving. Hell, we've even discussed getting a bus route going through town. Not a free one. It *is* a business. We'd have to establish a rate and a means of payment."

"Might be easier to use bus passes," Jim said. "Let people barter for a pass, then you don't have to negotiate a rate for every single ride."

"Good point," the man said.

Cat smiled and twirled her hands in the air like a witch casting a spell "That's exactly what we're trying to do here, Jim. We're trying to help each other. We're offering feedback and throwing out ideas. We're interacting. It's been great."

"I'll play along," Jim said. "This is my business you're sitting in here. The Reset Roadhouse was started as a way for my people to trade off things we didn't need for things we could use. It was more efficient than hanging out at the farmer's market all day, especially when that's so dependent on weather." He left out the part about the roadhouse being an intelligence gathering operation.

"So you want our feedback on the roadhouse?" Cat asked. "The assessment of this group of business-minded individuals?"

He hesitated for a moment, but he'd already said he was willing to play along. He couldn't back out now. "Sure. Go for it."

The people at the table looked around the room with a more critical eye. Up until then, the roadhouse was just a convenient location for a meeting. Now they were examining it with the assessing eyes of prospective businesspeople. Jim could see their gears turning and hoped they weren't going to throw out any comments that pissed him off. He didn't want this to become an adversarial situation because the information he was obtaining from this table was useful. Knowing what businesses might be opening in the community, what resources were available, was valuable intel.

"Now that you have power, I'd focus on getting some more atmospheric lighting in here," one woman said, gesturing at the lights above them. "Everyone is glad we have power again, but those fluorescent lights are too harsh. No one likes a bright bar. Either take out some of the bulbs or use something different."

"Good point," Jim agreed. "It's been such a miracle to get lights that it's been hard to quit staring at them. They are a little much though."

"The place needs pool tables," one of the men said. "This much space and no pool tables is a crime."

"Movies!" another said, snapping her fingers. "Find a projector, hang a sheet, and show movies. They could just be playing in the background. People might enjoy that."

Another of the men continued to look around the room, but Jim could tell he wasn't actually looking at anything in particular. Mostly it was as if he was trying to avoid looking at Jim. The guy's name was Aaron Rose and the only reason Jim knew him was because he worked for the local paper. Anyone who read the paper local paper knew his name, because he wrote half the stories and took most of the pictures.

"What is it, Aaron?" Jim asked. "You can spit it out. I have thick skin."

Cat looked at Jim and cocked an eyebrow as if she'd heard differently, though she didn't say anything.

"This place has a bit of a reputation." Aaron had hidden his distaste up until this moment, but Jim caught a flash of it as he spoke. "It's a bit...rough and tumble."

Jim shrugged. "Uh...yeah. There's an apocalypse going on. Rough comes with the territory."

Aaron held his hands up defensively. "Oh, I know. The world *has* been like that, but we're hoping that the arrival of power ushers in a new civility to our community. At some point we have to quit carrying guns, quit shooting each other, and act like human beings again. Among most of the people I talk to, we're ready to throw down our weapons and put this Old West era behind us."

Jim was tired of hearing this. He talked to at least one person a week who espoused the same beliefs. Sure, he agreed it would be nice to not have to kill people on a regular basis, but he didn't think the country was there yet. It was still a violent nation full of desperate people.

Jim considered his words carefully before he responded. "Good men can't lay down their weapons until bad men either lay theirs down or have them taken by good men. Everyone in this building—including most of you, I'm sure—have had to do things you regret to survive the collapse. I know I have. When the worst is over, I'll be holstering my weapon, but I won't be throwing it down, nor will I be surrendering it. If we ever return to these dark times again, I'd like to be ready for them."

Perhaps sensing that this debate could turn hostile, Cat intervened. "This is the point where we agree to disagree. We have bigger problems than a philosophical argument about gun control. Jim has a point that things might be a little too violent right now for people to totally disarm, especially in the more remote areas."

"Things will remain violent *until* people disarm," Aaron said. "I don't think it should be up to them. There should be an ordinance. There should be rules."

The majority of the table groaned at the use of the word "ordinance."

"That's the one thing I haven't missed about government," one man griped. "The last thing we need is more rules."

Aaron held up his hands in surrender. "I apologize. My bad. I know we agreed to some ground rules at the beginning and avoiding politics was one of them. I'm sorry if I derailed the conversation."

Cat offered him a smile. "This is a good example of why we set rules like that, Aaron. Political discussions are like a riptide. Stray too close and you can get sucked in. Once you do, it can be tough to extricate yourself."

Jim stood from his chair. "I appreciate the ideas. Well, most of them." He shot Aaron a look. "I'm impressed with what you all have accomplished in one meeting. You're welcome to meet here anytime."

"Thanks, Jim!" Cat said, retaking control of her meeting.

Jim headed for the bar, feeling like he needed another cold beer. Before he got there, the radio clipped to his belt chirped. *"Roof for Jim. Roof for Jim."*

Jim recognized the drawl as belonging to one of Hugh's security team, a nineteen-year-old named Conway Twitty Atwell. The kid's mother had been obsessed with the country singer Conway Twitty to the point she'd implied the singer might actually be the boy's real father. No one really believed her. The woman had never strayed more than twenty-five miles from town in her entire life and no one had ever heard of Conway Twitty dropping into the Sinking Springs Trailer Court.

Despite his unfortunate name, Conway was a good worker, though unsophisticated in a way that was obvious even in this small Appalachian town. He'd quit school, didn't read books, and never paid any attention to the news, so a lot of things had to be explained to him. If it didn't happen in his trailer park, he didn't feel an obligation to pay any attention to it. He was loyal to a fault, though, and worshipped Hugh like the father he'd never had.

"What's going on, Conway?" Jim asked.

"Dude, I have a helicopter headed straight for us."

29

Jim stopped in his tracks. "Are you sure?"

"Uh, I ain't a genius, Jim, but I'm pretty damn sure I know a helicopter when I hear one. You want me to shoot at it?"

"No! It could be Hugh. He left earlier today to run an errand and it's possible he's in that chopper. Do not shoot at it. Do you understand?"

"Copy that. Don't shoot the chopper because it might be Hugh." Conway sounded disappointed. *"Conway out."*

Jim continued to the bar, placed his bottle on the counter, and signaled Shade to join him.

Shade drained his beer and placed the bottle under the counter to be reused. He slung his rifle and stepped around the bar. "Where we headed?"

"There's a chopper inbound. It could be Hugh."

"Lead the way."

Jim cut through the crowd to the loading dock and hopped down to the ground. Shade's wagon was still sitting there, the team of horses standing patiently.

"Reckon I should move those horses," Shade mused. "They don't care for helicopters."

"Howdy!" Conway said from the roof. "Can you hear it now?"

Jim and Shade both jumped at the unexpected voice from above.

"Little bastard startled me," Shade said. "I ought to toss his ass off that roof. That'd learn him."

Jim shrugged in one of those "what can you do?" gestures. "He's a good kid. Talks too much and thinks too little, but his heart is in the right place."

"Hell, he won't shut up," Shade complained. "He's got enough tongue for ten sets of teeth."

Jim laughed. "Sounds like that chopper is getting closer. If you're going to move those horses, you better get on it. I'm going to turn the dock lights on and see if it heads in for a landing."

Shade hopped on the wagon and in seconds he had his team headed around the side of the building. Jim stepped back inside the roadhouse and hit the same light switches he'd used earlier when Shade returned in his wagon. Again, those patrons loafing around outside recoiled as if they'd been hit with a death ray. Jim ignored them.

The helicopter closed in, then slowed to a hover high above the roadhouse. Curious what the arrival of this helicopter meant, some patrons were abandoning their tables to stand in the dock door. Just as Shade returned to the dock area, the helicopter began to descend to the illuminated parking lot near the loading dock. Everyone from the wall-leaners to the dock-standers to Jim and Shade were forced to shield their eyes against the dust and debris stirred by the landing aircraft.

In seconds it had settled down in the parking lot and the pitch of the engines changed. The downdraft off the main rotor began to subside and Jim uncovered his eyes. The dock lights reflected off the windshield of the helicopter and Jim couldn't see who was inside. He prayed it was Hugh.

The main cabin door slid open and a man Jim didn't recognize climbed out. Jim experienced a moment of uncertainty. Just because this man was unfamiliar didn't mean anything had happened to Hugh. Jim gripped his rifle harder, ready to snap it up and fire if the situation required it, but he didn't want to present a threat if this visitor meant them no harm.

While Jim was struggling with his predicament, a second figure dropped out of the helicopter. It was a man in a boonie hat and he was holding a gun aimed at the back of the first man.

Jim breathed a sigh of relief at the sight of his old friend, then headed over to greet him. "Glad to see you made it back, Hugh! Who's the guest?"

"That's my ride," Hugh replied. "I promised I'd let him go once we unloaded, as long as he behaved himself."

Jim looked up toward the roof. Spotting Conway, he waved at him to come down. "Conway can babysit your prisoner, Hugh. Any luck finding converters?"

Hugh grinned. "I got a few. I also cut off the head of the snake. It doesn't mean there won't be other snakes crawling out of other holes, but this one won't be doing any more crawling."

Jim leaned close. "How many converters is a few?" He wasn't entirely sure there was any point in lowering his voice. Everyone in the roadhouse was standing around watching this conversation take place.

With a grin on his face, Hugh whispered, "Around five thousand, give or take a few."

Jim was stunned. He searched Hugh's face for any indication he was joking, but there was none. Hugh was dead serious. Jim could hardly fathom such a quantity of converters. To have gone from three hundred to five thousand was an exponential leap. It could well be enough to power the entire region.

When he recovered, Jim asked, "Are the converters marked in any way? Is there any indication of where the devices were stolen from?"

Hugh shook his head. "Not that I could tell. Maybe Lightspeed's people would know if we chose to mention it to them, but I don't think I would."

"Agreed. I'm going to go with the assumption that whoever lost these converters has already requested replacements."

"I'm here!" Conway announced, pushing through the crowd and hopping off the loading dock.

Hugh pointed at his prisoner. "Sit this guy down against the wall where he can't hurt himself. Babysit him until we get this chopper unloaded, then we might set the little bird free."

"Ahhh, sounds sweet when you put it that way," Conway said, taking the pilot by the arm. "Come on, little birdy."

"Great, hand me off to the simpleton," the pilot mumbled.

Conway lashed out and cracked his knuckles across the back of the pilot's head, causing him to flinch and shy away from his captor. When the pilot dared to look back over his shoulder, Conway wagged a finger at him.

"Let's not be ugly," Conway said. "Not everyone gets the same opportunities in life. Being poor doesn't make me simple."

"I'm sorry...it won't happen again." The pilot winced at the painful knot forming on the back of his head.

Conway gave the pilot a friendly pat on the shoulder and leaned closer to him, speaking in a voice no one else could hear. "I hope so. Otherwise, I'll run a pipe through you from tooth to tail, then roast you for dog food. We clear?"

The pilot nodded but couldn't form a response. He looked like a man who'd had all his worst suspicions of hillbillies confirmed in a single day. Brutal backwoods barbarians with man-eating pets who'd kill without hesitation.

Hugh slid the chopper door the rest of the way open. "I had to repack some of the boxes to make it all fit."

Jim was speechless. Behind him, the crowd chattered between themselves. Those who'd overheard the conversation between Jim and Hugh told others what the aircraft contained. Those people told even more people. Jim felt that the situation had the potential to go south and turn into a riot. If a single person rushed them to grab a converter, the rest would follow. He turned the situation over in his head. There was no point in putting all these devices in storage. Why handle them twice? Why put himself in between the converters and the people who so desperately wanted them?

"Can I have your attention please?" Jim asked. When the crowd didn't calm, Jim repeated himself to no avail. Finally, he drew his handgun and fired a shot in the air.

Immediately, it was silent enough that you could hear a pin drop.

"Can I have your attention please!" he repeated. "Who here needs power and has some mode of transportation with them tonight?"

Nobody moved or said a word.

Jim rolled his eyes. "I'm not going to kill you. I promise."

A man raised a tentative hand. "I have a bike."

"Me too," an older woman offered.

"We came on horseback," another woman said, pointing between her and the man she was with.

A few more people volunteered until there were thirteen folks who'd dared speak up that they had some means of transportation beyond their feet. Jim waved them forward.

"If you don't have power already, I'm going to give each of you a converter. Instructions for installing it are written on the back of the device. If you have trouble installing it, come back and see me tomorrow."

"Hey! How come they get converters and we don't!" a man at the front of the crowd demanded.

Jim took a calming breath, failing miserably. "If you'd shut the hell up for a minute you might get one," he snapped at the man.

The man shoved his hands into his pockets and huffed out a breath. He mumbled something in response but was careful to make sure Jim didn't hear it. One of the men with a bicycle stepped forward and stuck his hands out, eager to get his converter.

"There's a catch," Jim said. "I need you to head home and tell everyone you see along the way to come here right now if they need a converter. Shout it as you're pedaling down the street. Whatever you have to do to spread the word. Got it?"

He looked around the group of people with a means of transportation and they all nodded that they understood.

"Then here you go." He held up a converter in each hand, but no one moved forward to take one. While Jim sometimes appreciated it when people were afraid to approach him, at other times it was simply annoying. "Today would be nice!"

The people took the hint and lined up to receive their converters. As each person or couple got one, they departed, hopefully to carry out Jim's instruction to spread the word. When they were gone, he faced the rest of the crowd. He was lousy at estimating numbers but guessed there must have been two hundred or more people there staring at him expectantly.

"Who else doesn't have power?"

Half the hands shot into the air.

"Here's what we're going to do. Form a line with one person from each household. Once you have your converter, make sure your tab is paid up at the bar and get the hell out of here. I expect we're going to be overrun soon with people needing converters so we're going to close for normal business."

Hugh and Shade stood ready with their weapons, hoping their menacing presence would have a calming effect on the crowd, and it seemed to work. People talked among themselves for a moment as each family, clan, or cohabitating group came to an agreement as to who would stand in line for them. The rest of their group then cleared out of the way. Distributing the converters went smoothly and despite the crowd, Jim had them handed out in less than an hour.

That was far from the end of his evening, however. By the time those who'd already been at the roadhouse filtered off into the night, the townspeople alerted by those on bike and horseback began to stream in.

At the sight of this horde, Jim gathered his people. "Let's haul the rest of these converters to the storeroom before the place gets too packed again, then we can send this pilot on his way. I hope you've briefed him on the need to keep his mouth shut, Hugh?"

Hugh reached into his shirt and removed the pilot's driver's license, holding it up for Jim to see. "I'm going to hang onto this. I know where to find him if he runs his mouth."

"You heard that, didn't you?" Jim called to the pilot, slumped against the wall a short distance away.

The pilot nodded. "I won't say anything. You let me take my chopper and go, you'll never see or hear from me again. As far as I'm concerned, today never happened. I was never here."

"Perfect!" Jim collected a box from the helicopter and hauled it to the loading dock.

Hugh and Shade joined him, while Ian stacked the boxes onto a cart they used for moving supplies. In ten minutes, the chopper was empty and a crowd was lined up at the front door to the roadhouse.

"Tell those people out front we'll be ready in a minute," Jim told Ian.

While Ian hustled off toward the front door, Hugh helped the pilot up and cut his bonds. "I'm keeping your weapons. Consider that a small price to pay for your survival."

"Take 'em," the pilot mumbled.

"Remember, I know your address," Hugh added.

"My lips are sealed," the pilot said, rubbing his chafed wrists. "Can I go?"

"Go," Jim said. "Get lost."

The pilot didn't give them an opportunity to change their minds. He scrambled to his aircraft, climbed in, and secured all the doors. Seconds later, the engines began powering up. Jim and his people retreated into the roadhouse, closing the dock door behind them, and turning off the floodlights. Within minutes, the pilot lifted off and was gone.

"Hey, Jim, you have guests at the door," Becky called from the bar, grinning.

"Yes, I know. Thanks for being so helpful."

"De nada," Becky cackled.

"What time is it?" Jim asked. "Midnight?"

One of the few that wore a watch, Hugh checked it. "Only 2200 hours."

"God, only ten? I thought it was later. This is going to be a long night."

"It already has been," Hugh said.

Shade was posted at the front door. With his size and demeanor, he was a match for the burliest of backwoods hole-in-the-wall door-men. No one challenged him and no one gave him any crap.

Jim said, "Tell them I'm going to address them from the roof before we open the door."

"No problem," Shade called back. "We're just getting to know each other over here."

Jim knew the situation couldn't be as cordial as that. Shade often downplayed the situation when people were testing his limits. He made it easy for them. If they pushed hard enough, he would clearly and definitively show them where the line was.

Once he reached the roof, Jim went to the edge and propped a foot on the parapet wall. Below him, the building's exterior lighting illuminated a crowd of several hundred people. "Can I have your attention, please?"

The unexpected voice from above startled the crowd, most of whom had been focused on Shade at the head of the line. When they settled down enough that Jim could speak over them, he continued.

"I know everyone has been waiting on more converters. As many of you know, people showed up to steal our converters last night, and it didn't go well for them. In the aftermath, my friend Hugh took it upon himself to track down where the thieves kept their stolen converters. At great risk to himself, he made the trip to Northern Virginia and brought back enough converters for all of you. That's him in the boonie hat down there, standing by the door. If you get the opportunity, you might say a word of thanks because he didn't have to do what he did."

To Jim's surprise—and most certainly to Hugh's—the crowd in front of the door began to applaud. Some people called his name, which grew into a chant of "Hugh! Hugh! Hugh! Hugh!" The words rose into the night like the cheers of a crowd at a high school football game. Jim let it go on for several minutes. Hugh deserved it.

Finally, Jim managed to quiet the crowd.

"We have no way of knowing who these converters once belonged to, so there's no way for us to send them back to the communities they were stolen from. There wouldn't be any point anyway since Lightspeed promised to deliver more anywhere they were needed. The people who lost these have probably already received their replacements. The only reason I'm telling you that is that there's no reason for you to feel bad for the people who lost these. You're not benefitting from someone's loss. You can take your converter and use it with a clear conscience. Any questions?"

No one raised a hand or spoke up. Jim only saw eagerness in those upturned faces. Eagerness to share in the electricity that some of their friends and neighbors had already received.

"Okay, we'll keep this short and sweet. You get one converter per household. If you lie or try to scam us, you go home with nothing. Keep things orderly and clear out once you've received yours."

Jim climbed back down the ladder into the roadhouse and headed for the front door. Hugh had positioned a single box of converters there to begin with.

On his way toward the door, Jim called to Becky at the bar. "Can you bring us a couple of beers?"

"Excuse me? I work the bar, not the door. If you want a six pack of beer, get your ass over here and get it."

Jim altered his course toward the bar and leaned against the counter, resting his elbows on the scratched surface. "Remind me again of why I hired you?"

"My charm!" said Becky. "Wit. Personality. Should I keep going? Because I can."

"You sure there wasn't something in there about work?"

Becky screwed up her mouth and tapped her chin. "Eh, I don't think so."

"Just checking."

Becky opened the refrigerator and grabbed the beers Jim asked for. She placed them in a galvanized bucket and slid it across the bar to him.

Jim took it and headed toward his post. "Thank you, Becky."

"I might need a raise after this."

"Put it in writing," Jim said. "Then choke on it."

"Asshole!"

When Jim reached the door, he uncapped the beers and handed one to Hugh, Ian, and Shade. Everyone else in the roadhouse was helping to clean up for the night or preparing to head home. Jim wasn't sure when he'd be clearing out. It had the makings of a long night.

Jim drained half his beer in one long swallow, then nodded at Shade. "I'm ready."

"One at a time in an orderly fashion," Shade commanded.

People listened. They moved through the line at a metered pace. They were polite to the roadhouse staff and to each other. Some tried to engage in conversation or ask questions, but Jim kept them moving by saying their questions would have to wait until the next day.

The more converters Jim handed out, the longer the line grew, with no end in sight. As if some cruel God had determined that this would be Jim's punishment for his long list of misdeeds—to hand out power converters for eternity to a never-ending line of tired and dirty people.

They handed out more than four hundred converters before the line was gone. It was well after midnight by that point. Jim was a little drunk and a lot tired. The only tension in the whole process was when a single group of familiar faces passed through the line. It was Dr. Byron Nelson and Blake Justice, the two ringleaders of the group who'd originally come to steal the converters on the night they arrived.

Jim braced himself for some smart-assed comment at a minimum, but there weren't any. Just an outstretched hand, a neutral look, and then they were gone. Even though they were entitled to a converter just like everyone else, it pissed Jim off a little. These weren't the devices left by Lightspeed's people. Hugh had risked his life to bring them home and a little gratitude was in order.

Jim let it pass. This wasn't the time or place, and he was too tired to say anything about it. Of course, he wasn't the kind of man to forget such things, either. There was a chalkboard in his head where these things were tallied, and it was a damn big chalkboard. He'd make a note there and he'd always remember. Such slights might not be the kind of thing he killed men over, but they could make a difference in whether he was willing to lend them a hand or not in their time of need.

Right now, Jim was inclined to think...not.

30

Exhausted, Jim didn't leave for home until the wee hours of the morning. Even when he finally managed to escape the roadhouse, Hugh chose to stay behind, not wanting to let the precious converters out of his sight until they found their permanent homes. The security situation at the roadhouse had been heightened since the arrival of that first load of converters. Jim was anxious to put that behind them and get back to their normal state of paranoia. That had been comfortable to him; this was not.

Once he made it into bed, he slept a little later than usual, a sign that the stress of recent events was wearing on him. He rarely slept past daylight. When he finally got up, he had his regular glass of cold water to shock his innards awake.

"Sleep well?" Ellen asked.

Jim gave a weary nod that turned into a yawn.

"I didn't," Ariel said. "You snore like a lawnmower."

"I apologize," said Jim. "Maybe you should sleep in the barn from now on. I'm sure it's quieter in there."

Ariel fumed in mock anger. "Maybe *you* should. You *smell* like you belong in a barn." She cackled with delight. There was nothing she enjoyed more than harassing her dad.

Jim took a whiff of his shirt. "You're right, Ariel. Maybe I should hug you really tight. I bet the smell will rub off on you and then we'll smell just alike. The smell won't bother you as much when you're stinky too."

Jim took a step in her direction and she was gone in a flash, out the front door and into the yard. Jim was still smiling at her when he caught Ellen's eye.

"You do kind of smell ripe," she said.

Jim shrugged. "I've been a little busy."

"If you're not going into town today you should include a bath on that To Do list of yours. A long one with lots of soap."

"Speaking of town, where's my pack?"

Ellen shot him a look. "Change your mind? Heading into town after all?"

"No, I just need my pack."

"It's beside the gun rack in the living room. You left it in the middle of the floor when you got home."

"I was tired." Jim headed into the next room and found his pack on the floor by the gun rack. They'd never had a gun rack in the living room until the collapse. Most of their guns stayed in the gun safe in his bedroom, with a few exceptions. However, with the number of threats they'd had to deal with since the lights went out, it became necessary to keep weapons at hand all the time.

Jim retrieved his pack and took it back into the kitchen. He set it on the table, unzipped it, and rooted around inside. He found what he was looking for and came out with the round plastic device he'd brought home from the roadhouse.

Ellen stopped what she was doing and stared at him. "Is that…?"

He nodded. "It is."

"Are you…?"

"I am."

Jim headed down to the basement with Ellen hot on his heels. He turned off his primitive solar setup, then went to the breaker box. He left the main breaker on, turned off all the circuits, then left through the basement door. Ellen followed, staring over his shoulder as Jim approached the electric meter and used a multitool to cut the power company's safety tag loose from the meter base. He tossed the tag, opened the metal lid, and pulled the meter loose. Uncertain of what to do with it, he dropped the old meter in the grass at his feet, then studied the converter to orient it correctly. When he had it aligned, he pressed it into the socket that had once held the meter.

"Is it working?" Ellen asked urgently.

Jim pointed to the lights on the front of the converter. "It has to acquire a signal and go through some diagnostics, then it powers up. Once we get a green light, we go downstairs and carefully energize the house circuits one at a time."

Seconds later, the green LED illuminated and Jim replaced the metal cover on the meter base. The converter was sized so that the lid to the meter base would go back in place and hopefully prevent theft of the converter once the cover was secured with a lock. Jim was impressed at the thought Lightspeed had put into all this. Even aside from the miracle of wireless power, it was amazing how Lightspeed had considered every little detail. Once the cover was back in place, they returned to the basement.

When they reached the breaker box, Jim used a voltage detector to verify that power was reaching the main breaker. It was a device roughly the size and shape of a magic marker that beeped in the presence of electricity. The advantage of the detector over a tester was that it could sense voltage through the wire's insulation without making contact with an energized wire.

"Why did you have to turn every circuit off?" Ellen asked. "They all worked fine when the lights went out."

"Yeah, but we don't know what got left on. We don't want to turn on a freezer breaker if the freezer is empty and standing open. We don't want to turn on the water heater breaker if the tank is empty or the elements might blow. We have to make sure that each circuit is safe. The converter is supposed to detect shorts and faults, but that doesn't mean it will detect every unsafe or wasteful condition."

Ellen looked around anxiously. "Turn on something we can see. I need to see it working."

"The basement lights." Jim flipped a breaker. When nothing happened, he pointed to the wall. "The switch, Ellen. Hit the switch."

Ellen stepped over to the cinderblock wall and flipped the switch mounted there. Dusty incandescent bulbs illuminated, glowing yellow and casting a harsh eye on the messy chaos of the basement. "This place needs cleaned."

Jim laughed. "Maybe it's finally time we can do that. Having power will free us from a lot of chores."

"We might be able to go back to living something closer to a normal life."

Jim winced. "I hope so, but don't jinx us."

They worked together to go through the entire breaker box. They flipped a double-pole breaker and the heat pump kicked on, smelling up the house as it burned a year's worth of dust off the heating coils. They flipped another and the water heater—now confirmed as being full of water—gurgled and crackled.

Twenty minutes later, they walked through the entire house, amazed at all the electricity around them. Digital displays flashed multicolored numbers as they waited to be set to the proper time. TVs were on, showing nothing but static and playing their oddly soothing white noise. Somewhere an alarm clock beeped.

Jim shook his head. "We were born into this technology and were never without it for more than a few days in our entire lives. Hell, we used to take the kids camping to get away from it. Now I feel like I'm walking through an alien spaceship."

"I know this sounds crazy, but you can almost feel it in the walls, can't you?"

"Yeah, I *love* it but I'm not sure I *like* it, if you know what I mean."

"I know," Ellen said. "It's an odd feeling to want something so badly yet dread the impact it will have on your life going forward. The kids will go back to video games and the internet. We'll go back to Netflix."

"Yeah. At the same time, though, I'm not ready to give up on electricity. In one of his radio addresses, Lightspeed said there were these people called Luddites who'd made that decision. They didn't want it anymore, decided they were better off without it. Some of them were even sabotaging the power to keep other people from getting it."

"I can see their point, but I hope no one around here tries to sabotage it. I'm not sure I could take that. It was bad enough to lose it the first time. To lose it again would be...devastating."

Jim sighed. "Keep an eye on things if you don't mind. Make sure nothing was left on that's going to start a fire."

"Where are you going? I thought you were going to take it easy today?"

Jim jabbed a thumb toward the kitchen. "I plan on staying in the valley, but I have a stack of those converters in my pack. I'm assuming some of the other folks will want them too. I'm going to saddle a horse and make the rounds."

Ellen face clouded and she looked away.

Jim put an arm around her. "I'll be home as soon as I can."

Ellen shook her head. "It's not that you're going out. That's fine. I just got lost in my thoughts for a second. I was just thinking about things eventually getting back to normal one day and what that would mean for our friends in the valley. There are probably heirs out there who'll inherit the house Randi is living in and they might want it back. Same with the house Gary and his family are living in. Even Hugh's trailer."

"Of everyone, Hugh is the one I'm least concerned about. That guy is as adaptable as a chameleon. He'll always land on his feet. As far as those other houses go, it could be years before all that gets straightened out. A lot of records have been lost, and don't forget that the majority of the population died."

"That's hard to believe," Ellen said. "Every time you say that, it floors me."

"In one of his radio addresses, Lightspeed said it appeared that 85-90 percent of the entire country had died, just as the studies predicted would happen in a major disaster. On a national scale, imagine how many people are in the same situation as Gary and Randi, living in houses they don't have titles to. This problem might *never* be fixed in our lifetime."

31

Jim took his time getting his gear together and saddling his horse. When he was ready, he slung his rifle around his neck and mounted up. He steered his horse toward the open gate that stood between his backyard and Randi's place on the far side of a pasture. Since her house was the closest, it was the logical place to start. He'd considered sending a converter with Lloyd so he could install it, but decided there was no point. As safe as the device was, Lloyd would have found some way to electrocute himself *if* he ever got around to putting it in.

It was a beautiful day as late fall went. The nighttime temperatures had dropped into the low forties, but the day was headed toward the upper fifties based on the warmth of the sun. That was entirely a guess on Jim's part. He hoped Lightspeed had someone working on a weather app because the forecast was one of the things he missed the most. Without it, he'd been caught unprepared more than once. Now he was reduced to trying to predict the weather like a mountain granny lady, based on the shading of wooly worms, the behavior of wildlife, the number of frosts they experienced, and the intensity of a random pain in the small of his back.

All around, there were signs of one season reluctant to succumb to the next. The high pasture grass that had fed horses, cattle, and deer all summer had gone brown but refused to lie down and die. The colorful leaves that made this region so beautiful in the fall were all the same tone of rusty brown now and most had fallen to the ground. The deer Jim spotted at the treeline were dark brown as their winter fur came in. Squirrels were practically hysterical with the desire to store away acorns, walnuts, and hickory nuts.

As he closed in on Randi's house, Jim heard signs of life before he saw them. Randi's grandchildren were playing in the yard while Lloyd oversaw them, butchering a Chuck Berry song on the banjo.

"What the hell are you doing?" Jim asked as he got closer.

"Maybelline."

Jim gestured at the children. "With them. Are you supposed to be watching them?"

"I *am* watching them. I'm the responsible adult in charge."

"Well, that one is eating dirt with a spoon. He's drooling mud."

Lloyd waved him off. "I ate dirt too and I turned out just fine."

"The way you turned out, it must have had uranium in it. Where is everyone, anyway? How'd they get so desperate as to leave *you* watching the kids?"

Lloyd tipped his head toward the house. "Randi's roots were past her ears, and she managed to trade for some hair dye yesterday."

"Where are her daughters?"

"They're in there with her. Apparently, it's a three-person job once you get to a certain age."

"Your mouth will be the death of you, Lloyd."

The front door opened suddenly and Randi emerged from the house with damp hair and a towel draped over her shoulders. She looked at Jim and frowned, her customary greeting for him. "I heard the jawing and wondered who was out here."

Jim waved but Randi didn't return the gesture. "I don't know why you scowl every time you see me, Randi. You'd think a woman who kept company with the likes of Lloyd wouldn't be so particular."

Lloyd wagged a finger at Jim. "Don't you go blaming me for this. From what I hear, Randi had something of a reputation long before I came on the scene.

Randi's daughters both covered their mouths in shock. Randi stormed toward Lloyd, hands on her hips. "You did *not* just say what I thought you said. Tell me I misheard you before that stupid ass comment goes down as your dying words."

"So what brings you here this fine morning, Jim?" Lloyd asked, desperate to change the subject.

Jim didn't answer. Something had caught his eye and he was staring intently at Randi. She was in the sunlight now and it was easier to see the change in her appearance. He knew he shouldn't say anything, but he couldn't stop himself. "Why the hell did you dye your hair green, Randi? You entering your emo phase?"

Lloyd laughed so hard he nearly rolled off the porch. Randi spun around, cocked her head at Jim, and glared at him with venom in her eyes. "It. Wasn't. Supposed. To be. Green."

Jim shrugged. "Well, it is. With summer gone, you're probably the greenest thing for two hundred miles."

Randi yanked the towel off her shoulders, balled it up, and threw it at Jim. His horse flinched, Jim dodged, and the wet towel went sailing past him.

"Don't hate me for stating the obvious."

Randi balled her fists, sucked in a couple of deep breaths, and closed her eyes. When she reopened them, she spoke slowly. "Sherry took cosmetology in high school." She indicated her oldest daughter. "She thinks there might have been a reaction between the hair dye and minerals in the water here in the valley. It might not have been so noticeable had my hair not been so light in color."

"By light, do you mean gray?" Lloyd asked.

Randi lashed out with a foot, kicking Lloyd in the thigh. He howled and frowned at her.

"What was that, Lloyd?"

"I was saying how lovely your hair is," Lloyd corrected.

"Damn right you were."

"Kind of like lime Jello," he continued. "My favorite flavor. Nothing wrong with that."

"Don't push it." She turned her attention back to Jim. "Why are you here?"

Jim reached into the pack he had hanging from his saddle horn, extracted one of the converters, and held it up for Randi to see. "I come bearing electricity."

Randi's change in expression belied the gravity of the moment. Her irritation at Lloyd and Jim fell away. Her concern for her hair emergency was forgotten. While she'd known she would eventually get it, the arrival of power was a sobering moment. "Are you going to put it in?"

At the same time, both gave Lloyd a disappointed look. For Randi, it was to explain her request, pointing out that Lloyd was useless for anything that even resembled work. For Jim, it was further validation of why he'd chosen to go ahead and install the device for Randi. Lloyd was oblivious to their judgment, absently picking away at his banjo.

"Is the back door open?" Jim asked.

When Randi nodded that it was, Jim rode around back and dismounted. He tied his horse off to the rail and climbed onto the back porch. Like a lot of older farmhouses, the breaker box was located outside on the porch itself. Within a matter of minutes, Jim had turned off all the breakers and replaced the meter with the converter. He was waiting for the green light on the converter to illuminate when Lloyd came strolling out the back door. Fortunately, he'd left his banjo inside.

"You must have screwed it up," Lloyd pronounced. "Nothing is working."

Jim spoke with exaggerated patience. "There's a process and it involves a few different steps. That's why I'm the one doing it and not you."

"Was that an insult?" Lloyd asked.

"Most definitely."

When he got a green light from the converter, Jim made a quick pass through the house to make sure there was nothing blatantly amiss with the wiring. Randi's grandchildren were a bit on the feral side, and it wouldn't be out of the ordinary for them to have jammed a fork into a receptacle or even to have pulled the wiring directly out of the wall in an effort to strangle a cat.

As he made his tentative inspection, Randi's entire family followed him from room to room, finishing near the front door. There were the two grandchildren with their dirt-stained lips, the two daughters with their green-stained hands, and green-haired Randi looking like some punk rock grandma. Lloyd had settled into a recliner and was plucking his banjo. Of everyone, he was the least interested in the return of electricity. In fact, he seemed downright disappointed by it.

Finding nothing amiss with the home's electrical system, Jim went back to the breaker box and flipped the first breaker, marked "Living Room Lights." If he was going to do this, he might as well make it something dramatic. The cheers and applause from the living room told him that something noteworthy had indeed taken place there. He flipped a second breaker and the cheers got even louder. That one had energized the receptacles in the living room and Jim assumed something just as remarkable as the illumination of the overhead lights must have happened.

He kept flipping breakers. The cheers became more sporadic as some of the energized circuits affected parts of the home that were less obvious. All went smoothly until he hit the double-poled breaker for the kitchen stove. When he flipped that one, there was a loud popping sound from the house, accompanied by startled cries. The breaker immediately tripped.

When Jim went inside to investigate, Lloyd shot him an accusing look. "I knew this was a bad idea. Sounds like you almost burned the house down."

Jim ignored him and headed for the kitchen to see what had caused the fault. Randi joined him there and they found a thin tendril of smoke rising from the stove.

Jim shrugged. "I think something might be wrong with your

stove, but I'm sure we can find you another one. Visit the empty houses and pick one."

Randi stared at the smoking stove for a moment. "Boys!"

Her grandchildren obediently trotted into the kitchen.

"Have you two been messing with the stove?"

The oldest, still of preschool age, stuck out his chest and folded his arms across it. "Ain't a stove, Granny. That's a squirrel jail. We put them in there when we catch them."

"How many squirrels are in jail right now?" Jim asked.

"A couple," said the boy. "Some have been in there a long time, like my Daddy."

Randi lowered her face into her hands and slowly shook her head. Jim stepped forward and cautiously opened the door a crack. Inside, he saw that the buildup of feces and urine had completely covered the bottom element of the stove, likely shorting it out when he turned the power on. Five squirrels lay smoldering, having died from electrocution when the damp floor beneath them was suddenly electrified.

"They alright?" the boy asked.

Jim shook his head. "Dead as disco."

Randi swatted the oldest boy on the head. "What the hell were you thinking?"

"They were bad squirrels. Do the crime, do the time," the boy replied. "That's what you always say."

"Lloyd!" Randi called.

Jim heard the creak of the recliner as Lloyd climbed out of it and made his way into the kitchen.

"Yes, my prickly princess? My green goddess?"

Randi swatted him too, aiming for the belly. "Get this stove out of my house *now*."

"Smells funny," Lloyd said. He opened the door to peer inside. He recoiled and waved a hand in front of his face. "No wonder."

"I don't care what you do with it," Randi said. "Just get it out of here."

Lloyd swatted at Jim in the same manner as Randi had swatted him. "You heard the woman. Get this stove out of here, Jim."

Jim headed for the back door. "Not my circus, not my monkeys. My work is done here."

32

It took Jim several more hours to make the rounds to Gary's house and then to Buddy's old house, where Pete and Charlie were living. He also stopped at a few other houses in the valley belonging to neighbors who weren't part of his clan. He took the time to install the devices at Gary's and Buddy's homes, making sure everything was safe before he left. For those folks who weren't part of his circle, Jim carefully explained the installation but left them to do the work.

By the time he was done with his rounds, Jim was getting hungry. He didn't know the time but suspected it was well past lunchtime. He was also feeling a little tired after all the long days and late nights recently. He considered doing something he hadn't done in a long time and stretching out in the hammock in the backyard. The day was a little cool, but it should be perfect with a sleeping bag draped over him.

After letting himself through the gate at the end of his driveway, he was nearly to the house, visions of that hammock filling his brain, when he noticed three horses tied in his front yard. As he got closer, he recognized the horses, just as he recognized the three riders who sat waiting for him on the porch steps.

"Took you long enough," Pops said when Jim reached the house.

"Save the smart comments, Pops. I'm too tired and too hungry to listen to it. What are you guys up to?"

Pops looked off in the distance, pouting at Jim's harsh tone.

Jim looked at the other two people sitting on the steps. "Pete? Charlie? What are you guys up to? Did you come over for lunch?"

The two looked at each other before Pete answered. "Pops wants us to take him to his house. When he heard you were going around turning the power on, he decided he wanted his turned on at his house."

"This is your house," Jim said. "You live with us now."

Pops shook his head. "Our *real* house. Nana's house."

Jim sighed and tried to remain patient. He understood what Pops was feeling but he hadn't planned on him wanting to make the move so quickly. The timing wasn't great. When Jim was tired and hungry, it was not the time to spring surprises on him. "I'm guessing you need me to go."

"No one needs anything from you," Pops announced, still not looking at Jim.

"Sorry I snapped at you, Pops, but I'm starving to death," Jim said. "And yes, you probably *do* need me to come if you want the converter installed."

"You said the converter had instructions." Pops gestured at Pete and Charlie. "I figured those boys could do it if I was looking over their shoulders. I know my way around electricity."

Though he didn't say it, Jim thought this was a case of the blind leading the blind. Pete and Charlie were no more adept at electrical work than Pops was. The three of them installing a converter sounded like a disaster waiting to happen.

"I'll go with you," Jim said. "I need a second to get a drink and some food. Will that work?"

Pops shrugged. "I reckon. We waited on you this long. Not sure what difference waiting a little longer is going to make."

Jim gritted his teeth but held his tongue. Whatever he drank with his lunch probably needed a shot or two of liquor in it if Pops was going to keep this attitude. Jim climbed off his horse and handed the reins off to Pete. "Please water my horse while I'm getting something to eat."

Pete did as he was asked, taking the reins from Jim and leading the horse toward a watering trough beside the barn. Jim had a lot of questions for Pops, specifically around his plans and timeline for moving, but he didn't have the patience to get into that now. It would only lead to more debate and hard feelings.

Ellen was waiting for him just inside the door. "You spoke to the welcoming committee out there?"

Jim grabbed his water glass off the side of the sink and opened the faucet, filling the glass with cold spring water. "I did. I'm going into town with them. Where's Nana? I'm surprised she wasn't waiting on me too."

"She's taking a nap. It isn't like her, but she said she wasn't feeling well. And I'm glad you're going with them. They're good boys and they want to help Pops, but I don't want anyone getting hurt."

Jim drained the glass of water, then refilled it. "I don't want anyone hurt either, but I need something to eat first. I'm seriously hangry."

Ellen grabbed a collapsible lunchbox from the counter and held it out to Jim. "I went ahead and made you a lunch, just in case."

Jim took it reluctantly. "I'd really like to sit down and eat, but the sooner I leave, the sooner I get back."

Ellen leaned forward and kissed him on the cheek. "That's entirely true. Good luck."

"I'm going to need it." Jim opened a kitchen cabinet.

"I packed everything you'll need," Ellen said.

"Did you pack tequila?"

She frowned. "Uh, no."

Jim rummaged around in the cabinet until he found a bottle someone had brought into the roadhouse to trade. He used his shirt tail to wipe out a dusty shot glass, then poured it full. He downed the shot, recalling the days he'd done this with salt and lemon for fun. Now it was strictly "medicinal." It took a second dose to make him feel like he was up to the trip, then he put the bottle back and closed the cabinet.

"Better?" Ellen asked.

"Tolerable." Jim opened the lunchbox and grabbed a sandwich of homemade bread, cheese, tomato, and bacon. "I'm not sure when I'll be back. If I'm going into town I might as well stop at the roadhouse."

"I'll see you when I see you. Be careful."

Jim took a bite of his sandwich and, still chewing, returned to the porch. Pete was standing there with his horse as it slavered green strings of saliva onto the ground.

"I'm ready," Jim announced.

Pete handed over the reins to Jim's horse. Jim led it a short distance away and checked that the saddle was still snug after the morning's ride. He did a quick pass over his gear, making sure he had what he needed for a trip into town. When he was comfortable that he did, he hung the lunchbox over his saddle horn and mounted up.

Pete, the good boy that he was, patiently led Pops' horse to the porch steps and waited for him to climb on, just as Jim had done with Pops the other day. Once Pops was steady in the saddle, Pete took his horse from Charlie, and the four of them rode off down the driveway. Charlie rode ahead and held the gate open for them, then shut it once they were all through.

"I didn't realize you were in such a hurry to move out," Jim told Pops. "Young people these days. So impatient."

Pops laughed. "You'd be the same way if the shoe was on the other foot, chomping at the bit to get back to your own place. Nana and I worked for years to build that house. The plan was that we'd retire and spend our golden years there. This is *not* what we counted on. The years are more rusty than golden."

"No one counted on this," Jim pointed out.

"Maybe not, but we really need to be home. We've both been in a funk lately and I think that's part of it. Our time is running out and we want to die at home, doing the things we like to do."

"What the hell, Dad? No one's dying. What brought that on?" Jim cut a sideways glance at Pete, wondering how he'd handle such a frank discussion of his grandparents' mortality. He was a sensitive kid, or he had been before the collapse. Now, Jim wasn't so sure anymore.

"Fat lot you know," Pops said. "We're all dying every day. Even you."

"Am I dying too?" Pete asked, suddenly concerned.

There was the sensitive Pete Jim had been waiting on. Jim jumped in to smooth over whatever damage his dad had done. "No, Pete. You're not dying. You have an entire lifetime ahead of you. Pops is just experiencing a moment of dementia."

Jim shot his father a look telling him to change the subject, but Pops either didn't get the message or didn't care.

"Jim, a person senses these things. I've seen it all my life, especially when I was a kid and we were around the old folks more. I used to think there was something scary or mysterious about it, but it's not like that. I think the veil gets thinner—the barrier between this world and the next. You feel like the people you lost are a little closer than they once were. Like you can talk to them and they hear you. Sometimes you think you see them."

"You see Heaven?" Charlie asked. "Or ghosts?"

Jim knew what Charlie was thinking. Charlie had to be wondering if Pops could see his mother, Alice. She was an old coworker of Jim's who'd died getting Charlie to the valley because she thought he'd be safer there. Charlie rarely talked about her, but everyone knew he'd struggled to redefine his sense of family after losing his.

"It's not what I see, but what I feel. Like the dead want you to know they're right there waiting on you. Like they're swimming in a lake and telling you to come on in because the water is fine. There are things that I see, but it's not ghosts."

Jim asked, "What do you see?" A minute ago he'd been trying to end this conversation, now he needed to know the answer.

Pops shifted, resting both hands on the saddle horn, reins laced between his fingers and hanging loose. For the moment he looked like a man who'd spent most of his life in the saddle. Like he was the elder statesman of a cattle drive passing on a lifetime's worth of wisdom to the younger generation.

"It's more like a change in the quality of light. Like the sun breaking through after a storm or when you get some amazing sunset because there's a forest fire upwind of you. It's kind of like that, except it doesn't go away. It just shows up one day and I assume it's with you until you pass over."

"That's weird," Pete said. "It's freaking me out a little."

Pops laughed. "It is weird, Pete, but just because things are weird or uncomfortable doesn't change the fact they exist."

"But how can that *really* exist if you see it and I don't?" Charlie asked. "If something exists, wouldn't we all see it the same way? Like seeing that light you're talking about?"

"I used to think that," said Pops. "It's only been in the last year that I've begun to realize our experience of the world is pretty much just that. *Our* experience. It's filtered through a lens made of the events that shaped us, our memories, our beliefs, our biases, and many more things. You ever tell a story about something and have another person who was there tell you that things didn't happen the way you were saying?"

Pete and Charlie looked at each other, then grinned at the same time.

"All the time," Pete said.

"Both of you could be telling the truth," Pops said. "Just because your stories are different doesn't mean that one of you is lying. It just means that you experienced the situation differently."

"I'm getting lost here," Jim said. "Circle back around to the beginning. Why are we talking about this?"

"All I'm saying is there's a change in the air that you guys aren't old enough to see yet, but I am. I think Nana sees it too, though we don't really talk about that kind of thing."

"Can't imagine why," Pete said. "It's such a cheery subject."

Jim laughed. Pete might have his mother's soft heart, but he had a touch of his dad's smartass mouth too.

"Hopefully you all live long enough to understand what I'm

talking about one day." Pops tilted his head. "It'll make sense then and I hope you remember this day."

"What do you want us to remember, Pops?" Jim asked, curious how he'd summarize it.

"I want you to remember a road trip with family on a beautiful day. I want you to remember the feeling of helping someone who outlived their independence. I want you to remember being among people to whom you were bound by blood." Pops glanced at Charlie. "That includes you too, young man."

Jim made a note of what Pops said, but immediately pushed it far back into the recesses of his mind, into a dusty disused corner where he wouldn't trip over it. Although there might be a day when he wanted or needed that memory, he didn't have room in his heart for it now. It simply was too damned sad to dwell on.

33

The ride through town was a more relaxed experience than it had been in the early months of the collapse. People had been wary then and their fear made them dangerous. They had peered at passers-by from endarkened houses like the spectral inhabitants of a ghost town. During those days, Jim and his people went miles out of their way to bypass town. They didn't do that any longer.

The farmer's market had made people more accustomed to traffic again and they were less uneasy with each other. The arrival of the Reset Roadhouse had created yet another opportunity for people to interact with each other in a more conventional fashion. Despite the apocalypse, the existence of even a few familiar rituals comforted and reassured people.

It was a beautiful day and the town was active. The farmer's market was crowded with people selling end of the year produce, eggs, and baked goods. Now that electricity promised a return to refrigeration, some forward-thinking farmers were taking orders for meat. They displayed prices for cuts of lamb, pork, beef, bison, ostrich, and goat, which they would deliver to customers in the coming weeks. Though Jim, Pops, Pete, and Charlie didn't pass directly through the market, they saw people leaving with purchases tucked beneath their arms, in the baskets of bicycles, or crammed into backpacks.

As he typically did when travelling through town with Pete and Charlie, Pops delivered a running monologue about all the things around them. Pops had given up on telling Jim those stories and now directed them toward a younger, more enthusiastic audience. Although Pops hadn't been born in the town, by this point he'd lived there most of his life. It wasn't his hometown, but it had become home.

Decades working in education and politics had presented Pops with the opportunity to hear lots of stories and learn the history of the town. With Pete and Charlie being teenage boys, the more scandalous, sordid, or lurid tales were their favorites. Pops knew how to play to his audience, and he regaled them with stories of crimes that had gone unpunished and murders for which no one had ever been charged. He spoke of secret love and public madness and spun numerous examples of how money had insulated the guilty, while the lack of money had left innocent men unable to prove their innocence. He was in the middle of one of those stories, gesticulating wildly, when a man standing in the yard of a Main Street home called to him.

"Afternoon, Mr. Powell! You out seeing the sights today?"

Pops stopped midsentence and squinted in the man's direction, the bright overhead sun making it difficult for him to see the speaker. He shaded his eyes and a grin split his face. "Mr. Irving, how are you, sir?" Pops steered his horse over to the sidewalk and carefully leaned over to shake the man's hand. "I apologize for not getting down to shake your hand, but it's not the easiest thing to get back up here. My equestrian days should have been far behind me."

Mr. Irving was a little older than Jim, not quite as old as Pops. He'd retired from the Forest Service and lived in a neat, ordinary house along Main Street. It was one of the aluminum-sided ranch houses that sprang up on nearly every vacant lot when the town hit a growth spurt in the late 1960s. "I'd have said the same thing about my days of splitting wood, but as you can see, that's what I'm out here doing."

"Better to do it now than to be forced to scavenge for wood mid-winter," Jim pointed out.

"Wood is plentiful now," Mr. Irving said. "I got this from a neighbor. They spent all summer collecting it and splitting it, and now they're giving it away since the power came back."

"Really?" Jim asked.

Mr. Irving shrugged. "I grew up with wood and I've always burned wood. I'll burn it whether I have power or not. For some of these folks, wood heat requires too much sweat equity."

"I prefer wood heat also," said Jim.

"I'm going to have to side with the folks who gave you the wood," Pops said. "Once I have power at my house, I hope to never kindle another fire in whatever life I have left. I'll just stroll to the thermostat and push it as high as I want. Whatever allure the flame once had for me is long gone. There will be no more wiener roasts at a bonfire, no more smores or toasted marshmallows, no more chestnuts roasting upon my hearth. I want modern convenience for the rest of my days."

"What about you boys?" Mr. Irving asked, looking at Pete and Charlie. "You guys like wood heat?"

The two young men exchanged glances and shrugged.

"I grew up with it," Pete said. "It smells like home to me."

"It's growing on me," Charlie said. "It's cozy."

"Kids these days," Pops lamented. "Can't do anything with them."

"We better get moving," Jim said. "Our day isn't over yet."

The group didn't have to ride very far to confirm that what Mr. Irving had told them was true. Not only had the restoration of power energized the *homes* of Main Street, it had energized those residing in the homes as well. Several homes had windows open, airing out their musty, smoke-infused interiors. Music spilled from some of the open windows as various music sources were rediscovered. The boom boxes and cassette players from closets, record players from attics,

CD players from garages, and MP3 devices with their Bluetooth speakers.

Wood stoves had been dragged out onto front porches and either shoved up against walls or rolled out into yards with utter disdain. Sections of sooty black stove pipe had been discarded with abandon, as if evidence of some shameful period that no one wished to remember or discuss ever again. Firewood, a precious resource only weeks ago, was now evidence of an undesirable and ancient technology. Some stacks had scrawled signs stuck on them advertising wood free for the taking.

A man with an orange extension cord used an electric weed whacker to assault a waist-high lawn. It was slow work and of questionable quality, but the homeowner approached the battle with dogged determination. Despite his efforts, the yard looked like a child's attempt to cut their own hair. Another homeowner used an electric pressure washer to clean the front of his house, appearing to enjoy a task that would have once been mundane drudgery. Multiple people worked around their homes with power tools, making long overdue repairs with whatever materials they had available to them.

"It's like a Saturday morning back in the old world," Pops said. "All the weekend warriors hard at work."

"Or some scraggly, apocalyptic version of a Saturday," said Jim.

"It's nice to see people making an effort again," Pops said. "Everyone has been so defeated and beaten down by the events of the last year and a half. It's nice to see them caring about things again."

Jim wasn't impressed by the way everyone was quick to leap back into the trappings of normality. "They might be caring about the wrong things. I worry that we're getting ahead of ourselves. This isn't like restoring power after an ice storm. This is a new, unproven technology. I mean, it's working now, but it seems a little sketchy. We're entirely reliant on a big orange weather balloon, for God's sake. What if it fails?"

Pops shot Jim a disappointed expression. "You know, I've understood your pessimism and negativity throughout much of this disaster, Jim. While I didn't agree with it, I understood that you were trying to keep people from getting their hopes up. You wanted them to be realistic and deal with the problem in front of them instead of waiting for a rescue that wasn't going to come."

"Exactly!" Jim agreed.

"Well, rescue came," Pops said. "Now's the time for the negative Nellies to go sit in the corner and be quiet. Let people have their moment in the sun. Let these people clean, trim, repair, and whatever else they're doing."

"Hey, I'm not stopping them," Jim said in his defense.

"No, but you're judging them."

Jim smiled, but it was a worried smile. "Yes, I am doing that."

"Then do it silently. People need this moment."

Despite his harsh words, Pops wasn't angry or accusatory in his comments. Jim also understood Pops' comments had nothing whatsoever to do with any of the people they'd passed in town. His remarks were entirely about himself and his dream of restoring power to his home so that he and Nana could move back in there. He wasn't telling simply Jim to leave those people alone, he was telling Jim to leave *him* alone. If Lightspeed's wireless power grid really was fragile and might disintegrate at the first strong wind, Pops didn't want to know. He wanted to get back to his home with his wife and pretend that life was normal again.

From the corner of his eye, Jim saw Pete and Charlie watching him, waiting to see if he would present further argument. He didn't. He winked at the boys, a gesture he frequently made to them when he was humoring Pops. Even in his acquiescence Jim understood that the significance of this debate was far greater than most of the disagreements he and Pops had. This was about that last stubborn, tenacious thread of hope that kept everyone going through this dark period. It was about honoring the possibility of a future and a return to better times. If there truly existed the possibility that there might *not* be better times ahead, then it was about allowing people to maintain that illusion.

They rode in silence for several minutes. Jim finally broke it when they reached the center of town, with its red light and confederate statue. "It looks like someone has been cleaning up the downtown."

Someone had gathered all the leaves, debris, and trash from the main downtown area and burned it all in a parking space off to the side of the street. It was a small gesture that made the town feel as if it were occupied by people who still cared.

Pops smiled. "Yes, it does. It does indeed."

34

Pops and Nana's home had been relatively untouched since they moved most of their belongings out to Jim's place. When weather and time permitted, Pops had visited there with Jim, Pete, Charlie, or whoever else was going into town. Even when Pops couldn't come, Pete and Charlie had accepted the assignment as one of their ongoing responsibilities, making sure the windows were intact and no one was living there. Nana had never made the trip, however. Pops said seeing the place was too hard on her and only served to depress her further.

"We're here!" Pops said cheerily as their horses clattered into the asphalt driveway.

Normally the driveway would have been immaculate, but it was plastered with damp leaves at the moment, and small branches broken loose by the wind were scattered around.

"I might need to get one of you boys up on the roof," Pops said, pointing to more leaves and branches on the roof. "We need to make sure those gutters aren't blocked off."

"I'll do it, Pops," Pete offered. "I've done it before."

Everyone dismounted and they tied their horses off to the decorative split-rail fence that lined one side of the driveway. Charlie held Pops' horse steady while Pete and Jim helped him down.

"Let's get those lights on!" Pops crowed, dusting his hands together. He was exuberant, almost giddy.

Jim retrieved a converter from his pack. "Not so fast, Pops. It has to be done right so we don't burn the house down."

Pops looked surprised. "I thought you said these things were safe?"

"They are, but we need to turn the breakers off in case any of your wiring was damaged or compromised in the last year."

"The house has been empty."

"Mice could have eaten the insulation off the wiring or built a nest in a wall box. The water heater has to be turned off so the elements don't blow. I know what I'm doing, Pops. Be patient just a little longer."

Pops fished his house keys from a pocket and headed for the front door. He unlocked it and stepped inside.

"We're going to get the ladder and clean out the gutters," Pete called from the driveway.

"Be careful," Jim said. "Don't fall off or you'll get a beating."

Pete made a face, uncertain if his dad was joking or not. "Yeah, okay."

Jim followed his father inside the house. As weird as it felt for Jim to be in his abandoned childhood home, he knew it had to feel even weirder to Pops. When Jim had been making his way back from Richmond, Nana and Pops had hastily packed up the home and moved out to Jim's place to help Ellen keep an eye on things. Once Jim got home, they'd made several trips back out there to find particular things Nana and Pops needed to make their stay at Jim's more comfortable. Even with all those rushed trips in and out of the house, even with the hasty packing, Pops had insisted that everything be left in perfect order. No open closets or drawers. Nothing left on the bed or floors.

"Your mother isn't going to like it if she comes back to a mess," Pops warned. "We have to leave this house just the way we found it."

That's how it was—a stale and slightly dusty time capsule of the way the home looked when they had walked out to go help Ellen. The pantry and cabinets had been emptied of food. The refrigerator and freezer had been cleaned out and the doors propped open. Other than that, it looked like they'd simply returned from vacation.

Pops led the way to the garage and Jim followed, using a flashlight to navigate the gloomy space. He pulled the emergency release on the electric garage door and raised it up to allow more light into the room. Jim cut off all the breakers, then went outside to the meter base. Over the course of a few minutes, he installed Lightspeed's converter, just as he'd done at all the other homes.

Once the LEDs on the converter indicated that it was synced up and energized, Jim went back to the garage, methodically re-electrifying parts of the house. As they turned them on a few at a time, Jim went into the house to make sure nothing was amiss. After about fifteen minutes, they had all the important breakers on and confirmed that everything was working as it should.

In the kitchen, the compressor beneath the refrigerator hummed as it started to cool. The LED displays of various appliances flickered, demanding to be set to the proper time. Pops insisted on trying every lamp and light switch, smiling as each came to life like some new and individual miracle.

"Can I turn on the heat pump?" he asked.

When Jim nodded, Pops went to the hallway and began tinkering with the thermostat. There was a rattle and a whoosh of air as the unit kicked to life.

"I smell something burning," Pops noted with alarm.

"It's the heating element. It's burning off the dust that's settled on it while the house was empty. It'll go away."

Pops didn't appear convinced, though he took Jim's word for it. They opened a few windows to let the smell out. While they waited for it to clear, Pops settled into *his* chair, a recliner in front of the television. He reclined it and closed his eyes. "This feels like home."

Jim settled onto the couch, noting the cloud of dust motes rising into the air when he plopped down. Everything would need to be vacuumed and dusted multiple times. Curtains and bedspreads would have to be washed. Jim was sure there were probably mice and bug issues to deal with also. You couldn't leave a house empty for a year and assume nothing else would move in.

"We need to check the plumbing," Jim said. "If you're wanting to move in, you'll need running water. There's no water source nearby. Not even a decent place to haul from."

Pops said, "I thought about that already. There's a creek about a mile away, but it's obviously not drinkable water. It would have to be treated."

"I'm not sure how long it will be before town water is restored. A lot of the treatment equipment requires three-phase power and Lightspeed's converters only provide single-phase power. I'm sure people will rig up something eventually to get water restored, but there's no telling how long it might take. You still determined to move out here?"

"I'm determined to come home," Pops said, stretched out in the recliner, eyes closed. "I'm going to bring your mother home."

"Then we'll find a way to make it happen."

Jim sat there listening to the sound of air whooshing out of the vents. The sound was unnatural after a year of no power, but that didn't mean it was unwelcome. It was a sound that implied ease, convenience, and the lessening of the burden required simply to survive. The hum of the refrigerator was the same way—a comforting lullaby of electricity. Jim heard Pete and Charlie walking around on the roof, cleaning the gutters, sounding like oversized squirrels skittering across the shingles.

"You know the house has a well, right?" Pops said.

Jim said. "I remember us having well water when I was a kid, but I forgot about it."

"It reeked of sulfur," Pops said. "When you were a kid, you called it 'suffer water' instead of sulfur. When the town ran water out this way, we quit using the well."

"Where's the wellhead?"

"Out back near the storage buildings. The pump is still hooked to the power, although I doubt it's been used in thirty years. There's an electrical disconnect mounted to one of the storage buildings that kills the power."

Jim got up. "I'll go take a look at it and see what I can figure out. I have a few spare well pumps at the house if we need one. We should be able to figure out a way to make it work."

35

When the group gathered beneath the picnic shelter at the Little League field grew restless, Cookie decided it was showtime.

"Here's goes nothing," he whispered to his wife. He stood from one of the picnic tables and took a position at one end of the concrete slab, raised his hands, and waved to get the group's attention. Judging by the number of full tables, he estimated he had a crowd of more than a hundred people.

"Good evening, folks. I sure appreciate you coming out."

The crowd grew silent and turned in their seats until they could all see him comfortably.

"For anyone who doesn't know me, people call me Cookie. I used to work at the building supply company here in town and I see some familiar faces that I probably waited on over the years. The reason I wanted to have this meeting is so we could talk about working together to improve our living conditions. Ever since last summer, we've worked together to keep livestock, improve sanitation, and try to keep the town cleaner. Now that some of us have power back, it's time we turn things up a notch.

"This where you ask for our vote?" an old man asked. "I smell someone running for office."

There was laughter from the crowd.

Cookie smiled patiently and shook his head. "I'm not running for anything. In fact, I believe government usually causes more problems than it solves. Our system of representative government quit representing us a long time ago. Politicians started working for themselves and not us."

There was a murmur of agreement from the crowd.

"That's not what we're here to talk about. Some of you may have seen the projects we've been working on around town this week. My family and I, along with a group of volunteers, have been working on cleaning up the government offices, the library, and the trashier parts of Main Street. We've also been working with the church there by the hospital, moving in basic equipment so we can open a clinic there. We already have doctors and nurses lined up, ready to start as soon as they have a place to work."

"Still looks like a ghost town," a man in a red-checked hunter's jacket remarked. "There's more empty houses and buildings than occupied."

"It *is* a ghost town!" a woman with a raspy smoker's voice growled. "The dead have outnumbered the living for some time now. It's like a waste of time fixing up a ghost town."

"We can't do anything about that," Cookie stated. "Do we roll into the grave alongside the dead, or do we try to live the best life we can?" When no one answered, he asked, "Do we give up too?"

Still, no one answered. It was as if the idea of giving up had crossed everyone's mind at some point and the thought remained rooted there, like a stubborn weed that came back no matter how many times it was pulled.

"We have power now," Cookie said, trying to energize his audience. "If anything, we've crested the toughest part of the hill and we're ready to coast down the other side. We have momentum working on our side. Life should get better. I think you can all agree that the winter ahead will be much easier with power than without. We can run lights, our furnaces, and we can watch DVDs on those days we're snowed in."

A thin woman with tattooed eyebrows shook her head. "Power don't fix everything."

The man at her side was nodding in agreement. "My refrigerator might be cold now, but it's still empty. My stove might work, but I've barely got anything to cook on it."

Cookie spread his arms wide. "I'm not the government and I'm not here to save you people. I'm not here to fix all your problems and lie to you about how easy things are going to be from now on. All I can do is look for ways that we can work together to share the burden. That's what this meeting is about. If you're interested in sharing the load, then I invite you to stick around and hear more. If you're the rugged individualist type who's done working with other people, then you might as well go on home before I waste any more of your time. If you've been beaten down too far and you're ready to roll into the grave and die, I don't need you here either. This is a meeting for those who refuse to die, those who still get out of bed each morning with hope in their hearts."

Several dozen among the crowd did get up and leave, making Cookie wonder what had brought them out to begin with. Had they thought there were going to be refreshments, or perhaps some piece of vital information they didn't want to miss out on? He didn't know.

He didn't blame them for leaving. Some people were communal by nature and some weren't. Society was like a battery, with some residing on the positive terminal and others residing on the negative. Cookie had learned it was best not to force or mislead people into participation if it wasn't in their nature to work together with others. It only led to discontent later. Once the group had thinned out, Cookie continued.

"Like I said, I'm not from the government, nor do I have any interest in being part of the government. Representative government has failed us due to the weakness of the men we elect into those positions. They may start out with noble goals, but the next thing you know, they put their own interests ahead of ours."

A pinch-faced man with a thin beard and no teeth stood up at the back of the crowd, his arms folded defiantly across his chest. "You ain't about to start throwing out any of that communist bullshit, are you? Because I ain't about to stand for that."

Cookie smiled. "No, I'm not throwing anything out, especially any communist bullshit. I'm just trying to talk about some ways we can work together to improve things. You all have heard me talk about the projects we're working on already. What are some other projects we could take on? What are some of the things that you see people needing that we could help with?"

The pinch-faced man remained on his feet. "Well, let me ask you another question. How do we guarantee that everyone puts forth the same amount of effort on these projects you're talking about? Do the sorry people get the same benefits as people who work hard?"

Cookie shrugged. "Right now, no one is getting *any* benefits. We're just trying to make life better for all of us and we could use more help. But to answer your question, not everyone can do as much. There are folks in town who are weak, sick, or injured. There are other folks who are in full-time caregiver positions now because they have someone in their home who requires care."

The man shook his head. "Sounds like the same old thing. The labor of a few supporting everyone else."

Cookie heaved a patient sigh and walked back to the picnic table where his family sat. He picked up a notepad and scribbled a hasty note. "I'll add that to the list of concerns," he said. What he'd actually written was, "I'm trying not to punch this asshole."

Feeling as if he'd been cut short, the pinch-faced man sat down, grumbling.

"I know everyone has a lot of concerns, but we can't fix all of them immediately," Cookie said. "We have to try and focus on the big picture."

"What's the big picture?" a woman wearing a dirty blanket as a shawl asked.

"The big picture is things like getting the library open so people can use it to educate their children. The big picture is trying to figure out how we can make the water plant work with less power so we can have clean running water for our houses this winter. And even though we're getting power, we can't forget that we have livestock on the football field that need to be tended this winter."

"How much longer we got to do that?" shawl woman asked.

Cookie frowned. "What?"

"Take care of livestock?" the woman asked. "If we got power, won't we be getting food soon?"

"From where?" Cookie asked.

The woman shrugged. "I don't know. I was hoping you'd know."

"I hear there could be aid shipments available in some nearby communities, but I don't know if they're coming to us," said Cookie. "I haven't heard anything that told me we should give up on our livestock. The idea of depending entirely on government aid sounds risky to me. Did they step in a year ago and save all the friends and neighbors we've lost? I don't trust them. I hardly trust anyone outside of my own family anymore."

Around the picnic shelter, people shook their heads. They all remembered that no one had come to save them during this crisis. Those who'd made it this far had done so through their own determination, resourcefulness, and grit.

"So with that in mind," Cookie continued, "there's a value in us moving forward as if no one is coming to save us because they haven't yet. I don't think we can assume help is coming any time soon."

An old man in a dirty suit stood up. The elbows were worn thin and the front was discolored, as if he wore it nearly every day. "If we're going to clean up the town, there's a lot more than the trash in the streets needs dealt with. We got whores and whoremongers. We got people selling marijuana and liquor right there in front of God and everybody. They's men in this town who've taken multiple wives and don't even have the decency to try and hide it."

"Amen!" said the quilt lady.

"Multiple wives?" a man said. "Hell, I don't even want the one I got."

The woman sitting beside him, apparently his offended wife, rolled her eyes and smacked him on the back of the head. There was laughter around the room. Soon there was chaos as everyone shouted out their opinions either against or in support of all the vices the man in the suit outlined.

Cookie and tried to regain control of the group. "Can we get back on track here? We still have a lot to cover."

The man in the suit raised his voice, drowning Cookie out. "They is *murderers* walking the streets. Men carrying guns like this is the Old West."

"And they should be!" Cookie shouted, finally drowning out the old man. "It's not exactly like we can call the police if something bad happens. People have to be able to protect themselves."

"You support that?" the old man demanded.

"I don't support or condemn it," Cookie replied. "That's just how it is and it's not my place to judge other men for their actions."

The old man leveled a finger at Cookie. "I judge!"

Cookie lost his temper. "You better judge your ass on out of here before I throw you out! This is my meeting and you're pissing me off."

The offended old man huffed and walked off. Cookie was a foot taller and eighty pounds heavier than him, not to mention the forty-year age difference.

A tall, slack-jawed man in his late thirties raised his hand like he was in a classroom waiting for Cookie to call on him. Uncertain of what else to do, Cookie pointed at him and nodded encouragingly. Whatever the man had to say couldn't push the meeting any further off the rails than it had already gone.

"I live out on the east end of town. We run into a lot of folks that live between here and Tazewell County. I keep hearing rumors there's a cult up that way."

The entire shelter sat in silence staring at the man, waiting to see if there was more to the story.

"Uh, that's interesting, but I'm not sure how that ties into our topic," Cookie finally said.

The man shrugged. "Hell, I don't know either, but that old feller there was talking about whores and killers. If we can talk about that, why can't we talk about cults?"

"Except that's not what we're here to talk about," Cookie said through gritted teeth. "Not cults, not killers, not whores or whore-mongers, or people who shoot each other. We're here to talk about how we can work together to get more things done around town."

The slack-jawed man frowned. "Ah hell, I care nothing about that. I just came to your meeting because I thought it might be a good way to meet women."

"You're kidding," Cookie said, palming his forehead.

The man shook his head. "I got a good farm, livestock, and no debt. I'm in good shape and looking for a woman of childbearing age. I'm fine with homely or on the husky side, but I like them strong."

Cookie looked at his wife with a combination of shock and amusement. "He just shot his shot right here in front of everyone, didn't he?"

She offered him a sheepish look.

Cookie looked back at the group. "Does anyone at all want to talk about community projects?"

A homely woman raised her hand, making a point of flexing her thick bicep as she did so. "I'd like to hear more about the cult that attractive gentleman with the farm was just talking about."

Cookie threw his arms up in the air. "Meeting dismissed. You folks have a good night." He gestured at his family. "Let's get out of here. I can't take another minute of this."

His family got up and followed Cookie out into the late evening. His wife hurried to catch up with him, draping an arm across his back. His entire family could sense his disappointment.

"People are idiots," his son said, trying to be supportive of his dad.

"Yes, they are, son."

"They're butt brains," his daughter said, not wanting to miss out on the fun.

Cookie considered the comment a moment, then said, "Yes, honey, they're that too."

36

It was dusk when Jim buttoned up Pops' and Nana's house for the day. Pops insisted on leaving the heat pump on and the refrigerators cooling. He even left a few lights on to give the house a lived-in appearance. He wanted it to be ready and welcoming when he brought Nana home.

Before they even got out of sight of the place, Pops stopped and turned his horse several times, admiring the view of his house with lights on again. "You think it's okay to leave those lights on?"

"I guess so," Jim replied. "It used to be something people did without sparing it a thought."

They entered town in the gloaming, the horses familiar enough with the route that none of the riders need turn on a light. Jim had his rifle at hand, though he didn't sense any danger out there in the night. The arrival of electricity had changed things in the community. Even the most degenerate of the population suddenly had priorities beyond robbing, stealing, and killing each other. Even the wicked took a night off sometimes.

It was impossible not to notice the proliferation of electric lights around town. The illuminated houses also served to highlight the number that remained dark. It was a statement both to the death toll their community had experienced and how many people had simply disappeared over the last year. Jim assumed that the fate of some of those people would never be discovered. They'd simply walked out of their homes never to be seen or heard from again.

While there were no streetlights going, plenty of porch lights were illuminated. With the prospect of free electricity, people saw no reason not to light their homes up like Christmas trees. Jim understood there was comfort in that. Lights pushed the gloom away even when so many other things were missing.

In the silence of the evening, heat pumps hummed from roadside neighborhoods. Though windows were closed against the cool evening, muffled sounds could be heard coming from some of the homes. Music or the sound of movies playing on DVD. Occasionally they'd catch a flicker of movement when someone stepped outside to relieve themselves or investigate the sound of hooves on the street.

Once they were close to the center of town, the riders encountered more people, some of them in small groups. That wasn't all that uncommon these days, especially with so many people frequenting the Reset Roadhouse. When Jim spotted someone he recognized from the bar, he called out to them.

"Coming back from the roadhouse?"

An older man and woman stopped and shook their heads. The man replied, "Nah, we went to that meeting Cookie was having about organizing people. It was a waste of time."

"That's too bad," Jim said. "Cookie has some good ideas and he's a hard worker."

The old man shook his head. "Good ideas are pointless without a good leader to carry them out. Cookie is no leader. That meeting was like watching someone herd cats. People were throwing out one dumbass comment after another. Eventually he gave up and left."

"I'm not surprised," said Jim. "It's hard to organize people to do anything. Half the time people come to meetings like that because they want to be heard, not because they want to listen."

"That's true," the old man agreed.

"We best get on home," the older woman said. "We hooked up the old VHS and we've been going back and watching TV shows we recorded in the 80s. It's been a hoot. Tonight it's *Dallas* re-runs."

They said their goodbyes and continued through town. When they reached the intersection near the roadhouse, Jim reined his horse to a stop. "I'm going to check on things at the roadhouse. You guys get Pops home safely and tell Ellen I'll be home later tonight."

"Got it," Pete said.

"I'm in good hands," said Pops. "Two fine young bodyguards. Makes me feel like I'm someone important."

"You are," Charlie said. "To us."

The three of them rode off as Pops launched into another story. "Have I ever told you boys about the flood of '57? That was a bad one."

Jim was still smiling at the three of them as he approached the roadhouse, rode around back, and tied his horse off. Things inside sounded rather raucous, like a celebration of sorts was going on. Jim had imagined since people had power now, they'd stick close to home, but perhaps that wasn't the case at all. The return of power had given them something to celebrate.

He entered the back door to waves and people calling his name. Onstage, Lloyd was playing the banjo with a guy on guitar and a girl on bass. They'd played with Lloyd several times, though Lloyd was tough to share the stage with. He was prone to being the center of attention even when it was someone else's turn in the spotlight. They were playing some 1960s protest song. Even though it was a beautiful rendition, Jim always accused Lloyd of being a communist every time he played it.

When he got closer to the bar, Becky sniffed the air. "I think I smell Jim Powell. If it was a cologne, I'd describe it as horse manure and wood smoke mixed with the smell of gunpowder."

Jim laughed. "That's probably accurate, but I'm guessing you overheard someone calling my name. I doubt you could smell me among the odors of this place."

The roadhouse had come to develop a particular scent that all the employees carried with them even when they left the building. It was the smell of brewing beer and charred meat. It was the unique smoke that came from burning wood, smoked tobacco, and marijuana. As hesitant as Jim had been to start this enterprise in town, that smell had become part of him. He'd miss it when it was gone.

He spotted Cookie staring downcast at a mug of beer and settled onto a stool beside him. "Can I get a beer, Becky?"

"If you can get off your ass and get one."

"Thanks," Jim replied.

A few stools away, Shade cackled under his breath. Part of his attraction to Becky was her feisty attitude. She kept everyone at the roadhouse in their place, whether they were employees or guests.

When she finally gave in and grabbed a beer out of the refrigerator, Becky said, "Call out so I can find you, Jim. I don't have all day to fool with you."

Jim raised a finger in the air. "Marco!" It was a throwback to the old game he'd played in the town swimming pool as a kid, Marco Polo.

"Very funny," Becky said, placing the beer in front of Jim. "Don't forget to tip your server. You might pay my salary but that doesn't include tips."

"Duly noted," Jim said.

Becky wandered off to talk to Shade, leaving Jim with Cookie.

Jim took a sip of his beer. "So I heard your meeting was a real goat rope."

Cookie nodded, then drained the last of his beer. "Can I get another of these, Becky?"

She shot Cookie a hard look. "I was just down there. You let me walk my ass all the way back down the bar before you decide you need another one?"

"I'm sorry. It won't happen again." Cookie wiped foam from his lip with the back of his hand.

"You're damn right it won't," Becky snarled, grabbing another beer from the fridge.

"Can I get a fresh chilled mug?" Cookie asked.

Becky sighed and looked in Cookie's direction.

Reading her look, Cookie said, "That's okay. I don't need one."

"Damn right you don't." She placed his beer in front of him. "Anything else before I head back down the bar?"

"We're good," Jim said. "Cookie, you good?"

"I'm good."

Becky wandered off, mumbling to herself.

Cookie grinned in Becky's direction. "She's...full of personality."

"And she has hearing like the Bionic Man," Jim said. "Be careful what you say."

Becky turned her head in Jim's direction and gave him a thumbs-up.

"I see what you mean," Cookie said.

"So, about the meeting?"

"It was horrible, Jim. I can see now why you got so pissed off at everyone in this town."

"It's not just this town. It's the place our country was headed before the collapse. People are different than they used to be. They've lost that sense of sacrifice for the greater good. It's all about what they can get for themselves."

"I saw some of that today," Cookie said. "I also saw people who are unable to look at the big picture. They get lost in the minute detail of things and can't get past it. I was trying to talk to them about useful, practical projects and it was entirely wasted on them."

"So what's your plan then? You're giving up?"

Cookie shook his head. "I'm going to keep doing what I'm doing. I've got people who are willing to work—friends, family, neighbors, and other acquaintances. I'm just going to keep at it and lead by example. If people see us accomplishing things, maybe they'll want to be a part of it."

Jim took a long pull off his beer. "That's a good plan. Give people a forum in which to bitch and complain, that's what they'll do. Keep them busy and they won't have the time or energy for it."

Cookie shook his head with disgust, replaying the meeting in his head. "Everyone was concerned about someone getting something they weren't. They wanted to complain about all the vice and sin going on and what was going to be done about it."

"Anyone bring up the roadhouse?"

"Not specifically by name, but close enough."

Jim smiled at that. "Let them talk."

"It's really disappointing. I had a higher opinion of people before I started trying to organize them. Now I'm just kind of disgusted."

"It's like with the power restoration," Jim said. "When that crew was passing through installing the power station, they said that there had been multiple attempts on Lightspeed's life. How crazy is it that this guy has proven he can deliver power to the country and people still want to kill him? We've become a country that can't be satisfied by anything."

"The people or the government?" Cookie asked.

"Both."

"Well, they're sucking the enthusiasm out of me. I had been excited to get up each day and dig into things. Now I want to let those people rot in their homes."

"I've been there," Jim said.

"Maybe I just need a break," Cookie said. "A few days off might help me rediscover the enthusiasm I had a few days ago."

"I have an idea. Shade and I are heading to the east end of the county tomorrow to hand out some converters. Why don't you come with us? A little adventure will help clear your head."

Cookie furrowed his brow. "Is that dangerous? I haven't been out of town since the lights went out."

"Hell, everything is dangerous now," Jim said. "But it's less dangerous than it was a year ago."

Cookie mulled this over for a moment, staring at his mug. "That might be fun. What do I need to do?"

"Be here at the roadhouse at first light. You can ride on the wagon with Shade if you aren't scared of him."

Cookie leaned forward, then looked down the bar to where Shade was laughing with Becky. "He is a little scary."

"He's a *lot* scary," Jim said. "That's why he's a good man to have around."

"Do I need a bring a…gun?" Cookie asked, lowering his voice as if he was making a drug deal.

Jim looked at him like he was crazy. "Man, you need to be bringing a gun everywhere. I rarely step out of my house without one. Do you own a gun?"

"A Marlin .22."

"I don't know how much weapons training you've had, Cookie, but remember that grip is important when fighting with a .22."

"Really? I haven't had any training at all."

Jim nodded. "Yeah, you want a firm grip on the barrel when you're swinging it like a bat. It's more effective that way."

Cookie frowned. "You're making fun of me."

Jim laughed. "A little but bring what you have. If you ever decide you want to trade for a new weapon, we sell them here."

"I'm hoping the days of needing to take guns everywhere are almost behind us."

"I hope so too," said Jim. "But I don't think we're there yet."

37

The next morning was cool, with a light frost on the ground that disappeared as soon as the warm breath of the sun brushed over it. Cookie was waiting at the roadhouse just as he'd promised, his .22 rifle in hand and a pack slung over his back. He climbed onto Shade's wagon and settled into the comfortable seat beside him. Jim rode alongside the wagon on his horse. Hugh had also chosen to join them for a change of pace.

They left the town and headed east along the four-lane highway. Jim had only traveled this road a few times since the collapse. It was the way to Randi's house and to Gary's. It led to his office and on toward Tazewell County. It was the way Jim had returned to the valley after walking back home from Richmond.

The changes since Jim was last on this road were subtle. The abandoned vehicles they passed had all been broken into by now, looted for anything of value. Thick dust coated them and wind-blown debris was piled up against the tires. The vehicles looked as if they could have been sitting on that stretch of road for decades. The empty houses and businesses along the way looked no better. Windows were broken out and doors kicked in. There was a general look of desolation, as if anyone living this close to the road had moved or been driven out. It was like walking through a war zone long after the troops were gone and the bullets had stopped flying.

Without the highway department's mowing crews, the weeds alongside the road and in the medians between the lanes were overgrown. Fast growing poplars sprouted among the wildflowers and grass. Several times, they startled deer bedded down in the high grass along the road. In other areas, free-ranging cattle and sheep grazed the highway as if the beasts of the land had united to reclaim the land from modernity. As if they'd given man his opportunity to try and improve things and all he'd done was manage to screw it up.

"It's a good sign to see deer and cattle here," Shade said. "I was afraid people would decimate them."

"They've overhunted them closer to town," Cookie said. "At least the deer. Since we've been moving stray cattle onto the football field, we've been better able to manage them for the benefit of everyone in the community."

"These deer don't act too worried," Jim said.

After two hours, they turned off the main road and took a right along a narrow, paved road that led up the mountain. Jim knew a few folks along this road, though he hadn't seen any of them since the collapse and had no idea how they'd fared. This community was only a few miles from the office where he'd worked and several of his coworkers had lived here. Shade also knew some folks here from the livestock market.

"You remember me telling you all those people bitching at my meeting last night?" Cookie asked.

"Yeah, I remember," Jim said.

"Ninety percent of the population gone," said Hugh, "and it's just our luck that so many whiners survived."

That comment got a chuckle from Shade.

"Someone from this side of town said they'd heard rumors of a cult out this way," Cookie said.

"We've been hearing cult rumors since last spring," Jim said. "People passing through the farmers market mentioned all kinds of cults springing up around the area. Rapture cults, doomsday cults, fertility cults, Luddite cults, and even harvest cults."

"What's a Luddite?" Shade asked. "I've heard you mention that before."

Hugh said, "It was a name handed out back in the industrial revolution for a bunch of people who got pissed off because they didn't want machines to take weaving away from craftsmen. They started raiding factories and busting up machines. Now they use that word for anyone who is anti-technology."

"We don't have much technology for people to be against," Shade noted.

"The people they call Luddites now are against restoring electricity," Jim said. "They think we'd be better off without it and they don't want it to come back. Some of them are trying to destroy Lightspeed's equipment so none of us can have power again."

"That's insane," Cookie said, his eyes wide.

Jim nodded. "I agree. The harvest cult makes an odd kind of sense. When people's lives depend on a good harvest, they're liable to do anything to ensure it, even if it means dancing around naked under the full moon."

"Naked or *nekkid*?" Shade asked.

Cookie frowned. "What's the difference?"

"Naked is not having any clothes on," Shade explained. "Nekkid is not having any clothes on and being up to something. A great Southern philosopher by the name of Lewis Grizzard once said that."

Jim laughed. "I didn't realize you were a fan of Southern philosophy, Shade."

"Underneath this brutish exterior lies the heart of a poet, Jim. I grew up in a home without television and raised my kids that way too. We had a large library and reading was a regular evening activity in my home, especially in cold weather. Everyone sat around the fire with a book."

"Just when you think you know a man, he turns around and surprises you," Jim mused.

"What did you imagine?" Shade asked. "That I sat around on a bearskin rug picking my teeth with the bones of my enemies?"

Jim considered for a moment. "I pictured you sitting around sharpening knives and cleaning weapons. That's what I do. That's what Hugh does."

"That's only part of the time," said Hugh. "I also read a lot of technical manuals."

"I maintain my weapons too, but you can't do that all the time," Shade said. "What do you do in the evenings, Cookie?"

"Think about my life," said Cookie. "I think about all the decisions I made up until this point and how I might do things differently in the future. I make lists of what I want to do when the world gets back to normal and I add to that list every night."

"That would depress the hell out of me," Jim said. "I spend enough time second guessing what I'm doing now. I don't want to go all the way back to the beginning and question that stuff too."

"Don't dream your life away," said Shade. "We may never see normal again."

"Shade's right," Jim added. "Find some way to make peace with the world you're in now. Look for a way to enjoy this life and get some satisfaction from it. You spend your days wishing for a life that might never return and you may end up dreaming all your remaining days away."

"I've been working on that," Cookie said. "That's why I try to stay involved around town. It helps keep me out of a funk."

"That's good logic," Shade looked at Cookie appreciatively. "When I was coming up, you better not let my dad hear you complaining or even looking like you were in a mood. He'd damn well find something for you to do. He didn't believe in idle hands."

The road was lined with cornfields on both sides. Deer and cattle wandered among the dried stalks, hunting for stray ears of corn. Perhaps a half mile ahead of the riders was a cluster of houses and mobile homes. A Quonset hut had a sign indicating it served as a heavy truck garage. A 1970s model dump truck sat in front of a garage door with the hood tipped forward. A large engine sat in the gravel lot with a tattered yellow tarp stretched overtop it.

"Where do we start, Shade?" Jim asked. "You know this area better than I do."

"Too many houses to go door-to-door. We need to do something like Lightspeed's people did and leave some converters with a few select people. We can tell them if they need more they can come into town and pick them up at the roadhouse."

"You know a few people we might be able to trust?" Cookie asked. "People who might not shoot us for showing up in their driveway?"

Shade grinned. "We'll go visit my friend Bobby."

"He dependable?" asked Jim.

"Yeah, but he's the most cantankerous son-of-a-bitch the Lord ever breathed life into."

Hugh looked at Jim with a concerned expression on his face. "Hell, there's two of you!"

38

"I'd venture this is the place," Jim said.

The three men were stopped in front of a rusty red gate with a hand-painted sign affixed to it. The sign read "Go away or die!"

Jim couldn't help but grin as he read it. "I need one of those. Can't wait to meet this guy."

"I'm assuming we don't just ride on through the gate and go up to the house?" Cookie asked.

Hugh shifted in his saddle. "Well, *you* could."

"If I don't mind dying?" Cookie finished.

"Pretty much. In the country, the polite thing to do is to call from the edge of the property." Shade threw his head back, cupped his hands around his mouth, and issued a deep bellow that sounded like a warning issued by an angry bull.

"That was impressive," Jim said.

"Grew up calling cattle."

When there was no immediate response, Shade unleashed a second bellow, adding Bobby's name to the end of it. Shortly, a man appeared on the porch of the farmhouse. All Jim could make out at this distance was bibbed overalls and a white thermal shirt. Well, that and the shotgun in the man's hand. Bobby disappeared back into his house and reappeared a moment later, riding in their direction on a bridled but saddleless horse.

As the man got closer, Jim noted a scowl that could probably sour milk with no more than a passing glance. Bobby reined his horse to a stop at the gate and regarded the visitors, then nodded at Shade.

"Shade."

"Morning, Bobby. What you into today?"

Bobby spoke in a high pitch, his words coming fast, as if he was always in the middle of a rant. "Well, I *was* eating my breakfast until I heard the caterwauling down here at the gate."

"That would be me," Shade said. "These are my friends Jim Powell, Hugh, and Cookie."

Bobby nodded at the three strangers, never cracking a smile. His expression was that of a man always deeply contemplating some injustice done to him by a cruel world. His gaze lingered on Jim for a moment. "Jim Powell... I've heard tell of you. Can't remember the circumstances."

"You probably heard someone cursing my name," Jim conceded. "I've pissed off most of the county at one time or another. You might have even found flyers dropped from the sky that offered a bounty for me. Just to be clear, that bounty is no longer being offered."

"You're right on all counts," Bobby said. "I saw those flyers and got a laugh out of them. Anyone who's a pain in the government's ass is someone I can share a Moon Pie with. You're the one that caused a ruckus down at the farmer's market a time or two, aren't you?"

Jim shrugged. "Guilty as charged. I might have cussed out the entire town once or twice."

Bobby let out a high-pitched laugh. "Serves them right. *Town* people." He said it with the same disdain one might hold for a particularly foul odor.

"Yeah, I've butted heads with people a time or two," Jim said. "Things aren't so bad now. I run a bar and trading post in town and that's smoothed down a few feathers. I've also been handing out the power converters that allow people to get electricity, so that's made some of my worst haters a little more tolerant of me. Not all of them, though."

"Yeah, I heard the juice was coming back through," Bobby said, turning and looking at the big orange balloon floating above the ridge miles away. "Something to do with that big eyesore over there. Looks like a damn floating pumpkin from the Macy's parade."

"That's it," Shade said. "That *eyesore* sends power to a device about the size of a frisbee that replaces your electric meter. We're trying to find a person or two in each community who can hand them out to their neighbors. We have a lot of them to distribute and don't have the time to go from house to house."

Bobby tipped his head back and regarded Shade with a tight-lipped expression. "So you naturally thought you'd ask the crotch-etiest son-of-a-bitch in this part of the county to be the power fairy? Not sure that's a stroke of genius."

Jim laughed. He liked people who could acknowledge their own crankiness. He'd embraced his long ago. "The same was said of me when Walter Lightspeed's people dropped the first delivery of converters in my lap and asked me to hand them out to everyone. My friends and family got a good laugh out of that."

"Truth," Hugh said.

"Don't say much, do you?" Bobby said, looking at Hugh.

Hugh shrugged. "I say what needs to be said. I ain't one to keep rambling and fill the air with nonsense."

Bobby nodded. "I like a man who is sparing with his words. The world needs a lot more of them."

"You think you could do that for us?" Shade asked. "Hand out some of these converters? You have a better idea of who's left here in your neighborhood than we do."

"People in these parts fared well," Bobby said. "The town thinned out significantly but most of my neighbors did okay. I only know of a few empty houses, and the folks there either died or moved else-where to be with family."

"Can you estimate how many you'd need?" Shade asked. He set the parking brake on the wagon and climbed into the back.

Bobby began whispering names and counting them off on his fingers. When he was done, he said, "I reckon there's about twenty-eight homes I could hit here in my little area."

"That counting you?" Shade asked, digging into a box of converters.

Bobby's curmudgeonly expression grew even more sour. "I don't want one of the damn things."

"You sure?" Jim asked. "You can get some limited internet access with it. A little news of what's happening out there in the world."

"All the more reason to not want it," Bobby said. "My folks didn't have juice or indoor plumbing when I was born. I'd started school by the time we finally got power. My parents still didn't have a bathroom inside the house until after I was married and out of the house. As a matter of fact, I built their first bathroom as a Christmas present. Closed in part of the porch to make the bathroom and poured the septic tank myself. Took them a while to get used to it. Not sure my dad ever took to the inside bathroom until the old outhouse fell in and he didn't want to rebuild it."

"So you don't want power for sentimental reasons?" Cookie asked. "Remembering the good old days that weren't always so good?"

Bobby scowled. "Eh, maybe a little. Remembering how much better life was before the internet and cell phones is more like it. Don't have to go back to the 1940s and 1950s to get that. Just have to go back to the seventies and eighties to realize those were better times."

"Amen," Hugh said.

"Agreed," Jim piped in.

"I tell you what," Shade said, counting out the converters. "I'll give you thirty. I suggest you hang onto one of these. You don't have to install it now, but you might decide you want it later. That leaves an extra in case you forgot someone."

"Fair enough." Bobby nodded. "My wife and daughter fuss enough about not having power that I might give in and install it. Hoping it doesn't come to that."

"If you need more of these, just get a count and send someone to the roadhouse to ask," Jim said. "Right now we have plenty, but I can't say how long they'll last."

Shade carried the stack of converters to the gate and Bobby frowned at him.

"What the hell am I supposed to do with that stack? I ain't got a gunny sack or nothing. You're going to have to take them up to the house for me."

"I would if you'd open the damn gate."

"Fine!" Bobby sighed, used a key to unlock the chain from the gate, then swung it open, all without dismounting.

Shade piled the converters in his wagon and climbed into the seat. Once the riders were through and headed up the gravel road to the farmhouse, Bobby closed the gate so his cattle wouldn't wander, then fell in alongside the wagon.

Cookie cleared his throat and spoke loudly to be heard over the clattering of Shade's wagon. "So, Bobby, there are some folks in town talking about a cult out this way. You heard anything about a group like that?"

Shade laughed. "You're determined to find this cult, aren't you, Cookie?"

"I'm curious is all."

"There's only one bunch in this area that might describe," Bobby said in his high-pitched ramble. "I ain't sure if it's really a cult or not."

Jim asked, "If it's not a cult, what is it?"

"Buncha damn hippies or some shit like that," Bobby said. "Not really sure if it's what you'd call a cult or not."

"Why would people accuse them of being a cult?" Cookie asked. "They have some weird religion or something?"

"Not unless smoking that wacky tobacky and skinny dipping is a religion now," Bobby replied. "That's all I've heard tell of them doing out there."

"Pretty sure that doesn't make it a religion," Hugh said. "Otherwise there would be a lot more ministers in town."

"Where do these people live?" Jim asked.

Bobby consulted his mental map before replying. "On the opposite side of the highway. You go up the road a few miles, turn left, and go until you hit the Little River."

Jim studied his mental map and thought he had a rough idea of where Bobby might be talking about. "Is that close to where the old Rose farm is?"

"It's more than close," Bobby growled. "It *is* the old Rose farm. The left you take off the highway is Rose Farm Road."

Shade furrowed his brow. "I've known of Herschel Rose my entire life and he never struck me as the kind to start a cult. I've seen him at cattle sales all my life and can't picture him skinny dipping with a left-handed cigarette hanging out his mouth. He's kind of a quiet old country man."

"He's even quieter now," Bobby said. "He's dead as Dick Nixon."

Jim suppressed a grin. Bobby was about as sentimental about death as he was. There was just so much dying going on these days that it didn't hit you the same unless it was someone you cared about.

"Death does tend to silence a man," Hugh said sagely.

"Hell, it's the only thing that would silence some of them," Bobby said. "Most people are nothing but hot air and a waste of skin."

"Amen," said Jim.

"Herschel Rose is dead," Shade mused, turning the idea over in his head. "That comes as a little bit of a shock."

"I don't know why," Bobby said. "Old Man Rose was old when I was a kid. You can only keep getting older for so long before you throw a rod or blow a gasket."

Shade shook his head and sighed, still taken aback by the news of Old Man Rose's death. "When you notice that the old men you've known all your life are starting to thin out, it means you've become one of the old men."

"Anyhow," Bobby went on, "there wasn't no one but Old Man Rose and his grandson Hank living on the Rose farm when the lights went out. Old Mrs. Rose, God bless her soul, passed on to the great quilting bee in the sky a few years back. Hank wasn't getting along with his parents at the time and decided to come live on the farm with his grandfather. That worked out well for everyone. Old Man

Rose got some help around the farm and Hank got a break from his parents."

"And poor old Mr. Rose is dead," Shade mused. "I hate to hear that. What got him?"

Bobby snapped. "Jesus, Shade, the man lived ninety-four years. You going to spend ninety-four more going on about it? He died about over a year ago. Got a cold that turned into the *poo-monia* and he never snapped out of it."

Hugh grinned. "Damn *poo-monia* will get you every time."

Bobby cut him a sharp look, knowing he was being made fun of, and not liking it. "Bunch of damn smartasses! Anyway, right after things went all to hell, Hank Rose invited a bunch of his friends to come live on the farm with him and the old man. They needed help guarding the livestock and keeping up with the chores. In return, Hank's friends got a roof over their head, regular meals, and safe drinking water."

"I can see where this is going," Cookie said.

Bobby shrugged. "Maybe you can, maybe you can't."

"I'm assuming the grandson took over running the place and let it go all to hell," Cookie said.

"And you'd be wrong as sin on Sunday," Bobby said. "Hank and his friends kept the place up right nice. They've done a pretty good job for people who weren't raised on farming. According to the neighbors, they got an odd turn about them though."

"How's that?" Jim asked.

They finally reached Bobby's porch and Shade stopped the wagon. He set the brake and unloaded the converters, stacking them on the edge of Bobby's porch. Jim started to dismount but Bobby stopped him.

"Whoa, Nelly. They ain't a reason in this world for you to get down off that horse. You ain't going to be staying that long. I intend to get back in there and finish my breakfast if it's still fit to eat."

Jim settled back onto the saddle. "Well, at least finish your story about the Rose farm before you throw us out."

"Like I said, those young people have done a decent job of looking after the place, but the neighbors claim there's strange things go on there. Lots of hippie drugs like the reefer and those mushrooms that grow in shit and make you see shit. Now, I was alive back in those hippie days, but I never went in for any of that mind-altering nonsense. No time for that when you live on a farm because there's always work to be done. My point is that I don't think they're a cult, but their neighbors don't know what else to call them."

"What would you call them?" Hugh asked.

Bobby climbed down off his horse and tied it to the porch rail. "They're some kind of back-to-the-Earth hippie homesteaders, like we used to see in the seventies. That whole *Mother Earth News* crowd."

"We should see if they want power," said Cookie.

"You just want to see if the rumors are true," Jim said. "You're dying to know if there's really a cult up here."

"Maybe," Cookie admitted. "Don't you?"

Jim said, "I guess so."

"I hope Old Man Rose is buried there," Shade said. "I'd like to pay my respects."

Bobby rolled his eyes. "You'll have to go through their gate and ride up to the house. The old homeplace is so far off the road they wouldn't even be able to hear a bullhorn like Shade calling out."

"They armed?" Hugh asked. "Dangerous?"

Bobby raised his shoulders. "No idea, but I assume everyone is armed these days. It's safer that way."

"Indeed it is," Jim said. "Well, good to meet you, Bobby. I supposed we should be getting out of your hair so you can get back to your breakfast."

"I suppose you should," said Bobby. "Nice to meet you folks as well. I'd ask you to come back and visit again sometime, but I'd rather you didn't."

"I'll probably be back anyway," Shade said. "You don't scare me."

"Well, come alone next time," Bobby said. "Don't be bringing your whole entourage with you like you're some rock star."

Jim wasn't offended by such talk. He related to the old grouch.

"Stop in at the roadhouse if you're ever in town, Bobby. I'll buy you a beer."

"I hope it's a good beer," Bobby said. "I'm liable to turn a mite grumpy if I ride all the way into town for a bad beer."

"Yeah, I'd hate to see what your grumpy looks like." Jim turned his horse and rode off before Bobby could reply. Even as he rode away, he could feel Bobby's eyes on his back. Jim almost felt like he'd made a friend.

Almost.

39

Jim hadn't been down the dead-end gravel road to the Rose farm in years. He tried to remember when it might have been. Was it in high school when he was looking for a place to park with a girlfriend? When he was out drinking beer and cruising back roads? When he thought back on things like that it always seemed they took place only a "couple of years ago." Lately, Jim had discovered that the mirror used to look backward in time was unreliable. Sometimes those "couple of years ago" memories were actually as far back as twenty or even thirty years. Those revelations came like a slap in the face.

Even as his horse plodded down this barely familiar road, Jim plodded back through time. Most days, he was fully engaged in doing what he had to do and didn't have the time for dwelling on the larger implications of their predicament. He tried not to think about the future his children would have in a nation that had turned into a trainwreck. Sometimes, however, getting lost in those thoughts was unavoidable. Especially when he recalled his experience of growing up in the late 60s, 70s and 80s.

People hadn't used social media to blast their political and social views to their friends, and they'd observed a modicum of civility in their discourse. Political and religious discussions were only undertaken between close friends and family, and even then with the understanding that the relationship between you and those people was more important than the topics you discussed. More important than being right.

Perhaps it was that brief visit with the old curmudgeon Bobby that sent Jim's mind spinning off. The guy wasn't sure he wanted electricity. Jim had heard Lightspeed angrily dismiss Luddites, but there was a truth in what they and people like Bobby had to say. It wasn't particularly electricity that had destroyed the social fabric that held the nation together, but social media certainly had.

Jim remembered the early days of the internet, when email had been the primary form of electronic communication rather than social media posts or messages. It was like the old days of friends writing letters to each other, except it was instant and didn't require the additional step of going to the post office. Even then people were more polite. Social media made everyone an instant armchair political analyst. It gave them an over-inflated *opinion* of their *opinion*. It made people think that participating in all that noise was more important than relationships and civil discourse.

Even now, without social media, the lasting effects of its poison still impacted people's behavior. People struggled to look at the big picture because they'd become mired down in opinions and minutiae. Even the man now running the nation, Walter Lightspeed, wasn't good enough to satisfy people. He was restoring power to an endarkened nation while people tried to kill him for whatever flaws they felt were more significant than his achievements.

What kind of nation had America become when success was only tolerated if it came from within the existing channel? Did America now have a ruling class from which the president had to ascend? Jim understood this was why so many people didn't want Lightspeed to succeed. If anyone could step forward and lead the country, the entire system would be destabilized. The myth of elitism would be shattered. The center would not hold.

After a mile on Rose Farm Road they saw a wide pasture to their left. Soon they came to a gate with a fancy sign alongside it stating that the Rose Farm was a century farm, having been in the same family for over a hundred years.

"Guess this is the place," Shade said. "Bobby was right. You can't see the house from here."

"So we ride on in?" Cookie asked.

Jim shook his head. "Yeah, I hate doing that. It's a violation of basic rural etiquette, but we don't have a choice."

Cookie hopped off the wagon. "I'll get the gate."

When the gate was open, Jim and Hugh rode through, followed by Shade and his wagon. The gravel road continued through the pasture to a copse of trees that screened the farm from the road. Beyond those woods, Jim assumed they'd find the house.

"Road needs work," Shade said, steering his team around a soft spot.

"Maybe they don't like company," Jim pointed out.

Shade grinned. "Hell, who does?"

"No wonder you and Bobby get along," Jim said. "You aren't a people person like me."

Shade guffawed at that one.

A few minutes later, they passed through the trees that blocked the house from the road. The trees were mostly bare poplars, maples, and oaks, with a few shagbark hickories. Small piles of sawdust in the road indicated that people had been processing downed trees into firewood. Once they were through the narrow band of forest, another pasture opened up and, in the distance, a two-story white farmhouse sat overlooking the Little River.

A concrete pad in front of the farmhouse held a tall aluminum flagpole. While it may once had proudly displayed an American flag, there was now a Jolly Roger flying in the uppermost position with some kind of tie-dyed peace symbol flag below it.

"Just going by the flag, I'm thinking these people are more likely hippies than a cult," Hugh surmised.

"Guess we'll know more in a minute," Jim said. "Should we—" He was cut off by Shade unleashing another of his hillbilly yells. "Well, I was going to ask if we should hail them from here or keep riding, but that answered my question."

Shade cupped his hands around his mouth and unleashed another yell. Seconds later, a figure emerged on the porch.

Hugh raised a pair of binoculars to his eyes. "I don't see a gun."

"They wearing a black robe?" Jim teased. "Got some kind of creepy mask on?"

"Nah," Hugh said. "Bibbed overalls. He's waving at us. I assume that means it's safe to approach."

Jim nudged his horse and the group rode on. By the time they reached the front yard, there were four young men standing on the porch. Jim estimated them to all be in their early to mid-twenties.

"Howdy, neighbor," one of the young men said, coming down the irregular concrete steps from the porch. A handrail of galvanized water pipe was bolted to a porch post while the other end was cemented in the ground.

"I'm Jim Powell. I live about halfway between here and town, back along the mountain."

"I know the area," the young man said. "My name is Hank Rose."

Jim climbed off his horse and shook Hank's hand. He went on introduce all the members of his group. "I'm sorry to drop in on you unannounced, but have you all heard anything about power being restored?"

Hank turned around and looked at his companions on the porch. Everyone looked just as confused as Hank did. "Nah, we ain't heard nothing about that, but we don't get out much. The farm produces pretty much everything we need. What we can't grow or make, we trade for with our neighbors. Don't get to town much."

Shade turned around in his seat, leaned over, and plucked one of the converters from the open box. Jim walked over and retrieved it from him.

"Have you heard about Walter Lightspeed?" Jim asked. "He's kind of declared himself president. He's the one turning the lights back on."

"A little," Hank said. "We've listened to a few of his radio addresses. I recall him saying something about trying to get the power back on."

"Well, his power system reached us a few days ago," Jim said. "You just take this device, unplug your electric meter, and replace it with this. I don't know all the science behind it, but it works like a charm."

"You're selling those things door to door?" Hank asked.

Jim smiled. "No, they're free. Lightspeed's people gave them to the community and we're just trying to get them out to people."

Hank stared at the device in Jim's hand. "So all I do is plug that into my meter base and I get free power?"

"That's it," said Jim. "Of course, they want you to turn all the breakers off and turn them back on one at a time for safety purposes. Since we're here, I can give you a hand if you want. It doesn't take very long."

Hank continued to stare at the device, mulling over Jim's words. He looked back at his friends and seemed to take a long time reading their thoughts. Finally, he turned back to Jim and shook his head. "We don't want it, though it was kind of you to come by. I appreciate it."

Although these weren't the first people who didn't want power, Jim was still taken aback. "That makes you the second person we've visited today who didn't want power."

"Glad to know we aren't the only ones," Hank said. "That gives me a little more faith in humanity."

Jim furrowed his brow. "Can I ask why? Not judging, just curious."

"My friends moved onto the farm with me after the lights went out. There's fourteen of us living here now. It's a big house and a big farm so it takes a lot of people to keep things running. Things have been going well. We've found a simpler life and we like it. There's none of the stress and hassle of the old world, no negativity or rat race. I'm sorry so many people had to die to make all this happen, but it's the best thing that ever happened to most of us here. I don't really care if the power ever comes back on or not."

"You think you might get tired of this at some point and want your old lives back?" Jim asked. "Don't you miss games and apps and all that stuff?"

Hank shook his head and there was a smattering of laughter among his friends. "We grew up with that crap. It wasn't until it was gone that we figured out there was an alternative. Life didn't have to be that way. We got a little hydro power running off the creek and it keeps the things charged that we need, like batteries and flashlights. It's enough to run a few lights at night. Honestly, it's all we need."

Jim held up the converter. "You want to take one in case you change your mind?"

Hank shook his head adamantly. "I don't want the temptation. Take it with you. We've got a good thing going and I don't want someone screwing it up in a moment of weakness."

Seeing his determination, Jim went back to the wagon and tossed the converter back in the box.

"You know, people think you all are running some kind of cult out here," Cookie said. "It came up at a meeting in town yesterday. Apparently, there's a rumor going around and it tracks back to here."

Hank cringed. "Yeah, we know all about that rumor. It might not have been our smartest moment."

"What's that mean?" Cookie asked. "Is it true? Is this a cult?"

Hank frowned. "No, we're not a cult. We had a problem with trespassers when the lights first went out. People were coming down to fish in the river, which my grandfather used to let people do if they asked. He'd go down there and talk to them, explain the rules of being on his property, and they listened to him for the most part. When he died, people got bolder, and they started testing me. My friends and I would find them going through the barns and outbuildings, trying to steal stuff. Hell, some of them even killed sheep or chickens, running around like they owned the damn place. We didn't want to hurt anybody, so we decided the best way to deal with it might be to scare people into staying away from us."

"So you're *pretending* to be a cult?" Jim asked.

Hank nodded. "It was kind of a spur of the moment thing and maybe not our brightest idea. Some people showed up to fish the river one night. They had a bonfire and were raising hell, drinking, and carrying on. Breaking bottles in the river. That was the final straw. My friends and I came outside and danced around the fire naked, chanting a bunch of mumbo jumbo. Pretty soon, those fishermen packed up and left. Since that worked so well, we made these creepy little dolls out of old bones, string, and twigs. It was something we'd seen in a horror movie. We hung them up along the river, on our gate, and along our fences. It immediately put a stop to unwanted visitors."

"That works as long as the neighbors don't get scared and decide to burn you out," Hugh said. "Acting crazy can be an effective strategy, but it can also backfire."

Jim winced. "Yeah, I tried the same thing with being an asshole to people in town and it backfired on me."

Cookie wasn't done with the whole cult thing yet. "Hasn't anyone ever said anything to you about the rumors? Like the neighbors? Mine would. Heck, they'd show up with the preacher and the rest of the congregation to have a 'come to Jesus' moment with me."

Hank laughed. "The neighbors know the truth. They were dealing with the same trespassing issues I was, but I suppose they found their own way of dealing with them. The neighbors still come down here to shoot the bull and see how things are going, just like they always have. We have people we trade with and everyone here in the local community treats us the same."

"Well, I have to admit that the cult rumors made me curious," Cookie said. "That's part of the reason we're here."

"That's why *you're* here," Jim clarified. "The rest of us are handing out converters. I don't care if anyone has a cult or not."

Hank offered them a warm smile. "I thank you for your consideration, but we definitely don't want one of your converters. Everyone here would agree, I'm sure." Hank looked back over his shoulder and the friends who'd come outside with him all nodded.

"Then we'll get out of your hair," Jim said with a wink. "Let you get back to your ceremonies and sacrifices."

"One minute," Shade interrupted. "Hank, if I ain't being a bother,

I knew your granddaddy all my life. If he's buried here on the prop-erty, I'd like to pay my respects."

Hank pointed toward a cinderblock building a short distance from the house. The outside was surrounded by a circle of junk and cast-off parts, like some rusty force field. "My grandfather liked to spend time in his shop and he asked to be buried behind it. I told him I'd bury him out front if he'd rather, but he said he wasn't partial to people parking tractors and leaking vehicles on top of him."

Shade laughed. "That sounds like him." He set the brake on the wagon and hopped off. "I won't be but a moment."

Once he was gone, Hank said, "So, that's Shade Wolford."

"Yep, and apparently he was fond of your grandfather," Jim said. "He was all tore up when he heard he'd passed."

Hank shrugged. "My grandfather was old, tired, and ready to go. He was fond of Shade too. According to the old man, Shade had quite the reputation when he was young and wild. He was always telling stories about what Shade got up to at the livestock market or cattle sale or whatever. He sounded like a wild man."

"Still is," said Jim. "He's a good man to have on your side."

"Granddaddy said a man kicked Shade's dog at the livestock market years back. Shade knocked the man down and beat him nearly to death with the same boot he'd used to kick his dog. Pulled it right off the man's foot and set in on him."

"Sounds about right," Hugh said.

"There were a lot of those stories," Hank said. "Shade fighting, swarping, and raising hell. He didn't care for thieves or crooks, either, and he didn't bother calling the law when he ran across one."

"He hasn't told me much about his past," said Jim.

"You should have met my granddaddy. He had plenty to say about Shade, but it all came out of fondness and respect."

When Shade came back, no one mentioned he'd been the topic of conversation, nor did they call attention to the tears running down his cheeks.

"Do you all ever come to town?" Jim asked Hank.

"Not since the power went out. Haven't needed to."

"I'd love to talk to you guys some more," Jim said. "I run a road-house in town. It's a combination bar, restaurant, and trading post. We have live music too. You can get a cold beer, a hot meal, and some lukewarm entertainment, depending on who's on the stage that night. There are certain commodities we need and I've got a lot of trade goods I can barter with. I'm trying to build relationships with people who might become suppliers for us. I like your attitude and I like what you've done here. Maybe we can help each other."

Hank turned around and spoke quietly with his friends for a moment. When he turned back around, he grinned at Jim. "We'd like that. Might be a good change of pace to hear some music and have a night out on the town."

"I'll go you one further," Jim said. "Bring sleeping bags and you all can sack out at the roadhouse that night, so you don't have to ride back here in the dark. We keep the place heated and there's several people who live there full-time. It's a warm and safe place to stay."

Hank approached Jim and stuck out his hand. "Thank you, kindly. We'll drop in one evening this week. How do we find your place?"

Jim gave him some directions, searching for landmarks Hank would be familiar with. Over the next few minutes, they found enough common ground that Hank was comfortable he could find the roadhouse.

Once they were back on the road, Cookie said, "I'm kind of shocked, Jim. I can't believe you invited a cult to the roadhouse. I'm sure the town will have a lot to say about that."

Jim rolled his eyes. "Well, for one thing, we *know* they're not a cult now. For another, no one in town will be any the wiser unless *someone* runs their big mouth."

Cookie crossed his heart. "I won't say a word."

40

For the next few days, Jim felt that he got nothing done other than overseeing the distribution of converters. Shade helped by making forays into the outlying communities, tapping into his farming and livestock connections to find people willing to hand out converters to their neighbors. Other people came to Jim directly, stating they had family or friends outside of town in need of power. Jim didn't question them or ask for proof. By this point, he wanted the converters gone and out of his life as soon as possible. They had brought him nothing but trouble.

The stockpile of converters was shrinking, though was still far from depleted. Jim wasn't sure they'd even gone through half of what Hugh brought back from Northern Virginia. He quietly took two dozen to his home and stashed them in a safe place. He wanted the insurance of having spares in case any got stolen from the people in his group. He also wanted the ability to electrify a few more houses in the future if their group expanded. While he wouldn't have taken them if these were the converters delivered by Lightspeed's people, he had no guilt about hoarding away converters Hugh had risked his life for. They had plenty.

It was early afternoon later in the week and Jim had just handed out a half-dozen converters to a young man who'd only lived in town a short time. He rode in on an electric bicycle and was heading for a distant hollow where his cousins, aunts, and uncles lived in a jumbled assortment of houses and mobile homes. The young man assured Jim that they could see the big orange repeater from the hollow, so he handed over the converters. If they didn't work because the man lied about being able to see the repeater, that wasn't Jim's problem.

He was outside the roadhouse checking out the man's electric bike when Cat Anderson came weaving down the street on a pair of rollerblades. She stopped gracefully when she reached the road-house and sat down on the edge of the pavement. She took off her skates and swapped them out for sneakers she carried in her back-pack. With the skates in hand, she strolled across the parking lot.

"I'm impressed," Jim said. "Since the collapse I've seen many modes of travel. I've seen men riding horses, cows, bikes, and electric skateboards. I've seen scooters and even a man riding an ostrich, but you are the first rollerblader I've seen."

"I found these in my mom's attic. In junior high, I thought this was my future. I was going to be a competitive rollerblader and compete at the X Games. Obviously, that didn't work out."

"There's still time," Jim said. "Don't give up hope."

"Too late. I gave up on that dream a long time ago. Can I buy you a beer?"

"Sure."

They headed into the roadhouse and found seats at the crowded bar. It was early afternoon but with most people unemployed, drinking cold beer in a warm bar was as nice a way to spend the after-noon as any.

"The place is crowded for this time of day," Cat observed.

"It's been that way since the power came back. People are in a more festive mood. What are you drinking?"

"Is there a choice of beers now?"

Jim held up two fingers. "Yes, a lager and something darker that I can't pronounce."

"I'm impressed. I'll take the one you can't pronounce."

Jim grabbed a lager for himself and a bottle of the darker beer for Cat. Since they were reusing bottles, the beer came bottled in whatever they had available. Jim opened the bottles and took a seat beside Cat. "The power coming back on has been a big deal for Ed. It's a lot easier to brew beer with electricity, apparently. There's even the possibility I'll have beer on tap in a few weeks. Ed is collecting all the equipment now."

"That would be great." Cat took a sip of her beer, then held the bottle out admiringly. "This is good!"

"Ed says we might even be able to offer a different liquor now, instead of serving the same thing under several different names."

Cat laughed. "Power has changed things for this town in a big way. A lot of the people who came to my last meeting wanting to start businesses already have them up and running. That's part of why I'm here. I want to schedule another meeting but I'm expecting two or three times the people to attend."

"Geez, that's a big jump in attendance. Has there been that much interest?"

"Tons! People are as energized and enthusiastic as I've ever seen them." Cat took another sip of her beer. "I don't know if you've noticed this or not, but there's now an entire group of people calling themselves electrical contractors. Apparently installing the converters has created a need for people who can help with that."

"I've heard," Jim said. "Some of those 'contractors' have approached me and asked that I refer people to them if they have issues getting their wiring straightened out. Some of these guys know what they're doing. Others are jacklegs who know just enough about electricity to be a danger to themselves and everyone around them."

"There's a lot of demand for those people, and the repairs they're making have also created a secondary market for electrical supplies. The hardware and builder's supply stores ran out of inventory almost immediately. Now there are people going through abandoned houses removing receptacles, wire, and light fixtures for repairing occupied houses."

Jim smiled. "I like seeing that. I like seeing people reinvigorated. I like the enthusiasm and spark of life they have now. That kind of hope is contagious."

"Well, as you can imagine, even more people are getting ideas for businesses. They want to come to our meeting not just to brainstorm, but to network with other businesspeople. Some of these businesses are developing symbiotic relationships, as they would have in the old world. Like those electrical contractors and the people salvaging used electrical components. They need each other."

"You're doing a good deed by bringing them all together," Jim said. "For some of them, those meetings probably give them the push they need to take their idea to the next level."

Cat nodded. "I don't see this enterprise of mine as a business incubator any longer. It's more like a chamber of commerce. We need to find a new name for it. I don't want to step on any old-world toes."

"It's commerce un-chambered," Jim said.

"I like that!" Cat drained the last of her beer.

"Another?"

She shook her head. "No, I have things I need to do. I just wanted to see if you could accommodate us for a meeting later this week. We could have as many as fifty people."

"Not a problem."

"Do I still have enough credit from that bottle of pills I gave you last time to cover drinks and refreshments?"

Jim nodded. "As long as you don't have a hundred folks turn out, you should be fine."

Cat laughed as she slid off her stool and left. "No way."

Cat rollerbladed back down the street, and Jim checked the sun and decided it was somewhere between 3PM and 4PM. He went back inside the bar and found Becky.

"I'm going to take a quick ride over to my parents' house. They've spent the last few days making the place livable and supposedly they made the big move today. They wrangled Shade into hauling the last of their belongings over there in his wagon."

"They didn't have to *wrangle* him into it," Becky said. "Your parents are nice people. People gladly do things for nice people. There should be a lesson in that for you."

"I am nice. If you could see me, you'd be impressed by my halo and angelic smile."

Becky snorted. "I can see a lie when I hear it."

"As pleasant as it would be to stand here and argue with you all afternoon, Becky, I need to be on my way. I'll be back later, just so you have something to look forward to."

Becky sneered. "I can hardly wait."

Jim grabbed his gear from the storage room, slipped on his plate carrier, and slung his rifle over his neck. He carried his pack with him and tied it behind his saddle. Once he'd mounted up, he headed down the street, then paused to check that the street was clear before riding out onto Main. Once the fuel ran out, there hadn't been enough traffic that they had to pay much attention to whether anyone was coming or not. That had changed since people were more active now. There were golf carts, electric bikes, and scooters zipping along the street at a fast clip and barely making any sound. As much as the signs of progress pleased him, Jim wasn't excited about the return of traffic.

With each trip through town, the changes became more visible. People were making an effort to get their long-neglected homes in order. They were making repairs, cleaning up trash, and attempting to wrangle overgrown lawns into a more orderly state. People with electric lawnmowers or string trimmers were selling their services. People with electric chainsaws or tree trimmers were dealing with decorative trees that had been damaged or abused during the collapse. Broken windows in occupied homes were being replaced with windows from damaged or abandoned homes.

Most surprising of all, people waved at Jim as he rode through town. At various times he'd been the town outlaw and its most notorious citizen. He'd been Public Enemy Number One. Had the people of town been his high school graduating class, he might have been awarded the superlatives for "Most Likely To Die A Violent Death" or "Mostly Likely To Be Lynched By An Angry Mob."

He'd cursed the people of the town and called them out for their refusal to lift a finger to improve their conditions, and he'd killed several of them and made no effort to hide his deeds. Even today, while the residents of Main Street were working in their yards like it was a summer afternoon, Jim still wore his crusty armor with a loaded handgun on his side and a heavily worn rifle hanging around his neck. He had nine mags for his rifle and four for his handgun. While some in the town considered that overkill, Jim felt that was as light a loadout as he dared risk.

With no other rifles visible among the citizens of this town, Jim wondered how long he'd need to carry his. Maybe a better question was how long could he get away with openly packing so heavily? Already some of the townspeople had reverted to leaving their weapons at home when they were out and about. They came to the roadhouse unarmed and left in the darkness with no means to defend themselves.

Jim made it clear to his people that this was totally unacceptable. They were to continue carrying primary and secondary weapons until he told them otherwise. They were to carry enough ammunition that they could hold off an attack until help came for them. It would take a lot more than electricity to convince Jim Powell the world was safe again.

41

Jim's childhood home was bustling with activity when he arrived. Shade's wagon was backed up to the open garage door. Shade, Nooner, Pete, and Charlie were leaning against the sides of the wagon, taking a break after having unloaded. Jim tied his horse off to a tree and joined the group.

"Well here comes old Blister," Shade commented. "Shows up after the work is done."

"I tried to volunteer," Jim said in his own defense. "Pops said you guys had it covered."

"We do," Pete said. "Pops probably didn't want to spend the whole time arguing with you."

Charlie laughed.

Jim frowned. "Do Pops and I argue a lot?"

Nooner chuckled, filling the air with his high-octane breath. "Does fifty pounds of flour make a big biscuit?"

Jim shrugged. "Now I admit we *might* have heated discussions on occasion, but not all the time."

"There's not any 'we' to it, according to Pops," Pete said. "He told us you're the one who wants to argue with everyone."

"He says you've always been that way," Charlie added.

"Well, I came out here because I was concerned," Jim snapped. "I'll just head back to the roadhouse and let Pops figure the rest out on his own."

"What are you concerned about?" Shade asked.

"Mostly about them living out here by themselves. They don't ride horses unless they have to, so I don't know how they're going to get back and forth to the roadhouse or the valley."

Pete grinned. "Don't worry about that part. Pops has it covered. Go ask him."

Intrigued, Jim headed inside where he found Pops vacuuming and Nana dusting. Pops was sweating and looking fatigued. This was more activity than either he or Nana were used to, though Nana looked energized by it. She was like a cleaning whirlwind and Jim expected she'd have Pete and Charlie in there working just as hard before long. Those boys were going to be in for a long evening, but they both loved Nana and Pops. They'd be glad to do it.

"Hey," Jim said. "How are things going?"

Pops appeared relieved at having an excuse to stop. He turned off the vacuum and sagged into his recliner. "Hey, Jim. It's going fine. All the critical stuff is moved in and we're doing a little cleaning."

"I was talking to the guys out there about how you were going to get back and forth to the roadhouse. Pete said you had it covered. What's he talking about?"

Pops grinned. "I did some trading with a guy in town and he's giving me an electric golf cart for two riding mowers and a utility trailer."

"Sounds like a decent trade."

"Yeah, he said he's building electric riding mowers and wants them for parts, plus he needs the trailer for picking up old carts and delivering new ones. Worked out well for both of us."

"What kind of range does it have?"

"That's the best part," Pops said. "I should have enough power to get to your place in the valley and back. I'll definitely have enough to ride around town and visit the roadhouse."

"I'm glad to hear that. Just because you're back in your old house doesn't mean you should isolate yourselves."

"We won't," Pops said.

"I might," Nana chimed in. "Don't take it personally if you don't see me for a few days. Maybe even a few weeks. It's going to take a lot of work to get this place back into shape."

"As long as you enjoy it," Jim said. "Don't push yourself."

Nana smiled. "It's worth it to be back in my house."

"How's the water doing?"

Pops shrugged. "The pump you put in the old well has been doing fine and we have plenty of water. It still smells like sulfur, but I talked to a guy who says he can help with that. Says we need a potassium filter and he knows where I can get one."

"Just be careful who you let in your house," Jim said. "Things are better but they're not perfect. Don't assume everyone you meet has pure intentions."

"You never did trust anyone," Nana said. "Even as a kid. I'm not sure where we went wrong."

Jim rolled his eyes. "You didn't do anything wrong, Nana. Experience has taught me everything I need to know about people. I'm just saying you might not be able to trust everyone, okay?"

"Okay." Pops gave Jim a thumbs up. "Got it."

Jim knew he was being patronized. Pops would continue to take everyone at their word, whether they were trustworthy or not. He wasn't going to change. "Well, I need to get back to the roadhouse. Pete and Charlie are still staying with you for a few days, right?"

Pops nodded. "Yes. We'll keep them busy and fed."

"Good. If you need anything, just send one of them to get me. If you need supplies, send me a list. Since the power is back on, I have people coming into the roadhouse every day selling lightbulbs, appliances, and other things we had no use for a few months ago."

"Good to know," Pops said.

"I'll see you later, then." Jim hugged his mom and dad, then headed back through the open garage door.

When he got outside, Shade and Nooner were packing up their

gear. They'd folded the tarps they used to cover the loaded wagon and had them weighed down with several coils of rope.

"Our work here is done," Shade said. "And I promised Nooner a cold beer or nine at the roadhouse."

"That's where I'm headed too," Jim said. "I'll ride along with you."

"Bring a couple back for us," Pete said. "I could use an icy brew."

Jim spun around and frowned at his son, who was grinning from ear to ear.

"Just joking, Dad."

"You better be joking," Jim warned.

"Hell, they're old enough to drink," Nooner said. "I started smoking at four and drinking at eight and just look at me. I'm a hunk of a man, if I don't say so myself."

Everyone busted out laughing.

"What?" Nooner said, offended.

"You ain't got enough meat on you to hold your britches up," Shade said. "And them twiggy little arms of yours are so scrawny I'm surprised you can lift a bottle of liquor. Your skin hangs off you like a suit that don't fit and you're missing so many teeth you could eat corn through a chain link fence."

Nooner grinned. "None of that stopped the ladies from loving me. I got a woman in every town."

Shade cast him a doubting look. "You do, huh?"

Nooner bobbed his head. "Does a rocking horse have a wooden pecker?"

Shade held up a hand to stop him. "Before you start bragging about these women, you remember the last one you were holed up with?"

Nooner nodded.

"Why did you have to take her with you everywhere you went?" Shade asked.

Nooner looked sheepish. "So I didn't have to kiss her goodbye. She was ugly and had carcass-breath."

"That's right," Shade said. "So I don't want to hear any more lip about what a hunk of man you are. Keep running that mouth and you'll be buying your own beer."

Nooner pursed his lips shut and climbed onto the wagon seat. Shade laughed, then climbed in to join him. Pete and Charlie were laughing so hard their eyes were watering.

"You boys be careful," Jim said, hugging Pete, then Charlie. "If you need anything, come to the roadhouse. Otherwise I'll see you tomorrow."

"We'll be fine," Pete said.

"You have your weapons, right?" Jim asked.

Both boys nodded.

"Nana and Pops don't think you'll need them anymore, but you might. Don't let them tell you otherwise."

42

Nooner was on his thirteenth beer when Hank Rose and his "cult" piled into the Reset Roadhouse that evening. Of course, Jim and those who'd visited the Rose Farm with him understood that Hank and his friends weren't really a cult. To the rest of the crowd in the roadhouse that night, Hank and his roommates were simply more unfamiliar faces in the already bustling crowd in the busy roadhouse.

Hugh was the first to spot them and he radioed Jim, who was working the row of display cases that were part of the roadhouse's store. Jim was making small talk with a man in a canvas barn coat who was perusing the spare magazines for something that might fit the Raven Arms pocket gun he'd been carrying since the 1980s. So far, he wasn't having any luck.

Jim said, "I need to go talk to some people. If you find something you want to try in your gun, someone at the bar can help you." Jim stepped out from behind the counter and cut through the crowd, waving at Hank.

Hank looked relieved at finally spotting a familiar face and the two shook hands when Jim reached him.

"This place is hopping. I haven't seen anything quite like it."

"I'll take that as a compliment. If we have time, I'll tell you how this place came about later. You'd probably appreciate it. Like your cult story, there's a little misdirection and subterfuge in the tale of the Reset Roadhouse."

"Excellent," Hank said. "Can't wait to hear about it."

Jim led the group to a less-crowded section of the roadhouse and set up two tables for them. As they helped him set up the tables, Jim couldn't help but notice that they'd all cleaned up for the occasion. When he'd last seen them, they were just as scruffy as anyone else in town. The men had combed their hair and wore nicer clothes. The women wore dresses, nice coats, and even had on perfume. This was clearly a big night out on the town for the group of friends.

Once everyone was seated, Jim said, "I'm going to go get some beer for you guys. We also have liquor and water. That's about it for drinks. Do you need anything besides beer?"

Hank's people exchanged glances, then Hank acted as spokesman. "We don't need any water, but some beer and liquor would be nice."

Jim pointed toward the bar. "That chalkboard up there is the menu. It used to be that we could only offer one menu item every day, but we offer more now that we have electricity available. We've got freezers, ovens, deep fryers, toasters, and a lot of other kitchen stuff. Order early because we start running out of things before the night is over."

"Got it," Hank said, giving Jim a thumbs-up.

Jim headed for the bar and grabbed two buckets of beer, a bottle of liquor, and a few shot glasses.

"What are you doing behind my bar, Jim Powell?" Becky demanded. "I can smell you."

"I'm filling an order for a table so you don't have to."

"You should do that more often. Maybe then I'd be nicer to you if you worked once in a while."

"I doubt that.

Beckly cackled. "Me too!"

Jim hauled the drinks back to his new guests and placed them on the tables. "Remember, this is my treat. Eat up, drink up, and have a good night."

Hank crossed his arms and regarded Jim warily. "Although I appreciate the hospitality, a man always has to wonder if there's a catch. There's nothing free in this world. We just met the other day, and these aren't the kindest of times. Most people these days are looking for an excuse to kill someone and it's up to you to prove you don't deserve to die." There was no menace in Hank's tone, it was simply an honest question from a young man who tended toward directness.

"You're completely right," Jim said. "I'm generally the suspicious type so I understand your concern. There were two reasons I invited you folks down here. For one, I was impressed that you turned down power. You and your friends are making an effort to stick to your values, even if it means things are going to be tough. I respect that. Second, I can relate to a man whose life was shaped by his grandfather."

Hank smiled and grabbed the bottle of liquor from the table. He studied the label on the bottle, frowned, then poured two shots. He slid one toward Jim. "I don't know what hell this stuff is, but will you drink with me?"

Jim took the shot glass. "I will, and I'll explain to you later what you're drinking."

Hank took the other one. "Fair enough. Were you close to your grandfather?"

"Though I'm not sure 'close' is the word for it, he had a big impact on me. It's a long story, but he saved my life. He's been dead for years, and I was in a tight spot when the lights went out. Hearing him in my head is what kept me alive and got me home. He wouldn't let me quit, even when things were miserable."

Hank raised his shot glass into the air. "To grandfathers."

"To grandfathers," Jim repeated, hoisting his shot.

The two men tossed them back, winced, and scowled. While it was decent liquor by the standards of the day, current standards were painfully low. Hank immediately filled more shot glasses and slid them toward his friends.

Jim placed his shot glass back on the table. "I'll check back in a few and see if you've figured out the menu."

While Hank's group studied the chalkboard, Jim wandered around to see what else was going on around the roadhouse that night. Lloyd was playing the banjo on stage and had two younger men accompanying him on upright bass and guitar. They seemed like nice young men, but their choice of company was telling. At least the addition of their instruments to the ensemble helped tone down the dental drill abrasiveness of Lloyd's banjo.

Even without the music, the roadhouse was loud that night. They had a full house and people were drinking, conversing loudly, and laughing. It was everything a good bar should be and it amazed Jim that he'd managed to carve out this warm little niche in an otherwise drab, disaster-stricken world. He'd accomplished his goal of creating a station for monitoring community intelligence. He'd created a spot where his people were able to trade off their excess gear for items they needed, like diapers, toiletries, and medications. He'd also managed to give his people and the others he'd hired to work there a sense of purpose in a time when there were few opportunities to experience that.

Although he didn't often sit back and appreciate what he'd accomplished, Jim took a moment to do so. This was his doing. Certainly, other people had helped and were required to keep it functioning, but the Reset Roadhouse was his brainchild, and he was proud of it. Then he spotted Dr. Nelson, Blake Justice, and several of their cronies seated at a table near the stage.

Somehow, Jim had missed them coming in and hadn't spotted them among the crowd. He was a little surprised that none of the staff had informed him of their presence, and figured his people were probably trying to spare him the aggravation. They knew he wasn't fond of that particular group. Jim stood there for a moment trying to decide if he was going to approach them or just let it be and enjoy his night. A voice in the back of his mind encouraged him to turn away and let them be.

He almost did.

Then Blake Justice caught sight of Jim standing there in the crowd and met his eye. Blake grinned and nudged Dr. Nelson. Jim sighed and gritted his teeth. There was no way he could walk away now. Dr. Nelson twisted around in his chair and leered in Jim's direction. Yeah, Jim wasn't walking away. Some situations took on their own momentum and there was no altering it. There was no steering away or dragging his feet.

Time slowed down as Jim approached their table. "Good evening, gentlemen."

Blake's grin grew wider as he looked around the table as his companions. "He called us gentlemen."

"I'm shocked," Dr. Nelson said, taking a slug of his beer.

There was laughter around the table. Blake and Dr. Nelson were going to play this up for their audience, the people who felt obligated to laugh.

"I was giving you the benefit of the doubt when I called you gentlemen. Would you rather I address you as Dr. Dick and the Assholes? Is that the name of your merry little band?"

No one was grinning now. The tension thickened like congealed gravy and Jim was satisfied with himself. He wasn't going to let them come into his place of business and enjoy themselves at his expense or let them ruin his night. He had friends here and he was determined to have a good time.

Jim rested his hand on the back of Dr. Nelson's chair and leaned in. "Listen, I want you guys to finish your drinks and get out of here. Consider yourselves banned. Don't come back."

"What did we do?" Blake demanded.

"I don't like you. I tolerated you while we were handing out converters because you were entitled to them just like everyone else. Now you've got your converters and my obligation to you is done. I don't want to see you in here again."

Dr. Nelson's face was red and he was simmering. He wasn't used to being treated this way. "I've had enough of you, Jim Powell. You act like a badass with all those guns on you, but if we were to go toe-to-toe, I'd mop this filthy floor with you. Maybe it's time I show you that."

"I'm giving you the opportunity to finish your beer and leave quietly. I suggest you take it."

"What if I'd rather leave the shitty beer and *not* leave so quietly?" Dr. Nelson picked up his beer bottle and poured the contents onto the concrete floor.

"Kick his ass," Blake mumbled. "Teach him some respect."

Dr. Nelson smiled at his friend. "Oh, I'm about to."

Jim remained leaning over the table and kept his voice low. "My grandfather taught me a lot about fighting. You see, some men are scholars and others are men of science. Some are skilled tradesman while others are men of medicine, like you. My grandfather was a man of violence, and you bring to mind an important lesson he taught me."

"What's that?" Dr. Nelson snarled. "Are you going to entertain us now with tales from the Book of Inbred? Maybe you should do it from the stage so everyone can benefit."

Jim shook his head. "Nah, Doc, this lesson is just for you. My grandfather told me that it was just plain stupid to telegraph your intentions to an enemy. Never tell a man you're about to fight him. Never warn a man you're coming."

Without warning, Jim grabbed a fistful of the doctor's hair and slammed his face into the table so hard it overturned the beer bottles setting there. Jim did it a second time for good measure, then latched onto the doctor's collar, dragging both him and his chair over backward. Despite the doctor's threats, Blake and his companions were stunned by the explosion of violence. Blake finally broke the spell and stood up, along with the rest of men at their table. Blake only managed one step in Jim's direction before Jim drew his handgun and leveled it at Blake's face.

The sound of Dr. Nelson's chair hitting the floor stopped all conversation around the roadhouse. People craned their necks to see what was happening. As was his practice, Lloyd didn't let the excitement deter him. He kept banging away at the banjo and singing at the top of his lungs. His younger companions missed a few beats, uncertain of what was happening in the crowd, yet soon followed Lloyd's lead and kept going.

With his gun still on Blake, Jim dragged the doctor across the gritty concrete floor. Dr. Nelson was dazed, kicking, cursing, and grabbing at Jim. Hugh had watched the scene unfold from the bar and had security staged to assist Jim. Hugh closed in on the men's table along with Shade, Ian, and Conway. They searched Blake and the other men, took their weapons, and escorted them away from their table.

Jim didn't release the doctor until he reached the open loading dock door. He let go, then shoved the doctor with his foot, sending him rolling off the three-foot drop. He hit the ground with a thud and groaned. When the rest of the security team reached the loading dock, Dr. Nelson's party climbed down to the ground and helped the doctor to his feet.

"This is the last time I bump heads with you," Jim said. "You see me coming, you better cross the street. Better yet, why don't you just move and go somewhere else?"

"No one is moving," Blake snapped. "This is our town too. Maybe *you* should be the one packing up. Go back to the boonies with the rest of the hillbillies."

"Maybe you should stop talking," Hugh interjected. "Be a shame to die because your drunk ass couldn't shut up."

Blake shot Hugh a nasty look, then returned his focus to Jim. "This isn't over. You can't treat people this way and get away with it."

"If you can find someone who cares, file a complaint. You can send someone to collect your weapons tomorrow," said Jim. "None of you guys though. You're not welcome. Send your wives or something."

Dr. Nelson was almost too enraged to speak. He desperately wanted to jump on Jim and make him pay for the public indignity he'd just suffered. His rational brain tried to talk him off that ledge, warning him that it would only end badly. Finally, he said, "I'm going to shut you down. I'm going to get you banned from this town, then you'll learn what it feels like to be unwelcome. By the time I'm done, there'll be a shoot-on-sight order for Jim Powell. Mark my words."

"Good luck with that," Jim said. "People have tried it before. Besides, I'm thinking the people of this town would rather have a roadhouse than some outsider doctor who thinks he's better than everyone else."

When the doctor started to say something else, Jim hit the button on the dock door and it lowered, cutting off the doctor's tirade.

43

It was five days later when Hugh and Jim again rode through the gate at the end of Rose Farm Road. When Hank and his friends came to the roadhouse, he and Jim discussed this visit, though intoxication had made precise planning difficult. It was further complicated by the fact that they couldn't text or call each other to clarify the details.

They rode through the pasture, past the small stand of trees, to the old white farmhouse with its metal roof and poplar clapboard siding. A man and woman from Hank's group were in the front yard using a canoe paddle to stir a massive black cauldron suspended from a metal tripod. Jim thought their names were Brandy and Rick. A smoky fire beneath the pot had the water steaming in the cool morning air.

"Morning," Jim said. "What are you cooking?"

Brandy raised the paddle from the water, snagging a bedsheet, and lifting it into the air. "Laundry soup. Want some?"

Jim crinkled his nose. "Thanks, but I ate already."

Brandy shifted the paddle, extending the same offer to Hugh, a wicked grin on her face.

He held up a hand. "Nah, I'm good."

"We're looking for Hank," Jim said. "We made a plan when you guys were at the roadhouse the other night, but it was kind of loose. I don't know if he's expecting me or not."

"We were *all* kind of loose that night," Rick said. "That was a good time. Thanks again for the hospitality."

"No problem. I had a good time too."

Rick pointed at the river, to a rutted dirt path that ran alongside it. "Go downstream a little bit. You'll find Hank and a couple of guys working at the ponds."

"Thanks," Jim said. "Enjoy your meal."

Brandy laughed.

As Jim and Hugh rode toward the river, Jim said, "The river is nice here."

"It's about the same size as the river behind your house," Hugh pointed out.

"Yeah, they're closer to the river though. I wish I was closer."

They reached the river and turned downstream. The dirt road was rough, having grown rutted during the spring wet season. Jim stared out at the water. He didn't know much about this river, but it was wide, shallow, and fast-moving.

"There they are."

Jim followed Hugh's finger and spotted Hank and a couple of his friends working among a series of ponds, concrete tanks, culverts, and spillways. Most of the ponds were fully fenced and had metal roofs built over them. A collection pipe at the river caught fresh water and directed it through the ponds, then allowed it to rejoin the river a short distance downstream. When Hank's people noticed them, Jim waved, but it took several more minutes to reach them.

Hank stopped working and pulled off his high rubber gloves. "Greetings, Jim Powell! Glad you guys came. I wasn't sure if you'd remember or not."

Jim smiled. "I wasn't nearly so drunk as you guys. I remembered just fine."

"We appreciated you letting us stay the night at the roadhouse. That was way safer than trying to ride home drunk. Even if the horses know the way, there's a lot that can happen on a dark, lonely road."

"No problem. Anytime you guys want to come down there and blow off some steam, you're welcome to spend the night." Jim climbed off his horse. "I was surprised you guys were gone when I came into work the next day."

"We had work to do here at the farm," Hank said. "Once one of us woke up, they woke everyone else, and we boogied on home. That was something I got from my grandfather. You can stay out and raise hell as late as you want, but don't think that's getting you out of your chores the next day. When my grandfather was alive, I fed cattle when I was still drunk and puking off the tractor the whole time. My grandfather would be over there laughing his ass off, telling me I got what I deserved for staying out *tomcatting*."

"My grandfather was the same way," Jim said. "And you guys are welcome back anytime."

"Well, if we can make a deal, we'll be down that way more often, making deliveries to you." Hank gestured at the fenced ponds. "As you can see, these are our holding ponds. You probably couldn't get a permit to put a system like this in the days before the collapse. My grandfather was 'grandfathered' in, so to speak."

Jim smiled at the joke. "These are all trout?"

Hank nodded.

"You worried about them escaping?" Hugh asked.

Hank laughed. "You'd be surprised at the damage critters can do to a trout farm. Bears and raccoons will take a few, but birds are the worst. A heron will get in there and spear every damn fish you have just for sport. They can wipe out an entire pond in a single day."

"I'm surprised your neighbors didn't wipe out your fish," Jim said.

"There aren't many people that know about these ponds. My grandfather put them in back in the 1950s and he stocked a few local trout ponds for people. We ate a lot of trout and sold a few to people he knew, including some restaurants. Since the collapse, my friends and I have been eating them, and we haven't told anyone else about this resource. We didn't want word of it to reach the wrong ears, if you know what I mean."

"We won't say a word to anyone," Jim said. "There's a lot of *wrong* ears out there now. If you can provide fish to the roadhouse, we'll keep your name out of it."

"We'll figure something out. A deal like this would help us too because some of the ponds are overcrowded. A few weeks ago, we even turned some fingerlings out into the river because I didn't have room for them."

"That'll make some fishermen happy," Hugh said. "Eventually."

"That was my thinking too," Hank said. "Can I send some fish home with you for the family? A sample of the product?"

Jim grinned. "I'm sure they'd like that. I certainly would."

Hank used a big dip net to catch a half dozen sizable trout. He dumped them on the bank of the pond and one of his friends killed them by stabbing them in the head with a sharp knife. When he was done, Hank wrapped the bloody fish in a piece of fabric from an old round hay baler, then shoved them into a feed sack.

"Is that what you feed the fish?" Jim asked, pointing at the feed corn sack Hank had stuffed the fish into.

Hank glanced at the sack. "No, we used to feed them a special trout food, but we've been out of that for a long time. Now we feed them whatever we can find. We scour fields for old corn, then soak it until it's soft, and feed them that. It's not ideal, but it keeps them alive. The river also brings insects through that they can feed on."

"Have you ever tried a gut bucket?" Hugh asked.

Hank looked wary. "No, I'm pretty sure I'd remember a name like that."

"A lot of people use them for chickens. We didn't have much money growing up, so we always kept one going. Stank like hell, but it worked."

"What is it?" Jim asked.

"Basically a bucket of compost and old meat. We used to use roadkill, guts from animals we butchered, whatever we had. You drill some holes in the bucket and it basically becomes a maggot sprinkler. Chickens love it and I'm sure it would work for trout."

"Sounds amazing," Hank said. "Maybe you can help me set one up."

"I'll do it," Hugh said. "Get a dozen of them going and it would be a good supplement for you."

Hank handed the sack of fish off to Jim.

Jim hefted the bag and was surprised at the weight of it. "When do you think you can make the first delivery to the roadhouse?"

"We can bring them tomorrow if you want."

Jim shrugged. "Why not? We have refrigeration now. We can clean them and store them in a refrigerator if we have to. I keep forgetting we have electrical means for preserving foods now."

"If you don't want to deal with washing a bunch of silverware, I suggest fish nuggets," Hank said. "They're basically a fish version of chicken nuggets. It turns fried fish into a finger food."

"Hadn't thought of that," Jim said. "Sounds delicious."

Hank smiled. "With the right spices and breading, it can be."

"Maybe we can try that tonight?" Hugh said. "Research."

"As far as payment," Jim said. "Our biggest trade commodity is weapons and ammo."

Hank shook his head. "I appreciate the thought and I understand the need for security, but we don't want to turn this into an armed camp. We have a few rifles, some shotguns, and some handguns. That's plenty for us."

"Need any ammo for them?" Hugh asked.

Hank furrowed his brow and looked at his friends. One of them nodded.

"Sure," Hank said. "What else do you have?"

"We have clothing and medical supplies, a lot of camping gear, and knives."

"All this is in your store?" Hank asked. "These goods you're naming off?"

Jim nodded.

"Then how about giving us store credit?" Hank asked. "Instead of you having to pay for every delivery immediately, just give us credit. Me and my people can come in there and shop as needed. That might work better for us. Then we don't end up with a bunch of stuff we don't need."

"Credit would probably work better for us too. Can you bring us two dozen trout tomorrow?"

"Not a problem. Do you want us to clean them for you?" Hank asked.

Jim hadn't thought about this possibility. "You can do that? How does it impact the price?"

"We'd ask for twenty-five percent more trade value."

Jim looked at Hugh. "What do you think?"

"I'd jump on it," Hugh said. "Inexperienced people will do a lousy job of it and they're prone to getting cut. Not to mention all the complaining you're going to hear from whoever gets stuck with that job."

Hugh was right. Jim could easily imagine his staff complaining about the process. Whatever it cost to have the fish cleaned there would be worth it. "We'll take it. Sounds like a bargain.

Hank shoved his hands in his pockets. "Well, if you guys have time, I'd love to give you a tour of some other things we're doing."

"I'd like that," Jim said. "We've got plenty of time. Lead the way."

44

Over the next few weeks the pace of national recovery accelerated to the point it was evident even in their little community. Lightspeed's aid shipments finally began to trickle into the area. One day a convoy of military trucks from a local armory simply showed up out of nowhere and started handing out boxes. It was the first aid shipment the area had seen since the government showed up to try and sell Americans on the concept of Comfort Camps. The whole Comfort Camp system turned out to be a bribe in which communities would receive aid for laying down their weapons and allowing foreign troops to assist with the recovery. That idea died on the vine and was eventually shut down nationwide.

The soldiers had food, water, and medical supplies. They also had a doctor and a dentist who could provide rudimentary care and dispense medications. After all the supplies were distributed, the officer in charge of the aid convoy announced that supplies would be coming twice a week and people could let them know of any specific needs. People immediately shouted out suggestions, which the officer dutifully scribbled down.

The arrival of aid was not the only change taking place in the community. Cat Anderson's business incubator group had formally adopted Jim's tongue-in-cheek suggestion and were calling themselves Commerce Unchambered. The group decided to meet once a week at the same time to make it easier for interested parties to find their meetings. More and more people had expressed an interest in attending. Dozens of members of Cat's group had already gotten their businesses up and running. Without any large employers hiring a workforce, the local economy—such as it was—was dominated by small business.

As enthusiasm and hope returned to the community, people saw needs and rose to fill them. Not only were they starting businesses, but Cookie's volunteer workforce was restoring the appearance of the town. The sights and sounds of recovery were everywhere. These minor signs of progress were evident all down Main Street. During the day, people were outside repairing homes and buildings, cleaning up trash, debris, and vandalized cars. To the best of their ability, they were erasing the signs of damage done during the collapse.

The roadhouse was impacted by this vibrant atmosphere as well. As spirits were elevated, more and more people were frequenting the roadhouse. The menu, both in terms of food and drink, had expanded. They'd begun offering some mixed drinks, though the selection was still limited by what mixers they could find. On some nights, they had a version of sangria and on others they served an improvised wine cooler.

Ed was working like a mad scientist each day, brewing more varieties of beer, and bringing on an assistant so he could get more accomplished. Lloyd pitched in to help during the day, putting his background in moonshining to work. Ed developed a root beer to provide a non-alcoholic alternative for patrons, as well as an alcoholic apple cider that was a big hit. He also partnered with a local cannabis grower to offer a weed-infused beer.

Inspired by the success of Ed's cannabis brew, Randi's daughter's applied that same concept to food. They bought a supply of honey, repackaged it, and offered cannabis-infused honey. They did the same with jelly and canned apple pie filling. They offered infused cookies, fudge, and brownies. Not only did these products become big sellers for the roadhouse, they created a cottage industry that allowed Randi's daughters to work from home.

The fish nuggets made from Hank Rose's trout were a huge hit and Jim had even more contractors now supplying goods to the road-house. The lady who made tortillas for the roadhouse began offering bread, and another lady in the community began supplying the road-house with fresh cheese. By carefully coordinating with his meat, bread, and cheese supplier, Jim was able to add cheeseburgers and fries to the menu. Despite the simplicity and basic nature of this menu item, it introduced a normality to the experience of dining at the roadhouse that was exponentially more significant than it should have been.

"I never realized that this is what the apocalypse was missing the whole time," Jim said, holding his cheeseburger up in the air and regarding it as if it were a religious relic. He was sitting at the bar, eating one of those precious cheeseburgers and drinking some variety of Belgian beer Ed had come up with.

"Is it rocking your world?" Randi asked.

Jim groaned with satisfaction. "It's like falling in love all over again."

With an amused shake of her head Randi wandered off to check on the other patrons. The lunch rush had tapered off, leaving the roadhouse with the regular midday drinkers and a few late eaters. Normally, it would stay at about this pace until the dinner crowd started wandering in. Then it typically went nonstop until Jim ran everyone out and locked the doors for the night.

A kid walking into the roadhouse caught Jim's eye. They didn't get many kids coming in on their own. He had a stack of papers in his hand and looked around uncertainly before heading for the bar. He stood at the counter until Randi took pity on him and headed over.

She put her hands on her hips and glared at him. "What do you want, kid?"

He held up the papers. "I'm handing out these fliers and I'm supposed to give one to a man named Jim. Is he here?"

Randi pointed to Jim. "That's him. The ugly one. Approach with caution."

The kid nervously headed in Jim's direction. Jim assumed it was because of Randi's warning, but it wasn't. Once the kid handed Jim one of his flyers, he bolted and was out the door before Jim erupted in curses.

"What?" Randi asked. "Is that a wanted poster? Did Dr. Nelson put a bounty out on you?"

Jim scowled. "No." He slid the flyer across the bar.

Randi picked it up and read it. "That *asshole*."

"I might have said something to that effect already."

Randi rolled her eyes. "How was I supposed to know what profanity you were using? All I heard was this incoherent rant with the occasional word standing out above the others." She tossed the flyer back on the bar and it slid to a stop in front of Jim.

It read:

Grand Opening!
Doc's Place
The former Old Mill building
FREE beer and pizza tonight only!
Live music!
Enjoy dinner and drinks at the community's newest establishment.
Operated by Doctor Byron Nelson and Blake Justice, upstanding citizens you can trust!
Unlike Jim Powell's Reset Roadhouse, you will find none of the following:
Crazed, violent hillbillies; firearms; indoor smoking; random violence;
Rude staff; menacing employees; bad smells; offensive banjo playing;
Unappetizing food; bloodstained floor; and mediocre alcohol.

"I wonder if their pizza is any good?" Randi asked.

"You'd really go there? After he said our staff was rude?"

"Free is free." Randi shrugged as if that explained everything. "Besides, I'm sure he's talking about someone else."

"You eat *here* for free!" Jim snapped. "Your whole family does. And I'm pretty sure he was talking about you."

"Might have been Becky. She gets kind of feisty. But yeah, I'd go just to see what it's like."

"Well, it's a shame you have to work," Jim said. "Guess you won't have time to go dine with the enemy."

"You wouldn't let me run down there just to see? I could spy for you. Come back and tell you what I saw."

"No. Besides, I might sneak down there to do a little recon myself. How about I give *you* a full report when I get back."

Randi frowned. "Now that isn't fair at all. Besides, you should probably have backup with you."

"Surely those two won't try anything there in front of their customers."

"It's not him I'm concerned about, Jim. What if you have one of those 'stupid attacks' where you do something that you're going to regret later?"

"There wouldn't be anything stupid about kicking Dr. Nelson's ass," Jim said. "I should have done it a long time ago. The guy's an idiot."

"He's a doctor!"

"Then he's a well-educated idiot."

Randi gave a broad grin. "This is the Jim Powell I know and love. The one who kills people just because they annoy him."

"I do not! I've never killed anyone who didn't deserve it."

Randi winked at him. "It's okay, Jim. I know the truth and we can still be friends."

Jim groaned and shook his head. "It's impossible to argue with you."

"Yes, and a smarter man would have quit doing it a long time ago. Look at Lloyd. He knows better. As country people say, I finally learned him."

"Lloyd didn't quit arguing with you because he's smart. He quit arguing with you because he's too drunk to remember what you say half the time."

Randi wiped the bar down with a towel. "If Dr. Nelson and his crew were trying to get your panties in a twist, it worked. You're all bent out of shape over that stupid piece of paper."

Jim snatched the flier up from the table and read it again. "I don't care that they're opening a restaurant. People might go there in the beginning just for the novelty of it, but the guy is such a jerk I can't imagine people will keep going for long."

"If you don't care that he's opening a restaurant, why are you so mad?"

"I'm mad because he's only doing this to get back at me. This is personal. Everything this flier says is a jab at me. At us!"

Randi rested her elbows on the bar. "Then what are you going to do about it? The Jim Powell I know doesn't get this pissed off and let it go."

Jim laughed. "I can tell that you *want* me to do something about it. You're hoping I'll go down there, show my ass, and start a fight."

Randi bobbed her head. "Hell yeah, I am. I love it when you go full Jim Powell on someone. It makes my day."

"It ain't happening."

Randi gave Jim a smug smile. "We'll see."

45

There was no escaping the story of a new restaurant opening in town. Every customer coming into the roadhouse that afternoon tracked Jim down to make sure he'd heard about it. Then they wanted to know what he thought, which riled him up all over again. As his employees and family came in, they all read the flyer and asked the same question, which was whether Jim was going to attend the grand opening.

Ariel and Ellen had even shown up at the roadhouse, having been alerted by an anonymous employee that Jim might be headed for trouble that night. Ellen knew she couldn't talk Jim out of going, yet she did get him to agree to take Hugh along. Hugh was one of the few people Jim would listen to in a potentially volatile situation. Hugh was also someone Ellen trusted to drag Jim out of there if that was what needed to be done.

Shortly after sunset, Jim was at the bar having a final roadhouse beer when Hugh walked up to join him. Hugh didn't have a rifle, which was unusual for him, but they suspected they wouldn't be allowed in Doc's place carrying weapons. In fact, they weren't sure they'd be allowed in at all. Jim glanced at Hugh's hip, noticing the absence of a holster.

"I'm not sure I've seen you without a handgun in a long time," Jim said.

"No holster doesn't mean no handgun. Are you telling me you're not carrying any weapons?"

Jim glanced at him. "I didn't say that."

Hugh took off his boonie hat and held it out in front of Jim. "Aluminum knuckles in the hat. I have a non-metallic G10 dagger concealed underneath my belt and a .380 that only the most intimate of friends could find."

Jim grimaced. "Thanks for not showing me that."

"You carrying anything?"

"Knife in the boot," Jim said. "North American Arms Black Widow in .22 Magnum under the belt buckle."

"I'm also taking backup," Hugh said.

Jim frowned. "Having too large a presence there might set things off on the wrong foot. I'm sure he's expecting me or someone from the roadhouse, but he might not let us in with too big an entourage."

"They're not going in. I'm taking Ian and Conway and they're going to be waiting outside. They'll be armed and they're each carrying an SBR for us in case things get spicy. They're going to find a location where they can watch the building through a spotting scope in case we need them."

"Good thinking," Jim said. "You ready?"

"As I'll ever be."

They informed the staff they were leaving, then the two men went outside to meet up with Ian and Conway. They had the horses waiting so everyone mounted up and headed off down Main Street. They were passed by several golf carts along the way and saw other people on foot headed in the same direction.

"You know where they're going, don't you?" Conway asked.

"I can guess," Jim replied.

They scouted a good position from which Ian and Conway could see Doc's Place. Then Hugh and Jim left the horses with them and walked down the hill to the restaurant, noting that the broken windows had been repaired and the garbage around the building cleaned up. Doc's Place was illuminated with more lights than Jim had seen on a single building in some time. There were string lights and Christmas lights wrapping the porch and stretching along the exterior of the building. There were portable floodlights with different colors of bulbs.

"Sounds like a party," Hugh said, commenting on the loud music.

"Looks like a party too. There's a lot of people here."

"You can't blame them, Jim. Anything free is a big lure these days. Free pizza and beer would be hard to turn down."

"I don't blame people for that. I don't even blame the assholes who opened the place. There's a lot of people opening businesses around town and there will be even more as people find new ways to use electricity to earn a living. I just don't like these guys and I want to see what they have going on."

"Jim, did you even consider that they might try to lure you here just so they could have the pleasure of throwing you out?"

"I hadn't considered that," Jim admitted.

"It could happen. You really embarrassed them when you threw them out of the roadhouse. I'm sure they'll want revenge in some manner."

"Copy that. Consider me warned."

The two stopped outside the restaurant and took in the place for a moment. There were people arriving from all directions. The porch was crowded with people waiting for tables inside. Servers were handing out free beers to keep them entertained. Inside, the place was bustling, and there was standing room only. The smell of pizza filled the air and Jim had to admit that it was intoxicating. They'd experimented with pizza at the roadhouse some, but Jim didn't have a good source for dough ingredients yet.

"Hey, Jim, surprised to see you here."

Jim turned at the familiar voice to find his parents walking up. He frowned. "I could say the same. What are you guys doing here?"

"We heard there was free pizza and beer, so I brought the new golf cart into town."

Jim shook his head. "I had this same conversation with Randi earlier. You guys eat free at the roadhouse whenever you want. You could have had free beer too, but neither of you drink."

Pops shifted awkwardly. "Yeah, but we've been to the Reset Roadhouse a million times. There's not a lot of eating choices in town right now and we were yearning for something a little different."

"Fine," Jim said. "There's a line. You better get in it if you want your free meal."

"Thanks," Pops said. "We will."

After they'd left to get in line, Jim mumbled, "Traitors."

Hugh laughed. "Remember, you just said you wouldn't blame people for taking advantage of free food and drink."

"Yeah, but it hits different when it's your parents."

"It would be more than just your parents if the roadhouse wasn't open tonight. All the staff and customers would probably be here too."

Jim knew it was true, but he had a chip on his shoulder about this place. If it had been anyone else, he wouldn't have cared as much. Well, maybe.

"Good evening, everyone," came a loud voice from inside the restaurant.

Jim recognized it as being Dr. Nelson's voice amplified through the poor sound quality of a megaphone.

"I'd like to welcome you all to the grand opening of Doc's Place. I hear that Jim Powell is even in attendance tonight. That should tell you something folks. Even he doesn't want to spend his time in that smoky dive that he calls the Reset Roadhouse."

There was laughter among some of the patrons and Jim felt the sting of it. Even though he couldn't see Dr. Nelson inside the building, the laughter only increased his desire to pummel the man. Dr. Nelson pushed his way out the door and stood on the wide porch, staring directly at Jim with a bemused expression in his eyes. The doctor gestured at Jim as he continued, his words spoken for the benefit of his patrons, but aimed at Jim.

"I do have to thank Jim Powell for proving the concept that a bar and restaurant could thrive in this environment. He was a pioneer in this field, but let's think about what else being a pioneer means. The term is synonymous with primitive, antiquated, and outdated. Sadly, Jim Powell and his roadhouse are all those things. It's a horse and buggy in the day of the automobile. It's a locomotive in the days of air travel."

The doctor paused as if expecting Jim to speak up on his own behalf. Jim folded his arms across his chest, tipped his head back, and glared defiantly at Dr. Nelson.

Dr. Nelson continued. "I can imagine that some of you might continue to patronize the Reset Roadhouse in the same spirit of nostalgia that one experiences when visiting an historic site or a business that was important to you during your childhood. However, if you want a clean and modern evening out, Doc's Place is where you'll want to go. You won't find anything in here that relies on firewood or an open flame. You won't find any of the primitive technologies that we were forced to use to survive the last year. We're all sick of that crap and I don't know about you, but I never want to see some of that stuff again. It should be relegated to the past, just like Jim's roadhouse should be."

Again, Dr. Nelson paused to give Jim the opportunity to rebut his statements, to defend the honor of his establishment. Jim didn't take the bait.

Disappointed, Dr. Nelson shrugged. "Your silence speaks for itself, Jim Powell. As for the rest of you, eat up and enjoy the free beer. We also have samplers at the bar of some of the appetizers and dishes we'll be serving here at Doc's Place. I brought in a brewmaster from Bristol and two chefs from Abingdon. The food here won't just be tolerable, it will be delectable. I hope you all have a good evening and thanks for coming."

Dr. Nelson turned off the megaphone, then gestured for Blake Justice to join him. The music and the din of conversation resumed, and the two men walked down the front steps to where Jim and Hugh were standing.

"You coming over to welcome me personally?" Jim asked. "You did that already while you were playing with your Mr. Microphone."

Dr. Nelson smiled, though there was nothing friendly about it. "No, I didn't come down here to welcome you. I came down here to personally throw your ass out, just like you did to me a few weeks ago."

"I only came because of the engraved invitation I received today. Nice how you sent a kid to deliver it because you were too chickenshit to come do it yourself."

"Time to shut up and get lost," Blake said. "You're on our turf now. On this property, we make the rules."

Jim looked down. "I'm standing on a public street. You make *traffic* rules now, Blake? I'm not sure how you think you're going to make me leave. Pretty sure I can stand in the street if I want."

"You want to test that theory?" Blake growled.

"Ignore him," Dr. Nelson said, arriving at a decision. "If he wants to stand outside like a starving dog outside a kitchen door, then let him do it. Just make sure this is as close as you get, Jim. I'd welcome the opportunity to physically toss you off that porch." Dr. Nelson went back up the steps, shaking hands and smiling at customers as he went.

"This isn't over," Blake whispered.

"I agree," Jim whispered back. "Because you're still breathing."

Blake stormed off.

"Let's go, Jim," Hugh said. "We've seen what we came to see."

Jim was turning to go when someone called his name. He looked back to see Cookie walking in his direction, an embarrassed look on his face.

"I'm sorry about that whole thing, Jim. I had no idea he opened this place as a slam against you. I thought it was just another restaurant until I heard him spouting off."

Jim patted Cookie on the shoulder. "It's okay, man. Drink his beer and eat his pizza. If you avoided everyone in this town that had a problem with me, you wouldn't have very many friends at all."

"That's the truth," Hugh said.

"We're going to get out of here, Cookie," Jim said. "I wanted to see what he had going, but I'm not interested in standing around all evening glaring at him. I have better things to do."

The two shook hands and Jim turned, took one step, and the world went dark around him.

46

Jim reached inside his jacket and plucked a tiny flashlight from a shirt pocket. He thumbed the switch on the end and directed his light toward the ground. Hugh did the same. A few more flashlights came on throughout the crowd, but a lot of people weren't carrying them any longer. Up until a few minutes ago, there had been so many porch lights lit up on Main Street that it wasn't necessary.

"What the hell?" Cookie said.

Jim shook his head. "Maybe a breaker? They could have overloaded a circuit with all these lights."

"I don't think so," Hugh said. "The courthouse went dark too. That brick cottage over there was lit up until a few minutes ago and it's not now. There was also a porch light on that little ranch house over there, and it went out."

"So maybe this part of town?" Cookie asked.

"Doesn't work that way," Hugh said. "Every converter has a direct connection to the big repeater on the mountain. If all these places have gone dark, it must mean that—"

"There's an issue with the repeater," Jim finished.

Hugh raised his radio. "Hugh for Ian. Hugh for Ian."

"Go for Ian."

"Do you have eyes on other houses? Can you see anything still lit up?"

"That's a negative," Ian replied. *"Everything was lit until a minute ago. Now it's all dark. No lights anywhere."*

"Copy that," Hugh replied.

Jim raised his radio. "I'm going to see if I can reach the roadhouse from here." Before he could speak, he was interrupted by a loud voice from the porch.

"Damn you, Jim Powell!"

It was Blake Justice. Jim recognized the voice. He directed his light toward Blake, forcing him to shield his eyes.

"What the hell did you do, Jim? You can't stand anyone else having a good time? Were you that threatened by our business venture that you had to pull the plug on it?"

Dr. Nelson appeared at Blake's side, his face red with fury. "Whatever you did, you fix it now. This is inexcusable and absolutely unforgivable."

When Jim opened his mouth to reply, Cookie stepped up to his defense.

"He didn't do shit, Dr. Nelson. He was standing here talking to me."

"It could have been one of his people!" Blake bellowed. "One of that feral clan of misfits he runs!"

"Interesting description," Hugh whispered. "I like that."

"The whole town is out," Cookie said.

Dr. Nelson fell silent. "What?"

"The whole town is out," someone in the crowd repeated. "All the houses we can see from here went dark."

"How does that happen?" Dr. Nelson said. "Who do we call?"

Jim almost laughed. "I guess we can send a message to Lightspeed, but this isn't like reporting an outage to the power company. I seriously doubt you'll go to bed tonight and wake up to power in the morning. It's not that—"

Jim's words were cut off by a distant explosion. Despite the blast being too far away to injure them, everyone recoiled out of instinct.

They felt no heat, nor was there any debris raining down around them. Then the significance of where the blast took place began to spread through the crowd. It was high in the air above Clinch Mountain. The location of Lightspeed's repeater.

The great pumpkin had exploded.

Everyone was silent for a moment, watching in awe, unable to believe or accept what their eyes had just seen.

"What the hell?" Jim muttered.

"Is that your doing?" Blake demanded.

Jim pointed to his chest. "Are you talking to me?"

"Who else would I be talking to?"

"Why would I do that, Blake? Why would I have disrupted my entire life to hand out those stupid converters if I was going to knock out the power? Why would Hugh have risked his life to bring us more converters? You're a damn idiot. I can't imagine there's anybody here that would intentionally destroy the power."

"Well, someone did," Dr. Nelson said.

"We don't know that," Hugh fired back. "This is experimental technology. There could have been a malfunction."

"Or it could have been sabotage!" Dr. Nelson barked. "I heard Lightspeed talking about Luddites! It could have been terrorism by those nutcases who don't want electricity."

Jim dismissed him with a wave. "We didn't come across any Luddites when we were on the road handing out converters. There were a few people who didn't want power, but they didn't care if the rest of us had it or not."

Cookie held his hands up, gesturing at everyone to stay calm. "Hey! Hey! Everyone shut up for a second!"

The crowd noise trickled to a stop at Cookie's commanding tone.

"We're not going to solve this tonight. Tempers are high and we don't have enough information to know what's going on. We need to get everyone home safely and sleep on this. We can try to figure out the rest tomorrow. You think we can get along for one freaking day so we can do that?"

Blake, Dr. Nelson, Jim, and Hugh stared daggers at each other.

Finally, one by one, they mumbled their assents. They could put aside their disagreements until they figured out what was going on.

Jim reached out and hooked Cookie by the arm. "You need to take the lead on this. You're neutral and the crowd will listen to you."

Cookie let out a long breath as the mantle of responsibility settled onto his shoulders. "How?"

"Get all the people with lights together," Jim said. "Figure out where they're going so they can escort people in the right direction."

"Got it!" Cookie climbed the steps onto the porch, a better position from which address the crowd. "Okay!" he barked. "I need all the people with lights to step forward."

As the crowd shifted, Jim leaned toward Hugh. "Check on the roadhouse, then get Ian and Conway to bring the horses down. I'm going to find my parents."

"Copy that." Hugh raised his radio and stepped away from the crowd.

Jim cut through the crowd to try and find his parents. They were sitting calmly at a table inside. "I need to get you guys out of here."

Pops was pleased with himself. "Everyone ran outside so we took the opportunity to grab a table."

Jim heaved a sigh. "Did you notice that the lights went out?"

"Of course. I figured they'd come back on in a few minutes. Then we're going to order some pizza." Pops rubbed his hands together eagerly.

Jim tried to remain patient. "There's not going to be any pizza, Pops. The power is out again and the repeater station up on the mountain blew up. There's no way of knowing when electricity will be restored."

"What blew up?" Nana asked. "What's a repeater?"

"It's basically the power station for this area," Jim said. "Until it's replaced, no one around here will have power again."

"When are they going to replace it?" Nana asked.

Jim sighed. "I have no way of knowing that."

"Will they work at our house?" she asked.

"No."

"How you do you know?" Pops asked.

When his parents made no effort to get up, Jim said, "Maybe I should take you guys to the roadhouse. You'll be warm there and we've got food. We'll get you back to the valley tonight or in the morning."

Nana shook her head. "I'm not going to the roadhouse or the valley. I'm going home."

"You can't go home," Jim said. "There's no heat, no running water, and no electricity. All the things that allowed you to go back to your old home are gone now, at least temporarily." He hoped it was temporary, anyway.

"You heard your mother," Pops said. "We're back in *our* home and we're staying there."

"Well, I don't have time to argue with you," Jim said. "You can go home and sit in the dark if you want to. Can I send Conway with you to help out? He can build a fire in your fireplace and haul wood for you."

"Sure," Nana said. "He's a sweet boy. That mother of his was a piece of work. I'm not sure how he turned out so well. You remember her, don't you, Pops?"

No one could bring up anyone to Nana and Pops without hearing the family tree of whoever was being discussed. As far as they were concerned, everyone was the product of the deeds, misdeeds, accomplishments, and failures of their predecessors.

"You all can finish that conversation on the ride home. We need to get out of here," Jim said. "Stay with me and watch your step."

Jim helped Nana to her feet and looped an arm through hers. Pops brought up the rear. By the time Jim got them out onto the street, Cookie had all the people with flashlights separated according to what part of town they lived in. He was pairing people without a light source with people who could help get them home.

Hugh was standing off to the side with Ian, Conway, and the horses. He was on the radio with someone at the roadhouse. "Well, let me relay this info to Jim. We'll be back your way shortly."

"How's the roadhouse?" Jim asked.

"Fortunately, the twelve-volt lighting system we used before the converters came along was still in place. When the lights went out, Gary switched the power to solar and the batteries took over. They're still open and serving drinks, though things are a little chaotic with people trying to figure out what the hell is going on."

Jim pulled Conway off to the side. "I need a big favor. My parents want to stay at their home tonight. They came in their golf cart, and I need you to ride back home with them. Stay the night and help them get set up. You can build a fire in the fireplace, shut off some rooms, do whatever needs done. I'll send Pete to relieve you tomorrow. Can you do it?"

Conway nodded, unable to stifle a grin. He was pleased at being entrusted with what he saw as a big responsibility. After all, what could be more important than keeping the boss's parents alive? "I just need to get my gear off my horse and I'll be ready."

"Thanks, Conway. I really appreciate this."

"Not a problem," the young man replied. He headed over to his horse and grabbed his pack. He opened it and removed the short rifle he was holding for Jim. He handed it over, along with a stack of magazines.

Jim took the short-barreled rifle and slung it around his neck. He stuck the spare mags in his back pockets, seated one in the weapon, then charged it. He double-checked the position of the selector switch before returning his attention to his dad. "Where's your golf cart?"

"In the parking lot around back."

"Conway, you have your gear?" Jim asked.

He nodded. "Ready whenever they are."

Pops threw an arm around the boy. "Good man, Conway. How about you drive us? I've always liked having a chauffeur."

"I'd be glad to."

"Conway," Jim said, "I'll have Pete bring your horse when he relieves you tomorrow."

"That's fine," Conway said.

Pops grinned. "Lead the way, young man."

Conway removed his headlamp and used it like a flashlight to better allow Nana and Pops to see where they were going.

Jim sighed, glad that his parents were taken care of temporarily. "Let's get to the roadhouse."

The men mounted up, Ian taking the reins of Conway's horse so he could lead it alongside his. As they rode off into the dark, the voices of the scared, the angry, and the confused rose into the night. Jim's gut warned him that the power might be gone for good. With that in mind, those voices melded into a chorus that tugged at his heart, pulling it downward into a cold, dark water like a drowning victim clawing at their rescuer.

47

The ride through town was much different than it had been for the last few weeks. The glow of electric lights in homes that had sat dark for so long had made things feel upbeat and hopeful. It was like a candle burning in a dark window. A fire on a cold night. Now the town had gone dark again and the mood was ominous. Jim felt anxiety gnawing at him. He had a sense of foreboding, a gut feeling that this was more than a hardware failure.

Along the way, the riders saw people with flashlights examining their converters, scratching their heads at the lack of glowing LEDs. People compared notes with their neighbors. When they were hailed by someone asking if they knew anything, Jim explained that it wasn't just their neighborhood. It was the entire town.

Jim's rising anxiety helped him understand that the collapse had traumatized him more than he understood or was willing to admit. The information vacuum took him back to the early days of the event when he was stuck on the road from Richmond with more questions than answers—with no sense of what was going on or how long it might last. He hadn't known what his family was going through or even if he'd see them again. All those memories came flooding back as he rode along Main Street, whirling around in his mind like a dust devil, full of dirt, trash, and tumbleweeds.

Hugh peeled off from the other riders before they reached the roadhouse. "If you guys don't mind, I'm going to head back to my place and get on my radios. If possible, I'll try to get word to Lightspeed's people on the frequency Danielle gave us. I'll also put out a general inquiry as to whether anyone has ever heard of a repeater failure like this. It could be a known issue."

"Do it," Jim said. "If you can, please raise Ellen on the radio when you reach the valley and let her know what's going on. Tell her I might be stuck in town for a little while, but I'll send Pete and Charlie home as soon as I get to the roadhouse."

"Roger that." Hugh clucked his tongue, nudged his heels into his horse, and the animal sped up to a canter. The glow of Hugh's headlamp was the only light visible in that direction, bobbing like a glowing buoy on a dark sea.

When Jim reached the roadhouse things almost seemed normal there. Though the bright exterior lights they'd been using recently were dark now, the windowless building still reverberated with the sounds of activity. Jim realized that all the things Dr. Nelson had been critical of—all the sights and smells that he'd so disparaged—were part of what made the roadhouse feel like a second home to Jim now. Those negative comments didn't hurt Jim's feelings. In fact, he chose to look at them as a list of the positive attributes he'd worked so hard to create. His roadhouse might not be to everyone's tastes, but neither was he, himself.

They settled their horses into the paddock out back and entered the roadhouse through the side door. It was a little quieter than normal because so many people had chosen to attend the opening of Doc's Place. There was the same persistent din of conversation, with less laughter. The tone of the discussions was serious, with people mulling over the loss of power and speculating as to the nature of the outage. Lloyd was on the stage, banging away at the banjo like it owed him money, playing without a care in the world.

"Forget to pay the light bill, Jim?" Randi asked, passing by him with a tray of beers.

Jim rolled his eyes. "Very funny."

When he reached the bar, he went behind the counter and grabbed two beers from the refrigerator, sadly noting that the light didn't come on when he opened the door. That meant the beer would warm up eventually unless they went back to storing it in the creek out back. He opened the beers and slid one to Ian, then took a slug of his. He could tell that one wasn't going to be enough. Not tonight.

"I'm going to check in with the security team and let them know I'm back," Ian said. "Call me on the radio if you need anything."

"Thanks for going with us tonight, Ian."

"Not a problem. Anytime."

"What happened to the juice?" Shade asked, strolling up with a beer in his hand. He'd been seated at the other end of the bar, talking with Becky. "My first thought was that you must have gotten into a serious scrap with those boys at Doc's Place and managed to kill the power."

Jim shook his head. "This isn't my doing. Blake and Dr. Nelson accused me of it when the lights went out. They got it in their heads that I'd knocked the power out to sabotage their grand opening. We were standing there arguing about it when the repeater blew up."

Shade's eyes went wide. "Hold up a second. Did you just say the repeater blew up?"

"Yeah. We were standing in front of the restaurant and there was an explosion over the mountain. You guys didn't see it?"

Shade winced. "No, we didn't see that. That ain't good. From my understanding of how this all works, we're dead in the water without that repeater."

"This isn't going to be a matter of simply rebooting the equipment from mission control and seeing if that fixes it. There's going to have to be a whole new installation. Who knows how long that will take."

"Can we radio them and ask?"

"Hugh is on it. He's headed back to his place to tap into the radio network and see what he can learn. Which reminds me, I need to find Pete and Charlie."

"They were in the kitchen last I saw them," said Shade.

Jim finished his beer, grabbed another, and headed off to find the boys. As he wove his way through the maze of tables, customers peppered him with questions about the power.

"It's the whole town," he said, not stopping to talk. It was all he had the stomach to tell them at this point. They'd find out about the repeater soon enough.

He found the boys in the kitchen helping the staff clean up. Without the ability to cook with electricity, many of the food items they'd prepped were now useless. Some of the staff were trying to figure out ways to store those items in hopes the power might come back on tomorrow. Jim knew better.

Pete stopped when his dad walked in, wiping his forehead with the tail of his shirt. "What's happening, Dad?"

Though Jim didn't have the stomach to tell them the truth, he had no choice here. These were his people. Even those employees who didn't live in the valley were his people now. He had an obligation to them.

"I was at the opening of Doc's Place," Jim began.

"How was that?" Charlie asked, rolling his eyes. "That doctor is a jerk. They should call their restaurant Jerk's Place."

"Thanks for the support, Charlie." Jim looked at the expectant faces around the room, then blurted it out. "The power is out all over town."

"Everywhere?" Pete asked.

"I'm afraid so."

"When do you think it will come back on?" Charlotte asked.

"Not anytime soon. The repeater they set up on the mountain—the big orange balloon—exploded. I'm guessing they'll have to put a new one in, and I don't know how long that might take." He didn't mention his gut feeling that it could be worse. He could let his mind go there, but he didn't want to take anyone else's into those dark places with him.

Although the staff kept working, Jim could tell the information hit them hard. They were distracted now, their minds racing through all the ways that this development impacted them individually. All of their lives had been improved by the return of electrical power. Awaiting this repair would be depressing.

"Pete and Charlie, I need you guys to get your stuff together and head home. Ariel and Mom are alone and might need some help. Like everyone else, we got a little slack when the lights came back on. They'll need a fire and more firewood stacked on the porch. The stove might have to be cleaned out. We'll have to go back to all the things we've been doing every day for the last year and a half. At least until we find out what's going on."

The boys dried their hands with a dish towel and Jim followed them toward the storage room. Like a lot of the staff, they kept their packs, coats, gear, and weapons there.

"In the morning I'll need you boys to pack up a few days' worth of clothes and gear so you can go stay with Nana and Pops," Jim said.

"Won't they just come back to the valley until the power is fixed?" Charlie asked.

Jim sighed. "You'd think so, but they're hard-headed. They say they're staying in their house. All I can do is send you guys over there to help them until we have more information. Then we'll figure out the next step."

"I don't mind," Pete said.

"Me neither," Charlie added.

When they reached the storeroom, they unlocked the door and grabbed their gear. In a few minutes, they headed out the side door to saddle their horses and head to the valley.

"You guys be careful," Jim said. "People may get weirded out with the lights off again. Try to avoid people until you get to the valley."

Like most of the staff, the boys kept their weapons unloaded while they were working, but they knew better than to travel that way. Both boys slapped mags in their rifles, confirmed that their selectors were in the Safe position, and chambered rounds. They mounted up, waved at Jim, and rode off into the night.

Jim felt himself being slapped in the face by the gravity of the moment. It was yet another sign of how events had changed all of them. Neither of these boys was eighteen years old yet, but like centuries past, the ways of the world had matured them. A part of Jim couldn't believe that he sent the boys out like this. Armed and in the dark, trusting that they could navigate their way home safely, regardless of what they encountered. Another part of him understood that these two young men were probably more prepared for the unexpected than most people in the community were. They'd seen a lot and done a lot. They'd both pulled triggers and watched men die.

Jim returned to the bar and exchanged his empty beer for a full one. He spotted Cookie wandering in, looking haggard. When Cookie joined him at the bar, Jim passed him a beer.

"On me, buddy. Looks like you need it."

"I do." Cookie dropped onto a stool and rested his forehead in his hands.

"Get everyone home safely?"

Cookie raised back up and took a sip of his beer. "As far as I know. It was a headache. People became too comfortable. They had power for a few days and forgot how to function without it. Only a few of them had flashlights. Then, before they left, they started hitting me with questions that I had no way of answering."

"Like what?"

"Anyone who was outside saw the same thing we did, Jim. They saw the repeater blow up, and they were asking *me* when the lights were coming back on. Like I'm in charge of the electricity. Hell, I don't know. None of us know. Then they started pissing me off, asking about things that were their own damn fault."

Jim came around the bar and settled onto an empty stool beside Cookie. "Glad I missed that. I'd have got pissed off all over again."

"It pissed *me* off and I'm a patient man. All the people who got rid of their woodstoves or pulled down their rigged-up stovepipes wanted to know what they were supposed to do about heat. The people who'd given away their firewood wanted to know how they were supposed to get it back. How the hell do I know!" Cookie gave an angry shake of his head, as if trying to clear the screen of his mental Etch-A-Sketch.

"What did you do?"

"I finally cracked. I started yelling, and once I did, I couldn't stop. I told them I didn't know any more than they did, that it was their own damn fault if they gave their shit away and wanted it back now. I think I said a few more things and used more bad language, but I kind of blacked out and I don't remember it all."

Jim let out a hearty laugh. "Dude, I've been there. Remember, I'm the man who stood on top of an RV at the farmer's market and cursed out the whole damn town. Sometimes you get on a roll and it's hard to stop."

Cookie said, "That's never happened to me before."

"Being confronted with too much stupidity can bring it out of you," Jim said. "Trust me on that. Enough stupid questions come your way and you'll snap. Everyone does unless they're stupid too."

"Apparently." Cookie took a depressed pull off his beer.

"Blake or Dr. Nelson say anything to you after I left?"

Cookie shook his head. "When I left Doc's Place, they had their little group gathered up on the porch. All their cronies. Dr. Nelson and Blake were bitching about how much work they'd put into that restaurant only to have the power go out on opening night. They were still trying to find a way to blame it on somebody. They couldn't accept it was anything random. They were calling it *terrorism*."

48

Jim closed the roadhouse early that night. With the evening having gone sideways from the loss of power, no one was in as festive a mood as they'd been for the last few weeks. Certainly, there were some who were more interested in liquor than lights, but Jim and his people still ushered them toward the door a little after midnight.

"You can do it all again tomorrow," Jim said as he walked them out into the cool, dark night. When he locked the door behind them, he felt his energy falter. The long night was catching up to him too.

It took them another hour of working together to get the place in order for the next day. Sometimes it took more time, others less, depending on how rowdy, messy, or destructive the patrons had been that night. When the kitchen was straightened out, Gary's people gathered their gear and headed for the side door that led to the paddock. Even when Gary wasn't working at the roadhouse, which he wasn't that evening, he showed up to escort his family home around closing time. When Jim filled him in on his visit to Doc's Place, he found Gary was already aware that the repeater had exploded. He'd been outside trying to figure out why his converter had gone dead when the explosion cut through the night.

The rest of the valley crew, including Jim, left with Gary's people. Becky and Shade headed off in his wagon, back to her home in the center of town. Ian, Ed, and two more of the security staff remained at the roadhouse for the night watch. No one expected trouble, but Jim liked to keep enough people there that they could hold off an attack if one came. Four shooters on the roof would make the old brick building difficult to breach.

Riding in the bubble of light created by their headlamps, the group made small talk on their ride back to the valley. Some nights they compared notes on the crazy things they'd seen or heard at work that night. Tonight was more somber. Even though this group was more prepared than most, the loss of grid power stung, and it was hard not to feel it on a personal level. The first time, over a year and a half ago, it had been more terrifying than anything else. This time, amid the atmosphere of hope and renewal, they were all gutted.

When they passed through the gap in the hills that led to the valley, Jim was finally within radio range of Hugh. "Jim for Hugh, Jim for Hugh. You up, buddy?" Jim knew he would be up. Some people lived on a regimen of a good diet and lots of sleep. Hugh lived on no sleep and nicotine.

"*I'm up.*"

"Any scuttlebutt on the power situation?"

There was a long pause before Hugh asked, "*Who's with you, Jim? Where are you at?*"

"I'm riding home with our people. We're just entering the valley."

"*Copy. Just wanted to make sure of who might overhear this transmission.*"

Jim's horse stopped walking and he wasn't sure if it was his idea or the horse's. All the others stopped too, circling around Jim so they could better hear the radio.

"Is it that bad, Hugh?"

"*It wasn't just our repeater, Jim—it was* all *the repeaters. Every one of them.*"

Hugh's information blindsided them like an ax handle to the side of the head. Jim looked around at his people and they were stunned. Everyone's eyes were locked on him or the radio in his hand. It was absolutely devastating news.

Jim finally found his voice. "How is that possible, Hugh?"

"No idea. There's not enough information at this point. No one knows if someone hacked the devices, causing them to self-destruct, or what. There's more. Worse."

Gary muttered a rare curse. His daughter Charlotte wept softly. Randi lit up a cigarette.

Jim keyed his mic. "How the hell does it get worse, Hugh?"

"People in northern and coastal Virginia are reporting missile attacks, including one on Camp David."

"Camp David? What's the significance of that?" Jim asked.

"Lightspeed and his top people were living there," Hugh replied.

"I thought Lightspeed was living on some fancy yacht? Didn't he say that in some of his addresses?"

"He was, yes. There are multiple sources, both civilian and military, reporting that Lightspeed's yacht was damaged recently in some kind of attack. The yacht had to go in for repairs, so Lightspeed temporarily evacuated his core people to Camp David."

Jim could barely bring himself to ask the question weighing on his mind. "Is Lightspeed dead? Don't tell me Lightspeed is dead."

"No one knows, Jim. Someone living near Camp David reported that there were two missile strikes with explosions. Also some reports of gunfire. I'm going to continue monitoring the radios. This isn't good, Jim. This can't be good."

Jim wasn't even sure how to end the transmission. As important as this information was, he couldn't bring himself to thank Hugh for delivering it. Finally he said, "Good work, Hugh. Jim out."

Jim pocketed the radio and everyone sat on their horses in silence. Jim's horse heaved a breath, then snorted.

"If Lightspeed is dead, surely there are people on his team who can fix this, right?" Randi asked.

Jim had no answer.

"Maybe," Gary said. "Unless those people were killed too."

"Don't say that!" Charlotte snapped.

Jim clucked his tongue and reined his horse into a walk. "We better get on home. It's late."

49

Jim woke with the sun, feeling like he'd barely slept at all, which was pretty close to the truth. When he'd come in last night, he'd found Charlie on the couch and Pete sleeping in the room Nana and Pops had been using. Jim added a log to the fire then slid into his bed. He couldn't push the events of the night from his mind.

When he finally gave up on sleep, he dressed in the dark and went into the kitchen. He crossed his fingers and flipped the light switch. Nothing happened. The power was still out, just as he'd known it would be. He made a mental note to switch the house back to his small solar system later today.

Charlie must have been awake because he wasn't in the living room. Jim raked the coals in the stove, then removed the ash pan so he could dump them in the bucket on the porch. When he got outside, he found Hugh rocking in the porch swing, smoking a cigarette. Charlie was leaning against the porch rail, *also* smoking a cigarette.

"When did you start smoking?" Jim asked, staring at the boy.

Charlie shrugged. "I don't know. Not too long ago."

Jim frowned and dumped the ashes. "Those things will kill you."

Charlie laughed and swept his arm out, gesturing at the world beyond. "Does it matter?"

Jim knew what Charlie meant. He was reminding Jim of the state of the world, and he was right. In the face of everything, what was a cigarette?

Jim grabbed a chunk of firewood in his free hand. "I'll be right back." He went inside and replaced the ash pan, then stoked the fire. He pulled on a jacket against the cold morning and returned to the porch. "Any updates?"

"Chaos," Hugh replied. "No new information, only a lot of speculation, rumors, and prognostication. Everyone suspects the worst. Sabotage by the Chinese sounds like the prevailing theory on why the repeaters blew up. They're also suspected of launching the missile attacks. Apparently Lightspeed had been goading them."

Jim settled into a metal chair and felt the cold seeping into his body through his clothes. "We all heard him do that in those radio addresses. He said crooked politicians made deals with the Chinese and he wasn't going to honor them. If he's truly dead, there's no shortage of people who wanted to see him that way. He made more enemies than friends."

"No wonder you respected this guy," Charlie quipped. "Lightspeed was like your spirit animal or something."

Hugh laughed.

"Cigarettes must be making you a smartass," Jim fired back, winking at Charlie.

Hugh sat bolt upright. Although Jim hadn't noticed anything he went on alert in response to Hugh's actions. Then Jim heard the pounding hooves. Someone had come through their gate and was barreling toward them on a horse. Hugh casually took up his rifle from where it leaned against a porch post, steadied it on the rail, and sighted through the scope.

"It's a woman," Hugh said. "She's crying. She looks familiar, but it's hard to tell because she's got some scarf wrapped around her face."

Jim stood, wondering if he should retrieve his rifle. It was in a rack just inside the front door, only feet away.

When the woman got nearer, she spotted the men on the porch. The scarf dropped from her face and Jim recognized her. It was Brandy, one of the women living on Hank Rose's farm. She reined her horse to a stop in front of the porch. Her face was dirty and streaked with tears, her eyes red-ringed and filled with terror. The horse heaved and frothed, as wild-eyed as its rider.

Jim climbed down the steps and latched onto the horse's bridle. "What's wrong?"

"Men attacked the house early this morning." Her voice was hoarse, her sentences broken by gasps and choking sobs. "Hank knew we were outgunned so he sent me to find help and this was the only place I could think to come. I don't know any of the neighbors up that way."

Hank and his people had visited Jim's farm for a dinner recently. Brandy must have remembered the way in from the Rockdell Farms side of the valley.

"Hugh, can you help Brandy while Charlie and I gear up?" Jim asked.

Hugh leapt down the steps, grabbed the reins to Brandy's horse, then helped the young woman down. Jim rushed back inside, Charlie on his heels. Jim didn't want to alarm Ariel, but he woke Ellen and hastily explained the situation.

"I need you to look after Brandy," he said. "She should stay here with you."

Even as he was speaking, Jim was dressing in warmer clothes. He rushed back to the living room, pulled on his plate carrier, his battle belt, and his go bag. He grabbed his rifle and stepped out the door.

"Charlie is saddling horses," Hugh said.

Jim put a hand on Brandy's shoulder. "You should stay here with my wife."

Brandy's eyes flared with anger. "To hell with that! I'm going back. I can't sit here wondering what's going on."

Jim pointed to her horse. "That animal is done. You going to ride it to death?"

"Do you have one I can borrow?"

"We're wasting time," Jim growled.

"We might need her," Hugh said. "She knows the farm."

Ellen emerged onto the porch, a coat wrapped around her. She gestured at Brandy. "This way, sweetie. You can warm up by the fire."

"Change of plans," Jim said. "She's going with us."

Ellen didn't question the girl's decision. She might have been the same way if the situation was reversed.

Charlie came out of the barn leading two horses. Hugh's was still tied up to the porch from his ride down this morning.

"Bring one more," Jim told him. "Brandy is going with us."

Charlie handed the reins over to Jim just as Pete emerged out the door, pulling the last of his gear on.

"I'm ready, Dad!" Pete said.

"Not this time, Pete," Jim said. "I need you to put this girl's horse in the barn to cool down. Get the saddle and bridle off. Then I need you to get to Nana and Pops' house and relieve Conway. You'll have to take his horse with you. Got it?"

Although Pete appeared frustrated at not getting to go along, he didn't challenge his father's decision. He'd matured enough to understand that he helped best by doing the assignment he was given. "Got it."

Charlie hurried from the barn with another saddled horse. Jim and Hugh mounted up. Charlie passed the reins of the fresh horse to Brandy and she climbed into the saddle. Charlie mounted his horse and placed his feet in the stirrups.

"Be careful!" Ellen called from the porch.

Jim swung his horse toward the porch rail, exchanging quick hugs with Ellen and Pete.

"I love you. Tell Ariel too."

Brandy took off, Hugh and Charlie hot on her heels. Jim nudged his horse into a gallop and caught up with them by the time they reached the gate.

50

Had they been in a vehicle, the drive from Jim's house to the Rose farm would have taken twenty minutes. Maybe fifteen if the driver pushed the limits on the curvy back road. On a horse, even at a gallop, there was no way to make the trip that quickly. Still, the riders tried, cutting through fields and across pastures, knocking miles off the trip. Thirty minutes later, they were well up the highway and closing in on Hank's community. That was when Jim noticed thick black smoke rising in the distance, cresting over the top of a wooded ridge.

He pointed ahead of them. "Oh shit!"

"It could be something else," Charlie said, trying to remain positive.

"No, that's the farm!" Brandy said, her voice cut with the acid of fear.

Brandy pulled ahead and they let her lead. In another mile, she veered off the four-lane highway, passed through a gate, and tore across a fallow cornfield. Jim, Hugh, and Charlie stayed on her heels, aware that she knew this area better than they did. A few minutes later, they caught a dirt farm road that led them to the Little River.

They hung a right there, ending up on the same rutted two-track that passed by Hank's trout ponds.

Ahead, the smoke rose, dark and churning. It was impossibly dense and swallowed the light of day. They could smell it now and Jim knew it wasn't a burning barn or grassy hillside. It wasn't wood or vegetation. It smelled of plastic, chemicals, and burning metal. If this was a house burning down, that didn't bode well for Hank and his people. There was no way Hank would have let that happen if he were in any condition to stop it.

Minutes later, they reached the enclosed fishponds. Beyond them, the farmhouse was a seething inferno, fully engulfed in flames. The uppermost floor had already collapsed. The metal roof had buckled and was glowing red from the heat of the fire. The paint on the first-floor clapboards bubbled and peeled. A window blew out from the fire, making everyone flinch. They slowed their horses and stopped as close as they dared. Their faces burned with the heat, their horses stomping and recoiling.

Though there was no more gunfire, that didn't mean there weren't threats remaining. Brandy didn't care. She screamed and leapt from her horse. Charlie moved closer and scooped up the reins before it wandered off.

Hugh steered his horse away from the fire. "I'm going to check the perimeter."

Brandy screamed again and Jim knew what that meant. It was the universal language of life-altering grief. He searched for Brandy and spotted her collapsed across an unmoving body. It had to be her boyfriend, Rick. Her screams became prayers as she implored to her God to not let this be true. To let it all be some bad dream from which she'd soon wake up.

"There's another one." Charlie rode a short distance away, dismounted, and tied his horse and Brandy's off to a fence. He raised his rifle, took a good look around, then wandered off to examine the body.

Jim swallowed a bad taste in his mouth. He climbed down and tied his horse off. "I'm bad at this. The worst."

Charlie turned around. "You talking to me?"

Jim blew out a breath. "I don't know who I'm talking to."

"What are you bad at?"

Jim didn't answer. He headed toward Brandy, resting a hand on her shoulder, and kneeling beside her. He struggled to find the right words, but there were none, not when the world was going entirely wrong around them. He kept his hand on her heaving back and took in Rick's body. Judging by the blood and ragged holes in his shirt, he'd been shot at least three times, probably with a rifle.

When Jim tried to pull Brandy away from Rick's body, she refused to move. She slapped at Jim and bawled in the unknown and tormented tongue spoken only by the slavering and grief-stricken. When Jim spotted Hugh returning, he left Brandy to her anguish.

"Find anything else?"

"More dead. Some of them burned before they were shot. Looked like they were trapped in the house, then shot when they tried to escape."

Jim shook his head. "Who the hell would do this? These were good people, Hugh. Nice people."

Hugh patted Jim on the shoulder. "I know you liked them and that says a lot. You don't like many people."

"I don't, and it's a big problem when somebody kills them. I don't have friends to spare. I need all of them."

Hugh lit a cigarette. "I get it."

"Any sign of Hank?"

Hugh shook his head. "Not yet. It's a big property and it's possible he engaged them from another position. He could be anywhere."

"Most of the gunfire is on the side of the house that faces the road. Let's head that way and see if we can find a clue to who did this."

"What do you want me to do?" Charlie asked.

"Check the barn and see if you can find some shovels," Jim said. "We can't do anything about the people who burned up in the house, but we can bury the ones who made it out."

"Got it."

"Keep an eye out," Hugh warned. "We don't know who else might be lurking around. The smoke could draw people."

Jim stared at the inconsolable Brandy, still trying to beg her boyfriend back from the dead. "Keep an eye on her. Grieving people don't always make rational decisions. She wouldn't be the first to try and eat a gun. If you need us, reach out on the radio."

Jim and Hugh left their horses tethered and walked down the dirt road that connected the farm with the county road. They kept their rifles high, their voices low. They were vigilant, well aware they might not be alone. The smell of death might draw buzzards, but a burning house drew other kinds of scavengers.

A swatch of trampled grass caught their eye as they passed the narrow band of trees that screened the house from the road.

"I wouldn't have expected this. Horses maybe, but not this."

The grass had been crushed by tires.

"Two vehicles," Jim said. "Several men."

"Two golf carts," Hugh clarified. "Narrow and short wheelbase."

"There's a golf course up this way. Probably a lot of carts floating around."

Hugh spotted the shiny brass of a spent shell casing and picked it up. He flipped it around until he could read the headstamp. "It's a deer rifle. A .270 caliber."

"There's more of them," Jim said, pointing to more brass glinting in the trampled grass.

They followed a path of crushed grass into the thin strip of trees.

Hugh stared at the burning house visible through the trees. "This position gives you a good view of the house, but it wouldn't help you at night. Without night vision or thermal, you'd have a hard time shooting accurately in the dark."

Bile rose in Jim's throat. "Unless you burn them out. Light the house on fire and it drives the occupants out while also giving you the light you need to shoot them."

They continued to follow the trampled grass along the strip of woods and soon came upon another body. Hugh crouched and rolled the man over.

"I don't recognize this one," Hugh said. "Reckon he stayed home when the rest of them came to the roadhouse or the dinner at your place?"

Jim shook his head. "He isn't from the farm. He's from town. He's one of Dr. Nelson and Blake's people. I saw him at the restaurant last night."

Hugh spat and stood up. "Son of a *bitch*!"

51

It was early afternoon when the last grave at the Rose Farm was filled in. Jim had sweated through his clothing and was already chilling by the time he angrily pitched his shovel to the side. He pulled on the coat he'd left hanging on a tree branch and flipped the hood up over his head. Brandy dropped her shovel and sank to her knees in the soft dirt. She somehow found more tears when Jim thought she'd surely exhausted them already.

Jim walked over and stood beside her. "You're welcome to come with us. You can stay at the roadhouse until you figure out what you want to do."

"Thanks," she said, her voice the exhausted mewling of someone who'd cried themselves out. "But I have family."

"You want to ride back with us to get the horse you left at my place?" Jim said.

"Wasn't my horse. It was Hank's. Just take yours back with you and you can keep the other one. I don't want the reminder."

Jim shifted from foot to foot. "I feel bad about leaving you here with no horse and no gear."

"Don't," she whispered. "I'm not your problem."

"You're not a problem, Brandy."

"And I'm not your responsibility."

Jim crouched down beside her. "Will you promise me that you'll come find us if you can't connect with family?"

"Maybe," she said, but her words were hollow.

Jim couldn't be sure if she even heard a word he was saying. He felt bad about leaving her behind, but what could he do? It was her decision. He couldn't force her onto a horse and keep her prisoner in the valley for her own safety. People made their own choices, bad or good. He was a perfect example of that, having made enough bad decisions for a dozen people and two lifetimes.

"Then we'll get going," Jim said, feeling as if he were talking to himself at this point.

Weeping, Brandy stretched out on her stomach, resting her cheek on the cool earth. She clawed her fingers into the soft dirt. Jim looked away, Brandy's grief too intimate, too personal at this point for an audience. He nodded at Hugh and Charlie. The three men gathered their gear, slung their rifles, and mounted up.

Jim chose to leave by the back way, as Brandy had brought them there. He didn't want to deal with nosy neighbors if he left by Rose Farm Road.

"What are you thinking about all this, Jim?" Hugh asked after they'd rode in silence for several miles.

"I'm thinking this isn't over. I need to talk to Dr. Nelson and Blake Justice. I need to know if they were part of this. Cookie told me last night that they were looking for someone to blame, though I'm not sure how that led them to Hank."

"The cult," Charlie said.

"They weren't a cult," Jim snapped.

"*I'm* not saying they were. *Other* people thought they were. Maybe that doctor thought they were the kind of cult that didn't want power."

"Luddites," Hugh said. "Charlie might be right. Maybe the doctor and his cronies thought Hank's people were Luddites and that they sabotaged the repeater to keep electricity out of the community."

Jim mulled this over. "Everyone heard those cult rumors, but we didn't know who they were about until we talked to your friend Bobby. I can't imagine anyone in town putting together that Hank and his people were this evil 'cult' everyone was talking about."

"There's a lot goes on at the roadhouse," Hugh said. "Someone might have seen them there and put the pieces together. Maybe one of Hank's people got too drunk and said too much, or perhaps one of the staff let it slip."

That thought was like a punch to the gut. "It's bad enough that all these young people died such horrible deaths. If they died over a misunderstanding, that's going to be hard for me to live with."

"What does that mean?" Charlie asked, turning Jim's words over in his head. "You have to live with it, right? What choice do you have?"

Jim said, "We can choose to make it right. You can't fix everything, but you can fix some things."

Charlie sniffed his sleeve. "How do you make something like this right? I'm going to smell like burned bodies for days."

Hugh gave Charlie a hard look. The dark resolve in those eyes answered Charlie's question without the need for words. He now understood how Jim intended to make this right.

"Oh," Charlie said.

52

At first, Pete felt bad that he'd been left behind. He knew it was because his father wanted to protect him, but it made him doubt himself too. What if his dad didn't think he was mature enough or capable of defending himself? He gradually got over that feeling as he went about the duties his father had assigned him. He had too much to do to sit there and feel sorry for himself.

He took care of Brandy's horse, then saddled his and Conway's. He grabbed his gear, then said goodbye to his mom and sister. "I have to swing by my house for more clothes if I'm going to stay with Nana and Pops for a while."

"Be careful," Ellen said. "When you're by yourself, you have to be twice as alert. Don't let your mind wander. Pay attention to what's around you."

Pete used to take these reminders personally, as if he was being treated like a kid. He'd come to understand that this was what parents did and they couldn't help it. He'd even seen his dad doing it with other adults, reminding them to be careful and vigilant when they were on the road. It wasn't a sign that people thought they were incapable—it was a sign they cared.

He hugged his mother. "I will."

Pete left the property and rode to the house that had once been Buddy's, then Lloyd's, and was now his and Charlie's. He dug around on his bedroom floor and found his cleanest dirty clothes, shoving them into his pack. His mother wouldn't have approved of his choice of clothing or the way he packed, but she wasn't here so he could do what he wanted. When he was done, he tied the pack behind his saddle and mounted up, his rifle hanging around his neck.

It was a cool, sunny day. Riding along the river, Pete understood the importance of his mother reminding him not to be distracted. It would have been easy to lose focus on a day like this. He saw herons, ducks, and a muskrat as he rode along the river. He spotted a fox on the opposite bank, then saw a skunk amble across the road. Even the sound of the river itself—that incessant, soothing burbling—seemed determined to hypnotize him. There were a lot of things to capture a young man's attention and lull him into complacency.

When he reached town, Pete checked the road for golf carts. Since the power came back on those things had been everywhere, zipping around with no regard for speed limits, lanes, or pedestrians. Even with the power out now, he had to assume there were still some out there with a charge being driven around. If the power was out for a while, he wouldn't miss those stupid carts.

It was rare that Pete got to ride through town alone. He was always with Charlie or someone else from the valley. With no conversation to distract him, he found himself thinking about his life before the collapse. He remembered when he was little and had those birthday parties at the fast-food place, recalled the houses where his friends had lived, and thought about the errands he'd run with Nana while she was babysitting him. Those trips to the grocery store, the post office, or the hair salon.

For the first time, it hit him that those weren't *just* his childhood memories, but memories of a world that no longer existed. There were so many things he'd once imagined while he was bored in school. Now he had to wonder how many things he'd never get to do. Would he graduate? Go to a prom? College? Hold a real job? Get to buy a car?

He had no way of knowing.

Ahead, sitting in the middle of the street was an electric golf cart. The sight of it sitting there disabled and useless made Pete smile. While the carts might have been a godsend for some, for those accustomed to riding horses and having the road to themselves, they were a nuisance. When he passed the cart, Pete casually glanced down at it and noticed there was blood on the seats and on the floor.

Pete had unintentionally become an expert on blood over the past year and a half. From the color and texture, he knew it was relatively fresh. That in itself didn't alarm him. The blood could have come from a dead deer. Of course, it could have come from a person. Pete checked the chamber of his rifle, finding the glint of brass comforting.

Conway's horse, its lead wrapped around Pete's saddle horn, snorted and shook its head. It was just as concerned about the blood as Pete. He spoke to it in a calm, soothing voice. "It's okay. We'll get moving."

A short distance ahead, he found a second golf cart looking much like the first. Blood on the steering wheel, on the seats, on the floor. Pete was more curious than ever about the source of this blood. He'd seen many things during the collapse, but people continued to surprise him. They were a violent and morally ambiguous lot, capable of terrifying depravity and shocking deceit. He knew people also had good traits, but it sure seemed that those were on display less often than the negative ones.

Continuing his ride toward the center of town, though Pete didn't fully understand what the signs told him, he knew that whoever was bleeding had gone this same way. There were frequent drops and splashes of blood on the dirty asphalt, bloody footprints left by several different types of boot soles. Sure, it could be a group of hunters, each of them carrying a haunch of fresh meat, however, that was increasingly unlikely. Would a butchered animal leave this much blood?

Pete caught up with the source of the blood near the courthouse. At least he caught *sight* of them. He stopped his horse in the street and dug around in his coat pocket for a pair of compact binoculars. His horse shifted beneath him. Perhaps it was wondering why they were standing there. Maybe it smelled the blood.

Pete stroked its neck. "Easy, boy."

When he finally got the binoculars focused on the men, he uttered a word his mother wouldn't have approved of. He recognized the men as being Dr. Nelson, Blake Justice, and a few of their buddies. Pete didn't know the entire story but knew these men to be among the many whom his father didn't get along with.

He could make out rifles, and some of the men wore backpacks. Nearly everyone wore bloodstained clothing. They walked with the stagger of weary men, bone-tired and pushed beyond their point of endurance. The tale of whatever had left them in this state was not told by the condition of these men, but of the prisoner they led behind them on some manner of leash.

For as bad a state as they men were in, their prisoner had fared much worse. His gait spoke of more than exhaustion and the waning of adrenaline. He limped along in blood-soaked and tattered clothing, looking like something that had been dragged rather than having walked through town.

The men turned off Main Street onto Mill Street, which Pete knew to be the location of the new restaurant Dr. Nelson had opened up to compete with the roadhouse. That had to be where they were going. Turning that corner allowed Pete to get a better look at the prisoner. His hands were bound in front of his body, so bloody it looked like he'd butchered an animal with them. His face was misshapen and distorted. Swollen protrusions on his cheeks and forehead lent the appearance of some alien and previously unknown craniofacial structure, as if horns rose beneath the surface of his skin and threatened to push through. He shivered incessantly, his clothing both wet from blood and inadequate for the cold temperature of the day.

Despite his battered appearance, Pete realized he knew this man. He'd seen him at the roadhouse with his father, then again when they recently had a gathering in the valley. It was Hank Rose, the man who brought them fish. The man they teased about leading a cult.

Did this mean it was Dr. Nelson and his men who'd attacked the Rose Farm? Were these the men that Brandy had asked Jim for help against? It had to be.

For a second, Pete felt a wave of panic. If these men were returning to town, did that mean his dad, Hugh, and Charlie had been killed? No, that couldn't be the case. This had to mean that Dr. Nelson and his people had taken Hank and headed back to town before help ever reached the farm.

Pete sighed and shoved the binoculars back into his pocket. Although he didn't know what was going on here, he knew it was wrong. He also knew his father would most certainly intervene on behalf of his new friend. While a part of Pete wanted to do the same, he knew he shouldn't. Despite the weary state that Dr. Nelson, Blake, and their friends were in, they still outnumbered him. Soon, they'd be inside a building, holding a defensible position that would be hard to overtake. Attacking it would be futile for a single man. A single kid. He could end up getting both himself and Hank killed.

A part of Pete wanted to turn and ride back to the valley, but he suspected his dad wouldn't be there. He was probably at the Rose Farm or somewhere on the road in between. As much as Pete wanted to do something to help Hank, he needed to stick to the plan. He'd get to his grandparents' house, tell Conway what he'd seen, and send him to track down his dad. It wasn't what his gut *wanted* him to do, but it was what his head was telling him to do. This time, he'd listen to his brain.

53

Jim, Hugh, and Charlie took their time riding back to the valley after leaving the Rose Farm. They'd pushed their horses hard on the ride in and they needed the slower pace now, as did the human members of the party. Their bodies were sore from digging graves and their minds were troubled by what they'd seen as they were filling those graves.

The riders turned off the four-lane highway and onto the road that led through Rockdell Farms and on toward the valley. They'd scarcely made it a quarter mile when they heard the pounding of hooves on soil. Perhaps numb from trauma and inattentive from exhaustion, everyone was dangerously zoned out, staring blankly at the road ahead of them. The sound of an approaching horse shook them from that state. Rifles were raised and the men scanned the broad pastures that stretched for miles around them.

"There!" Hugh said, pointing to a field to the south.

Jim narrowed his eyes. "Is it Pete?"

Hugh shook his head, looking through binoculars. "Conway."

Jim immediately assumed the worst. Conway had spent the night with his parents. Pete was supposed to relieve Conway. Did his appearance here mean that something had happened to one of his family members? Jim nudged his horse into a run, headed for the nearest gate, and reached it about the same time as Conway, Hugh and Charlie right behind him.

Jim dismounted to open the gate. "What's going on?" He did a poor job of hiding the fact that he was on the verge of panic.

"I've got a message from Pete," Conway gasped.

"Is he okay?"

Conway nodded. "When he was coming through town to bring me my horse, he said he came up on two golf carts stuck in town. Both had blood in them. By the time he got to the center of town, he caught up with the men who must have been driving them. It was Dr. Nelson, that Justice fellow, and some more of his crew."

Jim bristled. "Those are the assholes who attacked the Rose Farm. We just got done burying some of their handiwork."

"I know," Conway said.

"How did you know that?" Hugh said.

"Pete said they had that Hank guy with them. They had him on a leash and he was beat all to hell. They took him to Doc's Place."

Jim swung onto his horse. "I guess we're going to town."

"Let's go by your place first," Hugh said. "You have goodies in your house and in the Daddy Shack that we might be able to use." The Daddy Shack was what Jim's kids called the storage building where he kept the camping gear.

"They might kill him," Jim argued. "Can we spare the time?"

"There's got to be a reason they brought him back here," Hugh countered. "Otherwise they'd have killed him with the rest of his people."

"You're right," Jim said. "Conway, you head for the roadhouse. You and Ian gear up. You'll be going with us. Wait on us at the roadhouse. No cowboy shit. Got it?"

Conway nodded. "No cowboy shit. I got it."

"Go."

Conway spun his horse and cut across the field, taking a shortcut toward town. Jim, Hugh, and Charlie rode through the gate, headed back in the direction from which Conway had just come. Ten minutes later, they were at Gary's house. Much to the disapproval of Gary's wife, Jim secured Gary's promise to join them in whatever operation they were about to launch.

"I'll get my gear together and meet you at your house in a few minutes, Jim."

From there, another five minutes of riding got them to Jim's house. Jim tied his horse off in the front yard, then headed inside to gear up. Hugh and Charlie went straight for the Daddy Shack.

Jim stormed into the house, barking her name. "Ellen!" He forgot that his manner sometimes terrified the people around him.

"What's going on?" Ellen asked, her eyes wide with panic. "Is Pete okay?"

"He's fine. It was Dr. Nelson and Blake who attacked the Rose Farm. We thought everyone was killed, but Pete saw Dr. Nelson taking Hank toward his restaurant. He said he was beat up pretty badly."

"Conway was here a little while ago asking for you. He didn't say why," Ellen said. "I assume it was about that. I wish he'd said something."

"Hugh, Charlie, and I are going into town. Gary, Ian, and Conway are going with us. We're going to get Hank and finish this."

"Finish?" Ellen asked, her brow furrowed, her face tense.

"I'm going to kill those assholes," Jim said. "All of them."

Ellen looked away. "Don't do something the town can't overlook, Jim. Something they can't forgive."

"I had to bury a girl today who'd jumped out a window because she was on fire." Jim spoke through gritted teeth. "Her legs broke when she hit the ground and those bastards shot her. When I carried her to her grave, her skin came off onto my clothes, and her legs hung like…"

He couldn't finish.

Ellen covered her mouth, tears in her eyes. "Oh God. I'm so sorry."

"I have to go." Jim kissed her.

"Be careful," she warned.

When Jim got outside, Gary had just arrived. He was wearing his body armor and had a rifle hanging off his saddle horn. His .338 Lapua sniper rifle rode in a scabbard on his horse's side. Charlie was also wearing body armor, and Hugh was lashing a backpack of goodies to his horse.

"What did you get?" Jim asked.

"I borrowed some of your mags for my MP5. Got better plates for Charlie and some smoke grenades in case we need them." Hugh had an MP5 submachine gun that had once belonged to a law enforcement agency. Most of the time he carried it in his pack since it was primarily a close-quarters weapon. He'd taken it out of his pack and had it hanging from his saddle horn.

"Let's go." Jim was still shaken from recalling the burnt girl he'd carried earlier. He couldn't get the smell out of his nose. He was afraid if he talked about it too much, he'd lose it, either crying or vomiting. He didn't want to do either.

They cut through the back of the property, taking the shortcut to the river. They didn't use it much at this time of the year since the banks were muddy and there was a risk of their horse taking a spill in the river. They reached the crossing, then rode by the cemetery and through the east end of town.

When they reached the roadhouse, Ian and Conway were waiting for them, as prepared as the two of them could be. They were wearing body armor, were weighed down with mags for their rifles, and had small backpacks with extra gear.

"Ed will watch the place while we're gone," Ian said. "He's on the roof."

Jim looked up, scanned the top of the wall, and caught sight of Ed up there. "Conway, did you tell Ian what was going on?"

Conway nodded. "As much as I knew."

"No rules of engagement," Jim said. "The things Hugh, Charlie, and I saw today...the things we'll have to live with for the rest of our lives...are inexcusable. No one gets a pass for shit like that."

"So, shoot to kill?" Gary confirmed.

Jim nodded. "We don't leave anyone alive today. I'm assuming the restaurant is closed, so anyone inside that building is probably party to whatever went on at Hank's farm. They're complicit in the murders of those young people on the farm."

"Copy that." Gary took a deep breath and exhaled. He didn't like killing and tried to avoid it when he could. Sometimes they couldn't go around it though. Sometimes it laid down right in their path and there was nothing else that could be done.

"Let's get moving," Jim said. "We still need to go by Becky's and see if Shade is around. He'd be a good man to have with us." He spun his horse, nudged it with his heels, and sprinted away from the roadhouse.

$$54$$

"Just kill me," Hank mumbled. His lips were swollen, the insides of his mouth lacerated by his broken teeth. He looked like a man who'd eaten glass.

"Not until you confess," Dr. Nelson said.

They'd lashed Hank to a chair in the dining room of Doc's Place. Sunlight filtered in through the blinds, leaving alternating stripes of light and dark on an immaculate interior, empty of diners. Without power, nothing at Doc's Place worked.

Blake grabbed an empty beer bottle by the neck. He smashed it against the bar with a flick of his wrist, and menaced Hank with the jagged glass that remained. "You'll confess when I start peeling you like a grape. When your face is lying on the floor looking back up at you."

Dr. Nelson frowned at Blake and pointed at the surface of the beautiful wooden bar, now gouged from the glass of the broken bottle. "Did you have to go full barbarian? We might get to reopen this place one day and I don't want it trashed."

Hank raised his head, bloody saliva running down his chin, one eye completely swollen shut. He peered at Blake with the other.

"There's nothing to confess." He choked and began sobbing, tears streaking the blood smeared on his face. "Why did you kill my friends?"

"You and your friends are terrorists," Dr. Nelson spat. "I am of the opinion that someone sabotaged Lightspeed's equipment. We all saw the explosion and there's no reason that repeater should have exploded unless someone attached a bomb to it."

"How the hell do you know that?" Hank croaked.

Dr. Nelson sneered as if explaining it was beneath him. "I'm a doctor and it takes a degree of intelligence to become one. Right now my powerful brain is telling me that someone–likely you—destroyed our power."

"How would I even get a bomb on it?" Hank asked. "All the way up in the air?"

"It was tethered to the ground," Blake said, twirling the jagged bottleneck in his hands. "You could have used horses to pull it down, then attached the bomb."

"Where the hell would I get a bomb?"

Dr. Nelson blew out an impatient breath. "That's what I'm waiting to hear." He got in Hank's face. "You know, we've all been hearing those cult rumors for months. It made sense to me that a cult wouldn't want electricity back. You couldn't hardly have a cult around here if things went back to normal, could you? Power threatened you. It was going to destroy whatever weird little thing you had going out there."

Hank repeated himself for the hundredth time, wincing at the pain in his mouth. "We. Weren't. A cult."

"Then what the hell were you?" Blake asked.

"We were friends. Living together. Enjoying life."

"Your friends aren't enjoying it anymore," Blake quipped. "They aren't alive."

Dr. Nelson pulled up a chair and took a seat beside Hank, only inches from his face. "We had to shut this place down last night because the power went out. We decided that the people responsible needed to pay. Everyone said the cult was on the north end of the country, so we headed that way and started asking around. Guess whose name popped up? Then someone was nice enough to point us toward your farm. If you're not a cult, then why do all your neighbors think you are?"

"It was a joke!" Hank yelled.

Dr. Nelson lost it, lashing out with a punch, knocking Hank and his chair over. The chair smacked against the floor, followed by a dull thud when Hank's head hit next. "Do you see me laughing?"

"Hey, what's going on here?"

All eyes turned toward the door. Cookie had just entered the restaurant, blocking most of the doorway with his large frame.

"What the hell are you doing in here?" Blake asked. "We're closed and this is private property."

"I was coming by to see how you guys were doing without power. When I looked through the window, I saw you working this guy over."

"This *guy* is a terrorist," Dr. Nelson snarled, strolling toward Cookie. "We intend to make him confess, then hang him on Main Street in front of all the people he's hurt and inconvenienced."

"Bullshit!" Cookie snapped. "This is a decent young man. I heard all those cult rumors myself and wanted to get to the bottom of them. I tracked them back to this guy and visited his place with some friends of mine. They're good people and they're definitely not a cult. You need to let him go."

"Those good people are all *dead* people now," Blake quipped.

Dr. Nelson shot him a look, a warning to keep his mouth shut.

"Is that true?" Cookie asked.

"Perhaps," said Dr. Nelson.

"I'm not asking you again!" Cookie bellowed. When he made a move to untie Hank himself, Dr. Nelson blocked his way.

"They killed them all!" Hank sobbed. "They set my house on fire and burned my friends to death."

"Is he telling the truth?" Cookie asked.

Dr. Nelson shrugged.

Cookie lashed out, clamping a hand around Dr. Nelson's throat. Blinded by his anger, Cookie missed the man who'd slipped out the back door and circled around behind him. Then a rifle butt connected with the back of Cookie's head and he dropped to the floor like a falling tree.

55

"Tell me what to do and I'll do it." Shade grimaced. "I knew we should have done this the night they tried to steal the converters from the roadhouse, but we tried to be nice. This is what being nice gets you."

They were around the corner from Doc's Place, huddled against an empty house. They'd left Conway a block back guarding the horses.

"There's two men on the front porch with rifles," Hugh said, returning from getting eyes on the building. "No one on the back."

"Recommendations?" Jim asked.

"Kill them all," Shade growled. "How's that?"

Jim offered a grim smile. "I'm onboard for that. I was really looking for strategic suggestions."

Hugh tipped his head toward Gary. "The front of the building has those big plate glass windows. A man with a good scope should be able to see inside if they don't have the windows covered."

"You up for that, Gary?" Jim asked.

Gary nodded. "Just say the word."

"How about you circle around and head for the courthouse parking lot," Jim suggested. "That's about seventy-five to a hundred yards from the porch where the guards are standing. Scope the place and report back on what you see. Position yourself for a shot but only fire on my word. If we make entry through the back, I don't want you hitting us."

"Got it." Gary crossed Main Street and headed west, circling around to his assigned position, staying well out of sight of Doc's Place.

"Okay, we have five minutes or so before he's in position," Jim said. "We don't make a move until he reports back. We need to know who's inside the building and how many people we're dealing with. Charlie, I'm going to put you on the north side of the building. You'll need to circle the block and take a position near the feed store. Don't fire unless one of these guys tries to escape in your direction."

"Got it," Charlie said.

Jim locked eyes with the young man. "Get moving. Call it out on the radio when you're there. Everyone communicate your positions and your moves to your teammates. I don't want any friendly fire."

Charlie jogged off down the street then hung a left into an alley.

"Hugh, I want you and Ian on the back door. Do you have your entry tools with you?"

Hugh lifted a leg, displaying a tan combat boot. "Damn right I do. Size eleven."

Jim nodded. "That'll work. Once we hear back from Gary, we'll have a better idea how to go in. Until then, get in position and sit tight." Jim looked at Shade. "Big man, you and I are approaching the restaurant from the rear with Hugh and Ian. While they cover the back, you and I are each going to take a side and move toward the front. We'll stop just around the corner from the front porch and you'll hang there until my signal."

"No problem," Shade said. "Let's knock heads."

Jim gave him a serious nod. "We'll knock 'em until they pop."

A noise in Jim's earpiece caused him to pull his radio from his plate carrier and adjust the volume. "Go ahead, Gary."

"They've got the blinds open to let light in so I can see inside. Pete was

right. They have Hank in the dining room. He's tied to a chair and it's...bad. They've messed him up."

Everyone heard the transmission and winced at the news, struck by the injustice of it.

"Copy that," Jim said. "How many players do we have and where are they positioned?"

"Hank isn't the only prisoner," Gary continued. *"Somehow they have Cookie."*

Jim looked around at the rest of the group, uncertain if he'd Gary correctly. "Can you repeat that?"

"There's a second chair beside Hank. Cookie is unconscious and tied to it."

Jim let out a string of curses. "It would be just like Cookie to wander into this mess. What else do you see?"

"Two men on the porch just like Hugh said. Dr. Nelson and Blake are inside standing over Hank. Judging by their postures, they appear to be questioning him. Blake has a broken bottle in his hand, and he keeps waving it in Hank's face."

"Anyone else?" Hugh asked.

"There are two other men standing inside the dining room with Blake and Dr. Nelson. One has a rifle and both are wearing handguns. They have blood on them. Whatever happened, they were a part of it."

Jim thought for a moment before responding. "Guys, I'm not trained for this. I'm not a soldier or a tactician, so if anyone has a better idea, I'm open to it."

No one said a word.

"Then we go with my plan," Jim said. "Gary, do you have a clear shot on the man standing inside with the rifle?"

"Affirmative, Jim. I'm only eighty yards away. At this distance I can pick which pore I put the round through."

"Copy that. We need three minutes to get in position. On my signal, you're going to drop the man with the rifle. As soon as you've fired, Shade and I will swing around the front corners of the building and take out the two men on the porch. The porch is about eight feet high, so we'll be shooting uphill and slightly away from each other. There shouldn't be any issues with crossfire."

"Agreed," Shade said.

"Hugh, as soon as Gary drops the rifleman, you guys make entry through the back," Jim instructed. "Someone could try to escape out that way so be ready."

"Always," said Hugh.

Jim looked at Ian. "You good with it?"

Ian nodded. "Ready."

"Let's do it, gentlemen. Watch your back and watch your friends' backs so we all go home tonight."

With Gary and Charlie in position, the rest of the team advanced on Doc's Place. They approached from the rear of the property, using a retaining wall, a wooden fence, and abandoned cars for cover. Hugh and Ian dropped off at the edge of the back parking lot, concealing themselves behind a dumpster. Jim and Shade split off, each of them heading for different sides of the building. Both men flattened themselves out against an exterior wall, just around the corner from the front porch. Jim clicked his radio twice, a prearranged signal intended to get the attention of the rest of his team. That was followed by the whispered message that would initiate the attack.

"Jim for Gary. Send it."

Two seconds later, Gary's rifle fired, the *boom* of the report felt as much as heard. Almost simultaneously, the plate glass window on the front of the building shattered. The rifleman watching Hank's interrogation, standing with his finger inside the trigger guard of his weapon, caught the rifle round in his chest. The heavy projectile slammed him like a red-hot sledgehammer and spun his body, splashing everyone in the vicinity with warm blood. He fell backward with a gaping hole in his ribcage, dead before he hit the floor.

Before the echo from Gary's shot had even faded, Jim and Shade swung around both front corners of the building, firing their handguns almost simultaneously. Jim caught his target with a double-tap. Shade did the same, his follow-up shot taking a split-second longer because he was using the big .357 Magnum.

Jim's target jerked, then faceplanted on the tall steps, tumbling to the sidewalk at the bottom. Shade's man collapsed and crumpled on the porch. Jim sprinted to his target and put an insurance round in his head as he ran by him. A part of Jim's brain recalled that he'd casually known the man he just killed, perhaps having talked to him at a kid's soccer game once or twice. That had been a lifetime ago in an entirely different world.

Shade climbed the steps two at a time and confirmed his target was dead, staying clear of the shattered plate glass window. Jim joined Shade on the porch, each of them flattening out against the wall.

His action also initiated by Gary's rifle shot, Hugh put a boot to the back door of the restaurant. The old wood splintered and the glass shattered, raining to the ground. Hugh stepped inside, the MP5 at high ready. He hooked right and swept the room.

"Clear!" Hugh called.

Ian entered the room with his raised handgun, hooking left, and scanning for threats. Hugh kept the MP5 aimed at the swinging doors on the far side of the kitchen, the only interior access point to the room. The kitchen was the only way out of the building without going through Jim and Shade, and it wasn't likely anyone would be trying that.

56

When Gary's shot shattered the front window and rearranged the rifleman's chest, the rest of the men in the dining room experienced a moment of utter, paralyzing shock before panic took over. Suddenly, Hank and Cookie were the least of their concerns. Dr. Nelson backpedaled away from his prisoners, trying to wipe his friend's blood from his face. It was purely an instinctive move, the doctor's brain in survival mode.

Blake was so startled by the gunshot he dropped the broken bottle from his hand while simultaneously pissing himself. He too was caught by the spray of blood but made no effort to clean his face. As more gunfire erupted out front, Blake knew he was running out of time and options. He no longer cared about the prisoners, desperately scanning the room for a place to hide.

The remaining guard bolted toward the back of the restaurant, afraid there would be a second rifle shot, this one aimed at him. When he heard Shade and Jim firing at the guards out front, he made the split-second decision to escape out the back, through the kitchen. He charged through the swinging doors and directly into Hugh's line of fire.

Hugh paused long enough to confirm that the man wasn't a

friendly, then pressed the trigger and his weapon burped. A short burst hit the running man center mass. He staggered and fell, crashing onto a stainless-steel table and knocking over a stack of dirty dishes. Gravity took over and dragged the dead man onto the floor. Another stack of dishes toppled over, crashing onto the bloody man stretched out on the tile.

Hugh hurried forward to confirm the fallen man was out of the fight. He keyed the mic on this radio. "One down in the kitchen."

"Copy that!" Jim said. *"We're making entry through the front. Hold your fire!"*

"Roger that. Holding fire."

Jim glanced through what remained of the shattered plate glass window, spotting Hank and Cookie but no one else. Hank whipped his head from side to side, trying to make out what was going on in all the chaos. His swollen face and the blood in his eyes made it difficult to see.

Cookie's chair had fallen over and the gunfire had roused him to consciousness. He was in the fight. The big man snapped his zip-ties and lurched to his feet.

Out front, Jim caught Shade's attention and gestured toward the front door. "Kick it!"

Before attempting to kick the door in, Shade wisely reached over and twisted the knob. He gave Jim a wink when it turned freely in his hand. Shade shoved it the rest of the way open and stormed inside, unleashing the bloodcurdling cry of some hillbilly berserker.

Jim made a less dramatic entrance directly behind Shade. At nearly the same time, they spotted Dr. Nelson and Blake ducking behind the wide wooden bar. Jim only made it one step in that direction before one of the men whipped out a move he must have picked up in a movie, raising a gun over the bar and firing blindly.

The shots were wild, striking a wall, the ceiling, and a light fixture. Jim and Shade hit the ground. Unfazed by the gunfire, Cookie was now on his feet and charging toward the bar like some enraged defensive lineman determined to take out the quarterback. A sound emerged from his mouth, something between a groan of pain and a murderous squawk.

Still on the ground, Jim latched onto the back of Hank's chair, and dragged it toward the front door. The guy had survived too much to get killed by random gunfire from one of these idiots. When Jim got him safely outside, he unsheathed his knife, and sliced away the zip-ties.

Back inside, Shade was aiming his big revolver, trying to get a shot at the bar, but Cookie was in the way. Knowing there was a man attached to that gun-bearing hand, Shade was certain he would hit something if he could empty his weapon in that vicinity. Then, to Shade's surprise, Cookie threw himself onto the bar, slid overtop it, and dropped out of sight.

"Dammit!" Shade yelled. There was no way he could take the shot now.

There was a gunshot from behind the bar, the round striking the ceiling and knocking loose a chunk of old horse-hair plaster. There was another shot and this one knocked off a wall sconce. Shade took off running and launched himself overtop the bar. There was no way he was letting Cookie have all the fun.

When Jim got Hank cut loose, he stood him up and helped him down the steps. There was too much wild gunfire inside the restaurant to remain on the porch. At the bottom of the steps, Jim sat Hank down on the sidewalk and called into his radio. "Charlie! Gary! Close in and watch Hank."

Not waiting for an acknowledgment, Jim tore back up the steps, paused at the front door, then carefully reentered the dining room. The main space was empty, but it sounded like twenty men were brawling with a grizzly behind the bar.

"Moving!" Hugh called over the radio. *"We're coming in!"*

Jim barely registered the transmission. He was headed for the bar with his handgun leading the way. As soon as he reached it, he cursed and holstered his weapon. There was no room for a shot in the chaos of tangled bodies.

Shade had Blake Justice pinned to the ground, and Blake wasn't releasing his hold on the weapon. Shade got a hand clamped on it and wrenched it to the side, trapping Blake's finger in the trigger guard. There was a snap and Blake screamed. When he tried to pull his finger free, it wouldn't come out.

Shade dropped an elbow, then another on Blake's head, stunning him. He got a hand on the bar and pulled himself up. With Blake's handgun aimed skyward, Shade walked backward, tugging Blake along by his broken finger. Blake latched onto the grip of the handgun with his remaining fingers, trying to lessen the pain in the broken one. That worked until Blake's feet got tangled up behind the bar and Shade had to pull harder. Blake lost his grip on the handgun, consequently allowing all of Shade's force to be focused onto that one damaged finger. Shade bellowed, yanked, and the finger tore completely off. Blake screamed.

Out of patience, Shade shook the detached finger loose from the handgun, then shoved the weapon into his waistband. Reaching down, he grabbed Blake by the belt and hauled him to the center of the room. He dropped him in a heap and knelt on him, pinning him to the floor with a heavy knee.

Behind the bar, Cookie flailed on Dr. Nelson like he owed him money. The flurry of fists and the sound of solid punches made it sound like the closing seconds of a UFC match just before a merciful referee stepped in to stop it. There was no referee and no mercy today. With the beating he took, Dr. Nelson was paying a price that went beyond the events of the day. He was paying for Cookie's frustration with everything that had happened to him in a year and a half.

Once Shade had Blake clear of the bar, Jim waded in, finding that Cookie had thrashed Dr. Nelson to a pulp. Still heaving from the exertion, Cookie staggered to his feet, blood dripping from his pulverized fists. Grabbing Dr. Nelson's jacket, Cookie hauled him up and threw him across the bar.

Dr. Nelson cried out and landed on a nearby table. One table leg snapped immediately, dumping Nelson to the floor. Cookie closed in on the stunned man, laid a heavy boot across his throat, and applied pressure. Dr. Nelson grabbed Cookie's leg with both hands but couldn't budge it.

"These people attacked Hank's farm," Cookie choked out. "They killed his people."

"I know," Jim said. "How did you get caught up in this mess?"

Cookie heaved a sigh. "I was walking by and wanted a beer. I looked in the window to see if the place was open today and spotted Hank. He was tied to a chair, and they'd beat the shit out of him. I tried to intervene and next thing I knew, I was tied up and taking a beating too."

All heads turned toward the front of the restaurant, toward the sound of glass grinding beneath boots. Charlie and Gary walked in with Hank in between them. He was unsteady on his feet and they were each holding an arm to help support him.

"They killed my friends," Hank gasped, the words requiring great effort.

"I know," said Jim. "Brandy came and got us. We went up there to help, but it was too late."

Hank started crying again. He had nothing left. No strength with which to resist the welling of emotions inside him.

Gary cleared his throat. "Now that the shooting is over, people are starting to show up outside. They're wanting to know what happened."

"So?" Jim asked.

"He's right. There's a crowd gathering," Charlie said.

Jim looked at Dr. Nelson and Blake with contempt. "If they're so curious, let's haul this garbage outside and tell the people what happened."

Hank was the first to go outside, still being supported by Charlie and Gary. There was an audible gasp when people saw the damage to his face. Shade and Cookie hauled their two prisoners outside, and a murmur spread through the crowd. Though Hank wasn't really known to the townspeople, Blake and Dr. Nelson were. They weren't outsiders. They weren't criminals who'd strayed into town to rob and pillage. These were respected men, and they had friends and associates among the crowd.

Jim wasn't surprised when all eyes turned on him. That was always the way it went when he was involved. One by one, the accusing stares of the crowd focused on him, demanding an explanation. Jim's adrenaline was still up, his anger at a low boil. He turned the situation over in his head, trying to determine the best way to go about it, knowing he'd still end up picking the worst. It happened every single time.

"I don't know what the hell you people think I did," he snapped, "but let me tell you what happened." He could see the doubt on some of their faces, defiance and distrust. It was all he could do not to curse them out and go home. He'd done it before.

Jim pointed to Hank. "This young man's name is Hank Rose and he lived on his grandfather's farm in the north end of the county. Dr. Nelson, Blake, and some of their buddies decided this guy was responsible for the power going out. Last night they went to the farm where Hank was living with his friends. There were over a dozen young people living there. Men and women, farming and living a self-sufficient life. Now all but two of them are dead. Dr. Nelson and his friends shot some of them. They burned the rest alive."

"That doesn't sound like something he'd do!" someone yelled. "How do we know you're telling the truth?"

Jim pointed to Hugh, then Charlie. "Those two were with me. They helped me bury what dead we could find. I still reek of burned bodies if you want to take a whiff of my clothing."

The man declined to take Jim up on the offer.

Cookie spoke up and addressed the crowd. "What Jim Powell is saying is true. I met Hank and his friends a couple of weeks ago. I visited their farm and drank with them at Jim's roadhouse. They were good people. I came by here today to see if Doc's Place was going to open up because I wanted a beer. Instead, I found them torturing this young man, trying to get him to confess to sabotaging the power. When I tried to stop it, they knocked me out and tied me to a chair."

This revelation sent a ripple through the crowd. Cookie was

generally respected in a way that Jim wasn't. Everyone in town knew Cookie and his family. They knew he worked hard to improve conditions. Hearing such a story from the likes of Jim Powell was one thing; it was different coming from Cookie. He wasn't a heathen or barbarian, he wasn't a cold-hearted killer.

"Dr. Nelson was right about one thing," a woman called out. "Someone knocked the lights out. If it wasn't that fellow and his friends, who was it?"

Hugh stepped forward. "I'm an amateur radio operator and I've been working to find the answer to that. The news isn't good. It wasn't just us who lost power—it was the entire country."

Jim watched the crowd, wondering if that news would throw them into turmoil. He expected shouting and chaos, perhaps accusations that they were lying about everything from Dr. Nelson, to Hank's dead friends, to the widespread power outage. Instead, everyone fell silent. There wasn't a whisper, a murmur, or even any movement that Jim could detect. They were stunned.

Finally, a teenage girl broke the spell, raising her hand like she was back in school. "Does anyone know when the power will be coming back on?"

Hugh struck a less confrontational demeanor and tried to soften his delivery for this polite young girl, but there was no lessening the impact of what he had to say. "No one is sure if it *will* be coming back on. Lightspeed's people aren't answering and there are reports that the facility where they were living was hit with a Chinese missile attack."

The chaos Jim anticipated never came. The outrage, the shouting, and the hostility never materialized. One by one, the crowd began to disperse. It was as if the life had been sucked from them and they were blowing away like empty wrappers in a strong breeze.

Dr. Nelson spat blood onto the porch, coughed, and called to the departing crowd. He knew they were his only chance for salvation. His only chance of getting rescued from the situation in which he found himself. "I was just looking out for my community! I was trying to help you people! I was trying to find out what happened to the power so we could get it back."

Cookie glowered at Dr. Nelson. "How did killing Hank's friends help these people?" He kicked the doctor in the ribs for emphasis. "How!"

"Somebody destroyed the power," Dr. Nelson moaned. "Somebody had to pay."

"You made the wrong people pay," Jim said. "You killed innocent people."

"I-I thought...I heard that—"

"Shut the hell up!" Cookie roared. "You're lucky I stopped. I ought to kill you."

Jim met Cookie's eye. "We *are* going to kill him. We should have done it when they tried to steal those converters from the roadhouse. When I was a kid, my grandfather told me that you never leave an enemy alive to come back on you. Every time I've ignored his advice, I've paid for it. This time, Hank and his people paid for it."

Dr. Nelson swiveled his head around and glowered at Jim. "Your grandfather sounds like a savage, just like you and the rest of your people."

Jim ignored him.

"You can't just kill us!" Blake said. "I have people depending on me."

"I'm a doctor!" Dr. Nelson snapped. "The community needs me. I can save lives."

"You didn't save any today," Hank said in a low voice, carefully forming the words with his damaged mouth.

Jim unholstered his handgun, confirmed there were rounds remaining in the magazine, and held it out to Hank. "You want to do this?"

Hank stared at the gun, then at the two men on the ground. Despite the contempt on his face, he said, "I ain't never...killed anyone...before."

"This would be a good one to start with," Shade said matter-of-factly. "These two are about the most deserving sons-of-bitches I've seen in a long time. I doubt you'd lose a wink of sleep over killing them."

"I want to watch it, but I don't want to do it," Hank finally said.

Shade and Jim exchanged a look, their pact sealed. The group hauled their prisoners down the steps, into the street, and dumped them on the dirty asphalt. Cookie, Hugh, Charlie, Gary, and Ian backed a safe distance away.

"You can't do this!" Dr. Nelson cried. "This isn't the Old West. We're entitled to justice."

Jim unholstered his handgun and fired three shots from less than ten feet. All three were grouped around the doctor's heart. Blood blossomed and ran onto the pavement.

"There's your justice." Jim couldn't hear his own words for the ringing from the gunshots. There was something about shooting a person in this manner that made the shots sound louder, more jarring.

Blake raised his head to say something, to offer a final plea for mercy. Shade didn't give him a chance. A .357 round to the head silenced him in a way that nothing ever had before.

Jim turned away from the dead and faced his friends. Everyone had backed up in anticipation of the gunfire, except for Hank. He'd remained standing in close proximity, needing to see these flames extinguished, needing the closure that only a bleeding corpse provided. Shade opened the cylinder of his revolver and extracted the spent .357 casing. He handed it to Hank who, after a moment of consideration, pocketed it. Understanding the comfort that such a memento might provide, Jim scanned the street for his spent 9mm casings. When he found them, he handed them over to Hank.

Hugh nodded to the bodies. "We need to do anything with them?"

"Let 'em rot," Shade growled. "Maybe they got rats in this town with low standards. If they can eat them without puking, let them have at it."

Charlie cringed at the thought while Jim mulled it over.

"Normally I'd agree with you, Shade, but I don't want their families having to see them this way. We might as well take out our own trash. If people have to step over it all winter, they'll blame me."

"They'll blame you anyway," Gary pointed out.

Hugh nodded. "True."

His tone uncertain, Charlie spoke up. "I might have an idea."

Jim looked at the young man. "What is it, Charlie?"

"When I was hiding at the feed store, I noticed a black trailer chained up to the loading dock. Have you seen it before?"

"I've seen it," Jim said. "I don't know what the hell it is."

Shade started laughing, the sound a low rumble like that of a distant engine.

"It's a carcass incinerator," Charlie said. "My grandfather had to rent it once when a couple of his cows caught some kind of disease and he didn't want to bury them. It runs off propane."

Jim shook his head. "Hell, if I'd known there was such a thing in town, I might have hauled it home a year ago. Sounds handy."

"I hadn't noticed it," Shade said. "Charlie's right, though. It will do the trick. Won't leave nothing but ash."

"Let's do it," Jim said.

57

It was nearly dark when the exhausted group reached the roadhouse. Jim had experienced a day he wouldn't wish on many people. Well, maybe a few. He couldn't get the smell of burning bodies out of his nose and didn't know if it would ever leave him. People said it didn't and he now believed them. When they turned off Main Street, they could hear the sounds of the roadhouse in the distance. Laughter and loud voices, that infernal banjo.

"I'm not sure I have the energy for this," Jim said. "I'm not feeling it tonight."

Shade said, "It's oddly comforting to me. Despite everything that's gone wrong, things at the Reset Roadhouse are normal in an apocalyptic kind of way. I need that right now to recharge everything that got drained out of me today."

Jim mulled it over and found some truth in Shade's words. He supposed there was no rule that said someone couldn't be both a killer *and* a philosopher. Perhaps a man who killed for the good of his family and friends needed a fundamental philosophy more than most. "That's a good point, Shade. Thanks for changing my perspective."

"De nada," Shade laughed.

They dealt with their horses then went inside. Jim led the group straight to the back of the building rather than taking a table or seats at the bar. They'd converted one of the empty offices into a private meeting space. If fancy nightclubs could have backrooms for snorting coke, surely the Reset Roadhouse was entitled to a backroom for patching wounds, washing off blood, and topping off magazines.

"I'm going to head up front and get some medicinal spirits," Jim said. "I'll bring Randi back to take a look at you, Hank. Cookie, if you have any injuries, she can deal with those too."

Cookie tapped his head. "They hit me in in the best possible spot. I'm hardheaded."

"Hugh, can you get the medical kit?" Jim asked. "The big one?"

Hugh headed off toward the storage room, tugging a ring of keys from his pocket.

"Charlie, can you bring us a pot of warm water for cleaning up wounds?"

The young man nodded and followed Jim into the roadhouse. Jim scanned the crowd, then spotted Randi carrying drinks to a table.

"Hey, do you think you could get somebody to cover your tables for a few?"

Randi frowned, giving Jim the look that usually preceded a tongue-lashing.

Jim held up a hand to stop her. "Not the day, Randi. I've killed men and burned their bodies. I buried young people that I was laughing with last week. Now Hank is in the back room looking like he's been dragged behind a car and he needs help. I need you to be a nurse—not a waitress, not a smartass."

Seeing the look in Jim's eyes, Randi rested a hand on his arm. "Are you okay?"

Jim shook his head. "Nah, pretty sure I'm not, but I don't know what it's going to take to fix me. I don't think a bandage will do it."

Randi pointed to the bar. "That's probably where you need to start. Though it won't fix a damn thing, it might take the edge off."

Jim nodded wearily. "That's where I'm headed."

He cut through the crowd, not making eye contact with any of the patrons. If anyone called his name, he waved and kept moving. At the bar, he expected Becky to start giving him crap just like Randi had, but Shade had reached her first. He was holding her hand, giving her a sanitized and abbreviated version of what had taken place. The look on her face said it all—anger at what had happened to Hank and his people; grief that the power might be gone for good; and a dirty and complicated satisfaction that some form of justice had been served.

Jim searched beneath the counter for a bucket. Suspecting a one-gallon pail wasn't going to cut it this time, he chose a plastic five-gallon bucket, then placed a bottle of liquor and several metal shot glasses inside it. He went back through the roadhouse, out the side door, and to the fenced off section of the creek where they cooled beer when they didn't have power. He stacked the bucket with two layers of cold beer, then stood to go back inside.

When he reached the flaking concrete stairs, those five steps seemed an almost insurmountable obstacle. Jim set the bucket down, then sat himself down on one of the cool steps. He rested his elbows on his thighs, staring at the ground and letting the gentle sound of the creek wash over him. When he closed his eyes, it was all he heard. The sound filled his mind, then unfurled across time and space until it was all there was.

It reminded him of visiting his grandfather's house in West Virginia when he was a kid. They were plagued with flash floods that charged through those steep hollows every couple of years, cresting over the riverbanks, and rising into peoples' yards. When the water receded there were always things missing, carried away by the river. Broken bicycles, old appliances, tires, garbage, children's toys, even old vehicles. People often added to it, taking the flood as an opportunity to clean out barns, storage buildings, and their homes by tossing trash into the rising water.

When the river receded, it left behind mud, branches, and debris. There was a particular smell associated with it that was both pungent and prehistoric, as if soil from past epochs had been redistributed across the land. Yet even in that distribution of mud and debris, there was a freshness to the world, as if God had scoured the land clean so people could start anew.

Jim felt as if he needed to be overtaken by the same kind of flood. Something to carry away the death, the smells, and the memories the last year and half had left him with. The odor of the unburied and the burned; the slaughterhouse smell of fresh blood and cooling bodies; the sounds that came from the dying in that intimate moment of their expiration; the sight of people he cared about being taken from this world in ways that had been unimaginable a few short years ago. He didn't know what it might take to scrub these memories and experiences from him. After a certain point, it wasn't just his mind that they occupied. They spread to his soul, inhabiting his body like a ghost, like some resident demon that would resist exorcism until his dying breath.

Jim uncapped the liquor bottle and drank from it without ceremony. When he was done, he raised the bottle to the night, to all the dead and the lost whom he dared not recall by name. He tipped the bottle again, took a swallow, and placed it back in the bucket.

By the time Jim reached the back room, Randi was already working on Hank with some clean rags, antiseptic wipes, and bottled saline. Occasionally, Hank would wince at her efforts. Just as often, Randi would wince at some particularly painful looking wound she was hesitant to touch. Jim handed out beers, then set the liquor and shot glasses on a table they'd improvised out of an old door.

"Who wants a shot?" he asked.

Every hand went up, including those of Hank and Randi. Including Charlie.

Jim winked at Charlie. "A little young, aren't you?"

Charlie didn't say anything.

Shade had returned to the back room while Jim was outside and had a beer in each hand, drinking from both. "If he can fight with us, he can drink with us. That's my two cents."

"You're right." Jim poured a shot and passed it to Charlie.

Charlie downed it immediately, wiping his mouth with the back of his hand.

Shade grinned. "Like a pro."

Charlie handed the shot glass back to Jim. "With what I been through, Jim, I ain't sure anything can hurt me again. I buried everyone in my family. What can a shot of liquor possibly do to me?"

"May I have a beer?" Hank asked.

Jim handed one over and Hank didn't even open it, instead pressing it against his swollen face.

"Me too?" Conway had missed out on the action at the Doc's Place because he was watching the horses, but everyone had assured him he was better off for it. Although Conway didn't entirely understand what that meant, he took their word for it.

Jim poured him a shot and slid it across the table.

"Go easy on the alcohol," Randi said to Hank. "We have pain pills here that people have traded in for other things, which you don't want to mix with alcohol."

Hank made a noise that indicated he was unconcerned about any potential overdose.

"You should stay here," Jim told him. "We've got clothes and gear. We can get you set up. You're certainly welcome to stay with us long-term if you want. You can stay here at the roadhouse or we can find you a place in the valley. There's a spare room in the house where Pete and Charlie are living."

Hank used a single finger to point down at the floor, then nodded, which Jim interpreted to mean that the roadhouse would be fine for now.

"We'll set you up with a sleeping bag and everything you need."

"Speaking of the valley, I don't think I'm going home tonight," Charlie said. "I'm going to head to Nana and Pops' house in a minute. I'm sure Pete is anxious to hear if we got Hank back."

Jim smiled. "That would be great, Charlie. I appreciate you doing that."

"We had your parents set up pretty well when they had power. Now I'm afraid it's going to be more work than they're able to do," Charlie said. "They don't have any firewood put up and that fireplace of theirs won't heat the entire house. I'm not sure what they're going to do."

Jim sighed grimly. "I'm sure you're right, Charlie. I'll run out there tomorrow and see if I can talk some sense into them."

One by one, the people in the room gradually drifted off. Charlie had dinner in the kitchen, then headed off to take Pete, Nana, and Pops some food. Shade joined Becky at the bar and kept a beer in his hand until closing time, and for a good while afterward. Ian wandered off to his room to take a nap since he had to work the night watch. Gary had dinner with his daughters in the kitchen, then headed back to the valley on horseback. Hugh excused himself to smoke on the roof and Conway went with him.

"I might stay here tonight," Randi said. "I'd like to keep an eye on Hank. Everything you see will heal up eventually, but he's got a knot on his head and bruising to his midsection. We need to watch that he doesn't have a concussion or internal injuries."

"What will you do if he does?" Cookie asked.

Jim frowned at him. That was the wrong question to ask.

"What?" Cookie said. "I don't know what you do in those cases."

"They hold...my hand...until I die," Hank worded carefully.

"Oh," Cookie said sheepishly.

Jim stood. "Let's get a beer, Cookie. Yell if you need anything, Randi."

"Sorry about that question," Cookie said once they were out of the room. "A thick head is a blessing in a fight. It's not so useful when sensitivity is required."

"It's okay."

They took seats at the bar and sat in silence for a moment before Jim said, "Cookie, what I told Hank also goes for you and your family. There are a few open houses in our valley. You'd be a good fit for our community if you're tired of dealing with town people. You could work here at the roadhouse with us if you wanted."

"Looks like you guys will be in business a while longer since the power isn't coming back on."

"I guess so," Jim said. "Losing power a second time is a serious setback. It's going to be hard on people. Harder than losing it the first time."

"Let me think about it, Jim. While I appreciate the offer, I probably shouldn't decide without talking to my family. Whenever I do that, it always gets me in trouble."

Jim cracked a smile. "Yeah, I've been there."

58

The next few days were challenging ones for Jim's community. Already accustomed to the lack of electricity, things at the Reset Roadhouse continued on much as normal. It was the same in Jim's valley where people cursed and complained about the loss of power, but begrudgingly went back to the way they'd been doing things before Lightspeed's people sent the Great Pumpkin aloft over Clinch Mountain.

In town, the impact was more significant. Jim wasn't sure what the difference was. Were country people more prepared or were they simply more resilient? He didn't know. His own stoic acceptance of the loss of power wasn't rooted in pessimism or negativity. He simply approached most things with a "wait and see" attitude. In this case, he'd waited and he'd seen, and the results were emotionally devastating to most.

The people who'd taken out their woodstoves and given away their wood supplies were struggling to put things right again. It was already cold with winter nipping at their heels. For those who'd so optimistically cast aside the primitive survival techniques that had kept them alive for the past year and a half, this return to pioneer living was a hard pill to swallow. Some who'd left their stoves in place and continued to collect firewood, even after the arrival of power, were quick to point fingers and call their neighbors irresponsible. The once hopeful were now demoralized as they worked furiously to prepare for another winter without electricity.

Then the suicides began.

It started with a couple who'd rolled their stove out into their yard and given away their stack of firewood. The wife was a schoolteacher and her husband sold cars at a local dealership. They'd repaired their Main Street home, cleaned up their yard, and even repainted their porch. They thought they were doing everything right, only to be crushed when the wireless power grid failed. It was too much for them to take. Together, they slit their wrists in bed one night and bled to death holding hands.

Solutions could be contagious. It was human nature. If someone invented a better way of doing things, word spread. The same was apparently true even if the solution was a dark and grisly one. For many, death was more appealing than surviving another depressing winter. They were tired of this world and this life and were ready for a reboot. Several times a day people came into the roadhouse bearing news of someone who'd pulled the plug because the prospect of death was less ominous than the prospect of living.

Pete and Charlie were still staying with Nana and Pops while Jim tried to convince them to return to his home in the valley. They were adamant that they didn't want to stay with Jim any longer. At the same time, they had no plan for how they might be able to survive in town on their own. Jim hoped he'd be able to get through to them eventually. Then one day Pete and Charlie showed up at the roadhouse unexpectedly.

"What are you guys doing here?" Jim asked.

"Nana and Pops kicked us out," Pete said, a crooked grin on his face. "They said they didn't need us anymore and we should go home."

"They say why?" Jim asked.

Both boys shook their heads.

"They just said they'd figured it out," said Charlie.

"Figured what out?"

Pete shrugged one shoulder. "I don't know."

Jim furrowed his brow. This made no sense at all. There was nothing for Nana and Pops to figure out. The amount of work required to live at their house in town was more than they could manage alone. "Were they angry?"

"Just the opposite," Pete said. "They were as happy as I've seen them in a long time. They were looking through an old photo album when I left. I saw a picture of you with a mixing bowl on your head and icing on your face."

"I saw one of you in a turtleneck and vest," Charlie added. "You looked like the coolest kid in kindergarten."

Pete and Charlie cackled. Jim wasn't laughing. In fact, a thought was forming in his brain that left him chilled to the core.

"Tell Hugh to meet me at their house." Jim ran for the back door with no pack and no rifle.

"What's wrong?" Pete yelled.

Jim never answered. He sprinted out the side door and to the paddock where they kept their horses. He led his through the gate and sprang onto its back. By the time Pete, Charlie, and Randi reached the back door, Jim was already galloping away.

Randi rushed back inside. "Do what he said, boys. Find Hugh and find Shade too." She tossed her apron onto the bar and snatched up her gear.

"Take this!" Pete got his father's rifle and pack from beneath the bar.

Randi took it and hurried outside to mount her horse and head off after Jim. Though his horse was faster than hers, Jim wasn't the rider she was. She'd been riding her entire life and was as comfortable on the horse as she was on foot. Jim, on the other hand, always seemed to have an underlying fear that his horse was going to wipe out and crush him to death.

She caught up with him near the farmer's market and pulled alongside him. Jim turned around and met her eye but didn't speak. He couldn't put words to the thoughts going through his mind. They tore through the little town, reaching Jim's parents' house in about ten minutes. In the driveway, Jim dropped his reins and leapt off the horse. He bolted for the front door and found it locked. He cursed and pounded on it with his fist. There was no answer from inside. No sound of footsteps.

"Do you need me to try another door?" Randi asked.

"This is the only one they ever use." Jim yanked a keychain from his pocket and flipped through it until he found the key. He hurriedly unlocked the door and shoved it open, calling inside. "Pops! Nana!"

When they didn't answer, he drew his handgun and activated the weapon light. He moved into the dim entry, calling his parents' names. Although Pete and Charlie hadn't understood what they were seeing, Jim did. He'd heard about it many times in his old job at the mental health center. Sometimes depressed people experienced a euphoria before they committed suicide. They were elated that they'd found a solution and felt that the worst was over. They had their way out—their own permanent cure for something that their doctors and therapists had been unable to fix.

It had never occurred to Jim that his own parents might be suicidal. They were tough people, but these were extraordinary circumstances. Although he could understand why someone might want to take this step, he could never do it, and he could never accept that they would. They had it better than most. He'd made sure of it. Yet perhaps that was part of the problem. He'd be unable to see their suicide as anything other than a failure on his part.

Had he listened to them and paid attention? Had he understood that their idea of survival might be different than his own? Maybe surviving wasn't enough for them.

It was like his grandfather asking him to bring him a gun all those years ago. Jim had been a teenager, and his grandfather was hospitalized after a stroke. Jim knew what his grandfather intended to do with that gun and he didn't want to lose him. He also didn't want to play a role in his death. Yet how could he say no to someone he loved so much? He understood his grandfather not wanting to live paralyzed and wheelchair bound. That wasn't who he was, nor was it who he wanted to be for the rest of his life. He was done with life and wanted to leave on his own terms. Perhaps Jim's parents were done with the world in exactly that same way.

Outside, Jim heard the sound of hooves on pavement. He supposed it was Hugh, but it sounded like more than one horse. He started to call his parents' names again then saw no point. He was far enough into the house that one of them would surely have heard him by now. He'd come inside this very door and called to them thousands of times in his life and never once had they failed to hear him. If they were home, they'd know he was here.

If they were alive.

Jim reached the end of the entry foyer. The opening to the living room loomed ahead. The blinds where open, with natural light spilling into the room. He took another step, gripping his handgun tightly. His hands were sweating now, his breathing rapid and shallow.

He heard footsteps on the sidewalk. Someone called his name. He couldn't find his voice to answer. He took the corner into the living room and found his parents sitting on the couch together, an old photo album open across their laps. A revolver was loosely gripped in his father's hand.

"What's going on, Pops?"

His father cleared his throat. "Remembering."

Nana had a Kleenex pressed to her face. She was crying.

Jim holstered his weapon, then held out his hand for his father's revolver. "That's not the solution."

Pops made no move to hand it over. "It might be the *only* solution."

"You've survived this long."

"We've outlived our friends, outlived the world we knew," Pops said. "Where's the joy in that?"

"We can't live in our home any longer," Nana said. "I'm tired of living out of a room in somebody else's house. I can't go back to that. I need my space. I need my house."

"You know that living here isn't an option. You'd need a good bit of help to do it. More help than we can easily provide when you're this far away from the rest of us."

"That's the problem," Pops said, his voice flat and devoid of enthusiasm, the life already gone from it. "We feel like a burden, and that's the last thing we want to be."

"You use that gun and you become a greater burden. A physical burden is one thing. It will pass. Knowing that you killed yourself is an emotional burden that will never go away. It'll follow me, Ellen, and the kids for the rest of our lives. It'll follow Charlie, Hugh, and all the other people in the valley who've come to know and love you. We'll always feel like we failed you. So while pulling that trigger might make it easy on you, that spares the rest of us nothing. Just know that before you take the next step."

"They could take Pete and Charlie's house," Randi said from behind Jim.

He hadn't known she was there. He spun around, startled. She didn't look at him but continued speaking to his parents.

"I doubt I'm getting rid of Lloyd anytime soon, so he can get the rest of his crap out of that house. There are other houses around that we could put Pete and Charlie in. They might even want to live at the roadhouse with the rest of that crew. The house they've been living in is a good house. It's already set up for living in these conditions, and it's close to the rest of us."

"I don't know," Pops said.

Jim followed Randi's lead. "You'd have your own place. If we move all your stuff into that house, it could be a home to you two. It's close enough to the rest of us that people could check in on you several times a day and help out if you needed it. You could be in radio contact with us all the time and we can't do that when you're here."

Nana and Pops exchanged glances, though still appeared uncertain.

"Your grandchildren would have more time with you," said Jim. "You could pass on more of the things you've learned over the years. You'd be leaving us with a positive memory instead of a traumatic one."

Pops glanced over at Nana. She wiped her eyes with the tissue, then nodded. Pops reached out and gave the revolver to Jim, who stuck it in his back pocket.

The onrush of relief left Jim feeling lightheaded. "I have to go outside." He walked briskly out the front door, then ran for the corner of the house. He barely made it before he bent over and vomited. He was still heaving his guts out when Hugh and Shade walked over.

Jim wiped his mouth on his sleeve. "Ya'll here to hold my hair back?"

Shade laughed. "With that buzzcut, there ain't enough to hold back."

"More like a 'buzzsaw' cut," Hugh said. "Like someone set a drunk loose with hedge clippers."

Jim straightened uncertainly, his stomach still experiencing weird tremors. "You think you could bring a wagon and move my parents to the valley tomorrow, Shade?"

"I'd be glad to. Where are they going?"

"Pete and Charlie's place. I'll be booting them out."

Hugh nodded. "You okay, man?"

Jim considered his answer. How could anyone ever be okay after something like that? On the other hand, it was only one miserable moment in a vast sea of miserable experiences. "I'll be fine. Can you radio Pete and Charlie and get them headed back here? I'll need them to stay one more night."

Hugh wandered off, tugging his radio out of a pouch.

"Lightspeed said we'd lost about ninety percent of the population," Shade said. "We'll be lucky if suicide doesn't take out half of what's left."

"You're right, Shade. The people who made it this far were tough, but the people still standing in another month are going to be tough as nails."

59

Over the coming weeks, the random suicides began to taper off. There were fewer spontaneous gunshots coming from occupied homes. There were fewer frozen and bled out corpses found by friends and neighbors. Fewer people hanged themselves in dark basements, from tree limbs, or from backyard swing sets. Fewer took intentional overdoses of old medications stashed in their homes.

In the end, the community didn't lose half its residents as some had feared, though easily lost as many as a third. If only ten percent of the nation had survived the initial collapse, suicide had likely dropped that number down to six or seven percent. No one had an exact count, but most people didn't really want to know either. Those losses were too fresh and too painful. In the gloomy recesses of their own minds, nearly all of the survivors were secretly asking themselves if those who took their own lives had made the right decision.

Those who remained behind in the face of this psychological setback were hearty folks. They were fire-hardened and tempered, determined to be there when the lights came on for good, should it ever happen. Should it *not* happen, should those survivors spend their remaining days struggling to carve out a life for themselves in this endarkened world, they would do it with as much dignity and as much joy as they could find. They would not lie down and die. They would not be swallowed by depression, grief, and hopelessness.

Shortly after Jim talked his parents out of going that route, everyone in their clan pitched in to help Nana and Pops move back to the valley. Lloyd removed all his belongings from Buddy's old house and finally moved in with Randi. It was as close as he'd ever come to committing to a relationship and he had a lot to say about it.

"Where am I supposed to go if she throws me out?"

"Act like you have some sense and I won't," Randi countered.

"What if she gets tired of hearing the banjo?" Lloyd asked.

"Breaking news," Jim said. "Everyone is *already* tired of hearing the banjo."

"What if I don't bathe often enough to suit her?"

"Then you'll sleep in the barn until you can act civilized," Randi fired back. "I might be a momma, but I ain't *your* momma. If you act like a two-year-old, I'll treat you like one."

Pete and Charlie also cleared out of Buddy's old house. Pete didn't have very much stored there since most of his belongings were still at his parents' house. Charlie had a little more since he'd hauled several loads from his home on the other side of town and his grandmother's house on the western end of the county. With no family left, he'd wanted to salvage as much as he could from his old life.

An empty farmhouse between Gary's house and Randi's was cleaned out for the boys to move into. It was a tiny two-bedroom house from the 1940s with white aluminum siding over the old painted clapboards. The metal roof was thick with a silvery coating rolled on every few years to prevent leaks. It made a good home, since it had been built before power reached the valley and was designed for country living.

A central chimney accommodated a Warm Morning wood stove in the living room and an old cookstove in the kitchen. There was spring-fed water that didn't require electricity to flow through the pipes. Some of the plumbing had burst the previous winter when the house sat unoccupied. Those were simple fixes. The boys were excited about the house and looking forward to making it their own.

The last step in preparing Buddy's old house for its new inhabitants was to clear out the last of Buddy's belongings. As Lloyd, Pete, and Charlie had moved into his house, they'd shifted many of Buddy's possessions into his old bedroom, leaving them there out of some amalgamation of respect and superstition. The other part of it was that no one wanted to sort through the old man's life. It was simply too sad.

Buddy wasn't coming back. He'd been shot a long time ago while visiting his daughter's grave in town. That daughter had been the only family Buddy had left. No one would ever show up to claim Buddy's possessions. No one would inherit the house, the photo albums, or the medals he earned in Vietnam. There would be no estate to settle nor courts to oversee it. Buddy's legacy would only exist in the hearts and minds of those who'd known, respected, and cared for him. The family that had come to him late in his life. The people of the valley.

Jim, Ellen, and Randi took on the task of sorting through their old friend's life. They had been the closest to him. All of Buddy's household items would be left there for Nana and Pops to use if they needed them. If not, there were other families in their group who might. When they came across specific items that they thought someone in their group might need, they set those items aside, putting a note on them so they'd remember who to give them to. Those included shoes, clothes, coats, tools, and some personal items.

They had a fire going in Buddy's backyard firepit and tossed in bills, family keepsakes, and everything else there was no point in keeping. Personal correspondence, unidentifiable photographs, cards exchanged between family members on special occasions, and children's drawings that had likely hung on a refrigerator decades ago. They tossed in neckties, obsolete kitchen gadgets, and catalogs for products that might never be sold again. Black smoke roiled high in the air, carrying a life, legacy, and history.

They also kept a pile for those items that no one in their group could use, but they might be able to sell at the roadhouse. Some old guns and odd calibers of ammunition, old knives and fishing tackle, camping gear from the 1970s. Those items they'd sell went onto the porch where they'd load them onto Shade's wagon after he delivered Nana and Pops' belongings.

The three each picked a few sentimental items to remind them of Buddy, including some photographs. Jim kept the trunk that held the reminders of Buddy's military service—the medals, uniform, discharge papers, and stacks of curling black and white photographs. He had no real use for them but couldn't bring himself to toss them into the fire or hand them off to anyone else. That felt disrespectful, so he'd stick them in one of his storage buildings for now.

Once Jim's parents were settled in, the house in the valley ended up being perfect for them. Jim was grateful to Randi for coming up with the idea and felt kind of awkward about it. His appreciation caused him to be overly nice to her, which wasn't the normal tempo of their relationship. Finally, she had enough.

"Can we just go back to being the way we used to be, Jim? You're creeping me out with the whole 'being nice' thing. It makes me paranoid, like you're just trying to get me to let my guard down so you can attack. I like you better as a sarcastic asshole, because then I get to channel my inner bitch. That's where you and I connect. *That's* the nature of our relationship."

Jim did as she asked, going back to taking jabs at Randi at every opportunity. They were both happier when they were slamming, insulting, and cursing each other. Nana and Pops seemed happier as well. They had their independence, but they were close enough that they could be an active part of the valley community.

They could eat with friends and family, then return to their home at night. They had people who could check in on them if they were under the weather. When they wanted to socialize, they were close enough to visit with any of the families in Jim's clan, and they could even take walks along the valley road when the weather was nice. It was a sustainable arrangement, unlike returning to their isolated home in town.

Hank Rose took a small home in the valley and immediately set to work recreating the trout farm his grandfather had built. Though everyone encouraged him to take it easy for a while, he needed the distraction. He couldn't sit around because then all he could think about were the friends he'd lost and the horrible way they'd died. In between their other tasks, nearly everyone in their group lent a hand with his project.

Jim had found him a farm that already had a pond constantly fed by an inflow of cold river water. A little work to the intake and over-flow pipes was all that was required for Hank to begin stocking it with trout from his farm. Those visits were gut-wrenching experiences for Hank. Seeing the rubble of his grandfather's home was overwhelming. Recalling what had happened there was even more traumatic.

On each of those visits, they used waders and nets to catch trout and place them in water-filled barrels on the back of Shade's wagon. Hank also salvaged what he could from the barns and outbuildings. The project filled Hank's days, helped him heal body and spirit, and provided a consistent source of fresh fish for Jim's people. Pete and Charlie took a particular interest in the project and, over time, built a strong friendship with Hank.

For Jim and his people, the Reset Roadhouse continued to be the focus of much of their activity. Even without power, they had friends and family who built cottage industries around making products to be used by or sold at the roadhouse. Despite the loss of so many people to suicide, crowds continued to gather there each night for food, drink, and music. None of the regulars had killed themselves, which everyone found to be interesting. They all developed their own explanations for it.

Lloyd obviously attributed it to the power of the banjo. "Hell, it ain't much different than an angel standing up there on stage plucking a harp. It soothes the mind and heals the body."

Ed argued it was more likely due to the liquor he produced. "It's like those old-fashioned tonic medicines. A few sips a day keeps bad health away. Ask any doctor or liquor-drinking professional and they'll agree with me. It's science."

Becky insisted that it was her charm and personality that kept everyone alive. "They'd miss me if they were dead. I'm the sunshine in their otherwise drab existence. That alone is enough to keep our regulars from bathing with the toaster, so to speak."

Jim's theory was different. He felt that the roadhouse, as dirty, basic, and simple as it was, offered a sense of community at a time when that was hard to find. It gave people a chance to escape the oppressive sense of dread that overshadowed their days. It allowed them to destress and to push aside the ever-present worry over food, heat, and health. Jim felt awkward when some suggested the roadhouse gave people hope.

"I'm not in the hope business. Most people don't even understand what gives them hope. It's like they think it's some shiny object and they're going to hear this chorus of angels when they find it. I don't think it's like that. Hope can be dirty, rusty, and cast aside. It can grow where nothing grew before. Hope isn't a flower. It's a weed."

The End